# SEPTEMBER MORNING

## Rowena Summers

This first world edition published in Great Britain 1999 by
SEVERN HOUSE PUBLISHERS LTD of
9–15 High Street, Sutton, Surrey SM1 1DF.
This title first published in the U.S.A. 1999 by
SEVERN HOUSE PUBLISHERS INC of
595 Madison Avenue, New York, N.Y. 10022.

British Library Cataloguing in Publication Data

Summers, Rowena, 1932-
        September morning. - (The Cornish clay series ; v. 7)
        1.   Domestic fiction
        I.   Title
        823.9'14 [F]

        ISBN 0-7278-5446-1

Typeset by Hewer Text Ltd
Edinburgh, Scotland.
Printed and bound in Great Britain by
MPG Books Ltd, Bodmin, Cornwall.

# One

Almost crushed by the crowds in the swelteringly hot stands, amid the noise and rapturous applause, Celia turned to her companion and hugged his arm. She knew that solemnity should be coupled with the excitement of the event she was witnessing but, outspoken as ever, she couldn't resist whispering in his ear.

"What a funny little man he is," she said with a giggle.

Franz Vogl glanced round, shushing her at once. Besotted as he was with Celia, he couldn't let the slight to his hero pass. Handsome, fair-haired and typical of his race, Franz's nature was as passionate as that of the Cornish girl he adored, but his national pride in the Fatherland and its leader was paramount.

"You must be careful what you say, Celia. Would your English folk be so pleased to hear your King Edward described as a funny little man – especially as—·"

Celia pulled a face as he paused abruptly, but she knew what he was thinking. European and American newspapers were rife with the stories and rumours that Fleet Street had had strict orders to suppress – that of the scandalous affair between the British king and an American divorcee.

But even if it had nothing to do with ordinary people, Celia was prepared to defend her king and his right to love. It was so very romantic – and any hot-blooded seventeen-year-old girl could hardly think otherwise. All the same . . .

"*Verzeihen Sie* – I'm sorry. But I would never describe King Edward as funny, because he's not. He's very dashing and very royal. But your Mr Hitler. Well—"

She giggled again at the memory of the German Chancellor pronouncing the Games open with his rasping voice and sporting his weird little moustache. Try as she might, Celia was unable to distinguish him in her mind from Charlie Chaplin. She straightened her face at once as her mother nudged her, and whispered

1

disapprovingly, "Behave yourself, Celia, and remember that we're guests of Franz's parents while we're here."

Celia nodded. It was pure luck that she was here at all. She had only been allowed to take her stepfather's place at the Berlin Olympics because he was involved in an important legal case and had been obliged to stay behind in Cornwall while she and her mother travelled to Germany. Her sister had begged to be allowed to come as well, but they had only been offered two tickets, and Wenna had never been interested in sports anyway. Celia airily brushed aside the fact that it wasn't so much the sports that excited her, as the thought of all those healthy, virile young men who would be panting around the tracks or leaping over the hurdles.

She felt a momentary pity for her young brother Oliver. He would have loved all this – but two seats meant two seats, and the moment of regret for him passed quickly.

Her mother was now deep in conversation with their German host, whose company imported White Rivers pottery, the business she owned and managed so successfully. Celia greatly admired her mother for her business skills, and also for having learned the German language so fluently and easily. She and Wenna had struggled with its vowels and complicated sentence structure at their Swiss finishing school.

Both girls adored their American mother, Skye, and the smile Celia gave her now was almost dazzling.

Skye caught her breath at the sight of that smile, marvelling as always how alike all the generations of women in their family were.

Skye's uncle, the artist Albert Tremayne, had done a remarkable job of transferring their likenesses onto canvas. His paintings were now fetching handsome prices in Cornwall and beyond. Skye thought it a charming way for the heritage of the Tremayne beauty to be perpetuated. Especially in the case of her own mother's portrait. The empathy between Albert Tremayne and his sister Primmy had been particularly strong.

But this was no time for reminiscing, Skye reminded herself. Today was a wonderful day, the first of August with Adolf Hitler opening the Olympic Games. If the great American athlete, Jesse Owens, lived up to expectations, then she could take an extra pride in one of her own countrymen winning a gold medal. She felt a thrill at the thought. It was many years since she had left America for Cornwall to try to find her roots, and stayed for a lifetime. But deep inside her there was still that tug of home and always would be.

Since she had read some of the American newspapers, she knew very well what the more lurid ones were saying about the new king and Mrs Simpson. Rumours all, according to her husband, which she shouldn't pay any heed to.

"Don't believe any of it until or unless you hear it from reliable sources," Nick had advised her. "These scandal-rags will say anything to further their circulation."

"They can't say just anything, Nick," she had replied uneasily. "You, of all people, should know the legalities of printing libellous material."

"And you, my love, know very well how a clever journalist can get around that little problem with carefully chosen words." Her luminous blue eyes seemed darker in contrast to her pale face, and her classically beautiful features were drawn and anxious. He had already guessed the reason why. "Darling, you really can't take all this personally," he'd said quietly, "it has nothing to do with us."

"I know it," she had answered, forcing a laugh.

And of course it didn't. They lived in the far west of Cornwall and events in London and the rest of the country had always seemed very removed from their own small world. So it was impossible for Skye to try to explain her feelings to Nick, her clever lawyer husband with the so-logical brain that didn't allow for hunches and sixth senses. Nor could she really explain them to herself. It was crazy for a long-exiled American woman to feel this unnecessary defensiveness, almost bordering on guilt, for pity's sake, on behalf of a slicker, more sophisticated and worldly American divorcee.

Except, of course, that her countrywoman was no ordinary woman. She moved in high places – the very highest. And if all these foreign newspapers were shrieking out the truth, she could be the catalyst for the unthinkable to happen: for causing the King of England to abdicate, and possibly even to bring down the monarchy. Such a shameful eventuality would touch every one of them.

At that moment Skye had felt the American newspaper taken

out of her numb hands. She had smiled briefly at Nick, knowing she was seeing what wasn't there – might never be there. That was the Cornish part of her, her legacy, and she told herself severely that such problems were for others to solve.

"Don't they look simply marvellous?" Skye heard her elder daughter say, and she forced her thoughts back to the present and the parade of athletes through the vast Berlin Olympic stadium.

At seventeen Celia was boy-mad, Skye thought, and it was a relief to her that Franz was such a steady and upright young man. He had strong opinions of his own too, which wasn't such a bad thing and might curb her headstrong daughter.

While they were in Berlin, she and Celia were guests of his parents. The very middle-class Vogl family lived in a mansion situated in a cool shady avenue of old buildings that exemplified the very best of European architecture. Skye counted herself fortunate to have such good European connections, both in business and socially.

Skye saw her daughter lean towards Franz and his blue eyes lit up at the sight of her. His blondness was in sharp contrast to Celia's glossy black hair. She felt a momentary frisson of unease at the way the girl smiled so teasingly into his eyes. At times, Celia's nature was too tempestuous and passionate for her own good. Everything had to happen at once for her.

Skye smiled faintly. Celia was certainly her mother's daughter in that respect. It could take no longer than a locked glance between two people for them to fall in love. She didn't want that to happen to Celia yet. She had her whole life in front of her, and the opportunities for women were so much wider now. But tempting though it was, Skye knew she must not indulge her own dreams through her daughters.

Instead, she too concentrated on the fine parade of athletes and the seemingly endless preliminaries before the Games could officially begin. This was the spectacle they had come here for, as well as making a tour of the factories using Killigrew Clay and the shops selling White Rivers pottery. She felt a glow of pleasure at her own success – as important to her as anything these athletes would accomplish.

In just over two weeks all the ballyhoo was over. Tears had been shed for the losers and plaudits given to the winners. Jesse Owens

4

was the undoubted hero of the Games with a clutch of gold medals, but to Skye's disgust – and the fury of the American press – Adolf Hitler had refused to shake hands with him because he was black. It said much about Hitler, in Skye's opinion, but because of her obligations to her German hosts, she wisely kept those opinions to herself.

By the time they were well on their way home, Celia was declaring dramatically that she had fallen madly in love with Franz. She was trying to persuade her mother to invite him to Cornwall during early December, when she would be back from Switzerland to share in her belated November birthday celebrations.

It had already been arranged that Celia would return to finishing school next month for the winter term, even though her course was officially over. She had obtained a post as the school's art class assistant, to keep Wenna company for her last year, and to keep an eye on her – or so she said. According to Wenna, it was more likely to enable Celia to keep her eyes on the young French and German buckos who flocked to the area for the skiing every winter. It was so unlike Wenna to criticise anything Celia did that Skye was perfectly sure it was true. Celia was the one who needed watching, if anyone did.

"You will ask Franz to visit us, won't you, Mom?" Celia begged, as they finally reached the end of their voyage back to Cornwall.

Ahead of them they could see the twin castles on the headlands of Pendennis and Mawes, as the welcome outline of Falmouth harbour came into view from the prow of their ship.

"We'll see, honey."

"Oh, you always say that! Why can't you just say yes? It would return Herr Vogl's hospitality to invite Franz. We could invite his parents too," Celia added as an afterthought. "I'm sure they would like to see the pottery, and the Killigrew Clay works."

Skye laughed. "You're so transparent, Celia. I'm quite sure that's not the only reason you want to invite the entire Vogl family."

"Of course it's not. I've already said so," Celia replied candidly. "Oh, please, Mom. Say, yes, so I can write straight back to Franz and invite them."

"You've only just said goodbye to him, Celia."

"I know," she said, suddenly miserable. "But it already seems like years ago. The minute he'd gone I missed him. You wouldn't understand . . ."

Celia felt Skye's arm round her shoulders, and her mother gave her a squeeze.

"Believe me, I do understand, my love," she said softly.

Skye gazed at the familiar shape of the harbour and the many ships that jostled in its deep waters, but in her mind's eye she was seeing herself on another ship in another time approaching this very harbour. A time when she too had fallen recklessly in love with a man she had only known for the duration of the ship's voyage. A man who had been engaged to someone else at the time, but whose love for Skye Tremayne had been too strong to deny. A man called Philip Norwood who had swept Skye off her feet and had eventually married her and fathered her children.

Now the eldest of those children was declaring herself in love with a virtual stranger too. Skye gave a small shiver in the cool evening air. History had a habit of repeating itself, and the endless cycle seemed more pronounced in the long history of the Tremayne family than in any other. Or so it had always seemed to Skye, although she had no doubt that other families would say the same thing of themselves.

"Mom, are you all right?" she heard Celia say.

"Of course I am, and if it will keep you happy, then, of course, we'll invite the Vogls—"

Her reward was a cry of sheer delight. The next minute she was hugged tightly by her effusive and beautiful daughter.

Anyway, the German family might not come, Skye thought privately. Why would they want to leave their home at Christmastime to stay with virtual strangers? By then, four months from now, Celia's butterfly passion for Franz would probably have waned. At seventeen it happened, and absence didn't always make the heart grow fonder.

"Do you see them?" Celia was saying excitedly, craning her neck to catch the first glimpse of the rest of her family. It was barely dusk and the dockside was filled with motor cars and larger vehicles awaiting the disembarkation of the passengers.

"Not yet—" Skye began, and then her heart jolted as she saw the tall figure of Nick Pengelly on the quayside, with two excited young people jumping up and down beside him. Wenna, at

6

sixteen, was not yet too grown up to smother all her excitement, and the finishing shool had done nothing to change that. Skye hoped it never would. While Oliver, at thirteen, would be blatantly expecting presents.

"There's Daddy," Celia screeched.

"Yes," Skye said softly. "I see him."

There was no way her daughter could guess how her heart raced at the sight of Nick, or that Celia could comprehend that love became more constant when you were nearing your middle years. The young believed that love was invented solely for them, but the feelings in Skye Pengelly's heart for the man who had become her second husband, were as achingly longing as when Nick had been her clandestine lover for a few brief hours of stolen bliss.

He and the children caught sight of her and Celia then. They began waving madly, and Skye's wanton feelings momentarily vanished, but she knew they would return, and a shudder of warm anticipation ran through her veins. Once the family reunion was complete, all the talking was done and the excitement had died down a little, she and Nick would be alone at last, with the whole night ahead of them to spend in each others' arms.

"The Games apart, the visit was a success?" Nick asked her a long while later, when they lay, replete and fulfilled, their bodies as intertwined as if they shared the same skin.

"It was wonderful," Skye told him. "But I wish you could have been there, Nick. The showrooms are so elegant, and our goods are displayed with such importance."

"Why wouldn't they be? White Rivers is really on the map now, darling, and the shops here are flourishing."

Skye loved the way he was so pleased for her success. Many men wouldn't be, she thought fleetingly. Many men would resent having a businesswoman for a wife. But there weren't many men like Nick. There was no one like Nick . . .

She held him more tightly for a moment, knowing how lucky she was to have found such love twice in a lifetime. But at his words, the second most important thing in her life took prominence, and her enthusiasm bubbled over in the soft warm darkness.

"But it's nothing like the huge department stores and showrooms they have there in Germany. I can't wait to see Lily and show her some of the brochures I've brought back. They're so keen on advertising. They send out brochures to their regular clients – and they also have them available for indulgent papas to send out to prospective wedding guests. Isn't that a marvellous idea? Imagine all those new brides receiving a complete set of White Rivers pottery to begin their married life with."

Nick laughed. Her enthusiasm was having a different effect on him.

"I don't know about new brides. I would rather concentrate on the one I've got in my arms."

"Hardly a new bride," she murmured, feeling his mouth seeking hers, and thrilling to the fact that he could be so readily aroused again, even after ten years of marriage.

"But every bit as desirable," Nick told her, and as he matched the deed to the words, she gave up thinking at all.

The following day while Celia was busily regaling her brother and sister about the delights of her stay in Germany, and no doubt giving away a few secrets to Wenna about the attentions of the lovely Franz Vogl, Skye made a telephone call to her cousin Lily in Truro.

"You're back!" Lily squealed unnecessarily. "How was it, Skye? Was it marvellous, or were you a bit scared? Right in the heart of the enemy and all that."

"Lily, stop it," Skye said, laughing. "All that was a long time ago. They're not our enemies any more. They're our best customers, don't forget."

"Oh, I know. There are still plenty of folk who can't forget, though, and David's not so tolerant with all the rumours he gets to hear. Still, as you say, we need them."

"How is David?" Skye said swiftly. "And I'm longing to see my nephews. I thought of coming to visit this afternoon."

"Good. David's fine apart from his arthritis, and the twins are driving me mad as usual, so it'll be lovely to have some adult conversation," Lily added cheerfully.

Skye hung up, the smile still on her face at hearing Lily's no-nonsense voice. The twins had come late in her life, but she was coping with everything, the way she always had. It was good to know that some things stayed the same, no matter what . . . and why Skye should think such a thing at that precise moment she couldn't have said.

She was looking forward to seeing Lily, with whom she had such a good rapport, but part of her was also keen to learn any snippets of information Lily's husband may have given her on the Mrs Simpson situation. David Kingsley was the owner of the *Informer* newspaper, and as such, was privy to much of the information withheld from the general public. Personally, Skye thought it ludicrous that the British public were cushioned from important and dramatic events that might shape their nation. It was their right to know. This suppression of news would never happen in America.

Before his death, Skye's brother Sinclair's brief love affair with politics had revealed how many aspects of public life could be inspected under a miscroscope. It wasn't always desirable, but at least it was honest.

She put such thoughts out of her mind. The children were sitting in the garden now with Celia holding court as she discussed the finer points of the Berlin Games with Oliver, and still boasting about meeting the handsome Franz Vogl – for Wenna's envious benefit.

Skye left them to it, and drove her car into Truro, revelling in the warm sunshine, with the fragrant summer scents wafting down from the moors on her left, and the sparkling blue sea on her right. As always, this route gave her a lift of the heart just to be where her ancestors had always been, from the start of their association with Killigrew Clay, when her grandmother, Morwen Tremayne, had married Ben Killigrew, the owner's son. The same great clayworks that Skye now part owned. No matter how often she travelled this road, the memories never failed to stir her heart. And if ever there was any doubt that she had inherited her family's Cornish sense of romance, this was the place she knew it most.

" 'Tis called fey, my love."

She could almost hear Granny Morwen telling her now, as she had done so often years ago. She almost turned her head to answer her with a smile, and knew how foolish that was.

But it was a fact that a person didn't have to be physically near for someone to feel their presence. Even now, Skye was sometimes aware of and charmed by it. It wasn't spooky at all – to use one of Olly's favourite words of the moment – and that was part of the Cornish legacy too, she thought with satisfaction.

When she reached Truro, she paused for a moment after leaving her car to gaze with unabashed pride at the frontage of what had once been Albert Tremayne's artist's studio. This was where Albert and his sister, Primmy, had spent so many happy years in bohemian bliss before Primmy had married Skye's father and gone to America.

The place was completely transformed now. Skye hadn't known what to do with it after Albert had bequeathed it to her. She certainly hadn't wanted to keep it as a dusty museum or art gallery as some kind of ghostly memorial, but the answer had come so joyfully and realistically when her inspired White Rivers Pottery had begun to prosper. The old studio was now an impressive shop and showroom, frequented by all the best people in Truro and the surrounding district. But always mindful that poorer people needed plates and dishes, too, Skye had insisted that they kept a special section of the shop for misshapen and less than perfectly thrown pieces.

Together with David's advertising strategies in the newspaper, it had proved to be a winner. The gleaming window displayed the pure white pieces, which were produced from the finest clay from their own clayworks, with their distinctive winding river decorated on the base of each piece. At Skye's suggestion the back-drop for each wide shop window was a deep blue, showing the china off to its best advantage.

The door of the old studio burst open, and Lily's well-rounded figure rushed through. Lily managed the shop and she and her family lived in the rooms above it. She used to be quite gaunt, but a happy marriage and two enormous twin sons had put paid to that, and she looked all the better for it. The five-year-old boys were at her heels now, like two fat little butterballs.

"It's so good to see you, Skye," Lily exclaimed. "And you look so well! Different, somehow. You were always elegant, but I reckon the continental style has rubbed off on you."

"What rot. I can't have changed that much," she said with a laugh. "It's barely a month since I saw you."

"It seems longer," Lily assured her. "I missed you. We all did, didn't we, boys?"

She always referred to them collectively as boys, even though she knew perfectly well which was Frederick and which was Robert. Skye sometimes wondered if it was going to give them a complex, but then the rest of the family never knew which was which. At their mother's question they hurtled towards Skye, and she was nearly knocked over as they clamoured to be held in her arms.

"Good Lord, they're going to grow up to be boxers at this rate, they're so strong," she gasped.

"That's what David says," Lily said happily. "I can't think where they get it from. Anyway, now that they've seen you, they can go into the garden and play, while we have some tea and you can tell me everything about Berlin."

That was Lily: tell me everything, in one fell swoop. But Skye relished her cousin's sharp mind, for it matched her own.

"Did Celia behave herself?" Lily asked over tea and toast, but before waiting for an answer, she rushed on, "Which reminds me, I saw Betsy the other day, and she thinks you were very modern in taking Celia to Germany by yourself. I think she was admiring your courage, but you can never be sure with Betsy, can you?"

Skye screwed up her nose. "Betsy's getting old and crusty just like Theo," she said, knowing she would have to meet their mutual male cousin quite soon, since she and Theo were co-owners of their various enterprises. "Anyway, why on earth shouldn't two women travel alone? You and I and plenty of others did far more during the war."

"True, but it was acceptable then, because they needed us. Now that we've all become *respectable* again, for want of a better word, we're supposed to take a back seat and sit at home knitting socks for our menfolk."

Skye grinned at the thought, knowing it was quite alien to Lily's nature. Lily had been a foremost feminist, and she and her sister Vera and Skye had served together in France in the war. Travelling unescorted had been seen as a serving woman's right at that time. Now, it seemed that the male population was only too anxious to keep its women chained to the kitchen sink once more, as one progressive cartoonist had portrayed it.

"I hardly think we come into that category," Skye said. "And they can like it or lump it."

11

"Sometimes, Skye, you're still so deliciously *American*," Lily said with a chuckle.

"*Still?* I always will be, nothing's ever going to change that! Anyway, you wanted to know about Celia, didn't you? She found a beau, of course."

"Well, was there any doubt? She's a Tremayne, no matter what label she goes under now. They were never short of beaux, even though it took some of us longer than others to discover what we wanted. And did you see that horrible little man?"

"If you mean Mr Hitler, yes we did. And yes, he is—"

"David doesn't like the situation at all," Lily said, apparently going off at a tangent. "He calls Hitler a rogue character and quite unpredictable. David sees dark times ahead if we're not careful."

"You don't mean another war? There's no likelihood of that, surely. All the German people we met were exceptionally correct and genteel."

"But ordinary folk don't rule the roost, do they? Oh, forget I said anything. It's probably nothing."

The trouble was, Skye couldn't quite forget it. David Kingsley had access to too many sources denied to other people. And this nasty little Adolf Hitler had already stirred up more than one hornet's nest by entering the Rhineland in March, throwing the French into confusion over whether to keep their dignity and refrain from comment, with the more belligerent of them shouting for instant military action.

Warmongering had been evident then, and when one newspaper claimed that Hitler was merely re-occupying what was rightfully his, it was pointed out that it was also a hundred miles nearer to French territory. Skye felt a shiver of real unease, and tried to shrug it off as she drove home to New World, deciding to call in on Theo and Betsy on the way.

"Betsy's out visiting, so you'll have to put up wi' me. So how were the bastards?" Theo asked her, with his usual charm.

Nearing sixty now, he was more portly than ever, and wheezing with the extra weight he carried, which did not improve his looks or his habitual lack of finesse.

"If you mean the Germans, they were delightful people," Skye snapped. "Why must you always despise everyone, Theo?"

"My God, but you've got a short memory, girl. Have you forgotten how those young German workers wrecked the pottery and half killed one of the clayworkers into the bargain?"

"For pity's sake, all that was more than ten years ago!" she said, exasperated. "You can't keep dredging up the past for ever."

"Why not? If it weren't for the healthy accounts we get from our exports, I'd say good riddance to the lot of 'em. They were our enemies in the war, and as far as I'm concerned, they're our enemies now and always will be."

His son Sebastian arrived home from the pottery in time to hear his father's usual blistering onslaught.

"Pay no attention to him, Skye," he told her with a grin. "He's always worse when the gout plays him up. I only wish I'd had the chance to go to Germany with you and Celia. How did it go, by the way?"

"It was wonderful, Sebby," she said, thinking it a marvel that he had turned out so agreeable. As a child he had been as obnoxious as any youngster she had ever come across. But now, working at the pottery with the clay he loved, alongside her own young brother-in-law, Ethan Pengelly, Sebby had turned into a fine young man, albeit with a roving eye for the girls.

"And she got a glimpse of the chief bastard, so don't bother asking her," Theo snarled.

"What was he like?" Sebby asked, ignoring his father.

"Charlie Chaplin," Skye said solemnly, as irreverent as Celia, and within seconds the two of them were laughing hysterically at the image.

After an hour, when she had repeated yet again everything she had told Lily, she finally headed for home. By then she knew that all was well at the pottery, though she sensed a small hesitation from Sebby as he had said so. Skye guessed it was due to a little bit of healthy friction between him and Ethan, which was understandable in two such creative young men, and nothing to worry about.

At least there were no current complaints from Killigrew Clay. That was a small triumph in itself, she thought, knowing the volatile nature of the clayworkers.

The memory of the German Chancellor still wouldn't leave her mind. It was one thing to scoff at a person's appearance, but the power that the man held was indisputable. And he was greedy. Surely the impossible couldn't happen again, when the younger members of her own scattered family were of an age to be involved? She shivered, thankful that Celia and Wenna were girls, and Olly still only thirteen.

But Sebastian was nineteen now, and his brother Justin a hefty fifteen. Even Ethan at twenty-five, would be more than ready to go if the call came, avenging the brother he had lost in the Great War.

Skye tried to shake off the unreasonable sense of disaster. It was madness to let passing remarks dwell in her mind and fester. It was even crazier to start imagining events that would probably never happen. Hitler's desire for power would be just as likely to fizzle out and disappear when some new ambitious politician challenged his right to lead the German hierarchy.

She comforted herself with that thought, and spent the evening with her husband and children gathered around her, as if to assure herself that together they were a stronghold that no one could violate.

# Two

C elia knew she was taking out her ill temper on her sister. She also knew it wasn't fair but she couldn't seem to stop it, as a natural deflation after the visit to Germany replaced her exhilaration.

Wenna was by far the gentler of the two sisters and, though she was by no means spineless, she had always been a useful scapegoat for Celia's sharper tongue. But this time she was goaded beyond measure.

"If you're so mad about the stupid boy, why don't you just go and live in Germany?" Wenna finally burst out.

"I wasn't even talking about Franz," Celia snapped, ignoring the little leap of her heart at just saying his name.

"You don't have to talk about him. You've been mooning over him ever since you and Mom got home from Berlin. Where's the sense in wasting your time dreaming over some boy who's so far away? He won't come here so near to Christmas, anyway, and we don't want him. We have enough family of our own without having strangers in the house."

Celia curbed her rage with difficulty. "Well, we all know *you* dream about someone much closer, of course, and a fat lot of good it will do you. Ethan's not going to bother his head over a little ninny like you. He still sees you as a schoolgirl – which you are!"

It was the final moment of triumph, and she saw Wenna's face flush a deep red at the insult. It wasn't Wenna's fault that Celia was more than a year her senior, but her sister never let her forget it. Nor did Celia ever forget that Ethan Pengelly had always championed Wenna, and teased Celia in a mocking way that constantly affronted her, and made her feel more like a good pal than the desirable young lady she purported to be.

But Ethan was a man now, and Wenna must know he didn't

look at her in any way but as Celia described it. If anyone was wasting her life dreaming about the impossible, it was Wenna for ever thinking that a man of twenty-five would waste his time on a schoolgirl who had just turned sixteen. There was a limit to how long she could fool herself that Ethan was just waiting for her to become an adult.

At Wenna's suddenly downcast look, Celia's demeanour softened without warning. Her frown vanished, her blue eyes sparkled and her mobile mouth curved upwards in a laugh.

"Just listen to us, will you? Mom would have a fit if she knew how the family coffers were being wasted on a good education by the way we're always bickering. We're supposed to be turning into young ladies, aren't we?"

Wenna laughed back, her sunnier nature never allowing her to stay cross with Celia for long.

"I wonder why a Swiss finishing school is supposed to be any better at that than anywhere else? At any rate, I always thought it was healthy for sisters to be competitive."

"Oh, is that what we are? I'll have to watch out when Franz comes to visit then." Celia grinned, complacent about her own sensuality and confident that such rivalry was never likely to happen. She hugged Wenna's arm. "Anyway, we're supposed to be looking round Mom's old pottery today, so that should please you, seeing dear Ethan up to his bare elbows in wet clay!"

She felt an odd tingle in her veins as she said the words. She had no particular feelings for Ethan Pengelly, her stepfather's brother, but she had to admit that if Wenna fancied someone like mad, she felt it was her bounden duty, as the elder sister, to prove that she could attract him too. It never meant anything as far as Celia was concerned. She treated her male cousins in the same way. It was just harmless flirtation, and it had the safety valve of being within the family. It was nothing at all compared with the way she felt about Franz Vogl.

Ethan Pengelly and Sebastian Tremayne were inspecting a particularly fine set of tableware they had just completed for Skye's approval. It was an experimental design, and Sebby knew he would have to win his aunt round to agree to it. She preferred to stick with tried and trusted methods, but you had to move on or you became stagnant.

His aunt was in _his_ mid-forties now, and in his opinion a little
staid in some respects, though hardly in the way his mother was.
Skye was still considered a beauty, while his mother had always
been old, even as a young wife, and when he was a child Seb had
been perfectly aware of his father's little peccadilloes. He
doubted that they still continued, what with Theo's gout and
his preference to stay at home at night, or to frequent the local
hostelries rather than going further afield. But Seb had been
blessed, or cursed, with his father's roving eyes for the female sex,
and was well aware of the way his beautiful girl cousins were
growing up.

Cousins or not, it was a good thing, as far as he was concerned,
that they spent so much of their time in Switzerland, he bragged
to himself, or . . .

"What's put that stupid grin on your face?" Ethan asked him.
"If you're planning how to win Skye round with your nonsense,
you'd better think again. If this new design is not going to be a
viable proposition, she won't agree to it, and we'll be accused of
wasting time and materials."

Seb scowled at once. Ethan had a knack of putting things in a
sensible perspective and, although they rubbed along remarkably
well, he was the more headstrong of the pair. Since Ethan's
brother Adam had retired from the business, Ethan was in charge
of White Rivers now. He had been persuaded against his will to
produce the set of tableware that now bore an entwined W and R
at intervals around the edge of the plates and the base of the
cups. It was elegant, but it wasn't Skye's design. It was Seb's.

"My father agreed with it," he reminded Ethan.

"Of course he did, since he was sure Skye would oppose it,"
Ethan said, knowing Theo's contrariness only too well. "When
did you ever know him to be happy to think a woman had the
upper hand in his business dealings – and especially an *American*
woman?" he added.

"She does though, doesn't she?" Sebby said thoughtfully. "She
always has, the way they said her grandmother did."

Ethan, paused, sluicing his hands under cold water to rid
himself of the wet clay remains that clung to them.

"You never knew her, did you, Seb? Old Morwen Tremayne, I
mean. That's how folk always referred to her, even though she'd
had two husbands."

"Well, since I was only a baby when she died, no, I never knew her. Why – did you?"

Ethan shook his head. "Not really. My family weren't involved with them then. I saw her once, though, when she was a very old woman. She had these amazingly blue eyes that seemed to look right through you, even though she must have been about eighty years old at the time. I was about seven, and it scared me, I can tell you. It was just as if she knew every damn thing I was thinking. Of course, they always said she was more fey than most."

Seb stared at him. It wasn't exactly the way his father had described Morwen Tremayne to him. Theo was Morwen's grandson, and he had loved and feared her in equal measure, but his aggression was mostly because he could never accept the idea of a woman being in charge of business. And what a woman. Seb was well aware that no one who had known Morwen Tremayne had ever been in doubt of her strength of character. She was practically a legend around St Austell and the Killigrew clayworks.

This was why he knew damn well he must never under estimate Skye's reaction to his new pottery design. She walked only too well in Morwen Tremayne's footsteps. So Seb knew he must tread cautiously, even though he and Ethan had worked bloody hard to bring the new design to a perfect finish before displaying it to her. But even so, he couldn't forget his father's sarcastic aside that if Skye hated it, then Sebby would just have to give the set to his mother for an early Christmas gift.

"Bloody cheapskate," Seb muttered beneath his breath.

"Thank you for that!" Ethan said indignantly.

"I didn't mean you. Anyway, you'd better perk up. Aunt Skye has just arrived with the girl cousins."

They both looked through the workroom window to where Skye was getting out of her car with Celia and Wenna. Contrary to most of the large and scattered Tremayne family and their descendents, neither the sisters nor their brother Oliver had the remotest interest in clay. After finishing his education, Oliver was determined to follow in his stepfather's footsteps and become a lawyer.

"My God, but Celia improves every time I see her," Seb commented. "It's at this time of year you appreciate that women

18

are wearing shorter skirts. She's also growing outwards as well as upwards, if you see what I mean. What a luscious pair – and I don't just mean her and her sister."

His coarseness hid the sudden nervousness he was feeling. He had hardly realised himself how vital the acceptance of this new pottery design was to him until he saw Skye. He had been in his father's shadow all his life and, although working under the Pengelly brothers had been perfectly acceptable to him while he served his apprenticeship, he never forgot that he was a Tremayne. He was now as skilled a potter as any man, and he needed to assert himself in the family business.

He ignored Ethan's snappy rejoinder to mind his manners. Pengelly had better mind his, Seb thought, and to remember who he was – and more importantly, who he wasn't. He strode through into the pottery showroom to greet his relatives.

"It's good to see you again, Aunt Skye, and I hardly need to ask how the world is treating my lovely cousins. You both look blooming, girls."

"Now then, Seb, enough of the flattery," Skye said with a laugh, aware he was sizing up her daughters. "Your father tells me you've got something to show me."

"Did he? It was meant to be a surprise."

"Well, since I have no idea what it is, it's going to stay a surprise for ever unless you show me, honey," she said coolly. "And how are you today, Ethan?" she added as he entered the showroom, hastily pulling down his shirt sleeves to cover his bare arms.

"I'm well enough, thanks," he said, still wiping the remnants of clay from his hands. He wondered how it was that Seb could always look so spick and span moments after finishing work, while he always felt as though he looked as dishevilled as a dishrag, especially in front of finely turned out folk like these three.

"Have you heard about our visit?" Celia asked him, cutting across the formalities. "If not, I'm sure Wenna's dying to tell you everything at second-hand."

"Seb's passed on most of it," Ethan said, "but I'm always glad to hear anything Wenna has to tell me."

"All right, you two, stop this bantering and let Sebby show me the surprise," Skye said briskly, seeing how Wenna's face began

19

to colour. The poor girl had always looked up to Ethan, and her adoration had never wavered since she was a child.

I wish it would, Skye thought suddenly. There was far too much intermarriage in the family already, and she didn't relish any more. She immediately thought how foolish she was being, to interpret a childhood fantasy in such a way.

"Before I do, I'd be glad if you would say nothing until you've counted to ten," Seb said.

"My goodness, what have you done, Seb – set fire to the workroom?" Celia giggled.

"Be quiet, Celia," her mother said sharply.

There had been a time, long ago, when these very premises had been reduced to ashes in a blistering and maliciously started fire. But they and the business had risen, triumphant and phoenix-like to begin again, and she wanted no reminders of that time.

The three women followed the young men into the workroom. They were *all* women now, Ethan realised, even little Wenna was the epitome of the fabulous Tremayne beauty. She was no longer a child. He felt a throb of desire in his loins which he thrust away. The girl was no more than sixteen, for God's sake. No matter how much rapport had always existed between them, it wasn't right to think of her in that way.

He caught the glimmer of mockery in Celia's eyes right then, and knew she had been perfectly aware of the way his thoughts were going. Bloody knowing wench, he thought savagely, reverting to the earthier speech of the clayfolk, as if to relieve the feelings in his surging lower regions.

Seb had arranged the set of tableware on a dark blue cloth, the way the sale pieces were displayed here and in the Truro shop and showroom. Their own Killigrew clay produced the finest and whitest of Cornish china clay, and their pottery was acclaimed country-wide and beyond. He had no doubt of the quality of his work, just Skye's reaction to it.

Once they were all assembled in the workroom, he pulled off the covering cloth with all the aplomb of a magician pulling a rabbit out of a hat. He looked anxiously at his aunt, his heart thumping. He truly didn't want to displease her, but he couldn't miss the frown on her wide forehead as she looked at his new design.

"My father says that if you absolutely hate it, I must give it to my mother for an early Christmas gift, and forget all about creating any new designs. It was no more than an experiment, you see," he heard himself say quickly, despising himself for doing so.

He was normally a brash and self-confident young man, but these three women, with their glorious blue eyes gazing on his work – his creation – were practically dissolving his innards.

"It's beautiful, Seb," Celia declared, breaking the silence. "Isn't it, Mom? And if no one else wants it, I'd be glad to have the set for my hope chest."

She challenged her mother to deny it. Seb laughed, more nervously than usual.

"Hope chest? You're hardly out of the nursery, cuz. It's far too early to be thinking about such things."

"It's never too early, providing it's no more than a distant dream," Skye murmured without thinking, while taking in the fact that the two men had been mighty busy while she had been away. But she had to be fair. "I like the result. But I'm not sure I want to go into production with it. People know what to look for with our goods."

"But that's just it. We've become too predictable, and perhaps the time has come to move forward, Aunt Skye," Seb persisted, becoming bolder now. "It's called progress—"

"I know what it's called, thank you. Anyway, I suggest you do as your father says and give this set to your mother, and I'll think about progress."

He had to be content with that for now, but there was something else he wanted to ask his aunt about.

"Would you object to my inviting Celia to a tea dance next Saturday afternoon at the Regal Hotel in Truro? If she'd care to come with me, that is."

Celia burst out laughing. "Dancing? You?"

"I do have some social graces, cuz, even if my father sneers at them. And I have been known to trip the light fantastic, as they say." He was cucumber-cool, but his eyes glinted dangerously, and her heart skipped a beat.

She composed her face, even though the image of her large cousin waltzing serenely round a ballroom was so unlikely. But she realised Wenna had drawn in her breath. Not that she had been invited, Celia thought at once. Everyone knew that an afternoon tea dance was at once respectable and slightly decadent, so why not? Even with Seb Tremayne.

There was always the chance there would be other handsome young men there. Dancing was so deliciously innocent a pastime, yet so intimate as well. The next moment she heard Wenna's explosive gasp.

"If Celia goes, can I go too, Mom?"

"I haven't said she can go yet," Skye said.

"She can't go without a partner, anyway," Celia put in at once. "It would look silly for one man to escort two girls. She'd have to sit at the side like a wallflower all afternoon."

"I wouldn't allow that," Seb said, though it hadn't been part of his plan to include Wenna in the invitation. It hadn't been his plan to go dancing at all, except that his mother was always urging him to do these things in her attempt to make him as different from his uncouth father as possible. He was already wishing he hadn't been so impetuous as to virtually kowtow to his aunt. It wasn't his style.

"You'd divide yourself between them, would you?" Skye said, her eyes beginning to twinkle at the way these three were revealing their feelings. Celia, aching to be grown-up and escorted to a dance . . . Sebby wanting a girl to himself, despite the way his father would probably mock him when he heard of the invitation . . . and Wenna, so envious that she wasn't old enough yet to be thought of as a suitable dancing partner, and knowing she would be only there on sufferance.

"If Wenna didn't think me too old a partner, I'd be glad to offer myself as a fourth person – or a chaperon, if you prefer it," Ethan said.

"I accept," Wenna said, suddenly overwhelmed at the thought of swaying in his arms to the strains of the waltz. "And I don't think you're too old to be my partner at all."

"Now, just a moment, young lady," Skye said sharply, and then saw the pleading expression in her daughter's eyes, and recognised her longing to be considered grown-up enough to do this. She looked at Ethan. "Can you dance?"

He coloured up at once. "No. Never tried. But maybe Wenna would teach me."

Celia hooted. "She couldn't teach anyone."

22

"Of course she could. Her music teacher says she has a marvellous sense of rhythm and timing—"

"That's piano playing, Mom! Teaching someone to dance in public would be just too embarrassing. You can't let her do it – I'll be mortified," Celia wailed.

"Then Ethan must come to the house every evening and we'll give him some private lessons," Skye said firmly.

It wasn't what Celia had had in mind at all, but seeing her mother's steely eyes, she knew she had to accept it.

As for Wenna, she had the dizzy promise that Ethan Pengelly was to be her dancing partner on Saturday and all the evenings in between, since she was quite sure that Celia would be set on flirting with Sebby Tremayne.

While they were at the pottery their brother Oliver was grumbling to Justin Tremayne from their moorland vantage point by the clay pool at Killigrew Clay.

"We've got to have this big eighteenth birthday party for Celia in December. You'll all be invited, of course, and now she wants to include this German fellow she met in Berlin," Olly complained. "I can't see what all the fuss is about. She'll be putting on even more airs and graces than usual once she's a so-called teacher at that finishing school of hers."

"At least you can bet Wenna won't get so stuffy," Justin said, skimming a pebble across the clay pool and watching it dance over the milky green surface.

"No. Celia was always the uppity one, even before she left Cornwall. From the moment she could talk, I dare say."

Justin laughed sympathetically. His older brother Seb had been the same with him once, until he discovered Justin had his own way of dealing with insults and had then simply ignored him. Justin had more than come into his own since then. He was two years older than his cousin Olly, but they had become as thick as thieves recently. Both were dark-haired, strapping youths, and more tolerant of each other than of their own siblings.

"You worry too much," Justin said. "You should be more like your mother or blood will out, and you'll end up as pompous as your father was."

"I hardly remember him. Was he really so awful?"

23

"Not awful. Just a picky minded professor. You have to forgive them for that, because that's the way they're made," Justin said easily. "Anyway, you get on all right with your stepfather, don't you?"

Olly's face cleared. "Oh, yes, Nick's spiffing!"

"Does he mind you calling him Nick?"

"Why should he? It's his name. The girls call him Daddy, but he's not my father and I believe in keeping things right – even though we all agreed to take his surname when my mother suggested it. But I'm still my father's son," he declared.

"My God, Olly, you're definitely a lawyer in the making, you pompous little twerp," Justin said with a grin.

Olly gave him a swipe across the arm, and the next minute they were tussling good-naturedly on the turf. They rolled over and over, and Justin finally declared himself the winner, sitting astride Olly and urging him to surrender.

"All right, you bastard," Olly squealed, and as Justin relaxed, he reversed their positions and sat heavily on his cousin, bumping up and down in triumph.

Justin felt a familiar and pleasurable surge in his groin. One of the more erotic discussions between his school contemporaries lately was of this discovery which could be so amazingly potent and produce such spectacularly joyous results under cover of the bedsheets. Sometimes it literally just happened . . . as if your mind had no control over your body, no matter whether you were a scholarly swot – which he certainly was not – or the son of a clay boss, which he was.

He tried to ignore the feeling as he rolled well away from Olly, and squirmed at the tacky dampness in his drawers, praying that Olly wouldn't notice it. Sometimes, close as they were, the two years between them could seem as wide as a chasm.

"Here, you two young uns, what are you about? Don't 'ee know this is private property?"

At the sound of the angry voice, the boys scrambled to their feet and brushed off the clay dust clinging to their clothes. They turned to face the burly man bearing down on them and, at the sight of his hard hat and shiny boots, they recognised the garb and suspicious face of the pit captain.

"We're very well aware of it, as a matter of fact," Justin said in his best school voice. He saw the man's expression change at once.

"Oh, I'm sorry, young sirs, I didn't see it was the two of you. We get some queer folk around here at times, see, and not always up to any good. Beggin' your pardons, I'm sure. But you should mind these clay pools all the same. They'm quite deep in places, and there's been more than one accident in 'em over the years."

"That's all right, Mr Vickery," Olly said. "You did quite right to question us, and thank you for the warning."

"Good day to 'ee both then."

As soon as the man had stumped off, Justin turned to his cousin. He frowned, his eyes squinting in the sunlight that dazzled on the mountains of clay waste – the pale sky tips glinting with the deposits of mica and other minerals that were a vivid reminder to upcountry folk from England that they had reached the far west of Cornwall.

"Why do you defer to these people so easily?" Justin complained. "You should remember who you are, Olly."

"I do remember, but I haven't had such a fancy education as you to put plums in my mouth. Anyway, things have changed since the clay bosses were kings around here. Even Killigrew Clay is down to one pit now, instead of four. I know your father still lords it over the clayfolk whenever he comes up here, but you're not the son of God, Justin."

"I'm not the son of a piddling pottery owner, either!"

"Well, at least we have something to show for the work that goes on there, instead of just piddling lumps of clay!" Olly said rudely. "You're a prize snob too, and if you want to know what I think, I reckon you and Celia are two of a kind."

His young voice, cracking with tortuous adolescence, rose higher. He was red with anger and always defensive of his mother, whom he adored. They had grown even closer over the years, especially since he had declared his intention to follow his stepfather's profession. To his secret shame he sometimes wished that his sisters would stay in their marvellous Switzerland, and never come home at all. Every time they did, things changed, and he had to share his mother with them.

Justin saw the sudden misery in his cousin's eyes and bit back the retort he had intended to make. Instead, he gave Olly a playful punch on the shoulder.

"Well, I haven't seen her since she came back from her visit to Germany yet. But I doubt that your high-and-mighty Celia will even deign to talk to her country cousins any more – especially Seb. She was always superior to him."

He grinned, remembering the spats they had all had as children, and since such occasions had usually ended in rough and tumbles, and then the inevitable pacifying parties from the grown-ups, he felt a passing regret that such a childhood couldn't continue for ever. And that was a bloody pathetic way for a healthy, red-blooded fifteen-year-old to be feeling.

It was a feeling that didn't last long though, not now that he was learning the new delights of approaching manhood, and knew there were so many girls in the world just waiting to be loved, and so many exciting experiences still to be tried. Not that he had done any of it yet. But he would, he thought confidently. In that respect he was certainly his lusty father's son, and so was his older brother.

"You've done *what*?" Theo asked Sebastian when the Tremayne family were sitting down to their evening meal.

Seb looked at him resentfully.

"I'm taking Celia Pengelly to a tea dance on Saturday, and Ethan Pengelly's bringing Wenna as well just to make it a family occasion and keep the numbers even."

"That's very nice of you boys, Sebby," his mother began.

"It's bloody poncey!" Theo exploded. "Working wi' the Pengelly fellow's one thing, but hobnobbing with him socially won't do your standing in the town any good at all."

Seb laughed carelessly. "Since when did you ever care what folk thought? And there's no need to cut Ethan down to size, not when his brother's married to Aunt Skye. Nick Pengelly's an important man in his own right in these parts."

Theo glowered at him. His foot was playing him up like billy-oh, and he could do without his son scoring points over him. T'other one could stop that stupid grinning too, he thought, and he snapped at Justin at once.

"What's funning you, then, boy?"

"Nothing. Well, just something Olly said."

"Oh, ah. And what was that?"

Theo heard his own voice coarsening, and knew it was

because, God dammit, he had sent the boy away to a posh school, and now he found his tidied-up accent as irritating as a cactus burr.

"Just that the pottery has something to show for the work they do, instead of just piddling lumps of clay. Maybe you should never have sold the pottery to her—"

Theo's eyes narrowed. So the little runt had been talking out of turn, had he? To Theo's amazement Seb suddenly turned on him, his eyes blazing.

"Olly's right. You should *never* have done that, Father!"

"Why the hell not?" Theo roared. "I'll do what I like and it'll take more'n the likes of you to stop me!"

"But can't you see what it means to me now?"

Theo leaned back in his dining chair, arms folded. He looked scathingly at his son.

"Why don't you tell me, if what I do with my business is so all-fired important to you?"

"You know damn well what the reason is," Seb flashed at him, ignoring his mother's tut-tutting. "When you sold out your half of the business to Aunt Skye it meant it would never come to me. All the work I've put into it all these years will be for nothing."

Theo crashed his chair forward again.

"And whose fault is it that you went straight into the potting nonsense instead of getting a proper education like your brother? You had the chance, but no, you had to do what *you* wanted," he yelled, not caring that he was totally backtracking on his opinion of what London schoolmasters were doing to Justin's speech.

"It was what *you* wanted, wasn't it? To have at least one of your sons knee-deep in clay."

"Knee-deep in it is one thing. Moulding fancy pieces of china for namby-pamby rich folk to enjoy is summat else. Especially bloody foreigners. And there's nowt wrong wi' clayworking, you young bugger. My father and grandfather all held their heads up high working in an honest Cornish occupation, not prissying about—"

Whatever else he was about to say was lost as Seb threw back his chair.

"If that's your opinion of me, then the less we see of each other, the better," he shouted back. "And I'm still taking my cousin dancing on Saturday, however prissy an occupation you consider *that*!" With that, he strode out of the room.

27

There was silence for a few minutes, as Theo strove to contain his anger and Betsy calmly continued to serve up three dishes of bread-and-butter pudding.

One of these days, she thought, eyeing her husband's puce-coloured facial contortions, his temper will get the better of him, and we'll all be happier when he's six feet under – and may God forgive me for thinking so.

As she anticipated, Theo's silence didn't last, though the words he muttered savagely beneath his breath were mostly unintelligible. This newly contrived habit was supposed to relieve Betsy from having to listen to his obscenities, but she didn't need to hear them to know how verbally inventive he could be in cursing anyone who angered him.

When they had all finished eating, she heard Justin clear his throat in the annoying way he had developed lately when he was about to make some clever pronouncement. Betsy gave a sigh, having looked forward to a quiet evening, and prayed that he wasn't about to enrage Theo even more.

"Father, I wonder if this would be a good time to discuss my future with you?"

# Three

W enna looked forward to Saturday afternoon with tremulous anticipation. It would be the first proper dance
she had ever attended. At St Augustine's Academy for Young
Ladies near Gstaad, rudiments of the dance was on the
curriculum as a desirable accomplishment for every well-bred
young lady. But dancing there had been confined to holding
another girl semi-close while meticulously following the instructions of an eagle-eyed dance mistress who considered too
much proximity with another person to be unhealthy, which
was why she had been given the secret nickname of the female
eunuch.

Now, true to Skye's promise, each night after supper, Wenna's
parents put a suitable record on the gramophone, and she
swayed to a waltz or a slow foxtrot in the arms of Ethan Pengelly,
which was like a dream come true. Or it would be, if only he
didn't have such clumsy feet and trod on hers more often than
not. Even more so, if her sister didn't hoot with laughter every
time they stumbled into one another.

"Does Celia have to stay here, Mom?" Wenna finally burst
out. "She's just being beastly, and she's putting me off."

"I agree. Go and do something else, Celia," Skye said firmly,
seeing Wenna's heated face, and her elder daughter flounced out
of the room.

"Now then, honey, you come and wind up the gramophone,
and Nick and I will demonstrate to Ethan how it's done. It will
probably be easier for him to watch the man's steps, and then
copy them."

Skye saw Ethan breathe more easily. Poor lad, she thought,
plunged into the middle of something he probably didn't have
the remotest interest in. But once her daughters had decided on
something, no man was safe. She smiled up into her husband's

eyes, remembering how he had once said the very same thing about all the females in the family.

According to Nick, they weren't wily, just irresistible. It was a long while since they had danced together and she had forgotten how very enjoyable it was. Maybe they should accompany the girls to the tea dance, but immediately she had thought it, she knew such a suggestion wouldn't be welcome. Young girls wouldn't want their parents around when they were doing their best to be alluring to two personable young men. The thought was only a fleeting one, but it startled Skye for a moment, relegating herself and Nick, as it did, to an older generation.

They *were* the older generation, for pity's sake, but you didn't always want to be reminded that time moved on more swiftly than you ever noticed. Here she was, with an almost eighteen-year-old daughter, when there were still times when she felt just as young and foolish as when she had been that age.

She was the one to stumble over Nick's feet then, and she forced herself to laugh.

"You see? We can all make mistakes, Ethan. But you'll be fine by Saturday, I promise you. A few more lessons and you'll be a proper gigolo."

"Good God, I hope not," laughed Nick.

"What's a gigolo?" Wenna said, frowning.

"Officially it's a male professional dancing partner," Ethan said, poker-faced. "But they sometimes do other activities as well."

"Do they? Well, I don't think there's much chance of you ever turning into one of them without more practice. I hope you never do, anyway," Wenna added. "You're much too nice to do something that sounds rather horrid."

She wasn't quite sure what those other activities might involve, but she blushed more deeply as she said it, and prayed that her heart wasn't actually throbbing on her sleeve as all the penny dreadfuls had it. If any of her family had the faintest idea of how passionately she had loved Ethan Pengelly all her life, they would probably be highly alarmed and forbid her to go dancing with him at all. At sixteen, they considered her still a child. Ethan was nine years older and already a man. But her feelings for him were far removed from anything childlike although she was mature enough to hide them – most of the time.

\* \* \*

Seb Tremayne and his father were at loggerheads again. Seb's own aggressive streak which always simmered just below the surface, was very much his father's legacy to him. When the two of them clashed their anger could sometimes blow up into volcanic proportions. He had a pretty shrewd idea that Theo was losing much of his interest in Killigrew Clay, which was a major shock to Seb, indoctrinated in it as he was.

He knew his family's sometimes violent history. He knew that Morwen Tremayne had been a young bal maiden working at Killigrew Clay when she had caught the eye of the owner's son, Ben Killigrew, and had eventually married him. He knew of her feyness and her reputed sixth sense, and although he would have ridiculed any such nonsense in himself, Seb knew what the future held for him if his father sold out his half-share of the clayworks, either to Skye, or to some other ambitious buyer. There were no supernatural fantasies about what such a prospect would mean to Seb: There would be no inheritance for him if the clayworks went outside the family. Even if it remained, prestigious though it was, it was long past its heyday, and Theo was cantankerous enough to sell out just to spite his son. He had already sold out his shares in the pottery to Skye, and although Seb loved getting his hands in the wet clay and producing something beautiful out of nothing, he was Tremayne enough to want the clayworks to continue within the family. It was their backbone, their strength.

Seb also guessed that in due course Ethan would be granted full control of the pottery by way of seniority, and he would be no more than a dogsbody employee. He seethed at the affront to his pride, but he'd put up with it, providing the Tremaynes were still the owners of Killigrew Clay as well.

He hadn't fully realised just how much he wanted the family continuity to remain. It occurred to him that he was the only one with the proud name of Tremayne who felt that way. Justin wasn't interested. But it was important to Seb that the name shouldn't die out and lose its meaning or its position in the community.

"I don't know you why you waste your time worrying about any of it," Justin said, when Seb sought him out later that evening. "Although, I admit that the clayworks are far bigger than any tin-pot business – sorry for the pun, bruth – and china clay sells everywhere for a multitude of purposes."

"You don't understand, do you? You never had any interest in any of it, unless you were thinking of trying to throw a pot or two as a pastime," Seb said, nettled.

Justin shook his head. "Of course not. But I've just had an interesting conversation with Father about my future."

"Oh, *your* future is it? I didn't think he was in the mood to talk sensibly with anyone, not even his blue-eyed boy. So what's going on? Don't tell me you're planning on becoming a clay-worker after all, and risk getting those nice white hands dirty."

"I'm going into medicine. I've been recommended by my tutors and I've just informed Father of the fact."

"Christ, Justin, why can't you talk in plain English for five minutes? *Informed* Father, for God's sake? What kind of talk is that?"

"It's something you wouldn't understand," Justin said, refusing to be riled. Then he grinned. "Actually, I thought Father would throw a fit about my wanting to study in London, but he was remarkably calm about it."

Seb snorted. "Why would you want to go to London? What's wrong with learning doctoring in Cornwall, if you *must* consider such an unsavoury occupation. Don't Cornish folk need their coughs and colds sorted out?"

Justin flushed. "I'm not being a snob, Seb, although you all seem to think I am. But Father's willing for me to go to university and then to medical school and who knows where I may end?"

Seb stared at him, seeing the determination in his face and a new authority that he'd never noticed before.

"My God, sometimes I wonder if I know you at all, bruth. Does your new best pal know about all this ambition?"

"If you mean Oliver, no, I haven't told him yet."

"Oh well, I suppose the future doctor and lawyer will make fine bedfellows – and don't take me literally."

Justin grinned. "You needn't have any fear of that," he said, thankful they were on sociable terms again and that the great trauma of revealing his budding hopes to his family was out in the open. He had to move forward, and Cornwall didn't hold him in spirit as it did the rest of them.

Unknowingly, he had a similar thought to that of his cousin

Oliver right then. Everything changed. Nothing stayed the same. But in Justin's case, it was a welcome thought.

It was the final weekend before Celia and Wenna were to return to Gstaad for the new term. Saturday was to be a highlight they hadn't expected, and they were both in a tizzy as they got ready for Ethan to call for them and drive them into Truro to collect Seb on the way.

"I wish I had jubblies like yours," Wenna wailed, as she tried in vain to push her bosom up higher into the white afternoon frock. "Mine are pathetic."

Celia preened in front of the mirror, admiring her own curvaceous figure in her best blue organdie afternoon frock. Then the pose softened as she giggled, standing with her hands on her hips for a moment.

"Now then, girrrls," she said, in a fair imitation of their Scottish female eunuch dancing tutor. "Young ladies should never refer to brrreasts in any shape or form. Indeed, we must try to forget we even have them. It's unhealthy to dwell too much on our bodies, and especially on our brrreasts."

Wenna giggled. "Well, you can't forget *you've* got them," she said. "I just wish mine would grow."

"Never mind, Ethan will love you just the same," Celia said lightly, meaning nothing, and not realising just how her sister's heart beat faster at the words.

At the sound of the motor-car hooter, they turned and raced each other downstairs, calling out goodbye to their parents and running out into the sunlight in a scrabble for the front passenger seat.

"And there go our so-called young ladies," Skye said with a laugh to her husband as they waved them off. "Have we wasted all our money on an expensive Swiss education, do you think?"

She felt his arm go around her and he nuzzled his chin into her neck beneath her glossy hair as she leaned back against him.

"If they turn out as beautiful and desirable as their mother, then we haven't wasted a penny of it," he told her.

She twisted round in his arms. "Why, Nicholas Pengelly, for a stuffy old lawyer, that was almost poetic."

"Oh, I have my moments," he said, following the words with a very satisfactory kiss.

Skye sobered a little. "I hope they enjoy themselves. I hope it's everything they expect it to be."

"Why on earth shouldn't it be?"

"With our family? You know better than to believe that everything will go smoothly, honey."

Celia smiled provocatively up into Ethan Pengelly's face. Seb had gone to fetch four glasses of lemonade and Wenna was nursing a sore toe from Ethan's enthusiastic dancing.

"So are you going to ask me to dance? There's no rule that says we can't change partners now and then, is there?"

Ethan laughed. "I don't think you'd want to risk it."

"Why not? I'm game, if you are," she said challengingly.

Truth to tell, she felt a small thrill as she said it. She had seen the admiration in his eyes as he had watched the way she and Sebby had whirled so expertly around the floor. She had been astounded at the way Sebby could dance, and privately congratulated her Aunt Betsy for pushing him into it. He was a very good partner, but he was just Seb, and she suddenly saw Ethan Pengelly in a new light.

"Ethan won't want to dance with *you*," she heard Wenna say. "You'll only make fun of him."

"No I won't," Celia said softly. "Well, Ethan?"

Imperceptibly, she held out her arms to him a fraction, and the next moment Wenna saw them moving slowly around the room together, and experienced the searing pangs of jealousy.

She felt a glass of lemonade being pushed into her hand as Seb returned, and saw his mocking glance towards the other couple.

"I pity the poor fellow. Celia will make mincemeat of him if he attempts anything other than a regular one-two-three."

"Don't you mind?" Wenna said, choked.

He looked at her properly then, and saw everything there was to see in her face.

"No, and neither should you, sweetie," he said roughly. "Pengelly's not our sort, however skilled he is at making pots, and Celia's going to run through beaux faster than blinking. It doesn't mean a thing to her, so get that jealous frown off your pretty face, and let's show them who can dance and who can't."

"You mean me and you?" she said, forgetting every aspect of correct grammar in her astonishment.

Seb laughed out loud. "Good God, is it so distasteful to you to be seen dancing with me? I'm not my father, cuz."

Wenna felt her face burn. "I'm sorry. I didn't mean to imply anything—"

"Then stop talking before your tongue gets into a tangle. Stick your nose in the air, and let's dance."

Wenna did as she was told. It was an extraordinary feeling to be championed so thoroughly by the cousin she had always thought had little time for either of then, but not disliking the feeling at all, especially when she she caught sight of Celia's piqued face as she and Sebby executed an expert twirl around the dance floor.

Dance classes in Gstaad were never the same after that. Not that Celia was involved with them any more, now that she was a part-time assistant in the art classes. But Wenna's contemporaries were eager to hear how she had been to an afternoon tea dance and danced with not one, but two eligible young men.

"Of course, one of them was my cousin, and the other was my stepfather's brother," she said, honest as always, even though she had never thought of Ethan as simply that.

"But you must have enjoyed it," her close friend Helene Dubois said. "Did you dance close – you know – the way Miss Macnab says we mustn't? Did they press against your jubblies?"

Wenna laughed, suddenly finding their way of referring to their bosoms as silly and childish.

"If you mean, did they press against my brrreasts," she said darkly, "well, there were so many couples dancing, they couldn't help it."

As Helene and the other girls gasped at this daring declaration, Wenna knew that she had suddenly gone up in their estimation. At the memory of the one time when Ethan had stumbled against her and held on to her tightly, she felt her nipples prickle against the regulation winter dress she wore.

"Is Ethan the one you always had a fancy for?" Julia Fletcher, the daughter of a church minister asked.

"He might be," Wenna said mysteriously, "and then again, it might be the other one."

"Well, you can't marry your cousin," Julia said.

"Yes I could – if I wanted to! But I don't – and you should ask your father about getting your facts right, Julia."

35

She was put out by the very suggestion that she might want to marry Seb Tremayne, and even more so by the suggestion that cousins couldn't marry at all. Of course they could. It had happened in her own family, and she wasn't having any self-righteous minister's daughter telling her otherwise.

Not that she could ever think of Sebby in that way. He was just, well, Sebby. She had always been a bit scared of him, but she had to admit that he was much nicer than he used to be. He didn't tease her about Ethan like Celia did.

Then the little group got into a more interesting discussion about the young men they had met during the holidays, and she forgot all about him.

Celia had forgotten the whole incident long ago. In her own room, away from the four-girl dormitory she had inhabited as a student, she was busily penning a letter to Franz Vogl. She implored him to come to Cornwall in December when the current term ended, and added her mother's invitation for his parents to accompany him for a week or so.

> My birthday will have come and gone by the time the term ends, but my mother is planning a big party for me, and I do so want you to be there, Franz. Mom is sure your father would like to see the pottery and the clayworks. The end of the year is never cold in Cornwall and I know you would enjoy the balmy weather and meeting the rest of my family.

She paused, wondering if it was quite true. The Vogls were so elegant and well bred, and some of her family were – well, she tried to be loyal, but for a start, her Uncle Theo could be guaranteed to let them down if he felt so inclined, or if he and Seb got into an argument. She ignored the thought and carried on with the letter.

"Anyway, please write back, Franz. It would be so nice to get a letter from you here."

Celia didn't dare to end it with love and kisses. It wasn't done, and she was sure his straight-laced mother wouldn't approve. She simply signed it with her name. Two weeks later she got a reply.

I would very much like to see your home, Celia, but my mother would prefer it if the invitation to include us all came directly from your parents. It would be more correct, would it not? So we will anticipate that event, and meanwhile I send you my best wishes and hope that we will see one another quite soon.

It was far more formal than Celia might have wished. There were no hidden messages that she could detect, nothing between the lines or any sign of the dashing young German she remembered. She felt oddly let down, but she had no intention of showing her disappointment. Instead, she wrote to her mother immediately, imploring her to write quickly to Frau Vogl, and issue the invitation to the family.

Once it was all a *fait accompli*, she could crow to Wenna and anyone else who would listen, about her handsome German beau who was coming to visit.

The weeks passed quickly for Celia in her new role at St Augustine's, and it seemed no time at all before she and Wenna were on their way back to Cornwall at the end of November. Franz and his parents would be arriving a few days later, and her party was fixed for the following Saturday.

Skye had seen to everything. It was to be a wonderful party, with all the relatives they could muster coming from far and wide.

"Not that there are that many now," Skye said sadly to Nick as they surveyed the final invitation list.

"There's enough of them," he said, scanning the names. "The house will be filled to overflowing if they all turn up."

"Oh, they will. When did you ever know a Tremayne or a Pengelly turn down an invitation?"

"And then there are these German folk," he said thoughtfully.

"It doesn't bother you, does it? You stood by me all those years ago when we had to hustle the German youths out of the country so hurriedly."

"I remember. I also remember the antagonism of so many local people when one of the German lads started messing about with a clayworker's daughter – and the ugliness that followed. There were always suspicions about just why she was hurried away into the country, so don't be fooled into thinking folk will have forgotten," he added.

"It's nothing to do with them," Skye said. "This is a social occasion, and anyway, the Vogls had no connections with us then. We all have to forgive and forget those bad times. I said it then, and I'm saying it now, and heaven help anyone who tries to interfere with my family."

The stupidity and short-sightedness of local folk had almost brought her business to its knees once, and she wasn't prepared to let it happen ever again. The bigots had objected to the young German lads coming here to work, and blood had been spilt because of it. But if they were foreigners, then so was she, and they would stand together if need be.

She began to wonder just what wildness was making her think this way right now. Her husband laughed gently at her vehemence.

"I doubt that any of them will forget the impact of Skye's Crusaders either, darling," he said softly. "You and David Kingsley together could conquer the world if you tried. It's a pity other folk don't have your kind of rhetoric instead of using their fists – or worse."

Skye smiled faintly. "David always said that more battles could be won with words if only people would listen to them – or read them – and he was right."

"But it was your words that won the day then. He had the wherewithal to publish the newspaper, but it was your skill and compassionate writing that made people see sense."

"Why, thank you, kind sir," she said, touched at this tribute. "So now, can we finish deciding on who to invite to Celia's party, and who we can legitimately leave out?"

As the evening of the party approached on the fifth of December, Skye realised she was looking forward to it as much as her daughters were. Such get-togethers had a sense of family solidarity about them. No matter what else failed, the family was always strong, and they were always there for one another.

There had been a party to celebrate her own arrival from America all those years ago, when she had met all these unknown relatives who were to become so much a part of her life. Her parents had urged her to come, to get to know Cornwall and to sense the joy each of them had known in finding one another in the place of their family roots.

The memory of that time was always an emotional one for Skye. She still remembered how she had had an almost hallowed feeling when she stepped onto Cornish ground for the first time in her twenty-three years. And then seeing all the places that her mother, Primmy, had told her about, and the mystical feeling she had experienced at one and the same time, at the strangeness and the familarity of them.

And now the house where she had discovered such an empathy with her grandmother, Morwen Tremayne, was to be host to another large gathering, and she was the hostess, the matriarch. She shivered suddenly, as the charm of it was replaced by a far less comfortable feeling.

The years passed, and with them the next generation took over the limelight, and the older ones began to fade . . . it was rightly so, and sometimes scarily so . . .

"Are you laying ghosts again?" she heard Nick say.

She realised she had been staring into the firelight in the drawing room for a very long time.

She spoke softly. "Just a few. But they're nice ghosts for the most part, Nick."

"Then let them be, and let's get ready to greet our guests," he told her, just as softly.

He took her hand and they went upstairs together to change into their finery for Celia's party. It was the last time they would be alone for hours and Skye savoured the moments. The girls were excitedly dressing and Olly was grumbling at having to look like a tailor's dummy, and the house guests were separately preparing to do justice to Skye's beautiful daughter.

She drew in her breath as she and Nick entered their bedroom, and she put her arms around him for a moment.

"We've always done right by Celia, haven't we, Nick? She's turned out just as Mom and Granny Morwen would have wanted her to be, hasn't she?"

"She's a credit to all of you, darling. She's a Tremayne woman to her fingertips, and I can't give higher praise than that. They would be proud of her, and I'm proud of you."

"I haven't done anything—"

"Then stop angling for me to tell you you're the most ravishing woman on God's earth, or I may just have to halt the party proceedings in order to prove it to you," he said, with a meaningful smile.

She laughed and moved away from him, the introspective mood broken and her spirits rising. Everyone would love both her beautiful daughters tonight, wearing the gorgeous evening dresses Nick had so generously bought for them. Celia's was the most luxurious, in a sensuous shade of deep blue velvet, and Wenna's was a stunning bronze shantung silk.

Skye's own gown was her favourite forest green, the shade that had so alarmed her cousin Charlotte when she had chosen to wear it as mother to the little bridesmaids when Vera had married Adam Pengelly. Skye had always refused to believe the superstitious nonsense that it was an unlucky colour. If anything was to prove to her that green was far from unlucky for her, that had also been the day that she and Nick had first set eyes on one another. The day they had both fallen instantly, and irrevocably, in love.

The German guests were ultra correct, and Theo's whispered aside that they resembled waddling penguins went thankfully unnoticed by all but his wife, who shushed him at once.

"Behave yourself, Theo," she said severely. "This is Celia's night, so try to be gracious for once in your life."

"Bloody women," he muttered, before trying to persuade David Kingsley to tell him what juicy bits of news were being kept from the general public.

The newspaperman looked at him coldly. Whatever there was, Theo Tremayne wouldn't be the one he confided it to. There was certainly something, and he intended to find a quiet corner to discuss it with Skye some time during the evening. But not now, when the Pengelly family was putting up such a happy and united front as their guests continued to arrive.

He felt an unexpected pang, watching them. The girls had the delicate yet sensuous beauty of all the legendary Tremayne women, but in his eyes nothing could match Skye. She was radiant tonight, and he could never quite forget how he had once wanted her for himself. He pushed the feeling aside as his little boys claimed him, overawed in such splendid surroundings and with so many people. He smiled at Lily, and his wife smiled back, and his world righted itself again.

"I wonder what's keeping Mother and Vera and Adam," Lily said. "I hope everything's all right. Vera said Mother was having trouble with her breathing the last time she saw her."

"None of us is getting any younger, my love," he commented, and for a man who avoided cliches as much as possible in his writing, he visibly cringed at the inanity. But he couldn't ignore the worried look on his wife's face, and he prayed inelegantly that her mother, Charlotte, wouldn't choose this particular evening to pop it.

He saw Skye smiling slightly at him, and knew she was guessing how he would sum up this party occasion for a brief mention in the *Informer*. Anything to do with Tremaynes and Pengellys merited a mention, and he considered himself very much small fry in the Cornish hierarchy of name dropping and heritage in this particular part of the county.

But he was doing his best to expand the dwindling family, he thought, as Frederick and Robert clamoured to know when they could have a drink of lemonade. If he had his way, he and Lily would have more children, but Lily was perfectly content with the two she called her late ewe-lambs.

"What are you grinning at?" she hissed at him.

"Just thinking how glad I am that I never married a pompous woman," he said. "And even more glad that you got all this feminist nonsense out of your system and married me."

Seeing the way her eyes sparkled, he knew it didn't mean that she didn't have a mind of her own. She was never afraid to use it either, and he was glad of that too.

He moved away with his boys and sought out the lemonade table, happy to be a part of this big, sprawling family in a way he had never expected to be. To his relief, his sister-in-law Vera and her husband arrived shortly afterwards, with Charlotte as well as ever.

As he gave Vera a dutiful peck on the cheek, David realised how enormously fat she had grown through compulsive eating, which Lily said was a compensation for not having the children she had wanted. Adam always said loyally that there was more of her to love, and all credit to him for that, but in his earthier moments David sometimes wondered how the hell they managed it with all those rolls of fat to contend with. Did they tuck them up and flatten them out, or . . .

*   *   *

"Ladies and gentlemen – and children," he heard Nick say some while later when they had all gorged their way through a mountain of party food. "This is not going to be a formal speech and we all want you to enjoy yourselves. But before we continue, Skye and I ask you to raise your glasses in an eighteenth-birthday toast to our lovely daughter, Celia."

As they did as they were told, Celia blushed and received kisses from everyone in the family until only the Vogls were left. She looked expectantly at Franz.

"May I be permitted to join in this expression of affection?" he asked.

"Of course!" Celia giggled, her heart beating wildly.

To her absolute mortification he took her hand in his and raised it to his lips in the continental way, clicking his heels together as he did so. She wasn't sure whether to be charmed by such old-world courtesy or enraged at the non-appearance of an acceptable kiss in company, when she heard Seb and Justin snigger. Even Olly managed a weak smile, knowing that he shouldn't, but unable to resist it as the three youths crowded together in a corner.

"Your young men seem to find our customs amusing," Herr Vogl commented to Nick.

"I assure you they mean no offence by it. The young are sometimes thoughtless, aren't they?"

"It rather depends on their upbringing, and perhaps we are stricter with our young men that in other cultures. *I* do not mean to offend either, sir. I merely make an observation."

"Of course," Nick said, privately thinking the man a bumptious ass, and praying that Celia wasn't serious about his son. If Franz Vogl turned out as prissy as his parents, his spirited girl would have a far less easy life than of old. He was glad when someone else claimed his attention.

Wenna had already joined her brother and cousins and was chuckling in a corner. They leaned together, their dark heads almost touching, in a solid family unit.

"Did you see it?" Olly said. "What a twerp."

"Shush, Olly, they'll hear you," Wenna hissed, happy to be included in their circle which excluded her sister. They had all had several glasses of fruit cup by now, and Wenna no longer minded quite so much that Ethan had asked to bring along a friend to the party, although initially she had been devastated to discover that the friend was female.

Seeing them together had made her cling to her cousins even more, as if to prove to Ethan that it didn't mean a thing to her that he was so attentive to the daughter of Tom Vickery, the pit captain at Killigrew Clay.

"Just look at that toe-rag now," Seb said, as if following her thoughts. Since lacing his innocuous drinks with a smidgin of brandy his voice was becoming slightly slurred, and it was making him bolder. He nodded in Ethan's direction as he spoke. "He's gooey-eyed about the Vickery tart, and we all know she'll drop 'em for a tanner. Mebbe that's the attraction."

It took a couple of seconds for what he meant to sink into Wenna's brain. When it did, she gasped, her face burning with embarrassment, and with it a sharp sense of loss for the feelings she had always attributed to her hero.

"How dare you say such things, Seb. You're disgusting, and you're spoiling everything, just like you always did. I thought you had *some* manners now, but you don't. You're just the same as you always were – a – a prize *pig!*"

The childhood name she had always given him came readily to her lips, which trembled visibly as Seb and the boys shook with laughter at her indignant face.

"Oh, come on, Wenna, he didn't mean anything," Justin said roughly, taking her arm. She shook him off.

"He shouldn't have said it then. And Ethan's not like he said. Nor is – is Jessie," she said, fighting to remember the Vickery girl's name.

"Oh, well, believe what you like," Seb said carelessly. "But you should grow up and open your eyes to the real world, Wenna. That posh school's obviously teaching you nothing."

The foursome broke up as Wenna flounced off, and Olly slunk away, not wanting to get into a family fight, especially when Sebby was in one of his belligerent moods.

Skye watched the little incident from a distance. She had heard nothing of what had been said in the general mêlée and excitement of the party, but she could read Wenna's body language. She knew full well the reason for her younger daughter's changeable moods that evening. The pangs of first love were never easy, but Wenna must always have known that Ethan wasn't for her, and that someone nearer his own age was far more suitable. Jessie Vickery was a pretty girl, and probably not as black as some people painted her, Skye thought generously.

"Can we snatch a moment to talk?" David Kingsley said, at her elbow and, as she saw his troubled eyes, her heart leapt with unease.

# Four

S kye always thought how strange, and how useful it was, that
two people could manage to hold a private conversation in
the midst of a crowd. From the back of the room, watching the
dancing from a distance, she looked at David Kingsley, seeing
from his face that his news had to be something momentous.

"What is it?" she murmured.

"My sources in London say the abdication is imminent," he
said abruptly. "An announcement is expected very soon."

Skye gasped. "Are you sure?"

But she knew he must be. He had the nose for a story, and the
integrity not to print it before it was proven. He also knew that he
could trust her above all people not to divulge what he told her.

"I expect the wire to come through at any time. I'm holding the
front page of the *Informer* each day until the very last minute.
The nationals have reported that the Duke and Duchess of York
have arrived in London from Scotland, which is a clear indica-
tion that something's afoot. It can't be long before the whole
thing is out in the open now and Beaverbrook will be unable to
stop it however much he tries. Why the devil shouldn't the British
public know what's common knowledge all over Europe and
America, anyway?"

"So once it happens, there will be a new king, and the two
young princesses will have their lives changed for ever." Skye
spoke slowly, ignoring David's sense of outrage at not being able
to do his job and report everything he knew.

She tried to take it all in, imagining for a brief, fantasising
moment, how it would be if her own daughters were to be
suddenly plunged into a situation none of them had ever
dreamed about.

"What are you two plotting now?" she heard her cousin Vera's
voice close to her a moment later. "Sometimes I swear that you

45

must both have printer's ink in your blood. Doesn't it make our Lily jealous?"

David laughed, making an obvious effort to sound normal. "It does not! She knows me well enough, and you wouldn't expect the glorious Skye to look at anyone else but her husband, would you, sister-in-law dear?"

Vera laughed too. Skye noted with a small stab of alarm how she wheezed as she did so. She resolved to speak to her cousin about her excess weight, and to try to convince her to eat a healthier diet. Though, remembering Vera's wonderful suet dumplings and her addiction to the bread-and-butter pudding that she and Adam loved, she doubted that her advice would have any effect. Her own mouth watered at the memory of Vera's steamy and aromatic kitchen.

As the other two drifted away into the party crowd, Skye became aware of someone else hovering close by. She smiled dutifully into Jessie Vickery's pretty face.

"I jest wanted to thank 'ee, Mrs Pengelly, for allowing me to come to the party. 'Tis real neighbourly of 'ee to let me come along of Ethan."

"Well, that's perfectly all right, Jessie," Skye said warmly, trying not to notice the clumsy speech of the clayworker's daughter, and trying even more not to feel snobbish about it, when her own family history was the very same as this girl's. Even Granny Morwen had lapsed into the soft, sing-song lilt of her clayworking background at times, which Skye had found endearing.

"Well, I jest wanted to tell you I 'preciate it an' all," Jessie persisted, as if determined to pin Skye into a corner with her voluptuous figure.

Her face was bold and vivacious. If you ignored the knowing eyes you could think she was just a simple country girl with no more ambitions than to wed a simple country boy, thought Skye. Why such a idea entered her head at that moment, she couldn't quite imagine. Jessie's next words clarified it all too well.

"Me pa says I'm not to get above me station, though, but there's nuthin' wrong in wantin' to better yerself, is there? And if me and Ethan want to go courtin', I reckon there's nuthin' he can do about it," she said, with a reckless giggle that spoke of having imbibed rather too well.

Ethan hustled his way through the crush of people and caught at Jessie's hand impatiently. Skye listened to his words with a sense of inexplicable unease.

"Come on, sweetness, let's show Seb Tremayne that me and my girl can do a turn or two on the dance floor. Anything he can do, we can do better!"

Jessie followed him with a laugh that was a mixture of excitement and triumph. Skye felt her heart skip a beat and a small frown creased her brows.

"What's wrong, darling?" Nick said as he came to join her. She composed her face at once and hugged his arm.

"Nothing at all. What could be wrong on a night such as this, when everyone's enjoying themselves so much?"

He knew her too well to be fooled, but she had no intention of spoiling the party by revealing her thoughts. Not for the world would she put into words the idiotic ideas that had swept through her mind at that moment. Ideas that were more like a presentiment, which was one of the Cornish traits her grandmother had bestowed on her.

Nor would she tell anyone, not even Nick, that just for one crazy moment she had visualised the likes of Jessie Vickery marrying her young brother-in-law Ethan. That between them and the influence of the clayworking community they would reduce *her* pottery and *her* clayworks to the humble beginnings of a century ago. If Theo were to insist on selling out, the clayworkers would rule the sophisticated empire that she still thought of as hers, by right, by her own efforts, and by the loving legacy of her grandmother, Morwen Tremayne.

"Sit down, Skye," she heard Nick say as if from a long way away. "What did David say just now, or can I guess? I warned you not to take this Mrs Simpson business too much to heart. Is that it?"

She clung to the lifeline he had thrown her. "I suppose so, and I promise to forget it, and mingle with our guests before Theo throws an almighty spanner in the works and outrages Frau Vogl with his coarseness."

She bit her lip, knowing she was doing it again. She was unwittingly separating herself from the very heartbeat of her family by thinking herself better than the rest of them. It had never occurred to her before, but it occurred to her very strongly now, and she didn't like what she saw. No wonder Theo had been so scathing about sending Celia and Wenna to a Swiss finishing school. If he sneered at his own son Justin for being a bit of a snob, then she was a worse one by far.

She and Nick made their way towards their house guests, currently being entertained by Theo and Betsy. The Vogls were clearly not at their most comfortable in their company, and Skye sympathised with both sides. Herr Vogl was stiff and starchy and although Betsy was a darling, she was a countrywoman to her bootstraps and unable to make the kind of conversation they would expect. And Theo was . . . she could hear him now, loud and bombastic as ever, and she groaned.

"Our china clay is the finest in the world, and 'tis a pity it never took on the Tremayne name when the Killigrews passed on. A real thorn in my side, that one, and if I had my time over again I'd probably insist on it. But female ownership had other things to say to it as usual."

"Theo, I'm sure Herr Vogl doesn't want to hear our family business," Skye cut in quickly as Theo's face darkened.

Jessie Vickery wasn't the only one who had had a drop too much to drink. In the girl's case it had merely emboldened her to speak to Skye, and she was now whirling on the dance floor with Ethan, while Theo was ready to do verbal battle with whoever encouraged him. Herr Vogl couldn't know that.

"I find it most interesting, as a matter of fact," the German said, his voice carrying. "In my country, we do not encourage women to enter into business in the same manner."

Every sentence was a speech with him, Skye thought. He had been a pleasant host in his own country and was a good business connection, but she didn't really like him at all. He continued speech-making, holding his small audience captive.

"I, too, believe that a man's name is most important. It's his personal attribute that no one can take away from him, and should therefore be preserved at all costs."

"Like Mr Hitler," came a smothered whisper from somewhere in the room behind him. "Preserved in aspic, perhaps, with his Charlie Chaplin face and his funny walk!"

Skye felt her face flame, and prayed that Herr Vogl didn't have such acute hearing as she did. Maybe he didn't, but Theo did. She heard him roar with laughter as he turned and clasped Celia around the waist, to her utter disgust as he breathed whisky fumes in her face.

"You've a witty tongue on you, girlie, but I doubt that our German friends will appreciate the insult to their leader. Charlie Chaplin indeed! But now that you mention it—"

He burst into more raucous laughter that started him coughing and retching, and had Betsy slapping him on the back. She led him off to the drinks table, her face puce with embarrassment, still apologising for him as they went out of sight. Skye also felt obliged to apologise for her loathsome relative. If Herr Vogl hadn't got the gist of Celia's words before, he certainly knew them now.

"Please forgive my cousin, Herr Vogl," Skye said, mortified to be doing this, and thankful that Frau Vogl was sitting with Charlotte and unaware of what had passed. Of Franz there was no sign. "Theo is a litle wild at times, and I'm afraid he always speaks first and thinks later."

"It would seem to be a national trait, I believe," he said, his voice stiff. Skye felt doubly mortified at this slight, said so icily and with so much meaning.

As for Celia, Skye seethed with anger at her daughter's indiscretion. Birthday girl or not, such an insult to their foreign visitors was unforgivable. Now was not the time to chastise her, but it later would be, Skye vowed. Of that Celia need have no doubt.

It was the early hours of the morning by the time the last of the revellers went home and most of the household had gone to bed. Only Skye, Nick and Celia were left downstairs, and Skye rounded on her daughter at once.

"What on earth did you think you were saying, Celia? Have you no consideration at all? The Vogls were your personal guests, and you went out of your way to insult them. I don't know what Franz must have thought of such rudeness."

"In case you hadn't noticed, I hardly saw Franz all evening," Celia exploded, her eyes sapphire-bright with tears she tried to hide. "Didn't you see the way he ogled that cheap Vickery girl? He even danced with her while Ethan was fetching her a drink. She's nothing but a miserable, common moors girl and she didn't belong here at my party."

Before Skye could stop herself, she had struck Celia's cheek. They both gasped, and Nick strode forward to intervene as Celia's hand automatically rose to defend herself.

"That's enough," he snapped. "The girl was a guest like everyone else, and you'll apologise to your mother at once."

"*Me*, apologise to *her*? She was the one who hit me!" Celia screamed. "I won't apologise for what I said about Jessie Vickery. I hate her, and so does Wenna."

She was ramrod stiff with fury, but Skye didn't miss the stark misery in her eyes. Nothing had ever thwarted Celia in her life before, and she felt it doubly hard. Dear God, it was not only Celia, but both her girls, Skye thought with a small shock, both of them were smarting and insulted by the Vickery girl, because both their young men had danced with her, and Ethan was apparently courting her.

First love could be traumatic as well as beautiful, and she felt her daughters' pain as if it was a physical thing, but before she could find any tactful words to try to make amends, Celia had twisted away from both her parents.

"I'm going to bed," she shrieked. "And thank you both for ruining my party."

There was silence for a moment after she had gone and then Nick folded his wife in his arms. Until that moment she hadn't realised how much she was shaking.

"Let it go, darling. A good night's sleep is what you both need, or what's left of the night. Things always looks brighter in the morning."

"You can guarantee that, can you?" she asked bitterly. She took a deep breath, suddenly very calm. "What I need more than sleep is to talk to you, Nick. I want you to call a meeting between Theo and the two of us, and to draw up a legal document to ensure the continuity of the family business that's absolutely watertight."

"It already is watertight. You know that."

She shook her head. "What I want is to add a codicil to the wills that Theo and I made, to the effect that if none of our children want to take over the clayworks or the pottery then they are to close down. Under no circumstances must anyone but our direct descendants inherit or make any offer to buy us out. When Theo and I die, our children will take over, or Killigrew Clay and

White Rivers will be no more. We have five children between us. We must persuade Theo to agree that one or several of them must inherit, without marital considerations, or we close down. Theo has no shares in the pottery now, but I'd have no objection to his sons being included in the arrangement if they wished."

Her thoughts came thick and fast and wild and without proper order, and she had to pause to catch her breath, but at her impassioned words Nick became white with anger.

"My God, is this all you've had on your mind at your daughter's party? Do you think Theo will agree to this ridiculous ultimatum?"

"It's not an ultimatum and I haven't thought it out at all. I'm just sure in my bones that it's the right thing to do. I'm protecting what has always been ours, and what must remain ours, or be no more."

"Oh, no, my dear, I think you mean what has always been *yours*," he retorted. "You and your womenfolk have always tried to undermine what's rightfully a man's prerogative, but no man is willing to be emasculated—"

"Don't try to blind me with long words, Nick. I know them all," she snapped. "And we do not try to emasculate you—"

"Really? I seem to recall that when you went on your crusade to keep the pottery open some years ago, Vera withheld her favours from Adam, even though they were newly-weds. If that's not emasculating, I don't know what is. You may think you're strong, Skye, but—"

"How did you know about that? Did Adam tell you? Do you discuss what does or doesn't happen in the bedroom in some public bar for everyone to hear?"

"Calm down, and think what the result of your proposal would be. Do you really want to throw all the clayworkers out of work because of a selfish female whim?"

She started at him, realising she certainly hadn't thought the idea through. And, as she looked at his angry face, she wondered how on earth this wonderful night had ended so painfully. She could hardly bear to look at him, knowing how little he must think of her. Her erratic plan to draw up a legal document that was watertight for the succession of the joint businesses had been for one reason only, but as he went to the door, she realised Nick had seen it entirely differently.

"You might also reflect over the insult you're doing to Ethan, Skye. And to me, since no marital considerations, as you call them, come into it. Not that I ever had any aspirations to be a clay boss, in case you were wondering."

She could easily dismiss his last ridiculous statement, but not the first one.

"What has any of this to do with Ethan?"

But she knew instantly. It had been at the back of her mind all along, even if she hadn't thought it through properly. All she wanted was to ensure that whatever little trollop married into the family couldn't get her hands on what her family had worked so hard to achieve. And that included Jessie Vickery. It was *all* on account of Jessie Vickery, who was courting Ethan Pengelly and hurting her younger daughter so.

"If you don't know, then you're more stupid than I give you credit for," Nick said coldly. "Ethan has given his life to White Rivers, and if you were to sell out, if anyone deserves to buy into it, he does."

"You're not listening to me, are you? I'm not talking about selling out. I'm talking about closing down, flattening the whole area, not letting anyone else take what's mine—"

"Exactly," he said, when she stopped abruptly.

Her heartbeats began to race. Suddenly it seemed as though she was staring at her own mortality, planning for a future when she no longer existed, and it frightened her.

"Nick, please let's sleep on it," she said. "I've obviously made a mess of trying to explain the way I feel, and anyway, we're talking about something that's hopefully years ahead. I'm not planning to quit this life just yet."

She tried to make him smile, but putting such thoughts into words always seemed like tempting fate, and she couldn't resist crossing her fingers as she said them.

"I sincerely hope not," Nick said curtly. "How the hell would I survive the humdrum of it all without these regular spats between us?"

She was too tense to see any humour in his reply. When they went to bed she curled up into a ball between the cold sheets, as far away from him as possible, wishing she had never said anything at all. She knew in her heart that she would never insist on her wild plan if Nick strongly disapproved. He always saw things so much more logically than she did, and of course she wouldn't want to put the clayworkers out of work. Whole families had given their lives to Killigrew Clay, including her own in years past.

She lay in the darkness, dismissing the whole crazy idea, but her last waking thought was the hope that Ethan would be as sensible as his brother, and marry someone far more suitable than the Vickery girl.

Celia was quick to apologise the following morning. She came into Skye's room and stood diffidently beside the bed.

"I'm sorry for everything I said, Mom, and I can't bear it if we're not friends. Please forgive me, and I'll grovel to Herr Vogl too – if I must," she added, with a watery smile.

It didn't really solve anything, but one look at her daughter's pleading face after a sleepless few hours, and Skye opened up the bedclothes and Celia snuggled inside them.

"You really were abominably rude," Skye told her. "You wouldn't like it if Franz said something horrid about the king, would you?"

"Everyone's saying horrid things about him and Mrs Simpson," Celia muttered. "Why can't they leave him alone and let him marry her if he wants to? What difference will it make to us, anyway?"

Skye gave her a hug. Celia was many things, but she wasn't intolerant of other peoples' relationships, except where it affected herself. In that she was certainly possessive and selfishly independent – just as a good Tremayne woman should be, Skye thought, wickedly cheered.

"Where's Daddy?" her daughter said suddenly.

"He was up early to attend to some business," Skye said vaguely. "We should get up too. What will our guests think?"

"They're already up. I saw Franz and Herr Vogl out walking earlier on."

"My goodness, they're energetic, aren't they?"

Celia shrugged. "It's the German way. A healthy mind in a healthy body, or some such tosh."

"Do I take it that the great romance is not as great as it was once expected to be?" Skye said carefully.

Celia turned to her. "Oh Mom, he's so *stuffy*! They all are. I didn't realise it until I saw him here among all our own folk. Even Sebby's like a breath of fresh air compared with Franz."

So obviously the little matter of him dancing with Jessie Vickery hadn't meant so much to her daughter after all. That was one relief, anyway. The last thing she wanted was for Celia's heart to be broken, but she had always thought that Franz Vogl wasn't the one for Celia. It was something her girl had had to find out for herself though, the way everyone did.

"Well, they'll be gone soon. Two more days and we'll have the house to ourselves again, and we can look forward to a peaceful family Christmas."

Providing she and Nick weren't at each others' throats, she thought. Life was too short to waste it on petty quarrels, and when she saw him later, Skye told him stiffly that he should forget the things she had said the previous night.

Was sacrificing the family businesses in all their glory really preferable to seeing them fall into the greedy little hands of the likes of Jessie Vickery? To her shame Skye knew that was the main reason for acting the way she had. She had simply been seeing things that weren't there.

She was thankful that she and Nick had patched up their differences and the house was harmonious again. The German family had gone home, making them all sigh with relief. The announcement they had all been anticipating was broadcast on the night of 11 December.

"At long last, I am able to say a few words of my own . . ." came the king's solemn voice, at which Nick muttered audibly beneath his breath.

"More like a dozen advisers putting the right words into his mouth," he commented, shushed at once by his womenfolk as they crowded near the wireless set.

Wenna, soft-hearted as ever, was openly crying as the tragic announcement unfolded, while Celia's voice was brittle as it came to an end.

"Well, I still think it's all wrong that he has to give up the throne for the woman he loves." As her sister wailed even louder, she turned on her. "Oh, do shut up, Wenna, you little sissy."

"Oh, you're hateful! Didn't you hear what he said? He

couldn't remain king without the help and support of the woman he loves. It's so tragic!"

"It's mad. Why should he listen to what the church and the government tell him? He should be strong and defy them all. What's the point of being king otherwise?"

"Well, he's not the king any more, is he?" her father pointed out, trying not to smile at her outraged face. "And even kings have to obey the rules, just like everyone else."

The girls were still in the middle of a heated discussion and solving nothing, when the telephone rang. Skye left the room thankfully to answer it. When Celia was in this mood, there was no changing her mind, and by now Olly was having his say as well, scoffing at them both.

She recognised David Kingsley's voice at once.

"I take it you heard the broadcast?" he asked, barely unable to contain his excitement. "Quite a turn-up, isn't it?"

"Is it? I thought it was what you were expecting."

"Yes, but not in quite such a way. The royals have never been known for expressing their feelings or emotions in public. He sounded almost human. It's quite a scoop to be able to print it word for word in the *Informer* – along with every other damn paper in the country, of course. Nobody gets an exclusive on this one."

But she could feel his enthusiasm as if it was tangible, and she could also feel a matching adrenalin in her own veins. Reporting a sensational story was every newsman's dream, and in this case it didn't matter that every other paper had the story too. They would all interpret the facts in their own way.

"Actually, I'm quite sorry for her," she said. "Whatever her aspirations, and however much of it was truly the king's own decision, she'll never be able to forget that she cost him his throne. That's a heck of a noose around anybody's neck."

She could almost hear the thoughts ticking over in David's brain before he spoke rapidly again.

"You wouldn't care to write it up for me from that angle, I suppose? As a favour, Skye. As a woman, and as an American. What do you say? It could be a stunner."

"Oh, I don't think so."

"Why not? You, of all people, know what it's like to be up against the rest of the community. Remember the German

workers' fiasco when the pottery was boycotted, and you organised Skye's Crusaders to keep it open with just yourself and Lily
and Vera to help until the other women joined in? Remember the
articles you sent home from the Front during the war that touched
the heart of every woman who ever agonised over what was
happening to her man? You're the best and most compassionate
woman reporter I know, Skye, and if Mrs Simpson has had a bad
press before, she's certainly going to get more of it now. You could
do a little bit to redress the balance, if you wanted to."

She warmed to his praise of her. It wasn't all flannel, of course,
he was too hard-hearted a newspaperman for that. She knew she
had it in her to do as he asked, too. Redressing the balance a little
– why not?

It took two people to fall in love and to commit themselves to
marriage and so far Mrs Simpson had had the worst of the
rumours, as the wicked witch who had schemed and manipulated
her man. By implication it had diminished the self-esteem of their
king – ex-king she reminded herself.

"I'll do it," she said quickly.

"Good girl, I knew you would. Get the copy to me first thing
in the morning, if not sooner."

"But that means I'l have to work on it all night!"

"Well, that's the way every good reporter is prepared to work.
Isn't it?"

"Yes," she said, laughing. "I'll see you in the morning."

Nick didn't approve of her involvement. She'd known he
wouldn't, even though the girls were intrigued by the idea of
their mother championing a romantic cause.

"You could be putting yourself in a bad light," Nick warned.
"The country has been divided against this liaison from the start,
however much it's been kept under cover."

"But you can't prevent people falling in love, and I don't see
how any sensible woman would think differently. I'm just going
to put my side of things as an ordinary woman, the way I've
always reported things."

"My love, an ordinary woman you're not, and never will be,
thank God," he said. "I just want you to think what you're
taking on, and to think carefully, that's all."

"Are you going to try and stop me?"

He gave a crooked smile. "I wouldn't even try," he said.

So she spent the next few hours in his study, among the familiar smells of leather and old books that always reminded her of the heady days when she herself had worked in the offices of a magazine in New Jersey. By the time she went wearily to bed, the article was ready to deliver to David the following morning.

"I'll drive in to Truro myself," she told Nick. "It will be interesting to be in the office at this time, and David wants the copy as soon as possible."

She just managed to avoid saying she couldn't resist being at the hub of it all, to be in on any news that was breaking over the wires.

David was delighted with her article, as she had known he would be.

"It's brilliant, as always. You have the common touch, Skye, with all the rhetoric of the skilled reporter. It's a formidable combination, and you're wasted out there in the sticks."

She had to laugh at that, but as always, his praise stimulated her.

"My husband wouldn't thank you for describing our life as being out in the sticks, thank you very much!"

"But you miss all this, don't you?" he said slyly, noting how she was avidly reading the newspaper columns and the incoming wires, and breathing in the pungency of the printer's ink.

"Of course I do, but if you think I could be lured back to work for you, think again," she retorted. "I've a business and a home to run, and three children to care for."

"Three adolescents who can perfectly well take care of themselves, you mean. The girls are young women now and don't need nursing any longer, and I gather that Olly already has ideas about his future, and good for him."

"Has Lily put you up to this?" Skye said suspiciously. "Does she think I should get out more or something?"

"No. I merely see the way those gorgeous eyes sparkle when you're involved in something other than domesticity, and I think what a waste of a good brain it all is."

And just for a moment he let his guard slip, and she knew instinctively he wasn't simply thinking about her domestic life. There was still a strong link between them, even if most of it was on David's side as it always had been.

57

"Anyway, I'm not here to discuss my future. It's the future of the country that should concern all of us," she said, more briskly. "What will happen now?"

"It's already happened. Our ex-king left Britain in the early hours of the morning to join his lady friend in France. We now have a new king, George the sixth, God help him. We know little about him and his family as yet, but that will soon change. The scandal-rags that have had their knives in Edward will soon want to show George as whiter than white."

"My God, how cynical you are!"

"And how right," he said drily.

With the release of the publishing restrictions ordered by Lord Beaverbrook, every newspaper in the country was full of the news, and Skye's article in the local Cornish newspaper brought mixed reactions. There were telephone calls, some praising and supporting her views, while others openly abused her for her disloyalty to the crown and siding with the woman they called the royal enemy. Some people turned their backs on her when they saw her in the street, but the final straw came when Ethan telephoned from White Rivers to say the walls of the pottery had been daubed with paint during the night with the words 'American Witch Lover' scrawled large.

"It's just like what happened when we had the young German workers here," she raged to Nick that night. "How short-sighted these people are. How *stupid* and insular—"

"Careful, my love, you're in danger of setting yourself above them," Nick said. "I warned you this might happen, didn't I? I'm afraid you've added fuel to the flame by reminding them that you're American and supporting your countrywoman."

"I don't see that she's done anything wrong, since the king chose her above his throne. And why shouldn't I remind them that I'm American and proud of it?"

"Because they're not, and some of them will always think of you as the colonial upstart. Remember how your grandmother used to talk affectionately in that way? Not against you, of course, but outsiders have always made Cornish folk close ranks. Feelings are running high, even so far from London, against what some see as the usurper stealing their king from under their noses."

"What absolute nonsense! They won't stop me saying what I think," Skye said. "No one has ever done so before."

She hadn't felt so mutinous for years, and was completely at one with her daughters in supporting the cause of true love. So it came as such a shock when Celia came home from Truro a few days before Christmas, her dress torn and her hair dishevilled.

"My God, what's happened, honey? Has someone hurt you?"

"You could say that," Celia said in a choked voice. "I took a walk over the moors on the way home to collect some greenery for the Christmas tree, and a couple of young clayworkers began taunting me about my mother being being a Yankee lover. I couldn't let them get away with it, Mom, so I yelled back at them, and they rushed at me and began pulling at my dress and hair—"

She stopped on a sob, and Skye hugged her tense body close. Celia was so unused to anyone opposing her in anything that this was doubly shocking.

"The sooner I get away from here, the better," Skye heard her say in a savage, muffled voice. "Don't you see what you've done? I can't wait for Christmas to be over so I can get back to Gstaad. This whole vacation has been a disaster. I hate Cornwall and all those dreadful people."

Blaming her sent a further shock through Skye. Dear Lord, but she had never meant this to happen. She had wanted to help, to put things into a sensible perspective, but it seemed as if her carefully worded article had backfired on her in a way she had never expected.

Those bloody, *bloody* clayworkers, she thought in a sudden rage, thinking they ruled the earth and taunting her daughter. They were to blame for this latest upset, turning Celia against everything Cornish, at least for the present. For all her brash ways Celia was as vulnerable as the next person when it came to wanting to be loved. She couldn't bear to be so hated, and blamed the taunting on her mother's interference. Oh yes, it was the clayworkers that were at the heart of it all.

But there was something far more urgent to think about right now.

"They didn't actually hurt you, did they, darling?" she asked carefully. "I think you know what I mean."

Celia gave a brittle laugh, more chilling than Skye thought possible from a girl of little more than eighteen summers.

"If you mean did they try to shove their hands down my dress or up my skirt, no they didn't. But there are more ways of being hurt than by sexual rape, Mother."

By addressing her in that scathing, adult way, Skye knew they had lost something precious between them for ever. It would be something to mourn in the long weeks ahead after the girls had gone back to Gstaad.

# Five

V era's illness progressed so violently that by early January everything else was forgotten. Interest in both state and business matters faded in view of the very real family crisis.

Skye made daily visits to her cousin's house to carry out the doctor's instructions, even though the cloying smells of coal tar medication and herbal chest rubs made her want to heave. But the chronic bronchitis didn't improve as the weeks passed, no matter what remedies were tried. By then Lily and Skye were taking turns in caring for Vera, since Charlotte couldn't face the journey up to the moorland house to make regular visits to her elder daughter. Skye and Lily even discussed the idea of resorting to the quack methods of the moors healing woman, but just as quickly discarded it.

In any case, Skye wanted no truck with any weird potions that could stun the brain to the point of hallucinating. In ages past these old crones would have been burned at the stake, and she wasn't so sure that the ancient woman who lived in the hovel on the moors now, wasn't in the same category.

Even if her evil-smelling concoctions might help Vera . . . but she shuddered, her conscience clear in that respect, knowing that neither Vera nor Adam would agree to it.

"Adam's mother swore by a bread poultice and red flannel to bring out any impurities, and mine always gave us a good dose of expectorant. But none of it's any good if your time's up. It's between me and God when that day comes."

Vera constantly wheezed out such words in between her agonising bouts of coughing and the disgusting bloody mucus she had to spit into a container for the doctor's inspection.

Skye shuddered squeamishly at the covered receptacle, wondering how she and Vera and Lily had ever coped with the sights and sounds and smells in the French field hospitals during the war. But that was then, when it had been a necessity and their sense of duty towards the poor soldiers and an endless procession of new cases numbed their senses. This was now, when she did it out of love and anxiety for her cousin, but with every day Vera got progressively weaker.

"It doesn't look good, Adam," Skye said, once they had left Vera tortuously sleeping. "If only she didn't have all this weight it would ease her breathing. As it is . . ."

"As 'tis, it looks as if I'll be losing my Vera quite soon, don't it?" he said, with the stark simplicity that couldn't disguise his agony at being without her.

Theirs had been such a love match, such an unexpected and spectacular love match, and one that had brought his clever lawyer brother Nicholas, back to Cornwall and into Skye's life. She could never forget that, and she always felt a special closeness to Vera and Adam because of it.

"It looks like it," she said quietly, not taking away his dignity by pretending otherwise.

She saw his shoulders begin to shake, and without warning he started to sob, great heaving sobs that tore at her heart and made her put her arms around his great bear-like body and hold him to her as if he was the child he and Vera never had. It took a long while for the paroxysm to cease and, when it did, he wiped his eyes and squared his shoulders, and made no apology for such an unmanly show, which only made the sense of heartbreak more poignant to Skye, knowing he loved Vera so much. Only a strong man would weep publicly for his wife and never mind who knew it.

"Would you like me to stay here tonight?" she murmured.

"Aye," he said. "In case I should have cause to go for the doctor. I wouldn't want her to be here alone."

But he faltered for a moment as he spoke, avoiding Skye's eyes. They both knew what he meant. This night was likely to be the last one on earth for Vera Pengelly.

In the early hours of a cold February morning she slipped from this world to the next, with her husband holding one hand and her best friend holding the other. It was over.

There was no possibility of Celia and Wenna coming home for the funeral, and Olly preferred to stay away since Adam said

62

roughly that it made no difference who was there and who wasn't. The only person in the world who mattered to him wouldn't care one way or the other. He was living in a twilight world of his own now, Skye told Nick worriedly, and seemed to want Vera buried with almost indecent haste.

"Everyone has their own method of coping, darling," Nick said, their own disputes a thing of the past in view of this far more fundamental tragedy. "Adam must deal with it in his own way. You know that."

Skye knew it was an obscure reference to the way she herself had coped with the deaths that had touched her life. Her brother Sinclair, hit by a crazed fanatic's bullet . . . her beloved parents . . . Granny Morwen . . . her first husband, Philip . . . All of them gone, reminding her of the relentless march and insecurity of a life span.

Lily was as stoical as ever at Vera's passing, but their mother, Charlotte, who had always resented Vera marrying a common man, as she put it, was vociferous in her show of weeping over the open coffin.

" 'Tis never right for the child to go before the mother, is it, Skye? 'Tis the wrong order of things."

"I know it," Skye said, not wanting to be the comforter for this elderly woman, but having no choice since Charlotte had begged to be told every detail of her daughter's passing. "So many parents had to face the same thing during the war, Charlotte. It's never right, but we just have to go on as best we can."

"Well, you never had to face such a thing, did you?" Charlotte said, suddenly aggressive. "You don't know what it is to lose a child."

Her innate selfishness overflowed as she glared balefully at Skye. Vera had been forty-two years old and hardly a child, but Skye couldn't find it in her heart to be angry.

"No," she said quietly. "Just a husband."

Charlotte crumpled then, and Skye let her sob against her, trying not to dislike her so much.

The small crowd of black-clad family mourners and friends was enlarged by the respectful clayworkers and their families who stood at a distance as Vera Pengelly was laid to rest in the moorland churchyard on a chilly afternoon.

"Turning out so ill-dressed for a funeral," Charlotte whispered to Skye, glancing at the clayworkers' everyday garb and dismissing them.

"They come to pay their respects, not to be a poppy-show," Skye said sharply, "and I shall make a point of asking one or two of them back to the house if they care to come."

New World was the venue for the beanfeast, as Theo always called a wake. He had ordered Killigrew Clay to close for the day, and Skye had closed the pottery and the Truro shop. She ignored Charlotte's outraged face as she walked across to the pit captain and other clayworkers and made the request.

"Thank 'ee kindly, Mrs Pengelly, but we'll get back among our own if 'ee don't mind," Tom Vickery said awkwardly. "My girl might want to go with 'ee though, if that's all right."

"Oh, yes, of course," Skye said, wondering how she could have missed Jessie's bright hair among the crowd.

Ethan's interest in her seemed to have waned partly due to the ragging he was getting about the flighty girl, Skye suspected, and a good thing too. But if she wanted to come to the house for a bite, she could hardly refuse her now.

Thankfully, it seemed that she didn't, and she saw father and daughter wrangling at the back of the crowd.

Jessie probably had other fish to fry by now, Skye thought fleetingly, while Tom wasn't ready to let the better-heeled Pengelly fish off the hook completely. She let the words slide in and out of her head, pushing aside the sadness of the occasion for the moment, and sought out her husband. It was time to return to the house and some kind of normality.

She saw Nick and Ethan supporting their brother Adam, taking him away from the open grave towards Nick's car before he totally collapsed with grief. There were other cars available, and she could return to the house with Lily and David. When she found them she spoke quietly about something that had been puzzling her.

"Do you know who that girl is? The one at the back of the crowd."

They followed her glance to where a slim young woman dressed all in black was standing motionless, as if intent on imprinting the scene on her memory. She wasn't a clayworker, and Skye had never seen her before, but from the top of her

64

beret-clad head and long dark hair, to the erect way she held herself, there was something dramatically familiar to her.

"Never seen her before," David said. "Do you want me to go and speak to her?"

"No, don't," Lily put in quickly. "We don't want strangers intruding today. This is a family affair, and it's getting very cold. Let's just get away from here, please."

Skye glanced at her. It wasn't like Lily to sound so agitated. Lily was always the calmest one of them all, the solid, no-nonsense one, who had kept Skye's swooning spirits in check when she had been near to collapse and horror in the French hospital wards all those years ago. Lily was as pale as death now . . . reminding Skye that she had just buried her sister.

"You're right. The sooner we get away from this place now and get something hot inside us, the better. Mrs Yardley will have hot soup and tea waiting for us."

The crowds were dispersing, and when Skye glanced back the girl had gone, as mysteriously as she had appeared. Or was she going crazy, seeing things that weren't there? A ghost, or an apparition, a phantom brought about by the rising mist that had already begun to shroud the moors so insidiously?

She shivered, colder than the February day itself, but if it had been an apparition, then David and Lily had certainly seen it too, and that was not the way of things.

She put it out of her mind and concentrated on being the hostess for Vera's wake, trying to be as cheerful as possible, and in particular, caring for Adam's welfare. He refused to stay at New World, and returned with his memories to the moorland house he and Vera had shared for more than ten years.

"He'll need watching," Nick said much later, when they were finally alone and in their own bed. "Vera was his life and I'm not sure how he'll cope without her."

"I know," Skye said, "somehow it always seems so much more tragic for a man to cope alone."

"Well, it's not going to happen to me, darling, since you're as fit as a flea."

"I'm not sure I like the comparison, but thank you anyway," she said, knowing he was trying to lighten the gloom that had descended on all of them on this sad day.

But it couldn't last for ever. Mustn't last for ever. Life had to go on, however trite it seemed, and she held him closer, wanting his warmth and comfort and to know that they were still alive, still in love, and still needed each other.

She remembered the girl the following day.

"Did you see her? I had the strangest feeling about her, Nick, and it was almost as though Lily recognised her."

"I doubt that. You know how that weird yellow daylight distorts things, especially when the fog is about to cover the moors, and we were all in a highly sensitive mood by then."

"Maybe," she said slowly. "But something tells me it was more than that."

"Or something Granny Morwen's telling you?" he said with a grin. "You can't blame everything on her, Skye!"

"Well, *I* didn't say it, *you* did," she retorted.

He moved away from the breakfast table. "I'm going to see that Adam's all right," he told her. "I'll fetch him back for supper tonight if he'll agree, and Ethan too. None of us should be alone at such a time."

She watched him go, loving his concern for his brothers. Loving him, and thinking how lucky she was to have found such love for the second time in her life. Not everyone was so fortunate. Only herself and Granny Morwen out of this whole, tangled family network, she reflected.

Halfway through the morning the housekeeper came to the sitting room where she was trying to compose letters to her daughters to tell them everything that had been happening recently. Mrs Yardley's creased face was anxious.

"There's a person to see you, ma'am," she said. "I told her 'tis a house o' mourning, in a manner of speakin', but she says 'tis of some importance. I think she's an Irish person."

Mrs Yardley's tone implied that this was comparable with being a tinker, and Skye hid a smile, as her own family had an Irish connection. Not that Morwen's brother Freddie had been Irish, nor her much younger son Bradley, but they had both lived in Ireland for many years until their deaths.

She gave a small sigh. "Show the lady in, please, Mrs Yardley. If she says it's of some importance then I'll hear what she has to say."

"You jest mind that she's not come here beggin'," the house-keeper muttered with a sniff.

The girl entered the room. She wore the same black clothes as before, and stood just as still and composed, apart from a slight tremor of her gloved hands. At a quick assessment, Skye guessed that she was about twenty-three or four. She was exquisitely beautiful, her hair long and dark in a completely unfashionable style, and there were dark shadows beneath her large blue eyes.

Skye rose slowly, a strange feeling inside her.

"Who are you?" she said, her voice unaccountably rough.

"My name is Karina, ma'am," the girl said, her accent soft and melodic. "Karina Tremayne."

There was silence in the room for a moment, and then Skye gestured to a chair, her heart thudding.

"I think you had better sit down and tell me what it is you want," she said at last.

As she did so, the girl's cool manner suddenly crumpled a little. She pressed a linen handkerchief to her eyes without any fuss or show, and quickly replaced it in the neat black bag she carried. The words tumbled out.

"I'm sorry, Mrs Pengelly, especially now I know of the circumstances here. When I made enquiries, the folk in Truro told me about your loss. I didn't mean to intrude, and I know I shouldn't have gone to the burying, but it seemed a way of observing without being observed, which sounds even more terrible to me now. But Mother of God, I didn't mean to upset anybody, and I don't think anybody really noticed me."

"They did. *I* did."

"Ah well, so be it then," the girl said softly. "But sure and I meant no harm by it."

"What do you want here?" Skye repeated.

The girl looked down at her hands. "My mother has recently died, God rest her soul. She left me some letters and documents. The lawyer gave them to me, but I didn't know what to do about any of it. He said I should come here and consult an English lawyer, but I don't know one."

"Don't you?" Skye said, her compassion over the girl's bereavement tempered by suspicion. It was a bad time to come here with some sob story, but then, what better time, when they were all feeling vulnerable?

The one thing she couldn't overlook, though, was what she should have seen all along. The thing that Lily had evidently seen, and that was the trademark of the Tremayne beauty. This girl had it all. Skye overcame her suspicion with an effort and asked gently if she would like some tea.

"Oh, that I would, ma'am. 'Tis a cold day and I've walked from Truro, so I have."

"My heavens, have you?" Skye said, startled.

That was something Morwen Tremayne would have done in her youth and thought nothing of it, in the days before people became soft and relied on motor cars to take them from place to place. Granny Morwen would have easily walked from the cottage at the top of the moors to the bustling streets of Truro for the thrill of the annual fair.

But she was more than thankful when Nick arrived home and took the questioning out of her hands. She was out of her depth for once, and didn't know how to handle this situation. As yet, she didn't even know what the situation was, since they had simply made awkward small talk after the girl's brief revelations. She seemed awed by the size of the house, and was reluctant to show her precious letters and documents to anyone but a lawyer.

"As I told you, my husband is a lawyer, Miss Tremayne," Skye told the girl formally. "Whatever you have to say I suggest you say it now, and we can sort out the mystery of why you're here."

It wasn't like her to remain patient for so long, but she was almost afraid to ask any more, and Nick had his own methods of dealing with clients, so she took a back seat while he dealt with their uninvited guest.

He scanned the letters and documents and opened the Dublin lawyer's letter which was addressed to whomever it may concern. Finally, he looked up.

"It all seems to be in order, and Mr Flynn affirms everything here. You are the daughter of the late Aileen Hagerty and Bradley Tremayne—"

He heard Skye gasp, and held up his hand.

"I am, sir," Karina said in a low voice. "But I had no knowledge of who my father was until my mother's death. It came as a great shock to me, but as you will see from some of his personal letters to her, he loved her and, unknown to me, he arranged for regular amounts to be paid to her for my upkeep.

68

You will see that he also wanted me to contact my Cornish family one day, especially if I was ever in need."

"And are you in need?" Skye said sharply, hardly able to take all this in.

"That I am not, ma'am," she said with quiet dignity. "I am well provided for. It's not why I'm here. 'Twas my parents' wishes that I contacted you and made my existence known, and now that I've done so there's no more reason for me to stay."

She stood up, holding out her hand for the return of her documents. Skye didn't miss the way her hands shook, and realised what an ordeal this must have been for her to carry out her parents' wishes.

"Of course you must stay. You're part of our family, after all," Skye heard herself say.

Karina gave a slight smile. "You're very kind, but I'm sure this must have been just as great a shock to you as it was to me. I have taken a hotel room in Truro for several nights, and then I must go back to Dublin."

"Do you have money?" Nick said, always the practical one.

"I have enough, but eventually I will seek employment, since idle hands do not suit me. I like to be busy, so I do."

Skye made up her mind. "My husband will drive you back to Truro to collect your things. I confess I know little about Bradley Tremayne and the Irish connection, but you can't simply pop into our lives and out again. I won't allow it."

"My mammie always said the Tremaynes were bossy folk," Karina said with an apologetic smile. "She took on my father's name in later years, although they never married."

"Was there any reason for that?" Skye asked.

The girl lifted her chin high. "My mother was already married. He was a wastrel who eventually drank himself to death and they had already parted when my father met my mother and I was conceived. I'm sorry it's such a sordid tale. According to the letters she left me, my father died when I was very young, so they had no chance of marrying. But I believe they truly loved each other, and of course, the priest always had to believe that I was her husband's child or Mammie would have been disgraced and ostracised by everyone."

"You'll be a Catholic then," Nick said.

"Lapsed, but none the less honest for all that."

Skye took control as she saw the strained look on the girl's face. She was exhausted. It must have been a shock to find herself in the midst of another bereavement so soon after her own. Fate sometimes had a strange way of dealing with folk and making them face up to things.

"I'd like you to stay here for a few days at least, Karina," Skye said gently. "My children are away from home, and it would be good to have a young person about the place for a while. Besides, the rest of the family would never forgive me if we didn't introduce you to everyone."

Although just how Theo was going to react to the fact of his Uncle Bradley having fathered a child, she couldn't think. She had met Bradley once when he had been on a visit to Cornwall years ago, and all she knew of him was that as a precocious and wayward child he had gone to Ireland to live with his Uncle Freddie and Aunt Venetia, where they had raised horses until the stud farm was sold after their deaths.

She would find out more later. First though, once Karina had returned from the Truro hotel, she would show her to a guest room and assure her that she was welcome, which, to Skye's surprise, she was. Karina was still grieving for her mother, but she brought a breath of fresh air into this rambling empty house.

*You can't keep her*, said a voice in her head.

Whether it was her own, or the echo of her grandmother's, she wasn't too sure at that moment. And of course it would be disastrous to try to replace her beloved daughters with this girl. Disastrous, and dangerous.

Nick's discreet telephone conversation with the Dublin lawyer confirmed everything Karina had said. He took her into Truro and collected all her clothes and cancelled the hotel booking, and that was enough for one day.

But later that evening, with the other two Pengelly brothers joining them at the dinner table, and the talk becoming more general than morbid, Skye was even more thankful for Karina's presence.

"I'd be glad to show you around the area, Miss Tremayne," Ethan offered. "You certainly can't walk everywhere, and I have a small car, even if Nick does call it a bone-shaker."

"Then I'd be glad to accept," she said shyly. "And my name is Karina."

70

"Karina it is then," said Ethan, the word as soft as a caress on his lips.

Theo was predictably coarse when he heard the news.

"Christ Almighty, I never thought old Bradley had it in him," he chortled. "Some even thought he was one of the limp-wristed brigade, what with he and old Freddie closeted up like two old women in that farm of theirs after Venetia died. Must have wanted to get his oats somewhere though."

"All right, Theo," snapped Skye. "You've had your fun, and you're not to say any of this to Karina. She's a lovely girl. Lily and David have met her and like her, so don't you dare put your evil spoke in, you hear?"

"Christ, but you're the spit of your grandmother when your eyes snap fire," he snarled. "All right. I'll be good – which is more than old Brad was," he couldn't resist adding. "So what's this meeting all about?" he asked, changing the subject.

They had concocted something to take his mind away from Karina's presence, though by now, Skye had seen the sense of not putting her previous plan into operation. Whoever Ethan or any of their children married they had to trust that they would have sense enough to keep the business in the family names, and that had to be ensured by proper documentation. Killigrew Clay would remain Killigrew Clay in perpetuity, and White Rivers, the name she herself had chosen for the pottery, would never be changed. If it was a compromise, it was a reasonable step to take. By arranging the meeting at Theo's house, they could kill the two proverbial birds, by also telling him about their new relative. Betsy, of course, had predictably been charmed at the thought of another girl in the family to fuss over.

Theo was surprisingly willing to listen to Skye's proposal, which made her increasingly wary. Theo being docile always meant trouble, and she didn't trust this mild-mannered attention for a moment.

"You do understand what Skye's proposing, don't you, man?" Nick said sharply, as if her own mistrust was fast transferring itself to him.

"Well now, I ain't too sure," he said, leaning back in his study with his arms folded behind his head, exuding a far from pleasant odour in the confined space.

"All I want is to ensure that the businesses continue with the family or chosen names, or not at all," Skye said before she could stop herself, and immediately bit her lips as he pounced on her words.

" 'Tis a mite selfish of 'ee, ain't it, cuz?" he said lazily, but his eyes were starting to flash now. "Seems to me like you'd happily put all the clayfolk out of work just because of a bloody female whim. Has this new Irish tart put more daft ideas into your head?"

Skye felt her face flush. "Karina doesn't come into it. There's no need to be insulting. I hadn't considered putting anybody out of work. Nick will vouch for that. Of course I don't want to sell out. I just want to keep the names intact. Is that too much for your pea-brain to take in?"

She should have held her tongue, she thought furiously. Instead she had implied that they might sell out if things didn't go her way, and she might have known what interpretation Theo would put on that: bloody female interference again.

Nick had warned her to let him deal with this instead of confronting Theo herself, and she hadn't listened to him. But why should she, when it was between herself and her cousin, she thought angrily? But now she was faced with Theo's smugly malicious face.

His hands suddenly left the back of his head and his fists smashed down on his fine oak desk.

"Well, I'll tell 'ee just what I think, cuz. I think you've gone too far above your station with your fine schools for your children, and your grand ideas, and 'tis the clayworkers who bring in the pennies for you to make your pretty pots, and don't you forget it."

"Why must you always twist my words?" she stormed. "I'm just trying to save everything we've always stood for, you damn idiot, by making sure that the registered names are a condition for the future. I know how hard Granny Morwen fought to stop another woman clay boss buying us out all those years ago and turning it into Pendragon Holdings or some such nonsense," she invented wildly. "All I want is to preserve Granny Morwen's values."

But God help her, she knew that wasn't the sole reason. It was seeing the covetous, greedy eyes of Jessie Vickery that had brought on all this frantic assessment of the future and prompted her to think so irrationally.

"Aye, and if Morwen and Ran Wainwright had sold out to Harriet Pendragon at that time, we'd all be sitting pretty by now, instead of having had to deal with depressions and strikes over the years, and having bloody po-faced Germans as our main markets," Theo said, turncoat in his thinking as always.

He just about managed not to hawk and spit as he said these last words. Others might be Jerry-lovers, but he was not one of them and never would be.

"He has a point, Skye."

Unbelievably, she heard Nick's comment, and felt her blood surge with rage.

"Are you siding with his bigoted views now?"

"All I'm saying is that you can't deny that china clay has always had its ups and downs, and in recent years the downs have taken precedence. I know you're shipping large quantities of raw clay to the German factories, and your own pottery exports continue to be good, which is to your credit. The new markets to America that you're so proud of are cautiously profitable, but in general, production is not at its best. The expensive electric machinery we installed seriously depleted profits for a long time, and they have never fully recovered. We're only just holding our heads above water."

Skye stared at him. She was no accountant, and neither was he, but he made regular visits to their Bodmin accountants, and knew their affairs better than anyone.

"Why haven't you said any of this before?"

He shrugged. "There was no need. I wanted to get Theo's reaction to your proposal first, and then put one of my own."

"What is it?" Theo growled.

In one respect he was in agreement with his cousin, and one respect only. He didn't want outsiders involved in their affairs. As far as he was concerned Skye would always be on the fringes as the American upstart, and even more so, her husband.

"Sell now," Nick said calmly.

"Are you out of your mind?" Skye gasped, and then she screamed as Theo shot around the desk like a streak of greased lightning and grasped Nick by the throat.

"What kind of backhander have you got your sights on, you

inferfering bugger? This is *my* business, not yours, and I'll see hell freeze before I let any snot-nosed lawyer tell me what to do with my business."

He was strong, but Nick was stronger and younger, and he had soon wrenched Theo's fingers from his throat.

"Sit down, you old fool, and listen to some sense," he snapped, pushing Tho away from him.

The thick-set man stumbled and fell, and for a moment Skye felt real fear in her heart when he didn't move for a moment. Then he scrambled to his feet and sat down heavily on his chair, no more than winded, his features puce with humiliation at this insult in his own home. His voice was harsh with derision.

"Whatever it is, it had best be good. Killigrew Clay has been in our family for nigh on a hundred years, and we ain't selling it on no lawyer's say-so. I thought your wife had some family feeling, but she don't need the money now, o' course, with her profits from old Uncle Albie's paintings."

His jeers stung Skye almost to tears. Albert Tremayne's paintings had become valuable assets after his death, and she had received a staggering amount of money for the ones she had sold. It was so like Theo to demean the things that other people held dear. He was a hateful, hateful man . . .

Nick spoke calmly and deliberately, ignoring the tension between them. "I'm no prophet, and far be it from me to foresee any trouble in Europe, but the fact that Hitler is building aircraft carriers doesn't make easy reading for those who remember the last conflict all too well. If the worst happened, all those overseas markets would be closed, just as they were in the last war."

"Good God, man, I don't have any truck with the heathen buggers, but you're away with the fairies if you're seeing another war coming up on the strength of a few goose-stepping idiots and the screechings of a madman," Theo sneered.

Nick ignored the jibe and went stolidly on.

"As you know, many of the smaller china-clay works that have struggled to keep afloat have decided to join the big conglomerates, and it may be time for Killigrew Clay to do the same. Selling now, and continuing to receive dividends through a central control would mean we wouldn't throw anyone out of work. Then, if anything untoward *did* happen, we would have the buffer of a shared business interest."

"And if that went down, we'd all go down," Skye said. "Granny Morwen never wanted us to be part of a large concern. It was her pride that Killigrew Clay always stood alone."

"Aye, it was the family's pride an' all." Theo added mutinously. "You're off on the wrong track here, Pengelly. We ain't merging with no big concern, and that's that. In fact, we ain't selling out at all, and as far as I'm concerned this here discussion is at an end."

He stood up. Skye glared at her husband and turned to Theo, swallowing her pride.

"We seem to have lost track of my original suggestion, Theo. Nick has turned this meeting into something quite different from what I intended. Perhaps you and I could talk about it together sometime? It seems a very simple matter to me, to make it a legality that the names of the two businesses never change."

So damn simple . . . no more than a few lines on a legal document . . . yet between them these two had turned it into an argument. She deliberately excluded Nick in her comment to Theo. She was seething with anger that he could have done this without warning her beforehand.

She sided with her cousin at that instant. They were family, and Nick was not. He was the outsider. She might bear his name, but at heart she was still a Tremayne and always would be, with a fine tradition behind her. Whatever happened, it would be a Tremayne decision.

"Come back tomorrow afternoon, cuz," Theo said after a moment, clearly finding a sly amusement in the conflict between them. "Bring the Bradley sprog with you if you like and let Betsy have a chinwag with her."

He went out, crashing the study door behind him, leaving them to make their own way out of the house. Once in the car, Skye looked at her husband, white-faced with anger.

"How dare you? Your role is to advise, not to issue me and my family with ultimatums."

"Thank you for putting it so succinctly, my dear. I thought my *role* as you put it, was to look after your interests and keep you happy, but it's obvious that I fall far short in both my marital and my professional roles."

"Don't twist my words, Nick. I feel very let down, and when

75

Theo and I decide what to do about the business – if anything – we'll be sure to inform you as our family lawyer."

"I never doubted it. And incidentally, I agree with the oaf in one respect. Are you quite sure old Morwen Tremayne expired nearly twenty years ago? If ever she had an influence on you she's exerting it now – or else she's doing a damn good job of reincarnation."

He drove off in a rage, while she stared dumbly ahead in the seat beside him. Far from enchanting her as it once would have done, his words chilled her. She didn't believe it was Morwen's influence telling her what to do. She was capable of using her own instincts. She was a level-headed American, not a fey-minded airhead like some of the spookier Cornish folk pretended to be for the benefit of upcountry strangers.

She didn't want to be anybody's reincarnation either, she thought fearfully, not even her beloved grandmother's, and she hated Nick even more for putting such disloyal thoughts into her head.

Things were still strained between them when she met Theo the following afternoon. By now Ethan was escorting Karina around, and she couldn't miss the attraction between the two of them. Skye simply refused to think how Wenna might react to it. There had never really been a future for her and Ethan but Wenna was too young and too romantic to be convinced of it. And in any case, Karina was so much more suitable for Ethan than the flashy Jessie Vickery.

Skye tried to push all of them out of her mind as she again faced Theo. The cousins were in agreement for once in total opposition to selling out on the grounds Nick had suggested, and Theo was adamantly pooh-poohing any idea of another war. Everybody knew the Great War had been the war to end all wars, and nobody would want to risk another, not even the power-hungry Nazi leader.

Theo had obviously had time to mull over the things Skye had said, and he agreed that they should make things watertight for their successors. The one and only thing she could admire in him was his loyalty to his family, and he had a strong second in Sebastian. Skye was sure his son would want to carry on the business, even if Olly didn't. She had more or less discounted her girls along with Sebby's brother Justin. And then Theo made her heart jump.

"Seb's the only fly in the ointment," he said, scowling.

"What? Surely he'd want to keep it in the family. He's passionate about his craft, and only Ethan's a better potter than he is."

"He's got restless lately. Wanting to travel and see a bit of the world some day, he says."

"He could go to Germany and see the other factories."

"Over my dead body, woman! You know what I think about them buggers. The only way I'd see him over there is in fighting gear, and that ain't going to happen."

"For pity's sake, don't say such things," Skye said quickly. "It's tempting fate, Theo."

"Anyway, I daresay 'tis all a long way off, but I'm just warning you that when the time comes to take over, it may be down to your sprog and not one of mine."

"Olly wants to be a lawyer, like Nick."

Theo became more thoughtful. "That don't stop him, or Seb, for that matter, being absentee owners, does it? What say we make a joint codicil to the effect that when we pop our clogs, the two of 'em are to be joint owners? That'll ensure that the names go on, and we'll insist on it legally if we must."

"Cut my girls out, you mean? Oh, I don't think so. It has to be the five of them or none at all."

"Done," Theo said, and she wasn't at all sure that she hadn't been. Or that they weren't back at square one.

Celia found it surprisingly easy to forget Franz Vogl. She would have hotly denied the suggestion that she was shallow, but her philosophy was that if someone didn't care for her, then she wouldn't care for them. It had the effect of sometimes making her seem harder than she was, but it also prevented too much heartache. And she hadn't really fallen for him . . .

Her new post at Gstaad was taking up all her energy and, besides, there were always new young men to talk to from a nearby college, who were only too eager to teach the beautiful young English sisters and their friends to ski on the winter slopes at the weekends. Even though she made a nominal protest at chaperoning her younger sister, Celia was secretly glad to have

Wenna with her, since she was far less sure of herself than her outward appearance revealed.

As the year rolled on, and winter gave way to a fragrant early spring, the experience at the hands of the jeering clayworkers faded, but she couldn't quite forget how vulnerable she had felt that day. Springtime in Gstaad and the surrounding area was exhilarating, with a plethora of brilliant wild flowers on the meadows and slopes, although by evening the temperature had usually begun to drop.

She and Wenna had got used now to the fact that there was a new female relative installed at home in New World, and Wenna in particular, had got over her jealousy when she had heard that Karina had taken on the job of nursemaiding Lily's little boys.

"Well, since Lily's boys are such a double handful, the new nursemaid cousin probably needs to be a dragon," Wenna had surmised. "Good luck to her, I say."

"She can't be that old," Celia said. "Mom says Olly's taken to her as an older sister, but then, anyone over twenty is ancient to him."

While the vagueness of Karina Tremayne's background was so intriguing to Wenna, Celia wasn't going to let on that Skye had also intimated in her letter that Ethan Pengelly was becoming ever more interested in her. For all their competitiveness, Celia didn't want to be the one to break her sister's heart.

"You have a letter from Berlin, Miss Pengelly."

She started when Madame Doubois, her immediate superior, handed her an envelope late one afternoon when lessons were over and the tutors were relaxing in the lounge in front of a unseasonably necessary log fire. All her life, Celia would remember the particular and piquant scent of those pine logs.

"Do you have a beau in Germany, Celia?" Monique, who taught deportment and elegance, asked teasingly.

"Not than I'm aware of," she said slowly, with a small leap of her heart.

She no longer had any contact with Franz, and was sure he wouldn't have written to her after so many months, but when she turned the envelope over, it was to see the seal and stamp of Herr Vogl's Fine Porcelain Distribution Company. She took out the letter at once, hoping there was nothing wrong. But if there was, she couldn't see why it would have anything to do with her.

My dear Miss Pengelly,

This letter will no doubt come as a surprise to you, but in recent correspondence with your mother through our mutual business concerns, I understand that you will be leaving St Augustine's Academy for Young Ladies in September of this year, and I have a proposal to put to you. I know how proficient you are in languages and your mother tells me of your interest in expanding your knowledge of Europe.

There will be a vacant post as personal assistant to one of my business managers in November in the company's central office here in Berlin. If you would be interested in the post a small apartment would also be available in the company hostel, which is securely supervised.

I have your mother's approval and knowledge that I am writing to you. Naturally, there is no need for a hasty decision, but please consider the matter and send me your thoughts.

With many felicitations, I remain etc., etc.

"Good Lord," Celia said out loud. "I've been offered a job in Berlin from next November, if I want it."

"What kind of job?" Monique said curiously. "You should be be careful in Berlin, *chérie*. I'm told it's a very bohemian and decadent city these days."

"Really?" Celia said, interested. "I can't say I saw anything like that when I was there with my mother last year. Anyway, I hardly think being a personal assistant in a long-established company is going to corrupt me in any way."

"Don't be too sure. There's personal and personal," Monique said meaningfully. "And of course, you were there with your mother at that time, weren't you? And well chaperoned!"

"Oh, well, I don't have to decide right away. I've got ages to think about it."

But she already knew she would accept. Living at home in a Cornish backwater, idyllic though it was, was already a long way behind her. This was a heady chance of adventure and independence she couldn't refuse.

# Six

O liver Pengelly's hand shot up that May morning as his
current affairs tutor related the news story of the previous day. Irritated at being interrupted in his dramatic
description of the *Hindenburg* disaster, the tutor told him to
be quick about it.

"I don't want to be excused, sir," Olly said, red-faced as his
classmates sniggered. "It's just that my mother was born in New
Jersey."

"Well now," the tutor said. "Perhaps she will be able to rouse
your interest in your lessons, young man. But for now, please
concentrate. As I was saying, the giant airship *Hindenburg*
exploded in mid-air in the state of New Jersey, in the United
States, killing thirty-three of its passengers and crew. She began
her flight across the Atlantic from Frankfurt. Who can tell me
the location of Frankfurt?"

As the voice droned on and more hands shot up, Olly lost
interest. He already knew about the disaster, anyway. David
Kingsley had telephoned his mother when the news had broken
the previous night. It had happened nowhere near the town
where she was born, and she had no relatives there now, but she
had been white-faced and shocked.

"I can't believe it! All those poor people," she had said. "I
always had a horror of those great airships. Travelling in them
always sounded horribly risky and claustrophobic. Just think
about all that terrible gas just waiting to ignite."

"I imagine that Herr Hitler will have to ban fuelling the things
with hydrogen, at least," Nick agreed. "Be thankful that we're
going to London by train," he added prosaically.

They were leaving for the capital on Monday, and Olly was
going with them for the royal occasion of the year. The drama of
the abdication was well behind them now, and the splendour and

pageantry of a coronation was just what was needed to raise the nation's spirits. Wenna had begged to be allowed to join them, and had been granted a special time away from the academy. She was wild with excitement at being included in a trip without her sister for once.

Olly's pal Justin hadn't been at all impressed at the idea of hob-nobbing with royalty, as he called it.

"Not that you'll get within miles of 'em," he said, as the two youths strode over the moors on the bright Sunday afternoon before the Pengellys left for London. "We'll see more of the procession through the London streets on my father's new television set, and you won't be allowed inside Westminster Abbey anyway," he added for good measure. "You'll just be squashed like insects by the crowds."

"You're just jealous," Olly retorted, refusing to let his pleasure be dimmed. The horror-filled accounts of the recent *Hindenburg* disaster were already receding in his mind as the excitement of London beckoned.

"What, of seeing all the fuss made of the new king and queen? It's for sissies."

"So you won't be watching it on your new television set with the rest of 'em then?" Olly said slyly.

"I might," Justin said. Then he grinned. "Oh, well, all right. In fact, my mother wants to invite all the relatives to come and watch it so she can show it off. Pity you won't be there. The new cousin's sure to bring Ethan as well."

Olly scowled. Since Karina Tremayne had effectively cut her ties with Ireland and looked like staying at New World with his family permanently he had been torn over whether to write to Wenna and mention Ethan Pengelly's attachment to her, but had decided against it. What brother wrote to a sister, anyway? That was for sissies if you like.

It would all have been for nothing, in any case. Now that Wenna was home, she seemed to have no particular feelings for or against their new Irish cousin, and she never mentioned Ethan Pengelly at all. Oliver simply didn't understand girls.

He forgot the lot of them as he and Justin raced across the moors, flattening the bracken beneath their feet. The stench of the old moorswoman's hovel reached them even before they saw the smoke curling from its chimney.

"Let's go and ask the old crone if Ethan Pengelly's going to marry Wenna or Karina," Justin said mischievously.

"I'm not going anywhere near her," Olly said at once. "My mother forbids it."

"And since when did you do everything your mother says?" Justin taunted him. "Are you scared of the witch woman?"

They heard a screeching noise behind them, and they whirled around to find the bent old woman leaning on a stick, her wisps of grey hair almost non-existent on her balding pate, her mouth full of blackened teeth.

"If you ain't scared, then mebbe you should be, my fine pretty boys," she said and cackled.

Justin spoke boldly. "We mean you no harm."

The cackle became louder. "*You* harm *me*? Now there's a dandy thought. So what do 'ee want old Helza to do for 'ee both on this fine May day? 'Tis never mere chance that brings 'ee this way."

"Yes it is, you old witch," Olly snapped, gaining courage from his cousin. "We're just taking the air."

"Oh, 'takin' the air,' is it?" she mimicked. "Well, mebbe you should mind and watch your feet instead of keepin' your snotty young noses in the air. There be plenty of ruts to catch 'ee unawares and stop your funnin'."

She went off still cackling, and the boys strode away as fast as they could so as not to lose face, before breaking into a run. They were on the downhill stretch, a stitch creasing their sides, when Olly gave a sudden yelp at a wrench in his ankle as he went headlong into the bracken.

"The old witch has cursed me with her talk of ruts," he moaned, trying not to cry out still more at the stinging pain and the sight of his twisted ankle rapidly swelling and bruising.

"Don't be stupid. There's not even a rut there. You just didn't look where you were going," Justin snapped, unnerved at the sight of him. "Get up and let's get home."

Olly tried, but the pain was excruciating.

"I can't," he whimpered. "I think my ankle's broken, and a fat lot of good you're going to be as a doctor if you can only stand there wringing your hands. Help me to Adam's place, Justin. He'll telephone my father to come and get me."

With Justin acting as a ungainly crutch, they somehow managed to cover the short distance to Adam Pengelly's house. Justin was practically hauling his cousin along, and Olly was near to swooning with the pain. He was trying to be manly and not to give in to tears but he knew his chance of going to London was gone. Even if it was only a sprain or a bad twist, he wouldn't be able to stand for hours among the crowds and cheer on the newly crowned king and queen.

Once Nick had collected him from Adam's house and the doctor had been called out, it was confirmed that it was a severe sprain, which had to be kept strapped up and rested for at least a week. Much later, his sister tiptoed into his room and sat on his bed, anxious and sad for him.

"I'm really sorry you'll miss our trip to London, Olly. But you should have taken more care on the moors."

"Oh, thank you very much for that advice, brainbox! But there's not much you can do against a witch's curse, no matter how much care you take," he muttered beneath his breath.

"What did you say?" She had caught the gist of the words but she wanted to hear them again.

"Nothing. I didn't want to see all the pomp anyway."

"Didn't you? You won't want to know what Daddy's been arranging for you then."

"What?" Olly asked, too sorry for himself to care.

"Uncle Theo has telephoned, and Daddy's arranging to take you to his house on our way to the train station. You're to stay there for the few days we're away so that Aunt Betsy can fuss over you, and you'll be able to see the procession on their television set!"

"I suppose that's the next best thing," Olly said grudgingly. "In fact, Justin says we'll see more that way. He was crowing over it."

"Well, it's not so bad after all then, is it?"

Wenna spoke cheerfully, as sunny-tempered as ever, feeling a mite selfish in thinking how good it would be to have her parents all to herself in London. She would never have wished Olly any harm, but it was odd how fate took a hand sometimes. And she scoffed at the thought that old Helza's words might have had any substance towards that end at all.

London was *en fête* on the day of 12th May, despite the threat of rain in the air. Nothing could stop the excitement and, with

84

everyone surging forward to get a glimpse of the golden coach and the royal procession, the Pengellys were squashed by the crowds. They had left their hotel early in the morning to be as near as possible to Buckingham Palace and get a reasonable vantage point.

Their feet were sore and aching by the time the unseen ceremony inside Westminster Abbey and the street pageantry was all over. But at last, their patience was rewarded. The roar of applause and excitement all around them heralded the appearance of the king and queen and their family on the balcony of Buckingham Palace, where they remained for some minutes acknowledging the crowds.

"They look just like the princesses in a fairy story," breathed Wenna, enchanted at the sight of the two little girls wearing their crowns. "How lucky they are!"

"Perhaps they are," Nick commented. "But they'll be living their lives in a goldfish bowl from now on. We're better off being anonymous."

"I'm not anonymous," she said indignantly. "And neither is Mom! She's far too beautiful to be anonymous."

"I'm not arguing with that," Nick grinned. "But I for one have had enough of all this standing about and adulation, so why don't we go off and find some tea rooms?"

"Yes please," Skye said feelingly. "It's been a heck of an experience to come all this way for a few minutes of actually seeing royalty. Olly will have had by far the best views on Theo's television set after all."

"You wouldn't have missed it though, would you, Mom?" Wenna said.

"Of course not. When will we ever get such a chance again?" she replied, as they fought their way through the sea of bodies still pressing forward as if to glimpse every last moment of history being enacted. It took an age to make their way through the crowds, and they thought they would never find a taxi, but by taking devious routes through unknown side streets, somehow they found one and fell inside it.

"Take us to the nearest Lyons cafe, please," Nick said.

"Righto, mate," the driver said cheerily. "First time up West, is it? You look done in. Big day though, ain't it?"

"A wonderful day," Skye told him, smiling.

It was as slow a crawl through the traffic as if they had been walking, but at least it was easier on the feet, and at last they drew up outside a Lyons. Once inside they were enveloped in the warm, crowded atmosphere, where all the talk was inevitably about the day's events. They ordered a welcome pot of tea and a selection of cakes.

"I was never so glad to sit down," Skye said. "As soon as we leave here, I want to get back to the hotel and take a hot bath. I feel as though I could sleep for a week. Thank goodness you persuaded me to stay for one more day before the long journey home, Nick. I simply couldn't face it tomorrow."

"We've got to do some more sightseeing, anyway," Wenna said determinedly. Skye groaned and closed her eyes for a brief instant.

There was a deafening mixture of voices and accents from every corner of the country all around them, as people outlined the events they had seen or missed that day. Then, through it all, one voice nearby seemed to ring out clearly in Skye's ears. A voice that was tantalisingly familiar, yet one she was unable to place immediately.

"Well, I tell yer, if I'd had to wear 'is bleedin' Majesty's crown on me 'ead for more than five minutes, I'd have keeled right over. Bleedin' 'ell, it must've weighed a ton at least!"

Skye turned her head sharply at the same time as Wenna did. It must have been ten years since either of them had heard the voice or the familiar phrase, and Wenna had been a small child, enchanted and awestruck by the daringly wicked words the flashy lady visitor had used.

"Fanny?" Skye said before she could stop herself. As she did so, the woman at the table near the window looked her way, and her heavily made-up face lit up with delight. She wound her way towards them at once, her arms outstretched, her fur stole sliding from her shoulders as she gaped from Skye to Wenna.

"Well, Gawd preserve us, if it ain't me old friend Skye. And this little beauty must be one of them lovely gels of yours, all grown up. Bleedin' 'ell, if this ain't a turn-up! You must come and meet my old feller," she chuckled.

"It's marvellous to see you, Fanny, but we were just going back to our hotel," Skye said, seeing Nick's frown, and remembering how he had disapproved of this old wartime acquaintance

86

who had burst in on their lives with one of her 'gentleman friends' some years ago – and acquainted their small daughters with words they had never heard before.

"Pity, but Gawd Almighty, yer like a sight fer sore eyes. Well, if yer doing nothin' tonight, come and see our little establishment. I've come up in the world now, see," she said, dropping her voice. 'Betcha never thought I'd end up hitched, did yer, gel? Me and my Georgie run a small club – nothing seedy, mind. We get some class acts in, and we've got a lovely torch singer for tonight. Look, I can see Georgie's wantin' to move on now, but you be sure and come along tonight and have a meal wiv us after the show – all right?"

She shoved a card into Skye's hand, and before she could reply Fanny had turned away in a whiff of cheap scent to join the insignificant little man waiting impatiently for her by the door.

"Bleedin' 'ell," Wenna said beneath her breath, smothering a giggle.

Thankfully, Nick didn't hear her, but Skye did. She kicked her daughter beneath the table, but there was laughter in her eyes as she did so.

She looked at the business card, as pink and flashy as its owner, and proclaiming the name and address of the Flamingo Club, with the name of the proprieter George Rosenbloom beneath it.

"You might as well tear it up," Nick said. "It'll be some awful dive, and we're not going anywhere near it."

"You haven't asked me if I want to go there yet," Skye said as Wenna gave a howl.

"Why can't we go, Daddy? I've never been to a club before."

"You're not going now—"

"Why not? Must you be so stuffy, Nick? I'm sure it's respectable if Fanny's husband is anything to go by. He looked such an odd little man."

"He's a Jew," Nick said.

"What's wrong with that? They're people, aren't they?" Wenna said, disappointed and ready to argue. "Why must lawyers always try to stop people having fun?"

Skye realised that people were glancing their way as their voices rose. She said calmly that they would discuss it further at their hotel and not in a public place, which would be far more suitable for the dignity of Nicholas Pengelly, Solicitor at Law, she thought in annoyance.

He agreed, as she had known he would, and after a couple of hours of female persuasion he had also reluctantly given in to their request for a short visit to the Flamingo Club.

"But if it's in the least bit dubious, then we're coming straight back here," he warned.

Skye and Wenna smiled at once another, well pleased, and determined to make a night of it, whatever he said.

The Flamingo Club was a pleasant surprise. True to Fanny's word, it wasn't seedy at all. The decor was that of a discreet little nightclub, with a small area for dancing, and a raised platform where the various acts performed.

Wenna was instantly entranced by the glittering costumes of the dancers who performed acrobatic feats to music, and the comedian whose jokes bordered on schoolboy humour with veiled references to Herr Hitler and exaggerated goose-stepping. But what thrilled her most was the female torch singer, imported from America who sang in a deep, soulful voice to a piano accompaniment. The singer wore a long, creamy figure-hugging gown, and trailed a wispy chiffon scarf through her fingers as she wandered among the audience, exuding the kind of perfume that hadn't come out of Woolworth's. She was glamour personified, and Wenna was bowled over by her.

"Wasn't she simply marvellous?" she said, almost choked with emotion when the rendition came to an end.

"Marvellous," her father agreed. "But don't go getting any ideas, darling. You need real talent and self-confidence to be able to perform like that."

Wenna stared into the distance, the subtle and intimate lighting of the club made the room very romantic. No ideas of trying to emulate such a star had even entered her head. Not until now. Not until her father had unwittingly put them there. She swallowed.

"It must be lovely to entertain people and send them home feeling so happy, though."

"You stick to your piano playing and singing at the academy, Wenna. It's much safer to be well praised for your performances and to leave it at that, than to risk embarking on a precarious stage career," he said lightly, never realising how his words had taken root.

He might not, but Skye had. Her heart beat a little faster at the glow in her younger daughter's eyes. Celia had always been the confident one, while Wenna had always lagged a little behind, uncertain, unsure of herself, even with the undoubted talent she had inherited from Primmy Tremayne's superb piano playing. But Wenna had even more. She had a husky singing voice that was a faint echo of the American torch singer. With the right training and direction, it could be as intimate as the star performer's here tonight.

Skye shook herself, knowing she was letting her imagination run away with her on her daughter's behalf. And knowing too, that it wouldn't be the kind of future Nick would want for his daughter. But no matter how much she adored him, Nick would always have the lawyer's reserve on that score, while Skye was a free-spirited American, where the moon and stars were there for the taking.

The show was over, and she saw Fanny weaving her way towards them, with Georgie in tow.

"You came then, ducks," she shrilled out gleefully. "So what did you think of the acts? Wasn't Gloria del Mar the absolute bleedin' tops?"

"She was wonderful, Fanny," Skye agreed. "Wenna certainly thought so."

"Good, 'cos she's joining us for supper in the flat upstairs. You can meet her prop'ly then. She might even give us a tune or two if we talk nicely to 'er. We've got a piano up there, though Georgie's a bit rusty on it. Your Ma used to play, didn't she, Skye?"

"She was semi-professional," Skye said with a burst of pride. "Wenna takes after her. She can play and sing too."

"*Mom!*" Wenna said, agonised. It was one thing to have stars in your eyes. It was quite another to visualise accompanying the glamorous Miss Gloria del Mar.

Georgie suddenly spoke up, in a quiet, slightly lisping voice. It was clear that he rarely spoke at all while his wife held court, and they all looked at him in surprise.

"Perhaps the little lady would do us the honour of trying out the piano first of all. It needs someone who loves the instrument to get the best out of it, and I'm afraid such a description does not fit myself."

Wenna caught his shy smile and found herself smiling back. He was such an incongruous match for the awful, yet oddly endearing Fanny. The warmth of his welcome was like that of an indulgent grandfather, and she loved him at once.

"I could try, if you really want me to," she said.

Her heart was still skipping beats with monotonous regularity when they finally went up to the elegant flat above the club, and discovered that Fanny and Georgie lived quite the high life. Georgie obviously had other qualities besides a placid nature to complement his wife. There was someone to cook supper, and someone else to serve it.

Fanny had evidently fallen very much on her feet, and not for want of trying, Skye confided to Nick later, ignoring his jibe that it was more likely the time spent on her back that had finally produced the goods.

But by then, Wenna had realised the possibility of doors opening to her that she had never in her wildest dreams considered before.

Supper was a noisy, jolly affair, and Georgie proved to be a congenial, witty man with a dry sense of humour that was a complete foil to Fanny's brashness. That they adored one another was obvious to everyone. When they had eaten their fill and drunk copious amounts of wine and coffee, Gloria was persuaded to sing for them without too much urging. She declared that she was going to sing a song dedicated especially to them both.

"Are you going to play for me, honey?" she asked Wenna. "I hope you can follow the sheet music, but you probably know the song. Try it first. It was all the rage last year."

She opened the lid of the piano stool, clearly very much at home with the Rosenblooms, and handed the sheet music to Wenna with a smile. Music lessons at the academy involved mainly classical pieces, but Wenna was well acquainted with the more popular songs of the day, and to her relief she already knew this one.

Her fingers rippled over the keys for a few experimental bars, and then launched into the haunting, expressive melody of 'The Way You Look Tonight' while the others listened. Then she nodded to Gloria, who began to sing, lingering over the words with all the heartfelt emotion of the torch singer, and Wenna felt her throat close up. To offset the feeling, she found herself humming the tune very quietly as she played. So absorbed was she in the sheer aesthetic beauty of the words and the music that she didn't realise that Gloria had stopped singing.

She stopped playing at once, scarlet with embarassment.

"No, don't stop," Gloria said softly. "Why don't you sing it, honey? I'd love to hear you."

"Oh no, I couldn't possibly." she said, totally confused now.

"Go on, ducks," Fanny said encouragngly. "Gloria don't sit back and let someone else take centre stage unless she thinks there's a star in the makin'."

"I'm hardly that!"

They waited expectantly and she swallowed, placing her fingers on the piano keys she loved, letting the melody flow out again, and putting her own husky interpretation on the sensuous words.

". . . Love me . . . never, never change . . . keep that breathless charm . . ."

There was silence for a moment when she had finished. She felt the same acute embarrassment she had felt before, but there was exhilaration too, because she had put her heart and soul into it, feeling the emotions of the composer and lyricist, the way she always did whenever she performed anything. And then she heard the applause.

There were only five other people in the room, but the applause was loud and unstinting. Gloria put her arm round her shoulders and faced the others.

"I'm no clairvoyant, and I don't know what you folks have got in mind for this little gal, but she's clearly destined for Broadway. She's an absolute natural, and with that talent and those looks she could make it anywhere."

Nick cleared his throat, seeing his daughter's eyes glowing like sapphires. Her Swiss tutor's praise for her musical skills was as nothing compared with the future that Gloria del Mar was dangling in front of her, and it had to be curbed before Wenna got completely star struck. She was too young, too impressionable, still his little girl, even though he had been startled and deeply affected by the depth of emotion she had put into the song. In those moments she had no longer been his Wenna, but a sensual young woman yearning for her lover . . . and Nick needed to squash the unwelcome illusion at all costs.

"It's very kind of you to compliment her so much, but it's far too soon for Wenna to think about a career at all. When she finishes her tuition in Switzerland she'll be coming home to Cornwall, and that will be time enough to consider what direction she'll be taking."

"Oh, Daddy, don't be so pompous," Wenna said with a nervous giggle. "I'm not going to be a stuffy old lawyer like Olly, that's for sure."

Skye put a restraining hand on Nick's arm. Before the tension rose any further, Fanny said, "Your boy was just a babby when I visited you all them years back, Skye. I never had no dealings with infants as you know. Never knew which end of 'em was worst, if yer gets my meanin'. Going to be a lawyer, is he? Fancy that. He's made up his mind already then. And what about the other gel? Celia, weren't it?"

"She may be going to work in Berlin as a personal assistant for a company that buys a lot of our pottery. If I'd known I was going to see you again, Fanny, I'd have brought some of it for you as a gift," Skye said, thankful to turn the talk away from the magic of a potential stage career.

Not that she had the reservations that Nick had. In his eyes, such a life was consistent with debauchery at the very least, and filled with unsavoury characters, which, he had to admit, Gloria del Mar certainly was not. She was charming and delightful, but she was clearly wise enough to say nothing more about it as the Pengellys decided they really must leave for their hotel.

"Georgie will run you back, Skye. You'll never find a cab at this time of night."

"Oh, we couldn't put you out like that."

"It's no trouble," the congenial Georgie said, and before they left to slide into the vastness of his big Daimler, Fanny hugged Wenna.

"If you decide you want to try yer luck, darlin', you jest get in touch wiv us. We know the best agents who won't rip yer orf, and you'd be welcome to have a spot in the Flamingo. You could lodge wiv us in our spare room, so no harm would come to yer."

"Thank you," Wenna said, dazed, aware that Nick was edging

her out of the room before she committed herself. Not that she would, or could, right now. She was only seventeen years old, and she had until the end of the summer to finish her time at St Augustine's, but after that . . .

"Fanny's heart's in the right place," Georgie observed to no one in particular as he drove them away in the sleek motor car towards the smart London hotel where they were staying. "She'd be like a mother to your gel, as well as an eagle-eyed chaperon. She'd be well looked after if she came to us."

Skye leaned towards him before Nick could reply.

"I have no doubt of it, Georgie, and I thank you for the offer, but Wenna's always been a home-living girl and might well decide that she's been away from home for long enough."

Georgie glanced at the girl in question sitting in the corner of the back seat as she gazed out of the window at London's bright lights and the throngs of people who didn't seem to want this wonderful day to end, no matter how late the hour. He thought that the girl herself might have ideas of her own about that. Such talent was far too good to waste in a Cornish backwater.

It was obvious that the Pengellys would have to purchase one of the new-fangled television sets, even though the programmes were so very few as yet. It was the thing of the future, Theo boasted.

Olly was making the most of his painful ankle while still confined indoors, and secretly enjoyed being waited on by everyone. But his relentless pleading for a television set of their own, coupled with his enthusiasm and lordly comments that he had seen *far* more of the coronation day on the screen than the others had seen, finally won Nick over. Besides, Olly added slyly in a final burst of triumph, they surely didn't want his Uncle Theo to continue crowing over the fact that he could afford the luxury of something the Pengellys didn't own.

"Your son has all the makings of a lawyer," Nick observed to Skye as they drove into Truro to see about arranging delivery and installation. But she could see he wasn't displeased at the thought. Olly could argue with the best of them, and that was Nick's forte too.

She wanted peace and harmony in the house. There had been a small fracas when Wenna had declared to Olly that she was going to be a stage star, and Nick had flatly refused to listen to any such ideas until she had finished her education.

Wenna had since returned to Gstaad in a considerably more aggressive mood than usual, asserting her rights to anyone who would listen, including her sister.

Celia grinned. "And the awful Fanny would be willing to give you a home, would she? I can't imagine what kind of a place she lives in."

"It's a lovely flat, as a matter of fact, and you wouldn't know her now," Wenna said, defending her. "She's perfectly respectable, and Georgie's a lovely man."

"Well, you'd better not let the tutors hear you say you're going to be a star of stage and screen, or whatever, or you'll be thrown out of here as a bad influence on the younger girls!"

Wenna laughed at the thought, but her eyes were pleading, wanting Celia's approval. "You don't really think it's such a daft idea though, do you, sis?"

Celia suddenly saw how intense she was, and how important all this was to her. The idea that had been no more than a small seed of ambition now burned brightly in Wenna's soul.

Uncharacteristically, Celia gave her sister a hug.

"If you want it badly enough, don't let anyone try to stop you. Make sure it's truly what you want, that's all."

"Mom showed me some portraits of her mother when she played the piano in concerts. Old Uncle Albie had painted some that I hadn't even seen before," Wenna said. "She was so lovely, and I know I want to be just like her."

"Then I'm sure you will be," Celia said, touched. "Just don't push it too hard with Dad, that's all."

There was no point in doing anything about it yet, except to dream of what might be. She was too young to be allowed that freedom. Another year, and her parents might just think of letting her go to London alone. In any case, in a few months' time they would be losing one daughter when Celia went to work in Berlin. It was far too soon for them to think of losing another. She would have to be content with at least a spell of life in Cornwall once she left Gstaad. Until then, academic and cultural activities had to take precedence over everything else if she was to get the same coveted certificate of excellence that Celia had won in her own final term. All thoughts of a future career had to be put firmly to the back of her mind.

But it was far from the back of other peoples' minds. In London, there were three people who had become excited over the huge potential of the girl they believed they had discovered.

"I'd be more than willing to promote her," Georgie Rosenbloom said, never slow to back what he saw as a winner. "She'd need a good agent, and Gloria already has someone highly reliable in mind."

"She'd stay here wiv us, of course," Fanny said. "I'd make good my promise to Skye on that one. We don't want no greasy-haired gigolos hanging round and causin' bleedin' ructions. She's a good girl, and she'd need to be portrayed as such. She's a proper bleedin' angel with that voice of hers."

"You're right, honey," Gloria del Mar said thoughtfully. "And with the right kind of promotion and backing, she could be really big. I think we ought to write a careful letter to her parents and put our proposals to them. We can't do anything without their consent, since the girl is still a minor. Thinking ahead though, it won't do any of us any harm to let it be known eventually that we discovered her right here in the Flamingo Club. Didn't you say her mom used to be a journalist? That's to our advantage. She won't be averse to some cleverly worded publicity when the time comes. What we have to do is assure them that it's Wenna's future we're thinking of, and that there's no question of our trying to yank her out of that posh school before time."

They smiled at one another, well satisfied with what had so unexpectedly come their way. Georgie was more than happy at the thought of having a hand in handling this potential gold mine, and each of them was genuinely excited at the thought of steering this very likeable little lady to fame and fortune.

# Seven

T heo swore vehemently as he scanned the official letter that had been delivered that morning. Coming hard on the heels of what that bastard Pengelly had been intimating recently, it smacked of intrigue going on behind his back. If there was one thing to get him riled up, it was that.

As always, when he was upset, his liver was affected, and he went about roaring and cursing at anyone who happened to come within earshot. It felt as if his entire guts were on fire and tied in knots on that fine June morning as his motor roared up to New World.

He scattered gravel in all directions as he hauled on the brake outside the house. He slammed the vehicle door behind him and hammered on the front door, bawling for admittance until Mrs Yardley answered him indignantly.

"Good morning to 'ee, Mr Theo, sir," she began, and then stepped hastily aside as he marched past her, hollering loudly for his cousin.

"If you'm wanting Mrs Pengelly, you'm out of luck, sir," she told him stiffly. "She's gone up to the pottery, and Mr Pengelly's away at Bodmin with the accountant. There's only young Master Oliver here and he's in his room with his books."

Her words as to Nick's whereabouts confirmed Theo's dark suspicions. He turned on his heel without another word, muttering obscenities beneath his breath. He shot away from the house in his motor, leaving the housekeeper sorely tempted to slam the front door behind him.

He arrived at White Rivers Pottery just as Skye was coming out, talking amiably with an important lady client, well pleased with her order for a dinner and a tea service that incorporated Seb's successful new design.

"I want to talk to you," Theo snapped, and Skye felt her face flame with colour.

97

"Certainly, Mr Tremayne. Please go into the office while I escort Lady Asher off the premises." She spoke pleasantly, but her eyes flashed dangerously at his crudeness. She walked on, her head held high, aware that Lady Asher glanced curiously at Theo's retreating back as her chauffeur opened her car door for her.

How *dare* he, Skye fumed, standing with her hands tightly clenched for several minutes until the car had moved smoothly away in the direction of St Austell. How *dare* he come here and disrupt her premises by such a display of rudeness? Lady Asher was as near to royalty as they would get in the county, and Skye was deeply honoured that she and her friends patronised the pottery. How *dare* Theo jeopardise that valuable clientele.

Inside the showroom, she ignored the huddled whispering of the two young women behind the counter, and went through to her office, where Theo was prowling, unable to keep still and barely able to contain his temper.

"Have you any knowledge of this, woman?" he bellowed, thrusting his letter under her nose. "And don't try to deny it, because I'm bloody sure your husband will have had a hand in it, and you'll be in cahoots with him."

"If you would kindly shut up for five minutes, Theo, we can discuss your outrageous appearance here in a civilised manner – if that's not asking the impossible!" she snapped.

Although she was shaking with anger, she sat down at her desk, forcing him to remain standing on the other side of it. Even sitting, with the desk between them she was still in control. In any case, she had the vocabulary to make mincemeat of him and he knew it. All he had ever had was bluster and blasphemies.

"*Well?*" he snarled, when she totally ignored the letter and declined to take it out of his hand.

"Well what? Or is all this dragon snorting supposed to be an unspoken apology for your rude behaviour?"

He crashed his hand down on her desk. She refused to be intimidated by him, and remained unblinking, her hands clenched tightly together. Only the whiteness of her knuckles revealed how she was controlling her temper.

"I'll see hell freeze over before I start apologising to a wench, and an outsider at that," he said explosively.

"Then we have nothing to say to one another," Skye said,

standing up so quickly that he stepped back a pace. As he did so, the door of the office opened, and Seb stepped inside.

"Is everything all right in here, Skye?"

Theo turned on his son at once. 'Don't come sniffing round my cousin's skirts and interfering wi' men's work, you milksop. Get back to your clay modelling where you belong."

Skye saw how Seb held himself in check with a huge effort. His father was a violent shade of red by now, and a fine candidate for a heart attack, Skye thought. The veins on his forehead stood out like purple ropes.

"You're a real bastard, aren't you?" Seb said at last, uncaring that it was his father he spoke to.

"Takes one to know one, boy," Theo roared, before he turned on his heel and went blundering out of the pottery. In the momentary silence in the office, they heard his car roar off with a screech of tyres.

"He didn't mean that, Sebby," Skye said quickly. "You know what he's like when he gets incensed."

"I know, I've had enough," the young man said bitterly. "I'm moving out, finding digs somewhere. I don't suppose . . ."

"If you're asking to move into New World, I don't think that would be a good idea, do you?" she said quietly.

"Probably not. After all, I'm not Irish. And I'm not female," he added, turning away.

When she was alone again, Skye sat down at her desk, drawing deep breaths, wondering just how this day had become so full of hate and resentment. The last thing she wanted to do was alienate Sebby from his father, and moving in with the Pengellys would certainly not help.

Trying not to dwell on that aspect, she re-read a letter that she too had received that morning. It would have been identical to Theo's. If only he didn't jump to hot-headed conclusions, usually the wrong ones, they could have discussed it sensibly.

With journalistic expertise, she ignored everything in the letter but the few sentences that mattered.

. . . and so this is our formal offer to purchase the part and parcel of the land and clayworks known as Killigrew Clay for the aforementioned sum. We would appreciate your early and considerate reply.

99

It was signed Zacharius Bourne and the address was Bourne and Yelland China-Clay Holdings Limited, Roche, Cornwall.

She shivered, wishing Nick had been there when the letter had arrived that morning, and just as quickly, glad that he was not. He had already suggested selling out, a suggestion that would have outraged old Morwen Tremayne and Theo's father Walter, who had loved the china clay with a passion only comparable with that for his wife, Cathy. Theo, Skye had long suspected, only loved it when it suited him, and when his covetous ownership was threatened.

But remembering the previous meeting between all three of them, she realised that Theo would naturally assume that Nick had been talking out of turn with Zacharius Bourne, and that this was the result. He would certainly think she had been allied with her husband. He had never trusted her or liked her comeuppance in the clay world, even though she was perfectly entitled to it. and now it seemed that Seb was against her too, with his snide reference to Karina.

Her thoughts shifted, wondering just how long Karina intended staying with them. She had cut her ties with Ireland, and was an undoubted family member, but she wasn't a substitute daughter. Skye had already sensed that Olly was tiring of her presence in his domain.

The uneasy question of what to do about Karina was taken out of her hands a few days later.

By then Nick had telephoned Theo and told him shortly that they need do nothing about the letters. He would send a formal reply on their behalf, if required, declining any interest in Bourne's offer. He had also assured him in no uncertain terms that he had had no prior knowledge of the matter, nor any personal interest in it.

But any ruffled feathers were forgotten when a frantic telephone call came from Lily one leisurely afternoon. Skye was sitting in the sunlit conservatory and reading the newspaper reports of the marriage in France of the ex-king and Mrs Simpson, now officially the Duke and Duchess of Windsor.

"It's Mrs Kingsley on the telephone, ma'am," Mrs Yardley said formally. "And she sounds in a right state," she added.

Skye went into the hall, and had to hold the instrument away from her ear as Lily's unusually shrill voice refused to make any sense for a few moments.

"You'll have to talk more slowly, Lily. I can't understand you—"

But it was impossible to quell Lily's flow, which continued to flood out in a long hysterical string of words.

"We were all sitting in mother's garden, and Karina was playing with the children, and mother was saying how she hoped the new Duchess would be happy now, despite all the fuss and upset she had caused, and then she just stopped talking in the middle of a sentence, and her head lolled to the side, and she was dead."

She stopped for breath with a huge shuddering gasp. Skye stared at the telephone for an instant, her mind unable to grasp the shock of such an unrelenting statement, and then her senses took control.

"Where are you now? Have you called the doctor?"

"I'm still here. At mother's. Karina's called David and the doctor, and has taken the boys home. I'm here with mother. Skye, I don't know what to do, and David's not here yet."

She was whimpering now, her earlier hysterical ramble reduced to short staccato sentences as shock took over. She had seen so much horror in France, stood up valiantly for women's rights and been a feminist long before her time, and now her nerves were simply shot to pieces by a second personal tragedy, coming so soon after her sister's death.

"I'll come right away," Skye said at once. "Hold on, darling. Just hold on."

She got into her car and drove to Truro like a wild thing, only pausing in her flight from the house to shout to Mrs Yardley to let Nick and Olly know what was happening when they returned from their ride along the sands.

By the time she arrived there were other cars outside Charlotte's impressive hillside house. It was full of a quietly dignified bustle as the doctor and the undertaker took charge.

Skye went into the terraced garden overlooking the sea, to find David holding his wife in his arms. She went to them and embraced them both, and the three of them stood silently locked together in mutual sorrow for some minutes.

"I need to get her home," David mouthed above Lily's head.

"She's had a terrible shock, and the doctor has given me a sedative for her."

"Not yet," Lily's voice came sharply. "And please don't talk about me as if I'm not here. I need to see that mother is taken carefully to the Chapel of Rest and made comfortable, and then I must tidy her house."

"You don't have to do any such thing!" Skye said, aghast.

"Yes I do. Mother hates an untidy house. She'll hate it if people come here and don't find everything in order."

"Lily darling, none of it will matter to your mother any more," Skye said gently.

"It matters to me," she said, as stubborn as ever. "Karina has taken the children home. My assistant can look after the showroom. It will be good for the boys to have a cheerful young person like Karina around them: I've asked her to stay with us for a while, since I'll be so busy here."

She almost faltered then, but her determination was strong, and she continued making plans as if needing to get the house ready for a party. She seemed driven, and after a while, David shrugged his shoulders and simply let her carry on. Everyone had their way of dealing with grief, and this seemed to be Lily's, Skye thought, horrified.

But more than a week later, when Charlotte had been laid to rest in the family vault beside her husband, Lily was still obstinately refusing to leave her old family home and resume normal living. David spoke desperately to Skye, knowing she was the one who always talked the most sense to his wife.

"She can't stay up there in that mausoleum for ever. In any case, it has to be sold. Charlotte made that clear in her will. The boys need her, Skye. They're fretting for their mother. And *I* need her."

"How does Karina feel about staying there?"

"She's a great girl, but I'm worried what people might be thinking. She's young and pretty, and she's living unchaperoned in my home with only myself and the boys. I don't need to tell you what gossips there are in a town like this, and a newspaperman doesn't attract the best of neighbours."

Skye knew she would have to tread carefully. "Lily is fond of Karina, isn't she? She trusts her with the boys?"

"Immensely fond. She thinks of her as a daughter, which is

why she sees nothing wrong in her being there with me. There *is* nothing wrong, Skye. You believe that, don't you?"

"Of course. But I can also see that you're worried about your reputation, and Lily should see that too. I'll speak to her and try to get her to come home where she belongs."

He leaned forward and kissed her. "What the hell would any of us do without you?" he asked simply.

She left him then and drove to Charlotte's house, where Lily was still industriously cleaning, as if to dare any speck of dust to defile her mother's memory. Skye stilled her vigorous polishing by putting her hand on her cousin's arm.

"Lily, it's time to go home. It's time to care for your children and to be a loving wife to your husband."

Lily gasped, her face burning with colour.

"How can you say such a thing?" she said, her wild eyes brimming with tears. "I've just buried my mother."

"I buried mine, and my darling grandmother, *and* my husband. But life goes on, Lily darling. We all have to go on. You'll still grieve for her, but your mother doesn't need you now. Other people do. Frederick and Robert are pining, and so is David. He deserves more than to be shut out like this."

The last thing she had intended was to sound like a bloody saint, Skye thought irreverently. But everything she said was true. And as Lily became sullenly silent, there was still more to say. "Karina has been a gem in looking after the children for these past days, Lily. Do you think it would be a good idea to ask her to stay permanently? She's already like a big sister to them, and it would give you and David time to go out by yourselves sometimes if she was part of the household. It's only a suggestion but you might like to think about it."

"I can't think about anything like that just now," she said mutinously, but Skye knew the idea would take root. Lily had been badly shaken by her mother's death, but basically she was the strongest person Skye had ever known. She would survive this.

"You're a bit of a miracle worker, aren't you?" Nick said to his wife at bedtime a few weeks later, when the whole thing had been settled, and Karina had moved all her things out of New World and moved into the spare bedroom in the flat above the White Rivers showroom on Truro's waterfront.

103

"There's nothing magical about getting people to see what's right under their noses. It's obviously the right place for Karina, and we should have seen it all along."

"But it took Charlotte's death to bring it to fruition," he said thoughtfully. "As if it was all meant."

"Don't say that, Nick!" she said quickly. "I don't like to hear such things."

"And you a Cornishwoman?" he teased her. "Even if only a colonially attached one."

She threw a pillow at him, which he tossed right back. A few loose feathers flew, making her cough and splutter with laughter. Then she was captured in his arms and held close to his heart as they fell together across the bed.

"Do you know how long it is since I've made love to you?" he said, his voice urgent and aching with desire.

"Too long," Skye said, her breath catching in her throat. "Much, much too long."

"Then it's high time we put that to rights," he said softly, his fingers pushing aside the straps of her nightgown and bending forward to press his lips to her breasts. She strained towards him, wanting him with all the fierce desire of a wife, and all the uninhibited lust of a lover.

His hand slid beneath the hem of her nightgown and his fingers moved upwards tantalisingly slowly until they found their goal, making her gasp aloud with pleasure. She reached for him, glorying in the rampant desire she knew was there for her, caressing him and holding him, and needing him so much. So very much . . .

"If there's anything better than this on God's earth, I don't want to know about it," he murmured a long while later when the sweet preliminaries were over, and he was forging into her, each erotic thrust interspersed with kisses.

She could taste her own musky scent on his lips as his tongue roamed round her mouth, increasing her excitement as they reached the climax of their lovemaking. She clung to him as he gasped against her, holding her tightly to him as she felt the surging heat of him filling her.

He didn't move away from her quickly. They lay, their bodies still close, still part of each other, until it became obvious that they must break away. Only then did Skye feel the strange tears of release on her cheeks, the way they always were when she had been in the grip of an almost unbearably strong emotion.

Nick saw the tears and touched them with his fingertips. His voice was softly teasing again. "If I didn't know you so well, I would say you regretted what had just happened."

She put her fingers over his. "I have no regrets for anything, ever, my love," she whispered.

She felt no disrespect to Charlotte for having encouraged Lily to resume a normal life, and as time passed, she was relieved to hear from Karina that Lily was behaving more rationally and taking an interest in life again. She and David had even been to the theatre one evening, while Karina had looked after the children. It was a healthy beginning.

The Cornish community was always considerate in its deference to a family bereavement. Several months passed before a second letter arrived from Zacharius Bourne. It suggested that if the owners of Killigrew Clay weren't willing to sell outright it would be advantageous for them to merge, and Bourne would be happy to arrange a meeting between them and their solicitors to discuss the matter.

"Damn cheek," Skye said, ripping the letter to shreds. "Why on earth would we want to be part of a company with that odious little man?"

"Because there's strength in numbers," Nick pointed out.

"Yes, but we don't need his inferior clay for the pottery. Ours is by far the finest, production is good, and we have more than our needs for export. We don't need the Bourne clay, and he's not getting his hands on ours."

"I didn't know you were so possessive," Nick said.

"Yes, you did," she replied smartly. "And so is Theo. He'll have had a similar letter, I suppose. I wonder what his reaction to it is this time. He's calmed down a lot since Seb did what he threatened and moved out of the house. It gave him a considerable shock."

Theo didn't care about the Bourne offer one way or the other. He had seen mortality staring him in the face when his cousin Charlotte died. There were very few of the older members of the family left, and he was now the most senior one. The fact that his elder son could so coldly turn his back on him had been a further blow to his pride and his nerves.

Like many a bombastic man, when he felt the shadow of mortality hovering about his own shoulders, he crumbled. He didn't even bother to get in touch with Skye to let her know he had also received a second letter from Bourne. If she wanted to negotiate, it was up to her to contact him. With uncharacteristic melancholy, he told himself that perhaps it was time for him to think of retiring gracefully from the race and preserving his strength – but how long such a state of mind was destined to last was another matter. He had always been a man of chameleon-like moods, as contrary as the fluctuating clay fortunes, and his long-suffering family were only too well aware of it.

The only one to benefit from his unusually placid mood was Betsy, who fussed over him like a mother-hen, knowing that, like the calm before the storm, it couldn't last, but ready to enjoy it while it did.

As the academy year in Gstaad was nearing its end, Celia also received a letter, this one postmarked Berlin. She had already written back to Herr Vogl, saying she would be very interested in taking up the position and accommodation that he offered, and that she had her parents' full approval.

It was stretching it a bit, since Nick had not been nearly as agreeable as her mother, but fathers always worried about their ewe-lambs, as she had told anyone who would listen. Nick wasn't even her real father, just a bolted-on step-Dad, she sometimes added airily, enjoying the Celia-like drama of the words.

This new letter was not from Herr Vogl.

I will be in the Gstaad area on business shortly, and I would be delighted if we could meet and discuss the position Herr Vogl has offered you as my personal assistant.

A place and time were proposed for the meeting, and it was signed Stefan von Gruber. Celia replied at once, and long before the arranged date, she and Wenna had conjured up all kinds of images for the man.

"He's sure to be old and crabby with a name like that," Wenna decided. "I wonder if there's a Frau von Gruber, and any little von Grubers," she added, starting to giggle. "What a name to land your children with. He'll have a large red nose and an enormous pot belly at the very least."

"Hush, the tutors will hear you." Celia laughed.

"I don't care. I'm leaving this place soon and going *home*. I never realised I would long for it so much!"

"Oh, yes? What ever happened to the prospective star of stage and screen then? Has the great ambition disappeared in favour of Cornwall and selling Mother's pots?"

"Certainly not," Wenna said. "I'm just biding my time, as the saying goes, until I can leave home without causing any fuss. I'll have my name up in lights one day, you'll see."

"And pigs might fly," Celia said inelegantly.

Only to herself did she admit how nervous she was becoming as the time drew near for her to meet Herr von Gruber. This would be her first real job as part of a huge production company in the heart of Germany with a connection with her mother's pottery and with Killigrew Clay.

The charm of it didn't escape her. She wouldn't be losing touch entirely . . . and at the thought she straightened her shoulders, telling herself not to be as soft as Wenna in feeling the tug of home. The entire world was her home, and the thought of the insular little corner of it that Cornwall represented was no longer the be-all and end-all of existence for Celia. Plenty of Cornish diehards refused to accept that they were even part of England, clinging to their quaintness and mystical heritage, their omens and superstitions, as if they were talismans. Celia found herself smiling faintly as the thoughts came into her head, because she was Cornish too, and she had a good feeling about this appointment. The first step was to make a good impression on the oddly named Herr von Gruber.

She dressed carefully, wearing her best grey skirt and a silky white blouse, her waist tightly clinched by an emerald-green belt. It was meant to stamp her as a woman of fashion, and she hoped nervously that it wasn't too flashy.

Sophisticated was the word she wanted to apply, and she pinched her cheeks and added a touch of lip colour to her mouth, standing back from her mirror and trying to judge the effect through someone else's eyes. Maybe she should have had her hair cut, she moaned. The new marcel waves were all the rage, and more suitable to a working woman that her own long straight hair with the fringe almost touching her eyebrows. But neither she nor Wenna could bear to have their hair cut. Like Samson, she believed it kept her luck intact – and who was being superstitious now!

She put on her matching grey jacket with shaking fingers, and left the academy for the hotel lounge where she was to meet Herr von Gruber.

The hotel was quite crowded. The area was becoming prominent now, not only for winter sports, but for the year-round health-giving Swiss air, as clear as wine, and fragrant with the scent of flowers. Celia felt a brief nostalgia at having to leave this place that had been her home for several years, and tried to work out who Herr von Gruber might be.

She prayed it wouldn't be the monocled gentleman in the corner, and was relieved when an elderly lady joined him. Wenna had said he would probably be a sportsman in lederhosen and a hat with a feather tucked in the side, and she choked back a giggle at the thought, trying to compose her face.

"Miss Pengelly?" a strong male voice said in perfect English, with just the hint of an accent.

She whirled around and hoped that her eyes didn't widen too obviously at the man smiling down at her.

She had always believed in first impressions, and her first impression of Herr Stefan von Gruber was a world away from the image she and Wenna had pictured. He was not old or middle-aged, and he certainly wasn't fat. His hair was a Germanic silvery blond, and his eyes were as blue as Celia's own with laughter creases at the sides. His face was craggily good-looking, his nose aristocratically long, and his smile . . . his smile was wide and welcoming. He wore a light brown business suit that was impeccably tailored, covering a lean, athletic figure.

He held out his hand to Celia as she inclined her head, momentarily dumb. She placed her hand in his, and even though she was not the type to believe in love at first sight, or all the romantic and euphemistic trappings that went with it, she swore that she felt a definite, tingling shockwave run up her arm at the contact.

"Shall we find a table where we can talk privately, Miss

Pengelly?" the adorable Herr von Gruber said. She blinked, wondering how long she had been standing there like a ninny, with her hand still held in his, while a flood of sensations had surged through her head. It couldn't have been more than seconds, or he would have been looking at her very oddly, wondering if he was hiring a maniac to work for him. Instead of which, he was smiling at her very appreciatively indeed. Her heart glowed as she took her fingers out of his grasp.

She could still feel their warmth as they sat near a large bay window where they could see the brilliant green of the slopes and the dazzling display of wild flowers, and the white-tipped mountains far beyond.

It was a memory to cherish, Celia thought, without knowing why she thought it.

"You are somewhat unexpected, Miss Pengelly," Herr von Gruber said, when they had been served with a pot of tea and had both declined anything to eat.

"Am I?" she said, her heart plummeting.

Surely he wasn't going to say she was too young for the job, or that she looked too flighty? She should have had her hair bobbed, or twisted it into a knot as she sometimes did, she thought frantically. She should have thought of how she would appear to a sophisticated Berliner.

"Herr Vogl told me of the legendary beauty of your family, but I found it hard to believe, until now. He called it the Tremayne beauty, which I did not quite understand."

"It's kind of Herr Vogl to say so," Celia said, embarrassed. "The legend arose with my great-grandmother, Morwen Tremayne. She was reputed to be wildly beautiful, and although she had humble origins she married the son of the Killigrew Clay owner – the clay works whose name you will be familiar with, of course. All the women in the family since then have had the same colouring and distinctive looks, and somehow the tag of the Tremayne beauty has stuck."

She stopped abruptly, feeling her face flush as she realised she was talking too fast in her nervousness, and identifying herself with that beauty.

"I'm sorry. You must think me terribly conceited." she said quickly.

"Not at all. I think you are charming, and your pride in your ancestry is something we Germans respect and admire. It's delightful to hear you speak of it so warmly."

As he spoke, he put his hand briefly over hers as it rested on the small table, and again Celia felt that frisson of excitement at his touch. But she almost snatched her hand away from his, feeling gauche and confused at the force of her own emotions. Whatever she had once felt for Franz Vogl, was like a drop in the ocean compared with the empathy she felt towards von Gruber. It also frightened her to think that she was not in such control of her emotions as she had always believed.

"Herr von Gruber, won't you please tell me more about the position I am being offered – that is, if you still think I'm a suitable person. If you aren't already aware of it, I should tell you that I will be barely nineteen when the vacancy arises. You may think I am much too young, and I will understand if you have second thoughts."

She was virtually asking him to agree with her. She was in a blue funk, but she couldn't seem to stop herself. If fate decreed that she shouldn't take this job, she wouldn't. On the other hand, if it decreed otherwise . . .

"So you are nineteen – barely," he said solemnly. "And I am thirty-six, unmarried, with all my own teeth and hair, no dark secrets in my past, and desperately hoping that you will come to work for me. I would deem it an honour if you would say yes. Will you – please?"

She swallowed. He had told her far more personal details about himself than any job applicant needed to know. He had also told her nothing about the job requirements.

She looked into his eyes, and said yes.

A long while later, when business matters had finally been discussed and explained, Herr von Gruber bade her farewell until November. Celia returned to the academy, glad that Wenna was still at her classes and wouldn't seek her out, agog with curiosity, for at least another hour. She needed to be alone, to think about the future and what it might hold. She wasn't merely thinking of the prestige of having a highly paid position in a well-respected company.

She caught her breath, still seeing those so-blue eyes smiling down into hers; still seeing the curve of his mouth, with the small creases at the sides that reflected his charismatic personality.

Of *course* she didn't believe in love at first sight, she told herself as she lay on her bed gazing up at her uncompromising white ceiling. That was for idiots, or soft-hearted romantics like her sister. And her mother ... her sweet, beautiful, romantic mother, whose wonderful story of how she and Nick Pengelly had looked into one another's eyes at someone else's wedding, and had just *known*, was indelibly imprinted on her daughters' minds.

Although she had known nothing of the magnetism passing between her mother and Nicholas Pengelly on that day, she could remember the occasion vividly. She and Wenna had been Vera's small bridesmaids. What Celia remembered most right now was Skye's beautiful shot-green silk outfit, and the way Aunt Charlotte had wailed that green was an unlucky colour.

It hadn't been unlucky for Skye, even though she had still been married to Celia's natural father, Philip Norwood. The colour and the sensual fabric of the outfit had enhanced her ethereal beauty. Skye had once confided in her daughter that despite her devotion to Philip, there had really been no turning back from the moment their eyes met, no matter how long it took for she and Nick to be together.

A long while after their father had died, when Skye and Nick had finally married, the children had mutually agreed to change their names to Pengelly. Celia remembered how her mother had worried that it was disloyal to Philip, but the children had insisted, and she had smiled ruefully, reflecting that no matter how many times the names changed, the old Tremayne spirit was still the same.

Unwittingly, her fingers touched the emerald-green belt at her waist. She shivered, wondering why she had chosen that colour, of all colours, to wear today.

She found herself whispering aloud, in a far deeper search for her inner feelings than usual.

"Oh, Mom, am I falling prey to what I've always thought was such romantic nonsense? Is this the legacy Granny Morwen left us; to follow our hearts, no matter where it leads us?"

Just like Morwen, and Primmy, and Skye.

# Eight

S ebastian Tremayne could hardly contain his excitement as
he reported to his father that night that his new pottery
design had been approved by the German firm of Kauffmann's
as well as Vogl's. Kauffmann's had been one of Killigrew Clay's
major markets for decades, firstly buying china clay for their own
pottery making and, more recently, importing finished goods of
excellent quality and workmanship from White Rivers.

"What's that you say, boy?"

Theo's gaze was fixed on the flickering television screen that
was now his passion, no matter what was showing on the very
few programmes the new medium boasted, and finding it hard to
concentrate on anything else.

"I thought old man Kauffmann had passed on years ago," he
grunted in passing.

"So he has. It's his son who owns it now, and he's sent me a
dummy of their new catalogue. My design is included in it as well
as in Vogl's display material."

He thrust the pages underneath his father's nose. His determination to make Theo take an interest was twofold. Firstly, he
wanted his father's approval of the way he was making a name
for himself in the world of potters. And secondly, he wanted to
stir Theo out of the alarming lethargy that seemed to have
descended on him recently.

"Won't you take a look at the pictures, Theo?" Betsy coaxed
him now. "Sebby's done so well, and is deservin' of a bit o'
praise."

"Oh ah, turning a pot's clever enough, I'll grant you, though
'tis not what my father had in mind when he took on his shares in
the clayworks. Walter Tremayne weren't afraid of gettin' his
hands into the clay at its source, not when it was all prettied up
for some fancy woman's table."

113

Seb's face darkened and he ignored his mother's warning look.

"That's true, Father, but a lump of raw clay's no good to anyone, is it? Until it's cleaned and refined and put to good use in medicine or paper-making, or turned into beautiful pieces of pottery or tableware, it's no more than it started out to be – a lump of raw clay."

He wasn't demeaning the basic material that had been their mainstay all these years, and his intention had never been to sneer, but he might have known his father would see it that way. Theo turned his eyes away from the television screen, and glared at his son.

"And mebbe that's what you think I be, too, just a lump of raw clay. If 'tweren't for all they who've gone before 'ee, there'd be none of it for 'ee now, and don't you forget it, you young whelp. I daresay you'll be hand in glove with the bloody Jerries next, with your fancy ideas—"

He was stopped by a bout of coughing, due not to any medical problem, but simply a lack of fresh air and exercise caused by the hours he sat hunched over the fire, no matter what time of the year, waiting impatiently for the next television programme until the day's viewing ended.

Despite his father's hawking and spitting, Seb's humiliation at such undeserved criticism made him lash out.

"My God, don't I know I did the right thing by moving out of here! You make me sick with your narrow-minded views. I envy Celia going to work in Berlin. At least the Germans know the meaning of civilised behaviour."

"Oh ah?" Theo shouted, snorting for breath. "Tell that to the poor buggers whose names are on the memorial crosses in St Austell and Truro. They weren't blown to bits and cut to ribbons through any bloody civilised behaviour."

Seb turned on his heel. His mother anxiously followed him to the kitchen.

"There's no reasoning with him any more," he raged. "He's a lout, Mother, and I don't know why you stay with him."

"He's my husband, that's why," Betsy said. "I promised to marry him for better or worse, and there's been worse times than this. He's got no taste for the wilder ways he once had, and he needs me now."

She had no intention of elaborating to her strapping son on

how many times in the past Theo Tremayne had come home reeking of cheap perfume, with the smell of another woman on his skin. It was enough, as she said, that he needed her now.

"Well, so much for showing him the dummy catalogue," Seb snapped. "I may as well throw it in the waste basket."

"No you won't," Betsy said more briskly. "You'll be proud of it, the way I am. But Sebby – you wouldn't go to work in Germany like Celia, would you? Your father would take it as a personal betrayal if you did. He does love you, you know."

She spoke awkwardly, because they were a family that didn't easily speak of love. Seb gave her a sudden hug.

"I promise you the only way I'd go there is wearing a uniform, and that would surely please him. But thank God that's not likely to happen again, is it?"

"Let's pray to God it never does," Betsy agreed, remembering to cross her fingers as she spoke.

Skye had begun to make regular visits to Killigrew Clay to discuss business matters with the site manager and pit captain. Since Theo had lost so much interest in the clayworks, she felt it was her duty to remind them that the family interest was still as strong as ever, no matter what some might still think of a woman clay boss.

That fine September afternoon, she walked the short distance across the firm moorland turf to the clayworks from the pottery, after a pleasurable time approving the German catalogues Seb had shown her so gleefully. She had no doubt both firms would be after similar stock once it was known that rivals were in full production of Seb's design.

Tom Vickery touched his hard hat as he saw her approach.

"Me and Mr Lovett were waiting for 'ee, ma'am. There's summat of importance we need to talk over."

"Oh dear, I hope that doesn't mean bad news," she said with a smile.

It was too fine a day to be hearing bad news. The girls were home from Switzerland, their school years over, and they were relaxing by taking a rowing boat on the river at Truro, having persuaded Justin and Olly to go with them.

"Depends," Vickery said in response to her comment.

Skye gave a sigh. Being closeted in the site manager's hut for even ten minutes was less than comfortable, with its rank smells of tobacco and sometimes steaming boots, as he dried the caking wet clay by his little fire. If this meeting went on for any length of time, she would as soon conduct it in the open air.

Once inside the hut, she tried to close her nose to the various unsavoury whiffs and shook Will Lovett's hand.

"I understand there's some problem that needs sorting out this afternoon," she said at once.

"It may take more'n an afternoon, ma'am," he warned. 'Tis this rumour that's going around, see?"

"What rumour? You should know as well I do, Will, that there's rarely any substance in rumours."

Although she knew only too well that there was frequently more than a touch of truth in them.

" 'Tis about we mergin' wi' Bourne's, missus," Tom Vickery broke in aggressively. "The clayers be up in arms about it, same as they've allus been when there's any such talk."

"And just where did you hear this?" Skye asked, amazed as ever at how quickly the moorland grapevine could transmit rumour and gossip. She knew she shouldn't be surprised. Families were so intertwined among the clayfolk that pillow talk could easily bring home the gossip from one pit to another, and it spread like wildfire.

"Don't matter where, Mrs Pengelly, ma'am," Lovett said. "The only thing that matters to we is whether or not 'tis true, and what 'twill mean to the clayers. One thing I can tell 'ee for certain sure, is that they don't like it."

"Theo Tremayne should be here explainin' things," Vickery growled. "The men 'ould listen to him—"

"And not to me?" Skye snapped.

He glared back at her, his eyes full of disrespect.

"I'll allow that they listened to your grandmother once, when times were threatening, but that was when another woman clay boss were in the runnin' for Killigrew Clay. This is different. Bourne's is a powerful name in Roche, and Zacharius Bourne's a hard man wi' money to burn. If 'tis likely you and Mr Theo are thinkin' of sellin' out or mergin', we've got a right to know of it – and what benefits we'd get out of it."

"You've got no such rights," Skye said, incensed. "Any

business dealings that my cousin and I choose to do are our business. We hold the purse strings here."

But his words made her go cold, intimating as they did that if Bourne offered substantially higher wages to the clayworkers, then a merger might be all too tempting if it came to a showdown between men and management.

"We do need to know where we stand, Mrs Pengelly, if only to prevent any talk of walkouts," Will Lovett said more quietly. "The autumn despatches are about due, and 'twould be a disaster if any were held up because of disputes that could be easily solved."

"Is that a threat, Will?"

"No. 'Tis common sense, ma'am," he said.

Skye took a deep breath. Despite the way her nostrils were closing up while being confined in this little hut, and her wish to get out of there before she threw up, she vastly preferred Will Lovett to the volatile Tom Vickery. He had the temperament to stir up trouble and strike action, while Will was more inclined to use diplomacy.

"You're absolutely right, Will," she said, appearing to back down. "Well, I can tell you that we have had offers to sell out or to merge with Bourne's –" she ignored Vickery's derisive snort at that point – "but my cousin and I have categorically refused both. There is no question of it, now or in the future, and you have my word on it."

"For what 'tis worth." Vickery muttered, and she rounded on him at once.

"Yes, Tom, and if my long and loyal family history in these clayworks mean anything, you will know that my word is worth everything to you – including your position here. I won't have men working for me who cannot trust me, or whom I can no longer trust. Do I make myself clear?"

"Aye, I reckon you do," he said sullenly.

"Then I suggest you and Mr Lovett relay all that I have said to the men, and get on with your work."

She left the hut, drawing in deep breaths of clean air, and began to stride back across the moors to reclaim her car at the pottery, more agitated than when she left.

Will Lovett called to her before she had gone more than a few yards.

"Thank you for that, ma'am," he said. "I'll smooth Tom over, never fear, and the clayers will be reassured."

"Good. It's all a storm in a teacup, Will, I promise you. It's a mystery how these rumours start, though."

" 'Tis no mystery. Young Jessie Vickery's courtin' one of Bourne's clayers, and she brought the news home to her pa."

So that was it. How much vindictiveness was in pretty little Jessie Vickery's mind at what she might see as scoring over the Killigrew dynasty – especially since Ethan Pengelly, very much a part of it, was no longer interested in her?

It hardly mattered, providing Skye had managed to squash any thought of uprising among their own clayworkers. It seemed likely, as the weeks passed without incident, and the autumn clay despatches got away on time to their various destinations, that she had done just that.

The weeks were passing all too quickly, she thought, as the time came for Celia to begin her new job in Berlin. They celebrated her birthday as a close-knit family event this time, just the five of them at home together as if this was an occasion that might never come again, not quite in the same way, anyway . . . the unwanted thought clouded Skye's mind. She was determinedly cheerful as she hugged her elder daughter as she prepared to leave.

"You be sure to write and tell us everything about your new life, honey. And you will take care, won't you?" Skye begged, hoping she didn't sound too much like clinging Betsy – but knowing exactly how Betsy felt now!

"Mom, I'll be just fine," Celia said, more than a little choked, but determined not to let it show. "And I'll be home for Christmas. You'll hardly have time to miss me."

She had to swallow hard as she said it. It was still a wrench to leave Cornwall and home, the way it had always been each time she left for Gstaad. But this time there was a new and exciting life awaiting her, and Stefan von Gruber was going to be a part of it.

As yet, she didn't know how great a part that was going to be. She knew she had to keep her feet on the ground, and remember that theirs was to be a working relationship. She also knew that in the past she had sometimes been too flirtatious for her own good, and she couldn't even be sure that the handsome German's attentions hadn't simply turned her head. After all, she had only met him once. The fact that he had filled her thoughts ever since, was no yardstick on which to base an everlasting love, Celia told herself severely, knowing herself too well.

As her immediate boss, von Gruber had arranged to meet her in Berlin and to drive her to the hostel where she was to live. It was far beyond his duties, and hardly usual for a managing director to take on the task for his new personal assistant.

He could have sent someone on his staff . . . or requested the *Hostel Frau* to meet her. Celia had been told she was a chaperone to the company employees, together with her husband, the hostel superintendent cum handyman.

But Celia didn't question the fact that Stefan had arranged to meet her himself. She only knew that her heart leapt the moment she saw him, and the pleasure in his eyes was far beyond that of a considerate employer.

"I'm so glad to see you again," he said, squeezing her hand. "The time has been long."

The simplicity and quaintness of the phrase charmed her. It wasn't over-gushing, but it said everything she would have said, had she dared.

As it was, for once, the sometimes arrogant, over-confident Celia Pengelly was briefly tongue-tied.

There was always a sense of strangeness when two people met again after being parted. A time of getting to know one another all over again, before they could fully relax and be themselves. But since they had had so little time to get to know one another before, there were no memories to share, save for that one afternoon in a hotel restaurant, with its view of the green slopes, the fragrant flower-filled valleys and the distant snow-capped mountains.

One memory of a stunning, evocative view, and a deep and certain knowledge that this was the man with whom she wanted to share the rest of her life. Celia's nerves prickled at the thought that hadn't even been fully formed in her mind, but which now seemed as inevitable as if it had been preordained.

She shivered slightly as she looked around the apartment in the hostel that was to be her home for the foreseeable future. The furniture was heavy and ornate in the German style, and more than comfortable.

"Is it to your liking?" he asked anxiously. "I saw you shiver.

Are you too cold? Perhaps the heating is not turned up high enough—"

She shook her head. "I'm perfectly fine, and the apartment is lovely," she said. "It was a goose stepping over my grave, that's all."

She gave a forced laugh at his puzzled look. "I'm sorry. It's an English expression. It means – well, I don't really know what it means, except that sometimes you get a feeling of fate taking a hand in your life, or of some memory of the past that intrudes into the future. It's a Cornish legacy, if you like. We all have this odd sense of *déjà vu* at times. It's silly, I suppose, to think Cornish people should be any more perceptive than anyone else, and now you'll be thinking I'm quite mad. I assure you I'm not normally scatterbrained, Herr von Gruber, and I hope you will be quite satisfied with my work."

He took her hands in his, laughing as she gabbled on, and stopping her by raising one of her hands to his lips and kissing it in the continental style.

"I'm quite sure I shall, Celia, providing you stop being so nervous and talking so much, and you will please use my given name except in the office building. I insist that you call me Stefan this evening when I take you to dinner."

Her eyes widened as he dropped her hands. "Oh, but is this usual? I mean, you're my employer—"

"It's my way of welcoming you to Berlin. I have every confidence that our association will be fruitful. So I shall leave you now to settle in, and I'll see you at seven thirty."

When he had gone, she watched him from her window as he got into his powerful car and drove away. Her heart was thudding as she saw him go and she felt momentarily alone.

A fruitful association seemed an odd way of putting it, but it was one more example of his beautifully correct continental phrasing.

She turned away from the window, took a deep breath and looked around her slowly. On her arrival she had met the motherly *Hostel Frau*, who had told her to let her know at once if she needed anything. She knew that the hostel was full of other employees of the Vogl empire, so she need never feel isolated in a new country.

The company offices where she was to work with Stefan were

120

literally around the corner on the next block, within easy walking distance.

She was here, in her new life. In *his* life.

The restaurant where he took her for dinner that evening was small and intimate and seductive with soft rosy-hued lighting. Not knowing the kind of place it would be, she had worn a softly draping afternoon gown of pale green, without heeding any significance. It was simply a favourite of Celia's that did double duty as a semi-cocktail dress, and she knew it flattered her colouring.

Stefan had called for her at the hostel and handed her a small corsage to pin to her shoulder. It was so very elegant and grown-up, she found herself thinking. It was hardly any time at all since she had been involved in school activities, albeit as part-time teacher. But now it seemed like aeons ago, and she was a different person now, with different ideals and prospects.

"Why do you smile?" Stefan asked, when they had been shown to an intimate little alcove and he was smiling into her eyes through the soft candlelight.

"I was just thinking how quickly life can change. Here I am, away from home and family – with you."

"Do you question the decision? I have been told that your Cornish intuition tells you when something is right." He spoke teasingly. "What is it telling you now, I wonder?"

"To enjoy the moment," Celia said, smiling back.

"Then you should always trust your intuition, for such moments never come again," Stefan told her.

It was said light-heartedly, but it was a remark that Celia knew she would remember. To enjoy the moment for it would never come again . . . it was at once poignant and prosaically true. He was a wonderful and sensitive man with the ability to put such things into words so uninhibitedly and without embarrassment.

He behaved, as she had expected, like a perfect gentleman, but they were so comfortable with one another, Celia felt as if she had always known him. By the end of that evening, she knew she was in already half in love with him.

She ignored the fact that there was a considerable age difference between them. As he had pointed out with admirable dignity on their first meeting, she was nineteen – barely – and he was thirty-six. To Celia Pengelly such statistics were unimportant in the great scheme of things.

Love was the only thing that mattered. Love, and the special rapport between two people who refused to let any outside interference come between them. Even though it went unsaid in the weeks that followed, Celia knew in her heart that their feelings were the same.

In business and in pleasure, they were soulmates, she thought, with a dreamy smile that would have done justice to her sister's romantic heart.

Christmas, when she had left Berlin to spend the promised two weeks at home for the holidays, cemented it all. Her family was ecstatic to see her back, wanting to know everything about the new job, the new boss, and how she was enjoying everything. In those first few hours, the excitement of being at home eclipsed the tug of longing to be with Stefan.

"Let me get my breath back!" She laughed. "Berlin is a wonderful city and the job is marvellous. Stefan has taken me round the warehouses and showrooms, Mom, and our goods are very prominent everywhere, including Sebby's new design. Vogl's are making a big spash with it for the new year trade, and Stefan says it will do very well indeed."

"Stefan seems to be saying quite a lot," her father said with a smile. "What about the other girls in the hostel? I hope you've made some new friends among them."

"Oh, yes," she said quickly. "There are two girls in particular – Gerda and Maria. We go walking in the nearby park when the weather's not too cold, and I've been to several concerts with them too."

She caught Wenna's glance, and gave a faint smile, guessing that once they were alone she would want to know far more about Stefan von Gruber than about Gerda and Maria!

"I've brought presents for everyone," she went on quickly. "I'll fetch them from my room as soon as I've unpacked properly and put them under the tree, Mom. The house looks wonderful, by the way. I guess you all went out on the moors gathering berries and stuff. I missed that!"

When she had gone upstairs, still chattering, with Wenna at her heels, Skye looked thoughtfully at Nick.

"She's different. In these few weeks, she's changed."

"It's only to be expected, darling. She's earning her own money now, and feeling her independence. None of them will stay your chicks for ever, you have to accept that."

Skye shook her head. "I know, but it's more than that. It's something in the way she spoke."

About Stefan von Gruber . . . it came to her instantly. It was the way she said his name, the way she lingered slightly over it, the way it seemed she had to say it more than once when it wasn't strictly necessary. Skye knew the signs. She knew her girl was in love, and she prayed that this Stefan person wasn't going to break her heart.

He came highly praised from Herr Vogl as a man of integrity and breeding, and with an impeccable background – which the Germans set such store by – but he was still a stranger, a foreigner. Skye found herself smiling ruefully at the thought, because wasn't she herself just that, in many a Cornishman's eyes? Even now.

"What's so funny?" Nick asked.

"Nothing, honey. Nothing at all," she assured him. "I'm just so happy to have all the family at home once more. It's a good feeling."

Wenna was always direct.

"So tell me, what's he really like? Is he as spiffing as you thought he'd be?"

Celia laughed. There were some things you didn't tell, even to a best friend or a loving sister. You didn't tell about feelings and longings, and the new range of emotions that you didn't know were in you until you experienced them.

"He's very nice and I like him a lot, which is just as well, as we have to work together every day."

Every single, beautiful day.

"So are you going to marry him?"

Celia laughed again. "Good Lord, what a question! I should think he'd want to marry someone of his own age, not a dizzy nineteen-year-old."

The instant she said it, she wished she hadn't put the thought into words. She didn't want to consider the possibility, and one of the new, emotions she was experiencing was a searing jealousy.

"Oh, well, there's always Franz," Wenna said easily. "How is he, by the way?"

Celia had almost forgotten Franz Vogl's existence by now, which frightened her in a way, making her wonder if she was really shallow, or had been, until Stefan.

"I've only seen him once since going to Berlin, when I was invited to the Vogl home for dinner one evening."

"And?" Wenna persisted.

"And nothing. He's nice enough, but I don't have any special feelings for him, and I'm sure he felt nothing special for me. And that's quite enough inquisition for now."

She picked up the armfuls of Christmas parcels in their Christmas wrappings, obliging Wenna to follow her downstairs. She put the gifts beneath the tree with all the others, but her mind was full of the small gift-wrapped box that she had promised Stefan she wouldn't open until Christmas morning. A small box could mean many things and her heart always beat faster every time she wondered what it might be.

It was a tradition that the family ate breakfast together on Christmas morning and then Nick ceremoniously handed around the gifts. But long before then Celia's shaky hands had opened the glossy silver wrapping round the jeweller's box, and she had caught her breath at the ornate silver and pearl earrings inside.

There was a small, handwritten note with them.

'For a special lady. I hope you are not superstitious about pearls. If they are meant to indicate tears, then they will be mine at missing you.'

Her throat stung. There could surely be no more meaningful words. He missed her. She knew by now that he didn't say things he didn't mean. He could be funny and amusing, but basically he was a deep-thinking, serious man, and he missed her.

They were to have a large family dinner that evening. Lily and David and the boys, along with Karina, would be arriving during the afternoon, and the Pengelly brothers, Ethan and Adam, would be there too. Celia wore the earrings with the elegant new dress her mother had bought her. They were noticed at once.

"Are those new?" Lily asked. "They're beautiful, Celia, and they must have cost a pretty penny."

"Oh no, not that much," she said in confusion. "I saw them in the jeweller's window, and I just had to have them."

"Your daughter's becoming extravagant," David said teasingly to Skye. "I hear the German shops are full of expensive items to tempt a young lady."

Celia laughed, and said airily that since she was earning it, she might as well spend it. But she didn't look at her mother as she spoke.

Because of their business connections the family were closely allied with the Germans, but she hadn't ever considered how any of them might feel if things got serious between herself and Stefan. She had never considered anything beyond the sweet sensation of being truly in love for the first time.

As if to bring her brutally down to earth, she overheard a remark David Kingsley's made to her father as they all relaxed after a gargantuan meal. The two men were taking a turn in the conservatory, and were well out of earshot of the games being played by the rest of the family and the excited screams of Lily's little boys. But Celia's ears were attuned to the sombre note in David's voice as she took coffee and brandies out to them while they finished their cigars.

"You know these plans for air-raid shelters are going through, Nick. These are strange times, and I've had it on good authority that all school children are to be issued with gas masks in the new year. What does that tell you?"

"Either it doesn't bode well for the future, or it's just scaremongering," Nick said.

"Whatever the truth of it, do you think it's wise to let Celia continue with this job in Berlin? It's one thing to keep the business contacts afloat, of course, but it could be fatal to leave her there in the thick of it if anything happened—"

Celia put the tray of drinks down on the small table beside them, her eyes blazing.

"I'll thank you to let me speak for myself, David. As for anything *happening*, as you put it, you seem to be the scaremonger. People in Berlin are going about their business the same as ordinary people everywhere. Anyway, if the government is going to put up air-raid shelters as you say, I think it's an insult to the Germans, as if we think they're going to start bombing us at any minute!"

She knew she was being unduly passionate, but it had nothing to do with governments or power-wielding leaders. It had to do

125

with the fact that if the unthinkable happened, as these two were intimating, then she and Stefan would be torn apart. There would be no future for them if their two countries were at war. As the word slipped into her mind, she drew in her breath. Nick put his arms around her.

"Darling, we have to face facts. Adolph Hitler is no fairy-tale prince, and who knows what will happen in the future? None of us can see that, but I know this job means a lot to you, and of course there's no question of our asking you to come home."

"Good. Because I wouldn't come," she said in a brittle voice. "I'm really happy there, Dad, and you two have managed to spoil that, and to spoil Christmas too."

She rushed away from them, her eyes stinging. She didn't want their image of the future clouding her lovely new life. She reached her bedroom and tried to compose herself, knowing she would have to go and rejoin the others before anyone came looking for her, but feeling as if everything she had believed was so safe and secure was slipping away from her.

"Celia, are you in there?" she heard her mother's voice a few minutes later. Before she could answer, Skye had opened the bedroom door. "There's a telephone call for you. The line's very crackly, but I think he said it's Herr von Gruber – are you all right, honey?"

"I am now," Celia said, her smile suddenly brilliant, leaving Skye in no more doubt of her feelings.

She ran down to the telephone and clutched it to her ear.

"Hello," she said huskily.

"I don't wish to intrude on your family festivities, Celia, but I wanted to wish you a merry Christmas," came Stefan's voice, as close as if he was standing beside her.

"Thank you. And thank you so much for the earrings. They're beautiful and I'm wearing them now," she said.

"When you return to Berlin we must have an evening at the theatre and perhaps you will wear them then."

"Of course I will, and I shall look forward to it very much. I hope you're having a happy Christmas too, Stefan."

"A quiet one with my parents. So goodbye, *liebling* – until 1938. It sounds so far away," he added ruefully, "even though it will be no more than a week, so enjoy your time with your family until then."

"I will. Goodbye."

She hung up slowly, missing the sound of his voice the moment it was gone. And turning to find her mother near enough to have caught her last breathless words.

"So he's the one, is he, honey?" Skye said softly.

She couldn't lie. If she'd tried, her luminous eyes would have given her away.

"He's the one, Mom."

# Nine

F anny Rosenbloom, née Webb, was nothing if not big-hearted. She didn't hesitate when her husband put the question to her.

"If yer frettin' about yer folks losin' their livelihood, then o' course we must bring 'em over here," she declared. "There's plenty of room in the flat fer yer ma and pa. You go and wire 'em to pack up the shop and leave Vienna before old Adolph gets up to any more anti-Jewish larks."

"You're a good girl, Fanny," Georgie said warmly. "They made pure gold when they made you."

"Go on wiv yer," she said, pink-faced. "I lost my own folks so long ago, it'll be nice fer me to share a ma and pa again. It ain't just bein' noble!"

But she was glad he couldn't see her troubled face as he went off to wire his parents to leave Austria as soon as possible and come to London. The new year of 1938 hadn't begun well for the likes of Georgie's people, and she knew he kept a sharp eye on every newspaper report about the situation.

By the middle of March, Adolph Hitler had marched into Austria amid cheers of adulation as he reunited it with Germany and increased the Nazi stronghold. Austria was his homeland, and now he was its undoubted hero.

Very soon afterwards Austrian Jews faced up to the fact that even their most dignified professions were being closed to them; shops had to bear the slogan that they were 'Jewish-owned' and theatres and music halls were forbidden to allow the great Jewish artistes to perform.

For Georgie Rosenbloom it was a time of great sadness as he begged his parents to come to London where they would be safe, no matter what the future held. Their long-established family grocery business would dwindle dramatically, as folk became afraid to patronise something that was clearly anti-establishment now. But his parents were old and proud, and even though he begged, they refused to be hounded out of their home.

"You can't force 'em, Georgie, love," Fanny said sadly. "We can send 'em money, though, even if the shop has to close. They should be takin' things easy now, anyway, and they won't go short while the Flamingo continues to do good business."

"And if any Jewish artistes are looking a venue, we'll never close our doors to them," he declared.

"That's right, my duck," Fanny said, though they both knew the Flamingo Club was small fry compared with the likes of the Windmill Theatre. Still, it had its loyal clientele, and Gloria del Mar was still their regular star performer.

"I was thinkin' about the little Pengelly sweetheart the other day," Fanny said thoughtfully, more to take his mind off his worries than anything else. "I wonder if Skye would agree to let her come up to the smoke for a spell, just to try her wings, so to speak?"

"Maybe," Georgie said, not yet able to be distracted so readily from his gloomy thoughts.

"We could take a trip down there when we close over the Easter weekend. You ain't never been to Cornwall, have yer, Georgie? What do yer say? Make a bit of a holiday of it, eh?"

She was more than thankful she had made the suggestion when the horrifying news leaked out in British newspapers in April that some of the most influential Jewish figures in Vienna had been sent to Dachau concentration camp.

Just for being Jewish, she raged and wept on the telephone to her friend Skye Pengelly, while making the arrangements for a brief visit. And for once, Skye couldn't find the words to comfort her.

"All I know is that the more I hear of Mr Hitler, the more uneasy I am about Celia living and working in Berlin," she said anxiously to Nick.

"She's a sensible young woman, darling. If there's any kind of conflict likely in the months ahead, she'll have to come home, no question about it. She's not of age yet, and she must obey our wishes."

It was easy for him to say Celia must obey their wishes, but as the weeks of the new year progressed, the euphoric letters Skye received from her daughter, told her that wild horses wouldn't drag her away from Stefan von Gruber's side.

However far the relationship between them had developed hadn't yet been confided to Skye in so many words . . . but sometimes mere words were the last things that were needed when a mother's instinct knew it all. Especially a mother who had been down the same passionate road as her daughter.

But there was no point in fretting over it, she decided, as she prepared for Fanny and Georgie's visit. And those two could be guaranteed to bring a breath of fresh air to the unease in the whole country after the government announcement that all Britons were now to be fitted with gas masks. Wenna had declared that she would rather die than be confined in such a hideous thing.

"You may very well die without it," her brother Olly retorted. He was fast changing his intention of becoming a lawyer, for the far more exciting one of newspaper reporting. He spent much of his spare time at the *Informer* offices and was well up with political and world events.

"Well, I can hardly sing behind a stupid gas mask, can I?" Wenna snapped. "And Mom says I can have my voice trained properly if I want to. I may have to go to Bristol to learn with a qualified teacher, but Dad knows some people there where I can probably stay."

Even though it sounded exciting, she wasn't too sure about it. Her father's ex-partner lived in Bristol with his wife, where they ran a small antiques shop. Wenna didn't know them or the city, and she would far rather have gone to London. The fact that Fanny and Georgie were coming to Cornwall for a short break was filling her with excitement, as she remembered the heady evening she had sung with Gloria del Mar and had a tiny taste of stardom.

The Rosenblooms descended on them with the force of a whirlwind. Their large Daimler motor car crunched to a halt in front of the house and it seemed to take forever for Georgie to transport all Fanny's bags and cases into the house.

Somehow they managed to bring with them an air of glamour and stability in a fast-changing world, with the certainty in some folks' minds that another war was just around the corner.

Fanny simply refused to discuss such things in Georgie's presence, determined not to add to his anxiety over his parents. Only to Skye, when they were alone, did she confess how much she grieved for him.

"He'd go over there like a shot and bring 'em back wiv 'im, but he knows they wouldn't come. They say the only way they'll be moved outa their place is feet first, and you can't argue wiv old folk, can yer?"

"It won't come to that, Fanny."

"Won't it? The way things are going, there's some in London predictin' it'll be months rather than years before we're at war wiv the Jerries again." She gave a wry grin. "Whaddya say to the two of us doin' our bit again, duck? Bit long in the tooth fer it now, I daresay!"

But Skye had three nearly grown children who weren't too long in the tooth for it.

"I don't even want to think about it, so let's talk about something else. I want you to meet more of my family while you're here, Fanny, including our niece from Ireland. And you must see the pottery, of course."

She quickly changed the conversation so as not to think of sending her children to war. The very idea of it chilled her. It wouldn't happen. Couldn't happen again in her lifetime, but into her consciousness came the echo of a voice she hadn't heard for a long time.

"What's so special about your lifetime, Skye Tremayne?" asked the ghost of Granny Morwen.

"Are you all right, duck?" she heard the more raucous and very alive voice of Fanny Rosenbloom say. "I didn't mean to upset yer wiv all this war talk. Anyway, there's summat else I wanta talk to yer about."

She tucked her hand in her friend's arm as they strolled in the garden in the sunny April afternoon, and Fanny outlined her proposal for Skye's younger daughter.

"Absolutely not," Nick said sharply when Skye broached the subject in their bedroom that night. "I won't hear of it. It's bad enough that Celia's gone to live in Germany, without sending Wenna off to London."

"You were ready enough to send her to Bristol."

"That's different. Bristol's not the capital. London would be an enemy's prime target if the worst came to the worst."

Skye felt icy cold all over. "You think it will, then. You do, don't you, Nick?"

"I'm no clairvoyant, but yes, if you want my honest opinion, all the signs are pointing that way."

"Then Celia must come home!"

"I thought we were discussing Wenna. And don't raise your voice. The Rosenblooms will hear you."

"They'll have to know our feelings, anyway. And Wenna has to have her say in it too."

"She certainly does not. She's too young to make any such decision for herself."

She glared at him. 'Oh Nick, how can you be so pompous? They're not children any more."

"They're not adults, either. And I suggest you sleep on the matter, the same as I intend to do."

With that he reached out to turn off his bedside lamp and turned away from her, leaving her staring into the darkness. She could her the wind whining softly through the trees outside, and to her over-sensitive mind that night, it seemed horribly ominous.

Wenna rarely dug her heels in, the way Celia did. This time, she was ecstatic with excitement.

"Oh Mom, it's such a wonderful chance for me to get the feel for performing without having to take any old voice training lessons. It's not as if I want to be an opera singer or anything stuffy. And Fanny and Georgie will take such good care of me, it'll be like having a second set of parents!"

"That's enough to damn it before it even starts," Nick said darkly. "I can't allow it. Wenna—"

"If you keep on being so beastly to me, I'll just go anyway. One day you'll come home and I'll be gone," she said, her eyes brimming with tears, her voice full of furious passion. "Can't you see how important this is to me? You didn't stop Celia going to Berlin, and I bet you're going to let Olly have his way about working for the *Informer* too. Why must I always be the one who's victimised?"

"Darling, nobody's victimising you," Skye said, seeing how

Nick was becoming incensed at this unexpected little firecracker. "And we know you wouldn't really go without our permission—"

"I would, and I will," Wenna said stubbornly. "I've never wanted to do anything more in my whole life, and unless you tie me to the bedpost and starve me, I shall go back with Fanny if she'll take me."

"Good God, I thought it was a budding songstress we had here, not a Sarah Bernhardt," Nick snapped. "There's no need to be quite so melodramatic, Wenna."

"Then let me go, and don't try to ruin my life."

In the heavy silence that followed her statement, Nick shrugged.

"We'll think about it. I won't say any more than that."

Wenna swept out of the room, leaving her parents wilting after her sudden onslaught. Nick rounded on his wife.

"You see what comes of inviting your worldly friends down here? They've put all kinds of forward ideas into her head, and now she's fired up with the thought of becoming an overnight singing sensation."

Skye was enraged by his words. "*My* worldly friends, as you call them, are respectable business people, and since Wenna has my mother's musical talent and the voice of an angel, I won't stand in her way."

"You approve of all this then, do you? It's not enough that one daughter is living in a place of potential danger, you want to send the other one away as well."

"For pity's sake, Nick, you're scaremongering again, and exaggerating things out of all proportion." She put a hand on his arm, feeling the tension in it. "Anyway, once she's standing alone in the spotlight and singing in front of a crowd of strangers, she may hate it so much that it will be out of her system for good and all. But at least let her find that out for herself."

She didn't believe it for one minute, but she wasn't going to let Nick see that. She could still remember the way her mother's face had glowed with an inner euphoria when she came home from one of her piano concerts, still in her own aesthetic world until her senses returned to normality, filling Skye with a kind of possessive jealousy that her brother Sinclair never even noticed, and her father Cresswell completely understood.

While Primmy Tremayne was lost in the sensuality of her

music, she was transported to a place no one else could ever reach. Skye knew in her soul that it would be like that for Wenna. The pleasure and the success had been as potent as a drug for Primmy, the way that painting had been for Albert, and it would be so for Wenna. They had to let her go.

"You mean it?" Wenna said later to Skye, her voice choked. "I thought Dad was completely against the idea."

As Skye held her close, she could feel her fragile young body was as tense as a fledgling bird ready and eager to fly.

"Providing you promise to keep in touch, and if there's the slightest sign of trouble, you're to come home."

"What kind of trouble?"

But Skye couldn't name it. Putting it into words made the foolishness of it seem far too real.

How could there be another war? Hadn't they all learned lessons from the last one? Thomas Cook was offering summer holidays on the French Riviera for £8 17s 6d. Would any travel business be so reckless as to send British people flocking to the continent if there was real danger there?

But she shivered all the same. The Spanish civil war had erupted mercilessly, and there was always conflict somewhere in the world. What made *them* so special, so God-protected? Was she deliberately flouting fate by refusing to let herself be intimidated into keeping her daughters in the womb-like safety of Cornwall?

So in early May she let her daughter leave New World in the care and custody of Fanny and George Rosenbloom, and her luggage contained several special evening dresses for her performances in the Flamingo Club, as well as her now obligatory gas mask in its cardboard carrying box.

Theo telephoned Skye a few days later, by which time she had done her private weeping at parting from both her daughters. By then, all the family knew of what Wenna had called her big chance and most had wished her luck. Skye knew that Theo could be guaranteed to take the opposite view.

"You've done a foolish thing in letting the girl go off like that," he informed her, making her bristle and defensive at once.

"Oh? And what about Justin leaving home? He'll be living in

London while he does his medical training. Is it any more foolish for me to let Wenna go, than for Justin to be there?"

"He won't be flaunting himself in flimsies for all to see," he sneered. "You never know what kind o' queer folk frequent nightclubs these days."

"I know the kind of folk my friends are," she said frigidly, thinking that if they were face to face right now, she would cheerfully wring his neck. "No harm will come to Wenna while she's in their care. And I don't see what business it is of yours, anyway."

"Only passing an opinion, that's all, cuz," he grunted. "Betsy wants to know what news of t'other one, and what's this I hear of young Oliver wanting to work wi' Kingsley at the newspaper? What happened to his fancy lawyering prospects?"

The inference that the one job was so much less prestigious than the other made Skye fume as much as his bloody nosiness into her business.

"Journalism is an honourable profession, and I'll be very happy if Olly goes into it, since it was once my profession too. As for Celia, she's doing nicely, thank you. Next month she and her boss are going to a trade fair and business conference in Cologne. Displays of White Rivers pottery will be included on the stands."

"You should be pleased," she added, drawing breath, "since the items and brochures on display will include Sebby's new design, as well as the new pottery figurines that he's been working on."

"Is that so?" he said, with apparent disinterest.

"What's wrong with you, Theo? Don't you care that Sebby's making a success of his work?" Skye asked angrily.

"Oh ah. 'Tis fine for now until the Jerries decide that making bombs and aeroplanes is more commercial than fancy pots, and close all the factories down. Then where will you be – and Killigrew Clay as well? It happened once before, and anybody with any sense can see it happening again."

"Don't talk rot, Theo."

"And don't go thinking 'twill never happen. I read the newspapers too, and if I were you, I'd pull my girl out of there quicker'n blinking. But that's not what I want to talk to you about. 'Tis about the offer to merge wi' Bourne's. I've been talking to people, and they're all of the opinion that we should do it now. Once the foreign markets close down on us, they won't want to know. They're willing to pay a handsome sum for coming in with us and I say let's take their money while the offer's still there."

"You've got no right talking to outsiders about our business," she snapped, furious that words might have been bandied about at local hostelries and the like. "And why are you so certain the foreign markets will close down? We haven't done so well for years."

"It won't last," he said prophetically, suddenly calmer than she was. "Your own man believes it, and so do I."

Skye felt a chill like a presentiment run through her veins. Theo sneering and at his bombastic worst was something she could cope with. Theo being serious and far-seeing was out of character, and only underlined the way the world was heading in so many minds now. She clutched at the telephone, and her hands were clammy.

"I won't sell out and I won't merge with Bourne's," she said stubbornly, as if her own determination was a talisman that would keep them all safe.

"Then you're a fool," Theo said, and slammed down the telephone on her.

Skye replaced her own instrument slowly. It always unnerved her when Theo became sensible, and she almost preferred his hot-headed self. When he put things squarely to her, it made her doubt her own intuition, and that was something Skye Pengelly rarely did.

At the thought, it came to her that in her own way she was being as arrogant as Theo. Believing she was always right, and the rest of the world was wrong. She had to admit that Fanny had certainly looked anguished when she told her about her husband's fears for his Jewish family.

She turned with a sense of relief as her son came into the house like a tornado. For the moment at least, she could put aside all the large-scale doubts and worries, and see what it was that had got Olly so excited now. But the moment she got the whiff of him, she knew.

His fingers were stained, and the familiar and pungent scent of printer's ink wafted towards her, taking her back and firing her blood. As David Kingsley had once said, 'once a newshound, always a newshound', and she remembered chiding his nonsense with a laugh. How long ago it all seemed now.

"I've decided," Olly declared.

"Have you?" Skye said, but knowing what was coming.

"I've been at the *Informer* offices all day," he said, with rising excitement. "David's got this little machine that sends through the latest news from various agencies, and it's even faster than telephoning. It's amazing, Mom! I've got to work there. I couldn't do the kind of boring stuff that Nick does all day when I could be part of everything important in the world at the click of a button on a machine. What do you think? Would he be very disappointed in me?"

Skye hid a smile. "So you think sorting out people's personal problems is boring, do you, Olly?"

"I didn't mean that – I thought you'd understand—"

At his flustered look, she hugged him tight. He was fifteen years old now, a young man who had blossomed in the last few months. No longer a child, but still her baby, and she knew well enough not to let on so! She let him go after a quick peck on his cheek.

"Honey, of course I understand, and I would personally be delighted if you went into the reporting business. I'm sure Nick won't be offended that you don't want to be a lawyer. In fact, I'd say he already had a pretty good idea of the way things are going," she added.

"Then if there's another war, I can go to the Front and do what you did in the last one, can't I?" he said eagerly.

Skye's magnanimity vanished at once, and she had a hard job not to slap him.

"Don't say such things! You have no idea what it was like, and I hope you never do."

"But you'll let me start as a junior with David right away, won't you?" he pleaded. "He says I'll learn more about life through that kind of work than anything a dull old school can teach me now."

"Oh, he does, does he? And since when did David Kingsley have a say in my children's education?"

Olly looked uneasy. "I'm sure he didn't mean it that way, Mom. But I know what I want to do now, and Celia and Wenna got their own way, so why can't I?"

138

"We'll see what your father has to say about it, but I'm not promising anything," she replied, knowing darned well that he was going to get his way too.

And then there were none.

If Nick was disappointed that Olly wasn't going to follow in his footsteps after all, he hid it well. And since Olly was so intent on starting his new career right away, his plea to be allowed to start as a junior in Kingsley's office instead of going to college, was finally agreed to. To Olly's surprise, it was his cousin Justin who was the most sceptical.

"I can't think why you want to be a reporter. There's no glory in that. Who ever heard of a famous newspaperman?"

"Who cares about glory? Is your idea of being a doctor because of the glory?" Olly demanded. "I thought doctors were supposed to have a sense of vocation, like priests."

"I do have a sense of vocation. I want to help people by making them well again."

"So do I, by giving them the truth."

They were glaring at one another, arguing on what was supposed to be a pleasurable walk along the sands on a blue and golden Sunday afternoon. Olly suddenly grinned, wanting to break the tension between them. Wanting to be friends. He spoke recklessly.

"Tell you what. If war comes, like all these gloom merchants say it will, we'll run away and enlist. Then while you're patching up some poor devil at the Front, I'll write down his dying words of praise for his surgeon hero, and report it back to the *Informer*. How does that sound? Then we'll both get the glory."

They both laughed at that, but there was a sense of desperation in Justin's laughter.

"I hope to God it doesn't come to that," he muttered.

He sounded so serious it seemed to Oliver at that moment that the warm air was chilled for an instant, as if a small cloud had shadowed the sun. It hadn't, but the feeling in his gut was just as shivery.

"Come on, I'll race you to the water's edge," he shouted, with the strangest urge to be a small child again when nothing mattered but being pampered and loved.

*    *    *

139

Being pampered and loved was the last thing Karina Tremayne had expected when she came to Cornwall in search of a family. Nor had she intended to stay longer than a week or so. The family she had met since her arrival was charming and welcoming, and she adored looking after Lily and David Kingsley's small boys and being accepted into their home.

But it wasn't her home, and as a mellow spring had merged into a blistering summer, and the moorland turf grew browner and more burnt by the sun, she found herself thinking nostalgically of the green hills and meadows of Ireland.

" 'Tis the rain that does it, me darlin'," the old men who sprawled about on wooden benches outside the ale houses would chuckle. "Tis not called the Emerald Isle fer nuthin', and no matter how often you leave it, you'll always come back."

Well, she hadn't been back, but neither had she expected the longing for it to be quite as acute as it was now. Not only because she missed it so, but because she thought of it as a refuge from her trouble. Her only refuge, if she was to escape the shame and disgrace of it all.

She would tell Ethan that very night. Not the whole of it, of course. She would merely tell him she could no longer stay in Cornwall, without giving him a reason, even though it would break her heart to do so. But she wasn't going to burden him with her trouble. It was hers and hers alone.

As she brushed through her glossy hair that evening before he came to meet her for a stroll along the Truro riverbank, she knew that only a fool could miss the way her eyes were huge and dark in the pinched pallor of her face.

"Mother of God, forgive me," her lips murmured imperceptibly. " 'Tis lie upon lie, but it has to be done."

If there was anything ironic in the words she chose, she refused to notice it. It was lying in Ethan Pengelly's arms that had given her the trouble, which in any other circumstances would be the most wonderful thing on earth.

She passed a hand lightly over her stomach, feeling the imperceptible roundess of it, and her mouth trembled. How could she ever confess to this so-respectable family that passion had got the better of her and Ethan, and that this was the penalty for giving in to sin?

Even so, she wondered briefly how anyone could ever compare

140

the love and the oneness two people had shared so spectacularly, with words like giving in? It had been a mutual passion that had taken them to the stars but now it had to end, before she ruined a good man as well as herself.

If ever the sins of the mothers were to be borne by the daughters, she found herself thinking, remembering her own shock at discovering that her mother had been Bradley Tremayne's lover for all those years.

Once Karina had decided that bearing her disgrace alone was her penance, she knew she had to deal with it in her own way. It wasn't so easy to be strong when she saw Ethan's tall, powerful form striding along to meet her on that summer evening. She felt her heart turn over with love at the sight of him. He took her hand in his as he murmured her name, and his eyes looked adoringly at her.

"God, but I've missed you," he said. "Do you realise it's three whole days since I've seen you?"

They had reached their favourite secluded spot in a grassy hollow and sank down together. His body was half covering hers, his arms round her, caressing her through her thin summer dress. His mouth was warm and eager on hers before she found the strength to pull away from him.

"Ethan, I've got something to tell you," she said weakly.

"God, that sounds worrying. What have I done?" he teased.

She tried to smile. He would never know what he had done – what they had both done. It wasn't fair to burden him with this. If she stayed, she would be disgraced and ostracised, and so would he. If she left, she could merge into obscurity with a cheap wedding ring on her finger and claim to be a poor widow. It was the only way.

"Well, come on," he said, when she fell silent. "It can't be anything too awful. You're far too sweet-natured and beautiful to have committed a crime, so what is it?"

She held him close to her, unable to look into his eyes and see the misery she knew would be there in a few minutes. She didn't intend to tell anyone except him her decision, only Lily was going to know before she was safely on the boat for home. No one was going to stop her.

"My love, I'm going back to Ireland very soon. I have to go, and I shan't be coming back."

141

She murmured the words against his shoulder, and it was all she could say before her throat closed up. She felt him go rigid and then his fingers gripped her arms so hard she almost cried out.

"What are you saying?" he asked roughly. "What's brought this on? Are you ill?"

She shook her head. "No, not ill," she whispered.

"Then *tell* me, Karina. I have a right to know. I thought we meant everything to one another."

"So we do. Oh, so we do . . ."

He stared into her eyes as if he would see into her soul.

"Then why are you leaving me?" he said at last. "Is there someone else? Someone you knew before you came here?"

"There is no one else – not in the way you mean." The minute she had said it, she knew it was a mistake. She bit her lip hard, tasting blood, her eyes were lowered, she was unable to meet his gaze, her whole body trembling.

"My God," Ethan whispered. Without another word, his hand went down to her belly.

She gave a shuddering sob as he folded her to him.

"Is this the reason? Are you having a child – our child?"

She had been prepared to lie, but he held her captive, insisting that she looked into his eyes, and it was impossible for her to continue the lie.

"Yes," she mumbled. "But 'tis my trouble, not yours. 'Tis my decision to go, and I'll not force you into anything—"

"*Trouble*? You call the creation of a child between us a *trouble*? Don't you think we share this? And how dare you call it a trouble, or think that I would ever let you leave me."

She looked at him through tear-drowned eyes.

"No, my love, I can't let you do this. Think what people would say. Your family – Skye and Nick – I couldn't face them. I won't stay here to be shamed, and to shame you."

He didn't speak for a few moments. He just stroked her cheek, holding her close and feeling her erratic heartbeat.

"It's no shame for a married couple to have a child—"

"I'll not force you into marriage," she said fiercely. "My mother did no such thing, and neither will I."

She knew she was reminding him that she was illegitimate. Unwittingly she had opened the door to everything he wanted to say since she had given him the momentous news.

142

"Nobody's forcing me, darling girl. But I've no intention of letting my child – our child – be born out of wedlock. But you're right. You can't stay here, and neither can I. Your father went to Ireland and made a new life for himself, and you want to be back there where you belong. So we'll both go, and before we do, we'll be married quietly. The respectable Pengellys will have arrived to make a new start."

"We can't! What would you do? Your life is here. Your family is here. You're a skilled man, Ethan—"

He shushed her with a kiss. "Don't Irish folk need pots? As you say, I'm a skilled man, and I'll soon find work. As for my family here – what would any of them mean to me without you? *You're* my family now – you, and our child."

Before she knew what he was going to do, he had bent his head, and kissed her softly rounded belly. As she held his head close to her, she could have sworn she felt the baby give a slight movement, but she couldn't have done – not yet.

She took it as a sign though, a sign that this was the right thing to do. That their love and their decision was approved by the Holy One above, and for a lapsed Catholic, it was a feeling that was at once awesome and unutterably sweet.

# Ten

T hey made their plans. They wanted no fuss. A number of
letters needed to be written which would be delivered after
the simple marriage service had been arranged, and they were
safely on their way to Ireland. All anyone would be told was that
they had married and decided to make a new life for themselves
there. The only people who were to know of their departure in
advance were Lily, and Ethan's older brother, Adam.

When Ethan went to see him, he was shocked at the uncared
for state of the house that Vera had once kept so spick and
span.

"What the hell have you been doing to yourself?" he exclaimed, seeing how unkempt his brother was, and seemingly
not even noticing.

"Who cares about me?" he shrugged.

"Well, I do and so does Nick," Ethan said, but he was filled
with guilt at the thought of how little he had seen of his brother
since Vera's death.

Apart from being prised out of his hermit-like existence to
spend Christmas at New World, Adam had insisted on being left
alone, and they had all honoured his wish. But the sight of him
and his surroundings was alarming.

"I'm going to open some windows. It's foul in here," Ethan
went on. "And then I've got something to tell you in strictest
confidence. I want you to do something for me."

"If you'm trying to get me married off again, you can forget
it," Adam said roughly.

"I don't want to get you married off, you old fool. It's me
that's getting married."

He hadn't meant to blurt it out like that, but at least it had the
effect of making Adam's eyes show a flicker of interest. But
before his brother could make some all-too emotive comment

145

like hoping Ethan hadn't got some young wench into trouble, he
rushed on.

"Now listen, Adam. Me and Karina Tremayne have been
seeing one another for some time and we want to get wed, but
she's homesick for Ireland, so we're going there to live. You
know how much of an uproar that will create in the family, so we
aim to do it quietly and without any fuss."

At his brother's gaping look, he smiled faintly.

"I know it's a bit of a shock, but before you say anything else,
there's no shotgun to my head. This is our choice, and naturally
we'll need money behind us. So that's where you come in."

"Well, I ain't got no money to speak of, but you can have all I
can spare," he said at once.

"That's not what I mean, Adam, but I thank you from my
heart," Ethan said, touched at the ready response. "I won't be
needing our old family house when Karina and me go to Ireland.
I want you to get Nick to arrange the sale of it, and then see that
the money's transferred to an Irish bank. Karina's getting in
touch with her old lawyer, and he'll contact Nick to make further
arrangements about the money."

"You've really thought all this out, haven't you?" Adam said
with grudging admiration.

"I'm not your kid brother any longer, Adam. I'm twenty-six,
in case you haven't noticed, and Karina's twenty-four, so we
don't need anyone's permission."

"So since you're a man, why don't you ask Nick about all this
yourself?"

"I told you. We don't want any fuss or arguments. We've
made up our minds, and we just want to be together as soon as
possible. You understand that, don't you?"

For the first time in a long time, Adam Pengelly's face
softened. Oh yes, he remembered only too well when he and
Vera only had eyes and hands for each other, and couldn't wait
to be alone together, desperate for each other's touch.

"Aye, I understand. So when is all this to happen?"

"We're leaving next week. We're getting married in Newquay,
and taking the afternoon ferry for Cork."

"You'll want someone to stand up for you," Adam said. "At
least let me do that."

Ethan squeezed his arm, aware of how thin it had got, but

thankful that there was a spark more animation in his brother now than when he had arrived.

"I'd be honoured, bruth. And there's one more thing you can do for me."

"Name it. If I can, I'll do it."

"You can do it better than anyone else in the county. Your skill was once legendary, long before I was knee-high to throwing a pot, and Seb will be missing a good work partner when I leave. I want you to go back to your old job and get back in the world again. I mean it, Adam."

His brother didn't speak for a few moments, staring at the chair where Vera used to sit, and where his strong young brother was sitting so tensely now, reminding him that life went on, and that if he wanted to be, he was still part of it.

"And you think Skye will want me back, do you?" he said slowly, as if still needing confirmation. "You think Seb will want me as a work partner?"

"Why wouldn't they want the best?"

Adam suddenly laughed. "My God, if that's the kind of flattery you give Karina, no wonder she's fallen for you."

Ethan grinned. "Then you'll do it? All of it?"

Imperceptibly, Adam straightened his shoulders, and Ethan knew what a momentous decision he was making. To come out of the shadows and face the world again couldn't be easy.

"All of it, bruth. You have my word on it."

They were married at twelve noon on a bright June morning, and as Ethan slipped the ring onto Karina's finger and said the words that would bind them together for life, he saw the conflicting emotions on his brother's face, and knew he was remembering another day, another time.

But Adam had already changed, smartened his appearance, cut his wild hair. He was preparing, this very afternoon when the newly-weds had sailed for Ireland, to carry out the rest of his promises: to deliver letters, and to talk to the people whose approval Ethan still needed.

At the last moment, once Karina had told Lily of her plans and vowed that nothing would change them, Lily had arranged for someone to look after her children and insisted on coming to Newquay to see her and Ethan married. And when they had left amid tears of mixed emotions, Lily and Adam drove back to the moors above St Austell together.

"Now to face the music, eh?" she said quietly.

She glanced at him, knowing of his heartbreak when her sister Vera had died, and wondering just how this day had affected him. "Is there anything I can do for you, Adam?"

He shook his head. "I have to see Skye and Nick first of all, and then I'll be calling on Seb Tremayne. I'm considering going back to work at the pottery. What do you think?"

"I think it's the best damn news I've heard all day – well, apart from the fact that the newly-weds looked so happy, of course. Good for you, Adam. It's time."

"I know." And already, ever since his brother had made the suggestion, his fingers were itching to hold the familiar, sensuous wet clay in his hands and transform it to whatever shape he desired. Her words were true. It was more than time.

"I can't believe it!" Skye said, after she and Nick had read the letters Adam delivered. "How could they go off and do this without telling us?"

"It was the way they both wanted it," Adam told her. "It was their choice. The letter to Nick explains everything about selling the house. You'll see to it, won't you, Nick?"

"Of course I will, and there shouldn't be any problem about selling it quickly, nor arranging for the proceeds to be paid into an Irish bank," he answered.

Apart from feeling a mild resentment that his younger brother hadn't confided in him first, he was more than thankful to see Adam behaving like his old self, rather than the recluse he had become.

Skye wasn't so ready to be mollified, having a woman's natural reaction to being done out of a family wedding. It would have been so lovely to have everyone there and given Karina a beautiful send off. She wondered how Wenna was going to take the news. Wenna had been crazy about Ethan ever since her childhood, although the feeling had surely waned of late. Skye turned her thoughts away from it, as something else came uppermost in her mind.

"And what about the pottery – the orders we've got – I

suppose Ethan realises he's left us in the lurch without a master potter to work with Seb?"

"Seb will still have a master potter to work with – if you'll have me," Adam said.

The reaction from Theo was predictable, saying he'd expected trouble from the moment he laid eyes on the Irish wench. At which point Adam froze him with a look, reminding him that that first time was at Vera's burying.

"Well, good luck to them, I say," Betsy said. "It's the most romantic thing I've heard in a long time."

"Romantic," Theo snorted. "If that ain't just like a woman to give no thought to what the pair of 'em are going to do. What's the plan — to raise horses like old Freddie and Bradley did? A fat lot they'd know about that!"

"Leave it, Theo," Betsy said sharply. "You've got about as much romance in your soul as a toad. What does it matter what they do? It's nothing to do with us."

Theo turned his attenion to Adam, as if noticing for the first time that he had come out of his shell.

"So what's to do with you, then? I thought you'd taken root in that place of yours."

"I was beginning to think so too. That's what I've come to see Seb about."

He wasn't going to explain to this oaf that his need to work was becoming more urgent by the minute. He hadn't realised how much he'd missed it. A man's wife and a man's work – they couldn't compare – but in the matter of need they were one and the same to Adam Pengelly right now.

"Seb's still up at White Rivers," Betsy told him. "He's taken to staying on later now that he's making these little pottery figures. Here, I'll show you."

Adam followed Betsy into the parlour where a row of pottery dolphins looked back at him: there were single figures; sets of connected dolphin families; others were perched on the rims of ashtrays. Adam's skilled eyes recognised that all were superbly made. They made his pulses race.

"These are excellent," he said.

" 'Tis Sebby's new ideas," Betsy said with pride. "He's come a long way since you taught him how to fashion the clay."

149

"He certainly has. I think the pupil could show the teacher a thing or two," he murmured. "Anyway, I'd best be off. I have several more errands to do before dark."

And one of them was to hightail it up to White Rivers before Seb Tremayne left the premises, and see what other interesting ideas the boy had developed.

As he drove away from the house and started back up the long road towards the moors, he felt a rush of adrenalin such as he hadn't felt in a very long time. It wasn't the same feeling that a man felt for a woman, but it was a good and honest feeling all the same.

Skye worded the letter to her daughter very carefully. She had had several ecstatic letters from Wenna in the weeks since she had gone to London with Fanny, and she always made a regular weekend telephone call to her parents. But this was something Skye didn't want to tell her over the telephone. This was something that Wenna needed to read and digest alone. She had the added thought that if she needed to weep, Fanny's broad and comforting shoulder would surely be at the ready.

Fanny saw the way Wenna's smile faded a little as she stared at her mother's handwriting.

"Bad news, duck?" she asked.

"No. Unexpected, though," Wenna said, surprised that the stab of jealousy she would have expected didn't come.

So much had been happening in the last weeks that her childhood passion for Ethan Pengelly had been the last thing on her mind. Besides, she had known that he and Karina only had eyes for each other, and had mutely accepted it.

She went on hurriedly as she saw Fanny's expectant look. "My stepfather's brother and my Irish cousin have got married and left Cornwall to set up home in Ireland."

"Good Gawd, you folks do believe in keepin' it in the fam'ly, don't yer?" Fanny said with a chuckle. "I never heard of such going's-on."

"It's not going's-on," Wenna said. "Mom says everyone was surprised, but maybe we should have seen it coming, since they always got along well."

"*Very* well, I'd say," Fanny commented, but wisely said no

more. Whatever the circumstances behind the hasty nuptials of
the couple, it was clear that this little sweetheart didn't suspect
anything other than a whirlwind romance. She was far from
dumb, but in some respects she was one of the world's innocents,
and as such, Fanny felt as fiercely protective of her as if she had
been her own. And for someone who had no maternal instincts
whatsoever, it was a feeling that surprised her.

It was those eyes, she thought, those bleedin' beautiful blue
eyes that could melt a man's heart and which were going to bring
hoardes of customers to the Flamingo Club as soon as she was
launched on the scene.

As yet, Wenna hadn't been tried out properly. She had to be
eased in gently to a very different way of life. Fanny and Georgie
had taken pains to introduce her first to the sights and sounds of
London, and to various acquaintances.

As a preliminary test, and in order to steady the girl's nerve, it
was suggested that she sang a couple of songs on several of their
quieter evenings early in the week. It had been an undoubted
success, especially when she had accompanied herself on the
piano and revealed her second talent. Fanny soon realised that
this was more than a good idea, it was a brilliant one. However
nervous Wenna felt when she stood alone and faced the dimly lit
audience, her nerves seemed to fall away when she had the prop
of her beloved piano keys beneath those sensitive fingers. She
caressed them and stroked them, putting all the feeling in the
world into the music. The combination of the rippling notes and
her soft, sensual voice was enough to send a shivery feeling
through the most hardened club goer.

Oh yes, she was going to be an asset all right, Fanny thought
lovingly. The customers already adored her. Gloria del Mar was
still the glamorous Saturday night star performer at the Flamingo, but it was obvious that Wenna wasn't simply a decorative
female who could sing in tune. It was clear to the talent-spotting
Rosenblooms that this girl had depth as well as beauty.

Fanny blessed the day that Skye Tremayne, as she had been
then, had come into her life during the Great War, and led her to
this singing discovery. It was weird how a chance meeting in a
war could lead you into directions you never anticipated, Fanny
mused. Wars weren't all bad . . .

Her thoughts were brought up with a jolt, remembering the

hazardous lives of Georgie's family in Vienna. If this was a hint of things to come, then her thoughts were downright wicked. There was nothing good about a war. *Nothing*. Georgie's own recent letter from his father had been full of pain and humiliation at the news that Adolph Hitler had now forbidden German children to speak or play with Jewish children. It was the work of an evil man, to recruit children into such hatred, Georgie had declared savagely. Fanny shivered, and made herself listen to what Wenna was saying.

"Are you all right, Fanny?" Wenna asked her. "You look a little green about the gills, as they say."

"I'm fine, lovey, just wondering what else yer ma has ter say. Anything more to report?" she asked, forcing her own worries aside for now.

"Mom says Uncle Theo is still urging her to agree to merging the clayworks with another company. Mom will hold out though. Oh, and Nick's other brother is going back to work at the pottery. He's a master potter," she added proudly.

Fanny gave a small smile. No matter how long Wenna remained with them in London, she would never reject her Cornishness. They all had it. Few of them moved away for ever, at least not the ones she had met, which weren't that many, she conceded. Just the Tremaynes and their close-knit family, by whatever name they used.

Which brought her to something else she'd been meaning to say for a while, and she spoke carefully.

"Wenna, have you ever thought of changing' yer name? Havin' a stage name, I mean, summat glamorous like Gloria's. Wenna Pengelly's a bit of a mouthful, ain't it? It'd take up a lot of space on a billboard, fer instance."

Wenna heard nothing but that one word. Billboard.

"I can't imagine I'd ever have my name on a billboard, Fanny. Like famous people do, I mean!" she added, momentarily dazzled by the very idea.

"Why not?" Fanny saw the sudden gleam in Wenna's eyes, and pushed home the advantage, while giving her time to mull over the suggestion. "Why ever bleedin' not, gel?"

Wenna laughed again. The first time she and Celia ever met Fanny, they had been enchanted by the racy and daring way the woman spoke, and had shocked their stepfather by repeating the forbidden word. But Nick wasn't around now, and Wenna wasn't a gullible child any more. She grinned.

"Well, I'll think about it. Why ever bleedin' not!"

She wrote to Celia that night. Celia might think it was a disloyal thing to do to change her name. But since all three Norwood children had changed their names to Pengelly when their mother had married Nick, she couldn't see the difference. But as ever, Wenna needed her sister's approval and advice – and any suggestions for the glamorous new name she might choose.

If she did it, then the entire world was at her disposal, she slowly realised. She could be whatever and whoever she chose. And it would only be a stage name. It wouldn't change her real self. She couldn't deny a shiver of excitement at the very words – stage name – they evoked a world of glamour Wenna had never known existed until now. As yet, she had only got the merest glimpse of it. Fanny was a far stricter chaperon than anyone might have suspected. She was a dear friend, but Wenna already knew there were far greater prospects than being involved in this delightful little club of Fanny and Georgie's. The stage, and the movies, where the handsomest of Greek gods worshipped at their golden goddesses' feet.

And at that wild and heady thought, she came totally down to earth and told herself not to be so dippy.

"You have something on your mind, *liebling*," Stefan von Gruber said to his dinner companion.

Their final day at the three-day June trade fair and business conference was over, and tomorrow they would return to Berlin from the beautiful city of Cologne, and report their success to Herr Vogl.

White Rivers pottery was only a part of the goods that the Vogl empire supplied, but to Celia's pleasure it had created a lot of interest in its pure white simplicity.

She smiled apologetically. "I'm sorry, Stefan. I didn't mean to be rude. I'm still feeling surprised at the letter from my sister, and wondering how to answer it."

"Ah yes. The budding singing star," he said with a smile.

"Do you believe that?" she asked. "That she'll ever be a star, I mean – and famous?"

"Don't you? Is it so impossible to imagine?"

"Oh, I'm not denying that she has a beautiful voice, and she plays the piano superbly. Nor am I in the least jealous of her," Celia said hastily, in case he should think otherwise. "It's just that – well, to me, I suppose she's just Wenna."

"That's because you know her so well. To her, you're just Celia, while to me, you will never be 'just Celia'."

She felt her heartbeats quicken as his voice deepened. These three days and nights away from Berlin had been for official purposes. The hotel rooms that had been allocated to them were on the same floor for the convenience of business contacts. Nothing improper was intended, or had happened.

But Celia would be a fool if she didn't know that as the days passed, the sexual tension between herself and Stefan was reaching fever-pitch. Their successful business dealings had been as potent as an aphrodisiac to them both, and this was the last evening, when they could relax and be themselves.

He reached across the table and took her hand in his. His eyes were dark with desire, and she caught her breath.

"Celia, you know what I want more than anything, don't you, *liebling*?"

"Yes," she said softly, because she had never been less than honest with her own feelings and whatever he wanted, she wanted too. And all these months he had behaved with such impeccable manners.

"But as I told you once before, you're nineteen, and I'm thirty-six—"

"And what in hell's name does that have to do with anything?" she said in a cracked, almost inaudible voice, not noticing the words she used until she saw him smile.

"My lovely, adorable Celia, you are totally delightful, and it is just as you say. What in hell's name does that have to do with anything?"

Celia awoke with a feeling of tremendous warmth and well-being, stretching her limbs as slowly and elegantly as a sleek Persian cat. For a few seconds she couldn't think where she was, until she felt the soft breeze of someone else's breath on her skin. Her eyes flickered open slowly, as if to preserve the moment, as if to hold on to this most intimate of moments before she looked into the face of her lover . . . no longer merely her boss, but her *lover*.

She heard his voice, the words whispered close to her mouth, his lips moving over hers so sensuously. "No other morning will ever compare with today, my love, when we awoke in one another's arms."

She felt his arms tighten round her, and her naked body was being moulded to his, the way it had been through the wonderful, erotic hours of the night. She had adored him then and she adored him now, for not moving away from her, or making her feel that this had been wrong, or a mistake, or cheap, or an expected part of a business weekend. She couldn't have borne it if she had looked into his eyes and seen any of that. Instead, she saw only love, and the yearning to be where they had been only a few hours earlier, before sleep overcame them.

She yearned too, to be so much a part of him again that they were truly one. She *ached* for him to love her again.

"Do I shock you for wanting you so much, my sweet girl?" he murmured next, as she seemed so silent.

"Of course not," she whispered back. "The wanting is not only confined to you, Stefan."

Even so, her face was fiery as she said the words, as the teachings of the Swiss school surged into her mind. *Nice* girls didn't go with men until they were married, and even then, they didn't admit to wanton desires. *Nice* girls certainly didn't have clandestine relationships in hotel bedrooms.

He bent his head and kissed the burning cheeks.

"Then I thank God that you are not one of those prissy young ladies, when I feel the need to explore every inch of your loveliness all over again."

She gave up thinking of anything then, and let the sweet sensations of his lovemaking take control of her. Touching, and tasting, and caressing, and discovering the unknown pleasures in reciprocating, until their mutual need for fulfilment could no longer be denied.

When he finally gripped her tight and gasped against her, murmuring words of endearment in German that she couldn't even begin to understand, she knew that none of it mattered. All that mattered was that he was here with her, and that it was where she wanted him to stay for ever.

He remained, spent, against her body, for some moments, until she simply had to shift his weight slightly, if only to breathe. Even then, they simply rolled sideways, still a part of one another, until nature decreed otherwise.

"You see what you do to me, *liebling*," he teased, as she felt him dwindle. "You have taken everything."

"And you have taken everything from me," she whispered. "You do know that, don't you?"

His fingers caressed her hot cheeks, gently moving the dark hair back from her forehead.

"Do you think I don't know that I was the first? Or that I would have wanted it any other way? A man who finds purity in his wife is truly blessed."

"His wife?"

He looked into her eyes. "You must know that I want to marry you, Celia. I have always wanted it, but it was too soon, and you were too—"

She put her trembling fingers over his mouth. "If you say that I was too young, I shall hit you," she said. But reality was fast catching up with her now. "All the same there are others who will say I am too young for marriage, especially since I would need their permission."

Her own words made her feel even younger and more gauche and vulnerable, and she gave a small laugh.

"Anyway, you haven't asked me properly yet!"

Stefan laughed too, folding her in his arms and refusing to let any sign of a cloud dampen this moment.

"Then I'm asking you now, my beautiful Celia. No matter how long it takes, will you marry me?"

She caught her breath. "I will," she said solemnly, "no matter how long it takes." Then she came down to earth and wrinkled her nose ruefully. "As a matter of fact, Stefan, I know exactly how long it will take. My parents will refuse to let me marry anyone until I come of age."

And that was not until November of 1939, almost a year and a half away. Celia's eyes were full of consternation as she realised the fact. What worldly man like Stefan von Gruber would be willing to wait so long for a girl to become officially a woman? Even though, to them, that deed had already been accomplished.

Stefan kissed her fingertips with the utmost tenderness.

"Then we must be patient, *liebling*, and do nothing to betray your parents' trust."

She looked away. Did that mean no more lovemaking? she thought tremulously. Now that she had experienced desire and fulfilment, how could she bear to forget the joy of it for so long? But she couldn't ask him, or broach the subject so blatantly, even now when they had been everything to one another. There were some things a young lady didn't do, and even the outspoken Celia Pengelly didn't go that far.

A second letter from Wenna awaiting her when she got back to the hostel in Berlin told her that Stefan had been absolutely right. However strong their passion, she couldn't bear to bring disgrace on her family, nor on Stefan's. She knew little about his background, she realised, except that his parents were elderly and lived somewhere deep in the German countryside. He never discussed them.

She read Wenna's second letter, which was more frantic in tone than the first. It was little more than a note, really, and bursting with indignation.

What do think, sis? Fanny had a bit too much to drink the other night, and got very talkative. She reckons that Karina and Ethan are expecting a baby, and that's why they got married so quickly and ran away to Ireland. I didn't know what to think, but if it's true, I'm glad I don't have to have anything more to do with either of them. I think it's absolutely beastly and disgusting.

I'm thinking about changing my name to Penny Wood for stage purposes. What do you think? Does it sound all right? I thought it was quite clever – a mixture of Pengelly and Norwood to keep the parents happy. Do you get it?

Celia stared at the letter for a long time, ignoring the final effusiveness of Wenna's choice of name, and thinking only of the first part. Beastly and disgusting were not words she would associate with her recent ecstatic time with Stefan. But if the outcome should be the same as Fanny Rosenbloom was surmising about the other two . . . Celia shivered.

As if to add fuel to Stefan's determination to keep passion at bay between them, there was an urgent message for him a week after their return to Berlin. Celia took the message and relayed it to him anxiously.

"You're asked to telephone this number immediately, Herr von Gruber," she said formally, for the benefit of anyone else who might be within earshot.

She handed him the slip of paper on which she had written the number. He immediately picked up the telephone, and spoke rapidly once he was connected. Celia's German was excellent, and she had no difficulty in understanding the one-sided conversation. When it ended, Stefan's face was drawn, and he began automatically pushing things into his briefcase.

"My father has had a severe stroke and is in hospital," he informed Celia, glancing at his watch. "There is just time for me to catch the noon plane. Please contact Gunter Schmit and advise him to take over my duties until further notice. I'll leave you to deal with anything else pertaining to the trade fair. And also inform Herr Vogl that I will be in touch with him personally as soon as possible."

Celia wondered if he realised just how remote he sounded. Her hands were rigid by her sides, thinking him a stranger again, even while she understood his reactions. Of course she did. His father could be dying, and he needed to be by his side, but all the same, she felt as if she had just been given a slap in the face, as if she meant no more to him than any other employee to be given instructions while he was away. He had shared nothing with her, other than the stark facts of what he had just been told about his next movements. His words were cold and curt, as only a German could form them. The thought was in her head before she could stop it.

Without realising that she did so, she stepped back a pace, not quite knowing how to react if he was to clumsily apologise for his abruptness. He did not. He merely glanced about him to check on the habitually tidy state of his desk for his deputy manager to take over.

"I'll attend to everything," she murmured, "and I hope your father makes a full recovery."

"Thank you." He looked at her properly then. "Celia, I'm sorry. I'll call you as soon as there is any news, but my mind is so scattered I can think of nothing else at this moment."

"I understand, Stefan," she said generously, but if this precision of thought was that of a scattered mind, then what on earth must he think of everyday scatterbrains like hers!

"I'll call you," he said again, as if he could think of nothing more to say. As he passed her he squeezed her arm, and she felt her eyes sting at his lack of tenderness, when she knew he was capable of all the love in the world.

"What an idiot I am," she told herself angrily a few minutes later, as she watched from the window of the high office building as he hurried to his car and drove quickly away. "How can anyone be expected to behave in a normal fashion after hearing bad news? I didn't really expect a passionate goodbye here in the office, did I?"

She chided herself severely, and got down to the business that needed urgent attention. The first thing was to contact Gunter Schmit and ask him to report to the office to take over Stefan's duties as soon as possible. She disliked the oily little man intensely, and hoped she wouldn't need to work with him for very long. Then she telephoned Herr Vogl.

His voice was cordial when he answered.

"How pleasant to hear from you, Celia, although I'm sorry for von Gruber's sad news. But it's fortuitous that you telephoned, my dear, since I have been meaning to contact you. Perhaps you would like to come to dinner on Saturday evening? I have seen your report of the trade fair in Cologne, and congratulate you and von Gruber on your successful dealings there. But now I have a proposition for you that I hope you'll find interesting."

"Then I thank you for the dinner invitation, Herr Vogl. I shall look forward to seeing you on Saturday evening."

She put down the telephone slowly. A dinner invitation from the company head wasn't so much an invitation as a royal command. Her brain whirled, wondering just what kind of proposition he had in mind for her. An increase in salary, or a bonus after their successful trade fair results? As long as it wasn't extra duties within the company. She certainly didn't want that. She was happy here with Stefan.

She turned with a forced smile as Gunter Schmit's weasel-like face appeared at her office door, already puffed up with importance at the thought of taking over Stefan's managerial role for a while. She shivered, as if the mid-summer day had already turned a shade colder.

# Eleven

"I've had very good reports of you, Celia, and you'll have discovered by now that I like to move my people around. It keeps them on their toes, as you English people say," Herr Vogl said easily, when dinner at the mansion was over, and the long-awaited proposition was finally about to be aired.

Until then, Celia had been in an agony of suspense, knowing better than to ask for information, and being obliged to listen to Frau Vogl's twittering praise of how Franz was now one of Herr Hitler's brownshirts. What little she knew of the fanatical rallies of this group smacked of a ghastly organisation intent on conquering and squashing lesser mortals, if not the world. But she smiled and tried to look interested, while being utterly thankful that her feelings for the arrogant Franz Vogl had long ago disappeared.

She turned her attention away from Frau Vogl to listen to her husband, and then she felt her face blanch.

"Our Cologne people were so impressed with you, Celia, that they have requested you be transferred to our office there for a time. I've now spoken at length with von Gruber on the telephone, and as his father is seriously ill, we have agreed that he must take indefinite leave until the situation is resolved one way or another. If the worst comes, he will need to remain there, of course. For the time being, Schmit will be in control of his department here, and it's reasonable for him to want to appoint his own assistant. So the way seems clear for you to accept the Cologne post, providing you approve the idea, naturally."

He kept smiling, but Celia knew that her approval was no more than a formality. She was being banished to Cologne to work with people she hardly knew. Stefan was out of her reach, somewhere in the German countryside caring for a desperately sick father, with all the signs suggesting he would stay there until

161

he died. She had found out by now that Stefan was no pauper, so he would certainly be needed to administer his father's estate when the inevitable happened, as Herr Vogl said.

But to Celia, still reeling at the swiftness of how things were changing, it all seemed so cut and dried, as slick and efficient as she knew these people to be. And for the first time since coming to work in Germany, she felt as if she was in an alien country among people whose culture she didn't know or understand.

She swallowed. "Do I have a choice?" she dared to say.

Vogl's smile never wavered. "Well, of course you do, my dear. You can always go back to England and work for your mother, or take up some other employment. No one is holding you here against your will."

God, he was colder than an iceberg, Celia thought furiously. "But if I stay, I must go to Cologne and work there? Is there no other position for me in Berlin?"

She spoke calmly enough, but inwardly she was like a boiling cauldron, seething, not only at the indignity and unfairness of it all, but at the way she was practically grovelling to this pompous prig. It wasn't Celia Pengelly's style, and she resented it bitterly.

"We like to think of our management people as a team, Celia," Vogl said. "You and von Gruber worked well together. If and when he returns to the company, then naturally we shall think again."

"Is there a real doubt about his return then?" Celia said, all else forgotten for the moment, as her whole world seemed to fall apart.

Vogl looked at her thoughtfully. "How much do you know of him personally, Celia?"

Her face burned, wondering just what he meant by that remark, but thankfully, Frau Vogl intervened.

"Now you've embarrassed Celia, *liebe*. Please explain yourself properly."

He held up his hand in apology. Celia guessed he rarely did so verbally. She remembered his family's stiffness at her eighteenth birthday party, and began to wonder why the dickens she had come here in the first place.

"The von Grubers are a very old and wealthy family, and Stefan von Gruber will inherit vast areas of productive vineries

162

on his father's death," he said. "He will not choose to leave it once he becomes the controller of the Von Gruber Estates."

"Why has he felt the need to leave it until now?" Celia heard herself saying numbly, tring to comprehend all he was telling her. "Why hasn't he always been the controller?"

She stumbled over the word, her mind spinning. She didn't know him at all, she realised. She didn't know any of them. None of them revealed more than they chose to outsiders. The insidious rise to power of Herr Adolph Hitler had proven such a trait only too well.

"His father insisted that Stefan made his own way in the world, and not to let it be known that he was due to inherit a fortune, for obvious reasons," Vogl went on. "Until now the estate has been managed by a caretaker controller. I'm sure that will change when the younger man is in charge."

"You knew nothing of this, Celia?" Frau Vogl asked.

"I did not. I was his personal assistant in the office, but we did not speak of private personal matters."

The distinction was bitterly ironic, when for one magical night they had been everything in the world to one another.

The memory of his whispered words when he had asked her to be his wife were like chaff to her now. Why would the wealthy and so cool-headed Stefan von Gruber, head of the Von Gruber Estates, ever want to marry a hot-blooded Cornish girl?

Especially one who might take advantage of the fact that he was due to inherit a fortune. The inference of fortune hunter did not escape her, and her face burned anew.

"May I have time to consider this offer, please?"

"Of course. There's no hurry. In fact, since Herr Schmit and his team will want to make their own arrangements in the office, I suggest that you take some time off. Go home for a month and decide what you want to do."

She kept her eyes lowered, wondering if she was really necessary to this company at all if he could so glibly offer her a month's holiday. She would damn well take it too, she thought furiously. There was no way she could work comfortably with Gunter Schmit and his team. He would have his own personal assistant, and there would be nothing for Celia to do. She had no intention of being passed over like a lost memo in the pending tray.

"Thank you, sir. I will take the month at home, and let you know my decision in due course," she said with dignity.

She cleared up her work at the office, and by the time she was ready to leave Berlin, she still had not heard from Stefan. She was bruised and shocked inside, and like a wounded animal she felt the need to run and hide, to be home where she belonged. She telephoned her mother in advance.

"How lovely that you're being given such a long holiday!" her mother said delightedly. "Tell us exactly when and where you'll be arriving, and we'll meet you."

Celia was choked at the warmth and pleasure in her mother's voice. Her pride hadn't let her reveal the whole situation, and she knew immediately she needed a little more time before she actually faced them all.

"Mom, would you mind if I stayed in London for a few days first? I haven't seen this place where Wenna's living, or what she's up to, and it will break the journey."

In the small pause before Skye answered, Celia knew her mother had heard far more than the impulsive words her daughter spoke. Her mother could always tell.

"I think that's a lovely idea, darling," Skye said. "Wenna will be thrilled to see you. I suppose you know she's going to go by the name of Penny Wood now?"

"So I heard. What do you think about it?" she said, making a huge effort to drag her thoughts round to the mundane question of Wenna's proposed stage name.

What the hell did it matter in the great scheme of things? What did anything matter but the fact that Celia was about to leave Germany, and that she would probably never see her lover again? She smothered a sob in her throat.

"She's sensible enough to know what she's doing," Skye said, "and so are you, my love. Come home when you're ready. Make it soon."

Skye replaced the telephone receiver slowly, more troubled than she wanted to admit. There had been desperation in Celia's voice and a resignation that wasn't healthy in someone so young – someone who had been on the brink of falling in love and having a wonderful life, if her mother had read all the signs correctly.

164

She didn't know what had gone wrong, but she was very sure that something had.

"It's surely unusual for her to be given an entire month's holiday, Nick," she said to her husband. "I'm tempted to contact Herr Vogl on some business pretext to find out if everything is all right. What do you think?"

"I think you should leave well alone," he said firmly. "Celia has been independent for some while now. Let her sort this out for herself – whatever it is. She certainly won't thank you for going behind her back and interfering."

"I know you're right," Skye said in frustration, "but it's never easy for a mother to know when a thing is interfering or just honest to goodness caring."

Nick put his arms around her. "Well, one thing's for sure, darling. She knows you care. You've always shown that you care for all of them. But you know it's important to let them go their own way. You didn't even raise your eyebrows at this damn nonsense of Wenna's about changing her name."

"Oh, Nick, you know the reason for that! If she's going to be a singer, she has to have a name that people will remember and can say easily. You must admit that Wenna Pengelly is a mouthful. I thought you'd be pleased that she combined both our names in the way she has."

His smile widened. "Of course I'm pleased. But the lawyer in me has to be objective and see every angle."

"Well then, you should see that this makes sense," she cut in neatly, guiltily glad to be diverted from worrying abut Celia for the moment. "Penny Wood is going to be a star. I can feel it in my bones."

"Just as long as she remembers she's still Wenna around here, and always will be to us," Nick couldn't resist adding.

Once Celia had made up her mind she couldn't wait to get away. Her decision to visit Wenna in London had been taken on the spur of the moment, but now it seemed totally the right thing to do, if only to get a little breathing-space before she faced the family at home. She never considered whether or not there would be room for her. She just knew that the warm-hearted Fanny would welcome her with open arms, the way she had welcomed Wenna.

She packed feverishly, and recklessly booked a flight to England rather than travelling by overland and ferry. The air travel was bumpy and scary and made her feel nauseous and, by the time she had gone the last miles of the journey in a hideously expensive taxi to the Flamingo Club, she was tired and tense and ready to burst into tears.

"My God, *Celia*!" Wenna exclaimed, as she opened the door to the flat. "What on earth are you doing here?"

"It's good to see you too," Celia retorted sarcastically. "So are you going to let me in or do I have to stand on the doorstep all day like a refugee?" she added, her voice cracking now, despite herself.

Still in shock at the sight of her sister unusually dishevilled, Wenna opened the door wider, noting for the first time the suitcase and collection of assorted bags. Celia never travelled light, she registered vaguely. Someone pushed past her and held out her arms to the visitor.

"Celia, by all that's bleedin' holy! Come on in and 'ave a cuppa tea and tell us what the bleedin' 'ell yer doing here and lookin' so done in, for Gawd's sake!"

Celia was suddenly enveloped in Fanny's welcoming arms, and held against her ample chest. Hearing the familiarly wicked expletives, Celia let her defences drop and burst into wild, angry and despairing sobs.

"Of course yer can stay," Fanny said, a long while later when the tears had been dried and several cups of strong sweet tea had been consumed. "Wenna – or Penny, I should say now – don't have anything much ter do in the daytimes, so she can show yer round." She cocked her head on one side thoughtfully. "You know, you two beautiful gels are the real spit of one another. I don't s'pose you ever thought of doin' a double act?"

It was enough to bring a watery smile to Celia's face. "I don't think you'd say that if you ever heard me sing! Thanks for the offer, but no thanks. Anyway, I'm not looking for a job, Fanny. Well, maybe I am. I don't know yet."

She hadn't meant to say any of it, but her words were so jerky and she was so clearly unhappy that Fanny wisely didn't say anything more. It was all going to come out later, Fanny was sure. Nobody could hold in such passionate feelings without

166

letting them erupt like a volcano at some stage or other. Poor little bleeder, she thought, with her usual rough sympathy. I'll bet there's a man involved. There usually was, in Fanny's knowledgable opinion.

"So what's happened?" Wenna said later, once Celia had unpacked her things in the tiny boxroom after insisting that she didn't want to muscle in on Wenna's space by sharing her room – a decision that relieved both of them mightily.

"I've been given a month's holiday to consider a change of job in the company, and I wanted some time to myself before I went home," Celia said, having rehearsed the words well.

"*And?*" Wenna persisted. "What does your boss say to that? The lovely Stefan, I mean. How will he manage without you?"

She smiled encouragingly, not meaning anything by her words, but virtually tearing open Celia's heart. Aghast, Wenna saw her sister dissolve as she threw herself face down on the bed and sobbed her heart out.

"Celia – darling – please tell me what's wrong," Wenna begged, white-faced now. "I can't bear to see you like this. You were always so much stronger than me."

"Not any more," came the strangled sound from the bed.

"Yes you are," Wenna said, wrapping her arms round her. "Whatever's happened, you'll survive it, like you always do."

Celia sat up jerkily. "Perhaps I don't want to survive it," she said tragically.

"Now you're just being a drama-queen," Wenna said, surprisingly brisk. "I've heard better lines at the theatre. I'll take you there one night to see a good play."

Celia stared at her once-timid sister, who was now far stronger than she, and was aware of how their roles had changed in so short a space of time. Wenna's growing confidence had probably been inevitable in her new life, while Celia's nerves were still raw and painful from what she saw as rejection and betrayal.

"You're a good girl, Wenna," she said huskily. "Or do I have to get used to calling you Penny now?"

"Of course not! It's only for my image, as they say." She added, with a giggle: "My agent thinks it will help my career."

"Your agent?" Celia echoed.

"Darling, you don't know the half of it," Wenna teased her airily in her best luvvie voice, thankful to see that Celia had shown a spark of interest in her fortunes, however incredulous, and was less agitated than when she arrived.

Celia stayed in London for a week, and during that time they contacted Justin and spent an afternoon on the Thames with him, which reminded them nostalgically of the times they had spent rowing on the Truro river at home. Wenna had instructed Justin not to ask too many questions about just why Celia was here, and to his credit he managed to refrain.

Celia was moderately surprised at how enjoyable life was in the city. The weather was glorious and the parks were full of summer beauty. Whatever anxieties there were about European affairs, it was confined to governments and apparently had no effect on ordinary people going about their business. Since Fanny and Georgie refused to admit to their own growing fears about his family, and resolutely hid the newspapers after they had scoured both the English and German ones, the two girls were in blissful ignorance of just how dire the situation was in Vienna for Georgie's parents.

The biggest surprise of all for Celia was the way her little sister was being acclaimed in the Flamingo Club. On Friday and Saturday evenings the glamorous Gloria del Mar was still the star attraction and drew the weekend clientele, but for three evenings during the week, they were treated to the sweet and husky voice of Miss Penny Wood, accompanying herself on the piano, as the new posters outside the club proclaimed.

Celia was impressed. Not only by the status Wenna had deservedly attained, but by the performances she gave. It had never been like this in Gstaad, she reflected. As always she hastily blotted out the memories, since they also evoked a special afternoon in a hotel restaurant with a wonderful view of soft green slopes and flower-filled valleys and distant snow-capped mountains, when she had first set eyes on the love of her life.

Her resolve was never to think of him now, unless it was absolutely unavoidable. Unfortunately, those times were only too frequent when Wenna sang the emotional songs of love that went down so well with her listeners.

Wenna was so independent now, and far stronger than herself, Celia thought enviously, despite the fact that her sister and the Rosenblooms fondly believed she had recovered herself since

Skye didn't raise an eyebrow to question her refusal to eat anything other than toast and butter.

"So are you ready to tell me what's wrong, honey?" her mother asked her quietly that afternoon when they were sitting together in the sunlit conservatory.

Celia gave a shuddering breath. She knew the question had to be asked, just as she knew she had to answer it.

"A lot of things. Everything. So much of everything that I don't know where to start," she said jerkily.

"The beginning is always a good place," Skye said. She cringed at the inane remark, but she didn't know what else to say, becoming increasingly alarmed to see her self-sufficient daughter so disorientated.

"The beginning," Celia murmured, as if looking far into the past, "occurred when I arranged to meet a man in a hotel restaurant in Gstaad."

"You mean Stefan von Gruber?" Skye asked when she paused.

Celia hesitated, then the words came out in a torrent. "I loved him, Mom. I thought he loved me, but I've had no contact with him at all since his father became seriously ill and he left Berlin to be with his parents. I've had a lot of time to think since Herr Vogl gave me this long holiday. It seems probable that Stefan won't return to the company at all. His father's almost certain to die, and Stefan will then be a very rich and important man controlling a huge vinery and country estate, so why should he bother about me at all? And I can't help wondering if he suggested this post in Cologne for me just to be rid of me."

"For pity's sake, Celia, slow down," Skye said, as her daughter's voice quickened and rose higher. "Why on earth should you think any of these things? If the poor man's distraught about his father it's not likely that he's going to be on the telephone to you every five minutes, is it?"

"I don't need to hear his voice every five minutes," Celia said, angry at this censure. "Just once would be enough. Just to know that he still cares."

Skye hardly knew what to say to her. Celia looked frozen, despite the heat of the summer day, and her face was pinched and white. Dear God, surely she wasn't . . .

"Were you lovers, darling? Don't think you'll shock me by admitting it," she added softly.

Celia didn't answer for a moment.

"Just once," she said. "And since I can see what you're thinking, no, nothing came of it. Thank God."

Thank God indeed, thought Skye, recalling her own feeings long ago when she too had had such misgivings. Celia couldn't be placated right now, however much Skye yearned to hold her in her arms as if she was a child and tell her that she understood so very well the mixture of relief that there was no child inside her, and the grief that there was not. They were feelings that only another woman who had experienced the same deep love would understand.

She spoke more casually, deliberately ending the subject. "I'm going up to the moors this afternoon. I want to visit the pottery. As it's so hot and humid here today, why don't you come with me? The fresh air will do us both good."

"What's this? Therapy for the poor rejected lover?" Celia said, with a feeble spark of her old spirit.

"Something like that. So will you come?"

"All right," she said grudgingly. "I know you won't let me wallow for ever, however much I want to."

As far as their family was concerned, the moors had always done more for restoring the spirits than anywhere else. Skye prayed that it would do the same for Celia. Not that she expected her to get over this trauma quickly. Miracles rarely happened, and how could she recover quickly, when her heart was so patently broken?

But even hearts didn't stay broken for ever. They healed eventually, though Skye was wise enough not to tell Celia so now, knowing that she simply wouldn't believe her.

"We'll walk," she decided.

"Are you mad?" Celia asked. "What's wrong with the car?"

"What's wrong with your feet? My grandmother used to walk from the top of the moors where she lived in a cottage with her family, right down to Truro Fair along with the rest of the young folk who used to work at Killigrew Clay. It was the highlight of their year. And they had to walk back again unless they got a lift on a cart or a hay wagon for part of the way."

Celia allowed herself a small smile. "You always did set a lot of store on those old tales of your grandmother, didn't you, Mom?"

"Why wouldn't I? Morwen Tremayne was a remarkable woman. They made them tough in those days," she added.

"She must have been strong willed as well as beautiful to have married the boss's son," Celia said without thinking.

Skye saw her lips tremble as the contrast with her own position struck her. She tucked her hand in her daughter's arm as they left the roadside and began the stroll up the sun-scorched moors, the bracken crackling beneath their feet.

"She thought, like most of us, that when we meet our destiny that was the end of it. She adored Ben Killigrew. But after he died she realised she could love again, and when she married Ran Wainwright, she was twice blessed by love."

"I know what you're trying to say, Mom."

"Then let me say it," Skye went on relentlessly. "I loved your father just as much as Morwen loved Ben, and I was devastated when he died. And I love Nick just as much, but without feeling disloyal to your father in any way. We all have the capacity to love more than once, darling, and if Stefan never comes into your life again, believe me, it won't be the end of loving for you."

For a moment she felt the guilt and shame of knowing that her love for Philip Norwood had already died before he did. But it was all so long ago, and a little white lie was far preferable to seeing the haunted look in her daughter's eyes.

Celia didn't say anything for a while as they went steadily up towards the moors, where the sunlight glinted as always on the majestic sky tips of china-clay waste.

"I'm sure you're right," she said slowly at last. "But that doesn't mean I've entirely given up on Stefan, Mom. I thought I had, but listening to you has clarified my feelings and I know I didn't imagine the love we had. I'm glad we had this little talk. Whatever happens, I shan't give up hope – even thought I'm still very angry with him, especially if he thought I was some kind of fortune hunter," she added for good measure.

She released Skye's hand from her arm and strode on ahead. Skye wondered if she had done any good at all, or if she had simply made matters worse in making Celia doggedly believe that someday there would be a future for her and Stefan von Gruber, and in doing so closing her mind to any other kind of love.

Her daughter would be here for three weeks, and in that time Skye was determined to revive her spirits totally.

But for all that Celia was trying to keep cheerful and positive for her mother's sake, she was just as determined that if she hadn't heard from Stefan in those three weeks, she wouldn't go back to Germany at all. It was the yardstick by which she would decide her future.

Gunter Schmit was now in charge of what used to be Stefan's large Berlin office. His blonde personal assistant, whom he had hoped would become far more amenable to his advances now that he was a somebody in the company, had been instructed to clear out everything that was extraneous to the new team, after scrutinising it all thoroughly. She wasn't a very conscientious employee, and the correspondence in the pending tray had piled up in the couple of weeks since Gunter took over. She glanced through it, more taken up with her broken fingernail which needed urgent attention, and tossed what were obviously mostly advertising missives from other companies into the waste-paper bin. She missed several letters that should have called for more scrutiny. One of them was a personal letter addressed to Fraulein Celia Pengelly.

The loss of it wouldn't change the course of world history. It just proved Celia Pengelly's despairing thought that she meant no more to the company than a lost memo in a pending tray, and no more to Stefan von Gruber than a brief and delightful encounter.

# Twelve

Seb Tremayne was openly glad to see Celia. He caught both her hands in his, ignoring the fact that her gloves were immediately covered in china-clay dust. Neither of them were too bothered about it.

"God, it's good to see you, Celia. It's been mighty dull here lately with none of you girls around."

She gave a slightly hysterical laugh.

"The day there are no girls around you I'll see pigs fly," she said, without thinking how, as children, she and Wenna as had always thought him a prize pig.

He wasn't now. He was tall and handsome, and his blue Tremayne eyes were admiring her slender figure and glossy dark hair, and noting how the exertion from the hill climb had made her cheeks glow and her eyes shine.

He laughed back. "There's none like you, though, cuz. I can't abide simpering females."

"You mean I've got an acid tongue, right?" she quipped.

"Something like that," he grinned, not sparing her. "So what are you doing here, anyway? I thought you were in Germany working with the enemy."

"Sebby, please," Skye put in sharply, her pleasure at the way Celia had become more animated dimmed at once by Seb's thoughtless remark.

"It's all right, Mom," the girl said now. "I'm home for a holiday, Seb, that's all. I needed a breathing-space and that's all you need to know."

"All right. If you're in Truro one evening, you can come and see a film with me if you like. No doubt you'll be doing the family rounds, and my mother's always glad to see a female relative. What do you say?"

"I'll think about it," Celia said airily, not ready to do the social rounds just yet. She thought that if she had any sense at all she would certainly not sit around like a love-sick calf, waiting for a man to call.

She managed to keep the smile fixed on her face as she greeted Adam Pengelly, looking far more like his old self now that he was working with his beloved pots again.

The women stayed at White Rivers for a short while, watching the potters' skilled hands shaping their wares and sliding them onto the shelves to dry. Celia didn't miss the way Seb's hands caressed the slippery wet clay, coaxing it into whatever elegant shape he wanted, as tenderly as if he caressed a woman. She was shocked as the thought slid into her mind, and willed it away. She had no intention of thinking of Seb Tremayne in that way, now or ever. There was no room for anyone else in her heart but Stefan . . . certainly not her cousin, Sebastian Tremayne!

"I knew the walk would do you good," Skye remarked when they began the trek over the moors towards Killigrew Clay. "It always has that effect on people. My grandmother—"

"Your grandmother has a lot to answer for," Celia said with a brief smile. "Sometimes I swear she's practically at your shoulder dictating to you."

"I wish she was," Skye said. "Even after all these years, I miss her. She was one of reasons I came to Cornwall in the first place. Well, Granny Morwen and my mother, of course. I desperately wanted to discover all the places I'd dreamed about since I was a little girl. All the stories were so romantic, and Cornwall seemed such a magical, mystical place."

She stopped, seeing her daughter's sceptical face.

"You can scoff, Celia, but if it wasn't for Cornwall, you might recall that you wouldn't be here at all. If I'd stayed in America and married a homebody instead of wanting to find my roots, you might have been the product of some hard-headed American businessman, or even a humble New Jersey fisherman!"

"And you think it was worth it – finding your roots and discovering who you really are?"

"Of course! A million times yes! I'm no philosopher, but I believe that we're all who we are on account of those who have gone before us, honey."

Celia said nothing for a few moments, staring straight ahead to where the clay-spoil heaps soared so magnificently skywards. She was as steeped in her Cornish background as anyone. The sky tips, such a symbol of that background, were part of her heritage, her legacy. But only part of it.

"Maybe that's what I should do too," she said slowly.

"What are you talking about now?" Skye said. "Have I missed something?"

Celia looked at her. "You went back to your roots, Mom. So where are mine?"

"Right here, of course."

Celia shook her head. "It depends on how far back you take this ancestor thing, doesn't it? This is where your Granny Morwen was born, *and* your mother and so many of the Tremayne family. But then your mom went to America after she married my grandfather and that's where you and your brother were born. *Voilà*! My roots are in New Jersey."

"My Lord, I always thought the Tremayne side of the family was complicated enough, but you've just complicated it still more," Skye said with a laugh.

"No, I haven't. I've clarified it in my mind, anyway."

Skye suddenly realised just what she was getting at and looked at her in consternation.

"Oh honey, this isn't for you! You're just getting over a traumatic experience. It would be the biggest mistake to go halfway across the world in search of something that doesn't exist any more. My family home was sold years ago after my parents and my brother died. There's no one belonging to our family in New Jersey now."

"Then come with me and show me where you were born and the places you used to know; where my grandparents are buried; the magazine office where you used to work—"

"Stop it, Celia," Skye said firmly. "This has been my home for twenty-five years now, and here I stay. Surely you're not serious about this. You'd be a stranger in America. Tell me it's no more than a whim, for pity's sake."

"All right. I'm not serious. I'm just crazy, so let's forget I ever mentioned it."

Crazy was the word for it, thought Skye, but at least her daughter was behaving more positively than when she had arrived home. She easily forgot the conversation, but Celia didn't.

If Seb Tremayne had been glad to see her, Lily was positively overjoyed when she turned up at the pottery showroom in Truro.

"I can't tell you how much I've missed seeing you girls, and Karina too," she told her. "I'm surrounded by men here, well, David, and now Olly's started coming back with him in the evenings sometimes, and it's all men-talk or newspaper-talk until I could scream. And then there are the boys . . ."

"You're not tired of these little poppets, are you?" Celia said, laughing as Robert and Frederick climbed all over her.

"No, but they do tire me out. I should have had them when I was much younger," Lily groaned. She shooed them off Celia's lap and sent them out to play. "Tell me what brings you home, how long you're here, and when you're going back."

Celia answered Lily's usual quick-fire questions in the same quick-fire manner, without stopping to think.

"I'm home on an extended holiday because of changes in my office, to consider my future within the company. I'm not even sure that I'll be going back at all."

"Good Lord," Lily said. "I thought everything was wonderful, or is that something I shouldn't even ask about?"

"I don't know. Has my mother been talking?"

"Not specifically. But you looked so glowing when you were home at Christmas, darling, and I'm not slow at putting two and two together. So what's gone wrong?"

"Nothing and everything. But I don't really want to talk about it. Let me ask you something instead. Would you think I was completely crazy if I went to America for a time?"

"Crazy! I should say so. Just give me the chance to be so crazy," Lily said. "But you're serious, aren't you?"

"Why do people keep asking me that? Yes, I'm serious, though I denied it to my mother. But the more I think about it, I think it's what I have to do. Mom came to Cornwall to find her roots, and I feel the urge to do the same thing."

"Are you sure it's not just an excuse to run away from something?" Lily said, direct as ever.

"Could be," Celia said, just as honestly. "But since I don't

September Morning

know what I'm running away from, maybe I'll find the answer there."

"Well, in my opinion, if you've got a problem, you just take it with you wherever you go. It'll still be here when you get back, darling."

"But maybe I'll have been able to deal with it then," Celia told her. "Anyway, it's just a hypothetical question. I haven't definitely made up my mind to go."

"Haven't you?" Lily paused while they both digested the rhetorical question. "Well, if you're thinking of staying here for any length of time while you make up your mind, I could really do with someone to help me in the shop. It's getting hectic now with so many summer visitors coming to Cornwall. I think we've been 'discovered' too."

"Come here and work in the shop with you? I might just do that," Celia said.

Nick was against it, as she had half expected.

"For heaven's sake, Celia, you have a wonderful chance to work your way up in the German company, so why on earth would you want to work in a shop?"

"Mom wasn't so damn snobbish about it when the town turned against her when the clayworks and pottery employed some young German boys years ago," she snapped. "I heard all about that, *and* the way the town's ladies came to her rescue."

"You don't know the half of it," he snapped back. "The whole area was practically divided on account of the loutish way those youths behaved."

"And who won? The *women* did, because we're stronger and have more sense in seeing people as people. They didn't give in to madheads like Uncle Theo who would have crucified the German boys just because of past prejudices."

Nick gave a tight smile. "Your education isn't entirely complete, my dear. Your young Germans almost caused a riot when one of the clayworker's daughters became pregnant. It wasn't only the women who got them out of the country before murder could be done. Ask your mother."

Celia turned away from him and sought her mother out at once, bursting with rage at his lawyer's pomposity. She loved him dearly, but sometimes, just sometimes she wanted to hit him.

\*     \*     \*

She found Skye in the midst of a fiery argument with her brother, and wondered hysterically if every family was like this, or only theirs.

Olly rounded on Celia at once, his eyes bright with fury, clearly intending to enlist her support.

"You don't think it's a stupid idea for me to want to move in with Lily and David, do you? They've got the room, and it makes perfect sense since David and I work together."

"My Lord, just listen to the little worm," Celia said before she could stop herself, in no mood to consider his needs. "Work with David indeed! I thought you were a junior tea boy, not a star reporter!"

The minute the words left her lips she saw the stricken look on Olly's face, and the shock on her mother's.

"Celia, that was unforgiveable. You will apologise to your brother at once."

"Don't bother," Olly yelled. "Everyone knows she's the favourite, anyway. Everything has to revolve around her, and I wish she'd never come back, making everyone creep around her as if she's half dead. I wish she'd go back to her fancy German employers where she belongs. And I *am* going to move in with David and Lily, if they'll have me. At least they see me as a person and not just as a tea boy!"

He stormed out of the room, and the next minute they saw him pedalling furiously away from the house on his bicycle.

For a moment the two women were too stunned to say anything. Then Celia held out her hands helplessly, hardly able to speak, her head throbbing with shame at the way she had humiliated her brother.

"Mom, I'm sorry. I didn't mean it. I don't know what's happening to me."

For once, Skye didn't take her in her arms and console her. This time, Celia had gone too far.

"What's happening to you is that you've become so self-pitying that you never consider anyone else's feelings, Celia. What's happening to you is that you think the world has to stop turning because you've had one little setback—"

"One little setback?" she said, choked.

"That's what I said. For pity's sake, pull yourself together and look at the world round you and see what's happening to other people. As a start, you might care to read the letter I received from Fanny this morning, and then tell me how important your little setback really is."

She thrust the envelope into Celia's hands and left her to it. Celia knew she had sought her mother out for a reason, but right now the memory had vanished in the shock of hearing her mother censure her so. It was so very rare. Simply to give her trembling hands something to do, she pulled Fanny's letter out of the envelope.

The words dazzled in front of her. Fanny was not an articulate letter writer, but as Celia read on, the one long ungrammatical paragraph made the horror all the more poignant.

We got a letter from Vienna a few days ago. It came from an old friend of Georgie's folks. You knew they was shopkeepers of course. Well it seems like the Jew-bashing bastards burned their shop down one night and Georgie's parents was still in bed and couldn't get out. It couldn't be proved who done it of course and anyway who would care about an old Jewish couple? The friend who wrote to tell us said it happened a couple of weeks ago and there was nothing left of them to bury properly. So some friends just had a secret service for them and that was that. They begged Georgie not to go there as everything's so bad now. But he's real cut up about it and he cries all the time when he thinks I can't see. He don't like folk to know any of it and Wenna thinks we've shut the club for a week for painting. We'll have to open again soon though. You can't sit back and let the buggers win can you gel?

Celia wept over the letter, knowing just why her mother had wanted her to read it. It put everything into perspective. Poor, poor Georgie . . . she wanted to run to the telephone and speak to him, but she knew it wouldn't be wanted. He was so proud, such a good man . . . and those terrible people had done this to his family, just for being who they were.

She found Skye in the garden and gave back the letter.

"I'm so sorry. I didn't understand," she said in a small voice. "Sometimes I think that for all my education, I don't know anything at all. Fanny – even Fanny makes me feel humble – and I know that sounds as snobbish as hell, Mom."

"Come here, honey," Skye said. "If you've realised that much, then I wouldn't say your education was wasted. Now what did you want to see me about? I know there was something."

She shook her head. "It doesn't matter now. I'm going into town to make my peace with Olly. That's more important than raking over old history." She hesitated. "You will let him move in with Lily and David, won't you? It would be good for him."

Even though the idea of working in the shop with Lily and suggesting that she herself should take the Kingsleys' spare room had been hovering in her mind, she knew that this was Olly's time, not hers.

A short while later, and with her mother's blessing, she got out her own bicycle and pedalled towards Truro. She caught up with Olly long before she reached the town. She caught sight of his own machine, thrown down on the grass above the cliffs, and saw his hunched shape, sitting with his hands clasped around his knees, a lone, miserable figure, and her heart went out to him.

"Olly, I'm so sorry," she said at once. "I didn't mean any of those things. Life has just been so bitchy lately, and I was just taking it out on you."

"Is that one of the fancy words they taught you at Gstaad?" he said, not yet prepared to compromise an inch, and staring resolutely out to sea, where a distant ocean-going liner was making its way steadily westwards on the calm, mirrored water.

Celia gave a small smile. "It's the way I feel right now, Olly. Why do you think I'm here?"

"How should I know?" he said bitterly. "Nobody ever tells me anything. At least David treats me like an adult and not like a baby."

"You want that room with David and Lily, don't you? And I think you should have it. You don't object to my putting in a good word for you, I hope. It's what older sisters do, and I know I can persuade Mom to let you do it."

So what if it was a little white lie as yet? Celia was damn sure she could swing it for her brother. The smile he gave her was worth any sacrifice she had to make. It was such a small sacrifice, anyway, she thought shamefacedly, still caught up with the dreadful thing that had happened to Georgie Rosenbloom's parents.

"You mean it?" he said eagerly. "But I thought you might be wanting to move there yourself."

"Not me," Celia said, her gaze also following the stately progress of the ocean-going liner. "I've got other ideas, and if you promise to keep it our secret for the time being, I might just tell you what they are."

She realised that never before in her life had she deigned to share a secret with her young brother. But seeing the look on his face she knew it was exactly the right thing to do to restore his hurt pride. It made her feel slightly better than she had for weeks. Life wasn't all bitchy.

A few days later, when she had made her peace with all concerned, it wasn't hard to wheedle out of Lily what had really happened all those years ago when a small group of German youths had been employed at Killigrew Clay and White Rivers, amid very mixed and vociferous reactions.

"Your mother was an angel then," Lily told her. "Though me and Vera didn't do so badly either. We became shopkeepers at White Rivers when nobody else would give us the time of day, and Vera withheld her favours from Adam, if you know what I mean. For a couple of newly-weds I don't think it went down very well with Adam," she added with a grin. "Anyway, Skye wrote a special newsletter that David published, saying how we should all let the past remain in the past and welcome good workers wherever they came from. Or words to that effect. I don't remember all of it now, except that it was addressed to the women of the area, and it turned the tide. The foreigners had to leave, of course. The situation was too volatile for anything else. But instead of Theo running 'em out of the country, your mum and dad smuggled them from their lodging house onto a ship in the dead of night and sent them back to Germany without any fuss. The poor little devils were terrified by then anyway, and all the fight had gone out of them."

Celia was open-mouthed at hearing all of this.

"We were all too young to know what was happening, and I had no idea it was such a traumatic time," she exclaimed. "You were all regular heroes, weren't you?"

"Oh, we had our moments, darling. Now what did you want to tell me? You know Olly's moving in and he's like a dog with two tails about it. I'd rather hoped it might be you, and that you'd decided to come and work for me. Are you?"

"I'm afraid not, Lily, but I'm not going back to Germany either. I've made up my mind and nobody's going to stop me."

"When did anybody ever try?" Lily said dryly.

Not everybody was so agreeable to her plan. Her stepfather thought it a mad idea to go to America in search of a dream, while Skye thought that Celia was simply putting as much distance as she could between herself and Stefan.

"I know why you're doing this," she told her daughter bluntly. "But you can't run away from your feelings for ever. At some stage you have to come back and face up to them."

"You didn't go back, did you? You came to Cornwall and you stayed. Why is it so impossible for me to do the same thing in reverse?"

Skye spoke softly. "I think you know the answer to that, honey. The time will come when you'll realise where your heart lies, and I don't believe it's in New Jersey."

Celia looked at her pleadingly. "I want your blessing, Mom. I feel too restless to stay here, and I can't go back to Germany, so where else is there for me to go? Anyway, the crossing only takes a little more than three days now. If I absolutely hate it, I can be back here in no time at all!"

Skye hugged her tightly, knowing that in the end she would give her blessing. Celia's complex feelings were tearing her apart, and the only place to sort them out clearly was as far as possible from everything familiar. Didn't she know that for herself?

"Then hadn't you better inform Herr Vogl that you won't be returning to Berlin? I'll write a separate letter to him explaining that you want to see something of the world and have decided to go travelling. I'll sort out some addresses and contacts for when you get to New Jersey."

"You're a darling, Mom," Celia whispered.

The plans were made, and nothing was going to change her mind. Celia stayed at home for the rest of her month's official holiday, but in early August she was a passenger on the *Queen Mary*, bound for New York. She left Cornwall with very mixed feelings, not least because of the letter that had finally arrived at New World a few days earlier, re-directed from the Vogl offices in

Berlin. She had shown it to no one, but the words Stefan wrote were imprinted in her heart.

I was devastated when you never replied to my earlier letter, Celia, and saddened that we had to part so abruptly. But if you wish to have no further contact with me, then I must accept your decision. Our paths are unlikely to cross again, since I have severed all connection with the Vogl company following the death of my father. My duty is here now.

I have been told that you declined to take the post in Cologne and have left the company. I can only assume that you preferred to be back in England with your own kind. My deepest regret is that I was clearly mistaken in the feelings I believed were genuine between us.

On my side, they were most sincere, but as I do not wish to put you under any obligation or sense of remorse, I will merely say that if ever you need me, I am here.

She couldn't read any more of it. It said so much, and yet it was so very stilted, and more like a formal office letter. Its tone was so unlike the lover who had held her and adored her, and even though she treasured his final words, she knew she would never contact him again.

Even his address, von Gruber Estates, heavily embossed in gilded letters at the top of the letter, set him apart from her. She should always have known it.

Where was this earlier letter she was supposed to have received, she raged? There had been no other letter, nor telephone call, nor message of any kind. Until now, she thought, he had forgotten her existence. This was his way of breaking all ties now that he was a rich landowner.

She clung to her anger. It was far safer than letting her emotions tear her apart. She told herself that he wasn't for her and never had been, and that she had to forget him, and travel to whatever fate awaited her on the other side of the Atlantic.

One thing was for sure. She wouldn't follow her mother's lead on her own long-ago voyage to Cornwall when she had met and fallen in love with Philip Norwood. This girl was keeping herself very much to herself for the few days of the voyage, and falling in love was not included in her itinerary.

"Well, that didn't last long, did it?" Seb asked his father when he heard the news. "I thought she was going to stay in Cornwall and get more involved in the business."

"She was always too high and mighty to think about throwing a few pots, boy," Theo said sneeringly.

"I didn't mean that. You never did have much time for Celia, did you?"

Theo scowled. "She was too sharp-tongued by far. And I've got no time for any of 'em while they remain so stubborn about mergin' with Bourne and Yelland. But I've got a trick or two up my sleeve that's soon going to change all that."

"Oh? And what's that?"

He laughed. "Oh, no, my lad. You'm too hand in glove with cousin Skye for me to give anything away. You'll all find out soon enough anyway."

He wasn't telling anyone about the deal he'd struck privately with Zacharius Bourne. The deal that was going to give him more say-so in what happened at the clayworks than he'd had since old Morwen Tremayne decreed that Skye should be a partner. He didn't know why he hadn't thought of it before.

The two partners at Bourne and Yelland, and himself, would be three-quarters of a thriving merger in which the fourth partner was not only a woman, but could always be outvoted. Once the two clayworks merged, Skye would be in the minority for decision making. The three men would hold the greater percentage of shares, which was the way it should be, Theo thought arrogantly.

Selected workers were already spreading the news at both clayworks that the merger was imminent. They said there was strength in numbers, and that all the clayworkers would benefit by it, especially from the fat bonuses the new combined company was prepared to pay as soon as things were settled.

That would be the clincher, Theo thought gleefully. Money talked, the way it always had. For the clayfolk, never the world's most affluent of workers, the golden handshake each of them would receive, would be irresistible. He and Zacharius Bourne had agreed to dip into their own pockets to see it through, which proved Theo's dogged intention to get his way over the American upstart.

He readily conceded that Bourne was a better negotiator than himself. The man had the gift of the gab without resorting to wild rages when things didn't go his way. This very day he was putting their case across to the two company lawyers far more eloquently than Theo could, which was why it had been decided that he would keep out of it for the time being. The fact that one of the lawyers concerned was Skye's own husband was a small fly in the proverbial, but Theo didn't anticipate any major problems now that he and Zach had sorted things out to their mutual satisfaction.

Nicholas Pengelly drove home to New World that evening at a greater speed than usual. There was no way he could object to the arguments that had been put to him today, and nor could he ignore the well-prepared documents that the Bourne and Yelland lawyer had produced. Private negotiations had clearly been going on for some time, and even though he was soured by the fact that Theo Tremayne had had a pretty hefty hand in it, he had to reluctantly agree that the conditions were fair and sensible.

As the fourth partner in the proposed merger, Skye wouldn't have any real choice about it, even though the entire workforces of the two companies would need to be drawn together to give a vote on it, the way they always did. To be seen to be fair and to give everyone their say, was the slogan, though in effect, it rarely worked that way. And there was little doubt what the outcome would be. The figures Bourne had produced for the bonuses, and the proposed rise in pay for the men, would see to that. Nick couldn't blame them. Nothing was stable in the world these days, and money in the men's pockets and food in their children's bellies counted for more than outdated principles.

He didn't relish the task of convincing his wife of it. She would see this merger as a betrayal of all her family stood for, despite the fact that Nick had been telling her for months that it made sense.

He waited until they had finished dinner before he told her he had something of importance to discuss with her.

"I think I know what it is," she said, looking at him unblinkingly in a way that he wished she wouldn't. That wide, blue-eyed gaze could always unnerve him, and it did his self-esteem no good at all to have to ask himself if he was a man or a mouse when it came to discussing things with his wife.

Right now she was looking at him as a businesswoman who knew very well he was about to destroy everything she had fought to preserve since the days when Morwen Tremayne had fought these same battles. *That* was what unnerved him, Nick thought savagely. This damn family thought they owned the world, and could do what they liked in it. The arrogant Theo Tremayne was proving that only too well. But in doing so, he diminished Skye.

"You can't know," he said briskly. "Unless you're able to read my mind, which wouldn't surprise me, with your so-called sixth sense," he added.

"I don't need a sixth sense to know why you're bringing your briefcase to the drawing room, and plying me with more wine than usual to soften me up."

"What a suggestion," Nick said, laughing.

Her voice sharpened. 'I don't need a sixth sense to know why Seb's been acting strangely for days now. He's been dropping hints as large as bricks as to why Theo's been spending so much time over at Roche lately."

Nick sighed. "This is like listening to your grandmother all over again."

"Thank you. I take that as a compliment, though I suspect it wasn't intended that way. But it doesn't get to the point of this discussion. So what is the proposal?"

"To merge," he said bluntly, "and to do it soon. Skye, you've seen the recent world figures for china clay. Prices are dropping alarmingly, and if it drops too far, then we'll have to lay men off, and if that happens we won't be able to fulfil our orders, and the pottery will suffer as well. We can no longer exist as a small company—"

"*Small?* Killigrew Clay was one of the largest—"

"It was once, but now it's one of the few independent companies left," he reminded her. "Others have merged and become stronger. Bourne and Yelland are offering excellent terms, and Theo's gone a long way to ensuring that the men get good bonuses. And before you say he shouldn't have done any of it

188

without your knowledge, when have you been ready to listen? You've simply closed your ears to any of it, but you can't go on burying your head in the sand, darling."

Skye bit her lip as his impassioned voice went on.

"Listen to me, darling. Bourne's strength is that they're allied to several paper mills which give them guaranteed orders, which will stand us in good stead if the European markets close."

"And you think they will, don't you?" she said slowly. "You're convinced that the war is coming."

"As convinced as anyone can be without a crystal ball. Perhaps you'd have more faith in what everyone seems to take as inevitable if you consulted your old crone on the moors."

"That's the last thing I'll do!"

"Really? I got the impression you took more notice of her than your own husband."

Skye recognised his growing anger. She turned away from his accusing face, her emotions very near the surface.

"Nick, please don't let's fight over this. My mind is in a turmoil lately, what with everything."

"What everything?"

She moved away from him and went to stand by the window, staring out at the soft blue evening light. The crescent moon was just rising, and the sky was alive with stars almost close enough to be touched. It was a beautiful summer evening, calm and fragrant, with no hint of any conflict anywhere in the world. Not their world, or the wider world. So peaceful, so for ever. Skye shivered at the thought, knowing that nothing was for ever.

Nick came to stand behind her, and his arms folded around her, holding her, keeping her safe . . .

"I've kept my feelings to myself, Nick," she said slowly. "But everything is changing, and suddenly I feel so alone."

"You're not alone. I'm here. I'll always be here."

She leaned back against him, feeling his strength. Loving his strength. Loving him so much.

"But now we're just two, where we used to be five. Oh, I know they've been away to school, but they were children then, and now they're not. They're making their own way in the world and and they don't need us any more, and it all seems so weird and final. Whatever you think of Fanny, I was happy for Wenna to go to London because I knew she'd be safe with her. I always

189

guessed that Olly had printer's ink in his veins, Nick, and Celia had such a future ahead of her in Berlin. But now . . ."

She paused for a moment as his hold on her tightened, knowing that it had to be said or she would burst.

"It's crazy I know, but it's as if I've only just realised that all our children have left home, and how much I shall miss them," she said, her voice catching. "The fact that Celia's assured future ended so disastrously makes me realise that I can no longer kiss them and make it better. We're not young any more, Nick, and we no longer have control over what our children do. Doesn't that frighten you?"

He twisted her around in his arms.

"Good God, woman, will you stop! If you're trying to say that we're in our dotage, then you'd better think again!" he said, making her give a half-smile.

"I don't mean that at all."

"Good. Then don't even think it. But I'll tell you exactly what I think. Our children are level-headed and intelligent. If Celia has to go halfway around the world to find what she's looking for, then so be it. Didn't you?"

As he echoed his daughter's own question, Skye felt his mouth on hers, warm and familiar, reminding her that life, and loving, didn't end because there were a few grey hairs in her still luxuriant black hair, and more than a sprinkle in Nick's. Love went on, passion could still be a flame. The kiss that began so tenderly was fast changing into something very different and demanding. His hands were pressing her into him, moulding their bodies together as he murmured against the softness of her lips.

"Since we seem to have wandered totally off the track, I think perhaps we had better finish this discussion about the clayworks in the morning."

"What clayworks?" she murmured back.

# Thirteen

B efore Nick left the next morning, Skye spoke quietly.
"If you really think the merger with Bourne and Yelland
is the right thing to do, Nick, then I won't oppose it."

She was grateful that he didn't make a big show of his reaction,
but simply accepted her decision. There would be time enough
for crowing when Theo got to hear of it.

"Right. I'll inform Theo first of all, and then we'll set up a
meeting between the combined owners and clayworkers. I don't
see any real problems, but there are always some old diehards,
and we don't want a strike on our hands because they don't
approve of the idea."

"They don't approve? Whose business is it, anyway?" she was
stung into saying.

"Yours, my love, but if you don't have willing workers, you
don't have a business at all, do you?"

She was weary of arguing. "I know it. Just don't let Theo come
crowing, that's all, or I shall throw something at him." Her
mouth trembled as she said it. Although she just wanted it settled
now, the enormity of it all was only just dawning on her. She still
couldn't quite dismiss the thought that she was betraying everything those earlier Tremaynes and Killigrews had fought so hard
to keep and, in particular, her grandmother's trust.

"Will you be all right?" she heard Nick say.

She forced a smile to her lips. "Of course I will. I'm not going
to fall apart. I'm made of sterner stuff, remember?"

But it wasn't the way she felt inside. When he had gone, she
wandered aimlessly about the empty house. Eventually she found
herself in the round turreted room where many years ago the
young Walter Tremayne and his sweetheart had hidden away,
wanting so much to be together that they were prepared to defy
everyone and risk a family scandal. If they hadn't been so

191

passionate about one another, finally forcing both sets of parents to agree to their marriage, there would have been no Theo.

But it wasn't only love that conquered all things, Skye thought contrarily. Her mother, Primmy Tremayne, had had such an early aversion to her American cousin Cresswell that never could anyone have foreseen such a lifelong passion between them. Hate and love were sometimes so closely allied, that you had to experience one before you found the other.

She shivered. How anyone ever in this world found their soulmate was a mystery that only a romantic fool would try to comprehend. Or were they all fools, anyway? Maybe there was no such thing as a soulmate, and it was no more than a chemical reaction that drew two people together. What did love have to do with it?

"I must be going off my head," she muttered to herself, feeling beads of sweat on her forehead.

It was hot and airless in the little room, and although it had been a secure lovers' hiding place all those years ago, it was making Skye feel claustrophobic now. There was a small window, and she tugged at the unused fastenings until it opened and let the cool morning air filter in and throw welcome beams of sunlight across the room. Dust motes danced in the rays, and she followed their movements in a kind of charmed daze for a moment, her gaze finally setting on the boxes of old photographs and documents stored here.

The documents were mostly all musty accounts and letters that should have been thrown away years ago. There was nothing emotive in them, as there had been in old Morwen Tremayne's diaries that she had left to her granddaughter. After reading only one of them, Skye had been true to her vow that they were private and not for anyone else's eyes.

Once, she had thought of writing a book about the fiery and passionate Morwen Tremayne, based on the diaries, but in the end she couldn't do it. A person's life was her own, and a diary encapsulated all the thoughts and dreams that went into it. They were the only totally private things a person had, and should remain so. So all the diaries had been burned, reducing a lifetime's dreams to ashes. At the time it had seemed a right and noble thing to do.

"And that was crazy and over-emotional, if you like," Skye

went on muttering savagely, as if needing the reassurance of her own voice. "There was always something in Granny Morwen's words to comfort and reassure me."

She lifted the lid on one of the boxes. The photographs were old and brown and crackling with age, the mostly sepia tints doing little to enhance the vivacious faces of the family. Some of the faces and names Skye had virtually forgotten, all the Tremaynes and Killigrews and the girls they had married, and their friends and confidantes.

She stared at a picture of two young girls, laughing together, their arms wrapped around one another in friendship. They wore the long-ago garb of the bal maidens who had worked in the Cornish clayworks of a century ago: long white cotton dresses and aprons; bonnets framing their pretty faces; black lace-up boots caked with clay. It was as if the photographer had just captured these two in a rare moment of glorious happiness away from their work. Two such pretty faces, with bold, laughing eyes and rosy cheeks from a life spent in the open air, high on the moors, working in all winds and weathers.

Skye turned the photograph over, even though she was certain of the identity of these two, anticipating the names she would see scrawled there in the faded handwriting.

"Morwen and Celia the day before Truro Fair," she read. "On the look-out for young men as usual."

She wondered who had added the last sentence, since it was written in a different hand. One of Morwen's brothers, perhaps. It might even have been her beloved brother Matt, who had gone to America to seek his fortune, and whose own son had returned to Cornwall years later and whisked Primmy Tremayne off to America and married her. And in time they had had a daughter named Skye.

God, was there ever such a tangled family as theirs! But Morwen's life had been more fulfilled than anyone might have imagined from her humble beginnings. Skye knew it, because Granny Morwen had charmed her so in the telling. She had certainly fared better than the tragic Celia in the photograph, after whom Skye's own daughter was named. Morwen's friend had drowned herself in a clay pool, unable to face the disgrace of being raped and then committing the mortal sin of allowing a witchwoman to induce an abortion and burying the child in an unmarked moorland grave. Morwen had been a party to it all.

At the sudden sound of a disembodied female voice, Skye jumped visibly, her heart thudding wildly, as if those other two women were about to materialise in front of her eyes.

"Skye, what are you doing up there? Where are you?"

She swallowed as her ragged senses returned to normal, and croaked out a reply.

"I'm in the turret room, Lily."

She hastily dabbed at her face, until then unaware of the tears that had streaked down her cheeks. A few moments later Lily appeared in the litle room and gaped at her.

"What the dickens are you doing in here? You look as if you've seen a ghost," Lily said, as solid as ever, and not remotely like anything supernatural.

Skye's attempt to sound matter of fact failed dismally.

"Don't take any notice of me. I always get emotional when I see these old things."

"Good Lord, are those old family photographs?" Lily exclaimed. "There must be dozens of them here."

"Granny Morwen was a bit of a collector," Skye said with great understatement. "If you want to see them we'll take them down to the conservatory and have some tea. I'm stifled up here and the dust is tickling my throat."

She half-hoped Lily would decline. The photos were hers, she thought fiercely, and then she knew how foolish and selfish that was. They belonged to all of them. Lily was as much a part of this family as herself. Besides, Lily was married to a newspaperman and was just as keen as David at sensing a story. She proved that a couple of hours later, by which time she had scrutinised every one of the photos, put them in order, and tried to sort out who was who and where they all fitted into the intricate pattern of the family. Lily sat back and stared at Skye.

"These are amazing. They're a marvellous record of a past era. You should do a series of articles on the Tremayne family and the Killigrew Clay involvement with it for the newspaper, Skye, and let David use the photos to illustrate them. I know he'd be keen to collaborate with you."

"Oh, I don't think so," Skye said at once.

"Why ever not? The pottery hardly keeps you busy these days, does it? You've become a backseat owner. It doesn't suit you to sit around and do nothing. Now that the girls have gone, it would do you good to work, Skye. I haven't said anything, but I've been worried about you lately."

"Have you?" she said in surprise. "I can't think why. There's nothing wrong with me."

"Nothing that a good dose of working on some project or other wouldn't improve," Lily said astutely "Believe me, darling, I know what I'm talking about. Look what it's done for Adam to get him out of that gloomy little house where he just sat about mourning Vera! God knows I miss her too, but endless grieving won't bring her back."

"Are you talking about you and Vera, or me and Celia?"

And Wenna, and Olly, Skye thought.

"I'm talking about wanting to see you the way you used to be, when nobody could hold a candle to the quick-witted Skye Pengelly. Your writing always proved that. You had such style, Skye. Don't waste it by turning into a cabbage. I think I'd better leave now, before you throw something at me."

"I won't. I'll save that for Theo," Skye said with a grin. "As a matter of fact, it might be exactly the time to commemorate the end of an era by recording it all, as you so rightly said. I'd better explain."

Theo telephoned her that evening and was surprisingly docile, though Skye had no idea how much pressure Nick had put on him to curb his tongue. She had fully expected him to crow over her, but instead he said she had obviously inherited a lot of good sense after all, and left it at that. She remarked to Nick that it was almost as if all the fight had gone out of him, now he had got his way, which proved that there must be a first time for everything.

"Don't you believe it. He'll be saving it for the rally on the moors when the combined owners and workforce get together to thrash things out. He might be in agreement to merge with another company, but he'll leave them in no doubt who has the loudest voice when it comes to cursing and lording it over the rest of them."

Skye's eyes sparkled. "Is that so? Well, we all know his bigoted views of women in business, but he'll have to account to two other equals as well from now on, and Bourne and Yelland aren't going to sit back and let him dictate the terms, any more than I am."

"That's my girl," Nick said, chuckling at her vehemence. "You've got some of your old fizz back, anyway, and I'm not sure that it's entirely due to last night, flattering though the thought is. So what's been happening today?"

She laughed. Her eyes glowed with the memory of just how erotically pleasurable last night had been, when she had lain in his arms and nothing had been more important to either of them than loving and being loved.

"I haven't entirely forgotten last night either," she said provocatively, "but I can't say that today has been entirely wasted either. Lily came to visit, and we had quite an interesting time."

She outlined her vague plans for using the old family photographs with a series of articles for the *Informer* to trace back the history of Killigrew Clay, and in particular the Tremayne family involvement with it. After all, there had been only one Killigrew son, and five Tremayne children, who had all helped to shape the dynasty it had become.

"I think it's a marvellous idea," Nick said. "I'm sure Olly would be keen to be a part of it too."

"Don't think that hadn't escaped me," Skye said with a laugh. "Though of course I still have to interest David in the idea. It's his newspaper."

"And since when did David Kingsley ever turn down any suggestion that came from you?" he said, so coolly that she looked at him sharply. He laughed. "Good God, Skye, do you think I haven't known that the man's been in love with you for years?"

Shocked, Skye spoke quickly. "Please don't say that. He and Lily have such a lovely, comfortable life together."

"I'm not saying they don't. I'm sure he loves his wife and his boys, but he's always been more than a little in love with you. There's a difference."

"Well, I don't want to know about it," she said, almost crossly. "Anyway, 'being in love' is never as deep an emotion as loving someone and making a commitment to them."

"That's all right then, isn't it?" Nick said.

But she wished he'd never said it, or had known it, although Skye knew that David had never quite lost his feelings towards her, even though years ago he had turned easily enough to someone else when she had rebuffed him.

Maybe that was what 'being in love' really meant. In love with the feelings, but not with the person. Whatever it meant, she was going to stop being so analytical. It made no difference to her need to be a creative wordsmith again. She hadn't quite realised how great this was until Lily had made the suggestion. She should have done, of course. Writing had always been her salvation, through good times and bad just as it had been Morwen's, in a different way.

Even though she hadn't been well-educated, Morwen had recorded her thoughts in her diaries. Skye had often wondered if her own instinctive need to write had come from her grandmother. It was a lovely thought, and one that she cherished.

"Anyway, I'm not in love with David Kingsley and never could be," she told Nick firmly. "So don't let it worry you."

"I wasn't, but it's good to know," he said, smiling. "And I think your proposal for the newspaper is an excellent one, darling, and well timed in the circumstances. It will be good to remind the community of just how powerful Killigrew Clay once was, and how your family helped to shape it."

"That's what Lily and I thought too," she said, hugging him, and marvelling, as always, at how lucky she was to have him.

The rally was arranged for the end of the month. If it went through smoothly it would be in good time for the autumn despatches, when the proposed new company would have a new name which was still to be decided. That would cause another headache since neither company would be willing to relinquish their own.

Skye was very much against them being called Killigrew, Bourne and Yelland Holdings. In any case there would be arguments as to which name came first. Other companies had amalgamated several names, but she thought it was just too much of a mouthful; something neat and memorable would be preferable. It was one of the things she intended to bring up at the initial meeting of the four proposed owners and their lawyers in the Bodmin solicitor's chambers. Statements, orders and accounts had already been properly scrutinised on either side, and each party was satisfied that the merger would be advantageous to all.

But she was nervous as she and Nick drove to Bodmin on that bright August morning. She knew Zacharius Bourne slightly. He was portly and middle-aged and as aggressive as Theo, but always ready with an oily charm when it was needed. They were two of a kind, thought Skye.

Gideon Yelland was slightly younger and more submissive than his older partner, and Theo clearly thought him a nonentity when it came to swaying votes. Maybe there was an underlying steel about the man, but somehow Skye doubted it. He clearly looked the weaker partner.

"Well now, little lady," Bourne said expansively, once the four of them and their lawyers were seated. "I hope you and I are going to get along very well."

"I hope so too, Mr Bourne," she said pleasantly, "and I'm sure we will get off to a good start if you will refrain from addressing me in such a ridiculous fashion."

"Skye—" Nick said warningly, while Theo guffawed, and the other lawyer, a Mr Pascall, merely sniffed disapprovingly. He was small and wizened and clearly took his lead from Nick when it came to summing up a situation.

"Told you to watch your tongue when dealing with my cuz, didn't I, Zach? She's no pushover." jeered Theo.

"Thank you, Theo," she said coldly, "but I can answer for myself, and I suggest that we get down to business instead of indulging in useless chit-chat."

It was dawning on her that maybe she held the upper hand, after all, or at least as good a hand as any of them. The other three all wanted this merger desperately. As a woman she was in a minority of one, but women had their own methods, and if things became sticky for any reason, there were still ways of persuading the clayworkers to see her side of things. The power of the press combined with the power that wives and mothers held was something men would be foolish to ignore. It had worked once before when, by subtle means, the womenfolk of the whole area had proved their worth to their men.

She felt an unexpected sense of exhilaration. She would not let these men forget that she was as much a partner in this merger as any of them. She was a woman in a man's world, just as her grandmother had been, but Morwen Tremayne had always stood up for what she thought was right, no matter how much the rest of them tried to manipulate her. Skye had every intention of doing the same.

Nick cleared his throat.

"Will you all please open the folders that Mr Pascall and I have prepared for you, and we'll go through the various stages one at a time," he said.

Each of them complied and studied the facts and figures. On the face of it, Killigrew Clay had everything to gain and nothing to lose. Bourne and Yelland Holdings were a much smaller company in terms of actual pit size and production, but their undoubted advantage was in being allied to paper mills, which would stand them in good stead if overseas markets for raw clay faltered.

Everyone knew that the initial decision to merge had been made in all but signature. It only remained for the clayworkers' approval to go ahead immediately. But there was something still nagging in Skye's brain.

"There's one thing I'm not clear about. The clayworkers don't take kindly to change, so what exactly are we offering them as an incentive? This seems no more than a very modest pay rise," Skye said.

She saw Theo and Zach Bourne glance at one another, and braced herself. There had to be something more, and these two had probably been in collusion for some time. She glanced at Gideon Yelland who was keeping his gaze fixed on the proposal forms and guessed that he knew something that she did not.

"Well, Theo?" she said sharply. "Will you please explain? I refuse to sign anything until I have all the facts."

And if her husband knew them, why the hell hadn't he already informed her?

" 'Tis nothing that had to concern you, cuz, since me and Zach are putting our hands in our own pockets to subsidise matters. Though, because of our goodwill, we have an extra rider to add to the proposal—"

"What's this?" Nick said sharply. "Why haven't I been informed of this? Pascall, did you know of it?"

The other man scowled, his face reddening. "Only recently, sir, and I have still been debating the ethics of it. Naturally I was going to produce the rider I have prepared before we get down to the signatures."

"Really? It seems to me as if it had been conveniently forgotten," Skye said, her blood boiling, disgusted by the underhand methods her cousin was prepared to use. "And if that had
happened, I presume the four signatures would have bound us to
the merger, no matter what these two have cooked up between
them."

"Now see here, little lady—" Bourne began aggressively, and
was immediately silenced as Skye got to her feet, the chair legs
scraping the floor behind her.

"No. *You* see here, Mr Bourne. Either you treat me with the
respect I'm due, or I'm out of here this minute, and the merger
will fail. My signature is of equal importance to my cousin's, and
you can do nothing without it. We're not partners yet!"

"Of course. And I apologise, ma'am," Bourne said, changing
his glower to an ingratiating smirk as Yelland put a restraining
hand on his arm. "I meant no offence, I'm sure."

"Please sit down, Skye," Nick snapped. "This meeting was
coming to an end, but it's clear that we have far more serious
matters to discuss now."

"And Mr Tremayne," he addressed Theo formally, "you will
please explain yourself. What exactly have you and Mr Bourne
been arranging between you? Surely you know that you should
have consulted me before any private arrangements were made?"

Theo immediately lost control and crashed his fists on the
table. The veins on his forehead stood out like purple ropes as his
face went a furious colour.

"You bloody snot-nosed lawyers think you rule the roost," he
bellowed. "We'm perfectly capable of sorting out our own
affairs, and I'll be buggered if I'll go cap in hand like a piss-
assed schoolboy to ask your permission as to how I spend my
money."

"Theo, for pity's sake, calm down," Skye snapped, disgusted
with him as always, and mortified that it was her side of the table
that was showing such a lack of control.

He glared at her, his eyes murderous. "Oh, ah, my fine wench,
you can play the lah-de-dah colonial as much as you like, but it
don't alter the fact that you came here and wormed your way
into my grandmother's life, and thought you could take over
what's been in my family for generations."

"It's my family too," she yelled back, furiously near to tears but determined not to show it. "What in hell's wrong with you, Theo? I never asked for any of this!"

But it was damn well hers now, and she'd fight tooth and nail to preserve her right to it.

"The deal's off," she announced tensely, standing again, and with her hands flat on the table surface as if to support every shaking nerve in her body.

"Skye, *no*," Nick said wearily. "I'm not going to let you back out of a sensible transaction on account of this buffoon's madness."

"Who the hell do you think you are to talk to me like that?" Theo rounded on him at once.

"I'm your lawyer and I suggest we all sit down again and get on with the business of the day."

"Damn right," Zach Bourne growled, seeing all their previous work dwindling away. Skye saw the flickering indecision on his face, and his jaw tightened as he went on. "Mrs Pengelly has a right to her opinions, and we must honour them. In view of all the dissension here today, I suggest that Tremayne and myself tear up the proposed rider to the incentives we've offered. For God's sake, let the bonuses stand but with no conditions attached."

The lawyer Pascall spoke cautiously. "Then before we go any further, do I have the meeting's permission to discuss the incentives, and the formal dismissal of the rider?"

"That would certainly seem like a good idea," Nick snapped, clearly wondering why the devil he had ever got involved with this volatile family in the first place.

Pascall continued. "Mr Tremayne and Mr Bourne decided to double the amount of the bonuses first suggested. They were prepared to pay these extra amounts themselves, which would undoubtedly have created goodwill among all concerned, and I trust they will honour that decision."

"I've said so, haven't I?" Bourne snapped.

"As to this rider," Pascall went on, clearly outraged at the implied slur on his reputation to be so involved in the first place, "it was to the effect that in consideration of these monetary offers, Mr Tremayne and Mr Bourne would each have a thirty per cent share in the new company, with Mrs Pengelly and Mr Yelland having twenty per cent each."

"They must have been out of their minds to suggest it," Nick said angrily. 'Show me the document, please."

Pascall handed it to him silently, while Skye was speechless. The rats, she raged, the double-dealers. It gave them more control than herself and the less dominant Yelland, who from the look of him, had been perfectly content to go along with it.

"This is not a legal document," Nick said. "It does not have the consent of all four parties, and I would strongly advise my wife to disassociate herself from it."

"You need have no fears on that score," Skye retorted. "What on earth were you thinking of, Theo? I always knew you were capable of some slimy dealings, but I didn't think you'd go so far as to cheat your own cousin."

"There's no cheating involved," he said, starting to bluster. "Twas merely a business arrangement that seemed perfectly fair, considering me and Zach Bourne were prepared to pay handsomely for the privilege."

"Bribing the clayworkers, more like," she snapped. "Well, this is what I think of it."

She picked up the document from the table, tore it in two pieces and threw it contemptuously towards her cousin.

"I think there's little more to be said here," Pascall began uneasily. "I suggest we leave things until another day."

Skye glared at him. "Certainly not. I think we all know a thing or two more about one another now. We came here to confirm our willingness to a merger, or do the other three parties wish to go back on it now?"

She heard Theo snigger at her vehemence, but his voice held the merest touch of grudging admiration as he spoke.

"Well, since 'tis clear that none of us will put one over on my cousin, and nor would we wish to," he added hastily, "I suggest we settle this deal once and for all, with equal shares between all four parties."

"Agreed," said Zach Bourne, with such alacrity that Skye guessed immediately who had made the initial suggestions as to what she could only see as a pay off.

"Then if that is the wish of you all," Nick said, taking charge as the senior lawyer, "it only remains for the new company to be given a suitable name. We can't present a *fait accompli* to the workforce without having it established. Have any of you given thought to it?"

Gideon Yelland made his voice heard properly for the first time. "It makes no difference, as long as the Killigrew folk don't shut us out. We ain't been established as long as they, but we've a good name in these parts."

"I agree, Mr Yelland," Skye said sweetly. "And neither do we want to lose the name of Killigrew Clay entirely. So what do you suggest?"

The man's face darkened with embarrassment, as she had suspected it would. He was the type to put forward a case, and then fizzle out because his thoughts never got past the first post. Pascall intervened quickly for his client in the small silence that followed.

"May I suggest that we get the initial agreements signed between all parties, and return here in a week's time? That will still give us a few days before the rally, and we'll have had time to choose a name that will satisfy everyone."

Nick nodded, more than ready to end the meeting.

"I agree. The agreement can be signed now, so the official deeds and documents can be drawn up before the new date, when the name of the new company can be inserted. After the rally, the final signatures and official seal will be put on the documents and the two companies will be officially one."

Just like a marriage, Skye thought. But with four partners instead of two.

"Thank God that's over," she said feelingly, when they were finally on their way home. "I couldn't have stood much more of Bourne's arrogance, or Yelland's fawning. As for Theo, well, he really overstepped the mark this time with his scheming."

"I think you made your point clear, and well done for seeing through him. At least you won't have to meet with the rest of them very often once the merger is finalised."

She glanced at him, seeing his set profile.

"You don't blame me for speaking up, do you? It was obvious there was something going on between him and Bourne, and I'm amazed that you hadn't already suspected it."

If he had, things might never have got this far.

"Are you blaming me for not doing my job properly?"

"Of course not! Nick, I didn't mean that—"

"It bloody well sounded like it, and I make no apologies for my language. Your family seems well used to it, anyway."

Skye gasped. "That was unforgiveable, and how dare you compare me with my loutish cousin! Oh, I wish – I wish . . ."

"What? That you'd continued hiding your head in the sand and thinking that Killigrew Clay could go on for ever? Face up to reality, Skye. It's doing little more than limp along at present, and you really had no option unless you wanted to close down like so many other Cornish pits."

"I never wanted that," she muttered. "I just wanted to preserve it as long as possible."

"And that's exactly what you did. Your grandmother would have been proud of you, but now it's time to let go."

She stared ahead as they drove over the moors and past the great silent sky tips that had never looked so calm and glintingly beautiful. No matter what happened, they wouldn't change. They would always be there, reminders of a more colourful age when the entire moorland was alive with the sight and sound of clayfolk, and the outmoded methods of extracting the clay from the earth. Skye remembered the tales of how the clay blocks had to be scraped by those white-bonneted women and left to dry for months in open air linhays before they were taken to St Austell port in huge, horse-drawn clay waggons, long before Ben Killigrew's little rail tracks had been built.

Oh yes, things had moved on since then. Nobody could cling to the past for ever. She had to be less possessive of her Cornish legacy, even though she knew she could never loosen all the ties that bound her to the past. Why should she? She was still part of it. But right now she would be better employed in thinking of a new name for the clayworks, and to start looking forward, not back.

# Fourteen

"You realise it can't be solely your decision, don't you?" Nick asked a few days later, by which time Skye had become totally frustrated trying to coin different titles for the new company, with a pile of screwed-up papers the only result.

"I know it, but I need to have something to offer, and I dread to think what the others might come up with."

How arrogant that sounded, as if she was the only one with any aesthetic ideas. Theirs would probably be far more practical and perhaps that was the answer; something plain and simple, like The China Clay Company. If only it didn't sound so damn boring. No, that definitely wasn't it.

"I've tried twisting the names around, combining the letters and so on, and nothing seems to work. KBY Holdings was one of them, but it seems too cold and impersonal. The best thing I've come up with is Bokilly Holdings. I'm sure Theo will object because our name doesn't come first, but Killboy as an alternative is hardly going to attract customers, is it?"

Nick agreed. "Actually, Bokilly Holdings has a certain ring to it. You know how to handle Theo, and if you're tactful enough he'll end up believing he thought of it first, the way he did with White Rivers."

"Well, I could try," she said. "I was thinking of going to Truro this afternoon, anyway. I want to take the box of photographs to show David and outline a few of my article ideas. I'll call in at Theo's on the way back."

In fact, the more she thought about it, the more Bokilly Holdings had a definite Cornish flavour and fluency about it, as if it had been established for ever. All she had to do was convince Theo of it so they could present a united front at the next meeting before the final documents were signed and sealed.

But first, she was meeting David at the *Informer* offices and outlining her plans for the articles. She felt a real lift to her spirits as she drove her car towards Truro, and blessed Lily for urging her to do this. She had needed something positive to do after Celia left for America. Though by the sound of her enthusiastic phone calls and letters, Celia was no longer pining, Skye thought thankfully. Either that, or she was a pretty good actress.

At that moment, in the early morning sunshine, Celia was halfway up a ladder in the apple orchards of New Jersey, laughing down at the boy who was holding it steady.

"If you make this ladder wobble once more, I swear I'll kill you, Jarvis Stone," she giggled, feeling more light-hearted than she had in months.

"I couldn't rightly hear you, ma'am," the boy said, laughing back. "Was that kill or kiss?"

Celia clung on to the branch of the tree where the gleaming red apples exuded such a heavenly scent, and spoke to him in mock severity.

"You know very well what it was, and I'll have your mom and poppa on my tail if I don't do what I'm being paid for, so just hold this ladder still and let me get on with my work."

"Only if you promise to sit by me at supper this evening," he persisted. "You talk real pretty, and I can't always hear you with the rest of 'em jabbering."

"All right, I promise." Celia grinned.

She wouldn't have said she talked real pretty, but her accent was very different from these delightful American folk who had taken her in so readily. She hadn't thought she had an accent at all until it had been pointed out to her. She sometimes cashed in on it now to their delicious amusement.

She hadn't known what to do or what to expect when she had taken the bus from New York to the small New Jersey town of Mainstown. She had visited the magazine offices where Skye used to work many years ago, and been given a warm welcome. But apart from one or two older members, the staff there had changed, and once the information about her mother and family had been exhausted, Celia felt it was time to move on.

She had followed the detailed directions to the house called the Appletrees where her mother was born, and which was appropriately enough now a thriving fruit farm.

The farm was advertising a room for rent in exchange for fruit-picking duties, and in taking it on she had discovered the large, warm-hearted Stone family, whose sixteen-year-old son Jarvis had already declared himself madly in love with her, and had to be kept firmly in his place.

"Shoo, Jarvis, or I won't get this basket filled before supper."

She watched him go, dragging the twisted foot that set him apart from his younger brothers and sisters, but did nothing to stop his puppy-like exuberance. He was a sweetie, thought Celia, then concentrated on filling her basket ready for market in the morning. She had never been happier, except for one time that she refused to think about.

Even the growing anxiety over events in England and Europe couldn't dim her spirits these days. The Stone family's easy-going philosophy was to ignore things they couldn't see and couldn't help, and it was a philosophy that was spilling over onto Celia. Whatever upheavals were beginning to erupt on the other side of the Atlantic, they were all far away, and couldn't touch them here. This was Utopia, and sometimes she thought blissfully that she would stay here for ever.

Skye sat opposite David Kingsley in his office and waited while he studied the family photographs she had brought, together with the outline of her article.

She had worked hard on it, realising more and more how much she needed this project – and David's approval. So it came as a huge shock when he said, "In principle I like the idea very much, and I don't doubt your ability to do it justice."

"But?" she said, her heart jumping as he paused. "I know that tone of voice, David, and I know when I'm about to be fobbed off!"

"Not at all. Now don't go all sniffy on me, Skye. If you're completely set on working up a series of articles then I'll be more than happy to go ahead and publish them. You have a lifetime of memories here, but I'm wondering if this is the right outlet for it after all. It deserves so much more."

She forestalled him. "I know what you're about to suggest, David. I once thought about writing a work of fiction based on my grandmother and the diaries she left me. But I couldn't do it, and what's more I don't want to do it, so don't even think about trying to persuade me."

"I wasn't thinking about fiction. Hell's bells, Skye, you people are all the same, aren't you? Tremayne or Pengelly, you all go off half-cocked at a second's notice without listening to what anybody else has to say."

"I'm sorry," she said with a rueful laugh. "You're quite right, of course. So I'm listening."

"I wasn't about to suggest that you wrote a novel." He paused again. "Incidentally, do you still have those diaries?"

"I do not," she said crisply. "I burned them all."

"Pity. Well, as I was saying, you know as well as I do that a series of articles in a newspaper will only end up as firelighters. They're not kept, Skye, the way a bound book is. Now that more folk are coming to Cornwall they'll be looking for souvenirs to take home. The proof of that is already happening in the pottery shop, so why not offer them a small booklet about an industry that is at the very heart of Cornwall, written by a member of an old-established china-clay family? What do you say?"

"A booklet?" she said sceptically. "Who do you think would buy such a thing? And where would it be sold?"

"Tourists would buy it, Skye. And where better to sell it than in the White Rivers shop right here, alongside your pottery? Lily could make a big feature of it."

"Do you really think so?"

"Darling, I know so," David said. "As for the publishing and printing side, my contacts can see to that. All you have to do is produce the copy and the photographs. And of course you can have access to our archive material any time you feel like going into the office dungeons for a few hours. I really think you could be on to a real winner, Skye."

"I don't want to make a career out of this, David," she said faintly, as his voice rose with enthusiasm.

"You don't have to. One booklet isn't going to make your fortune, either. But I'll guarantee that years from now, tourists will still be buying it. Cash in on what upcountry folk see as the quaintness of the place and its industries. If you don't, somebody else will. Think about it, Skye. Who knows the history of the Killigrews and Tremaynes better than you do – and who will handle it more sensitively?"

"All right, you've made your point, and I promise I'll think about it," she said quickly, not ready to be bamboozled into making an instant decision.

"Good. Then how about taking a certain young man out for some afternoon tea, since I know he's itching to know what brings you here," he said with a smile.

"How is he doing?" Skye asked, glad to get her thoughts round something else for the moment.

David laughed broadly.

"You've got a budding reporter in the making in young Oliver," he said, "and I'm no idle flatterer when it comes to business. He's very keen, although I'm sure he thinks the jobs I'm giving him are a bit tame for his restless nature."

"What's that supposed to mean?"

"Oh, just that I think he'd prefer to be out in the middle of a war zone where's there's real action and plenty of blood and gore. It beats reporting the cosy doings at local village fêtes and domestic squabbles."

"Don't even think about it," Skye said with a shudder. "He's far too young for any of that nonsense, thank goodness."

But he wouldn't always be fifteen.

She caught up with Olly in the print room, and offered to buy him some tea and fruit buns in a local tea room. She hadn't seen him for a week or two since he'd been at Lily's, and already he seemed different. He had grown taller and as he leaned over the press he already seemed a young man, Skye thought with a shock. She was losing them all, even Olly.

But at her offer of tea and fruit buns he washed his hands quickly, and rolled down his sleeves, always ready to be taken out and treated. He hadn't changed that much then.

"So how do you like being a working man?" she asked him lightly, once he had wolfed down two buns in record time.

"It's spiffing, Mother, although it can be pretty dull at times," he said, echoing David's words. "But maybe that will all change if I'm allowed to go with him to the clayworkers' rally. I'm looking forward to that."

"For pity's sake, how do you know about it already?"

"Uncle Theo called in to the office and said we should be there in case of fireworks." He looked at her uneasily. "He wasn't speaking out of turn, was he? It would need to be reported in the newspaper, anyway."

Skye sighed. Of course it would need to be reported. The merger and change of name of an important industry was newsworthy. She knew that. It was just that so far the news hadn't become public property. Until it did, she could believe that everything was going on as usual.

"In fact, I was wondering if you would give me an exclusive interview, Mother," Olly went on, pushing his luck. "Then I might even persuade David to give me a byline."

She looked at his young, hopeful face and had to laugh, even though the laughter was tinged with a hint of anxiety. Oh yes, the ambition was already there, staring her in the face, and how far it might take him, only time would tell. Time, and the growing threat of Adolph Hitler's European domination.

"What's so funny about that?" Olly said, full of resentment. "I have to start somewhere, don't I?"

She pressed his arm. "Of course you do, honey, and of course I'll give you your interview when the time comes. You'll be the only one to get an exclusive, and you can do something for me in return. When you've got nothing else to do, you can sort out a pile of old newspapers in the archives ready for me to come in and study. There's no hurry, the merger is the most important thing at present."

She explained why she was interested in archive material, and saw how his interest was caught by her proposed project. How odd, she thought, as she finally left him and drove to Killigrew House where Theo and Betsy lived, that Olly should be the one to follow so closely in her footsteps. There was no reason why he shouldn't have done so, but she simply hadn't expected it, and their shared interest warmed her heart.

She put these thoughts to the back of her mind, as she learned from a whispering Betsy that Theo was in agony with the gout this afternoon, and in a filthy mood.

"He's best left alone, Skye," Betsy advised. "I just thank God that the vicar ain't likely to call, what with his foul language and all."

"I've probably heard it all before," Skye said. "Anyway, I have to see him and it won't wait, so I'll risk it."

210

He was in the drawing room, glaring mutinously at the blank television screen, and didn't even turn around to see who had come into the room.

"Why can't the fat-arsed buggers think of folk who have to be indoors all day and give 'em summat to watch?" he bellowed. "I ain't paid out good money for sitting and watching a snotty square box that don't do nothing."

Skye was about to open her mouth and say something witty that she hoped would make him grimace at least, when he suddenly hurled the nearest vase at the screen, shattering it into a thousand pieces.

"Well, now you've really done it, haven't you?" she said calmly. He swung round in his chair and glared at her as his wife came rushing in.

"What on earth's happened?" Betsy gasped.

"He's let his ridiculous temper get the better of him," Skye answered while he was still gathering breath. "He's acted like the spoilt brat he always was, and this is the result."

Betsy's mouth fell open even more. Few folk ever dared to speak about Theo like that. They might think it, but not even Sebby was so openly scathing unless he was seriously provoked. Theo looked as if he was about to burst every blood vessel in his body. Then they realised that instead of shaking with a seizure, he was roaring with laughter.

"By God, girl, you drive me off my head sometimes, but I probably should have married you. What a hell of a life we'd have had then, sparking off one another—"

"I doubt that very much. I'd almost certainly have killed you by now," Skye snapped, mortified that Betsy should have heard his words. Not that she seemed to care.

"Well, thank God we can get rid of the ugly thing now, and I never want to see another," Betsy said stiffly.

For one ludicrous moment Skye thought she was referring to Theo, then realised with a sense of rising hysteria that she meant the television set.

Theo ignored his wife and stumped across the room, his heavily bandaged foot huge and cumbersome.

"Whatever you've come to see me about, girl, let's get it over," he growled, "while somebody gets this mess cleared up."

"Somebody certainly will," Betsy retorted feelingly. "And

211

then somebody will get the house reorganised to a normal place where folk can sit around and talk to one another, instead of gawping at that one-eyed monstrosity."

Skye hid a smile, admiring the way the old insipid Betsy had come out of her shell and tackled Theo in the only way that worked.

"Since I'm here on business, shall we go to your study?" she asked him, as matter-of-factly as if nothing had happened.

"Theo, I'm really sorry you're in such pain," she said, once they were settled. From his tortured face there was no doubting that it was genuinely excruciating.

"I'll live," he muttered. "A few more noggins of whisky and I'll be in never-never land. So what do you want?"

"To discuss the new name for the company."

"Bloody hell, I can't bother about all that now."

"It's important, Theo. Haven't you given it any thought at all?"

He scowled. "No, I ain't. But we don't want nothing poncey like White Rivers, mind."

"Well, that certainly hasn't done us any harm! But that's not the issue here. I've been trying hard to merge the two company names, since I think we should try to keep as much of them as possible so we don't lose our identity. But whatever I come up with it doesn't seem to work. I mean, what would you say to the Killboy Company?" she asked innocently.

As she expected, he let out a derisive roar of fury.

"I think we'd be the laughing stock of the county wi' such a poncey name, that's what I think, woman!"

"That's what I think too."

His eyes narrowed. "Oh ah. And what little game are you playing now?"

"I'm not playing any game at all. But it hasn't been easy trying to twist the names around. You try it, and see if you have any better ideas."

"It's a waste of my bloody time."

"No, it isn't. We have to have something to present, Theo. I'm damn sure Bourne and Yelland are thinking up something to suit them, and if they have their way it will seem as if Killigrew Clay never existed."

As his bloodshot eyes gleamed she knew she had got his attention at last.

"All right. So what else have you thought up?"

"Nothing really," she said slowly. "Unless – no, that probably wouldn't work."

"What? *What*? Dammit woman, speak up!"

"Well, Killboy is obviously awful. Boykill is just as bad. We might leave a few letters out, but I don't know where. Bykill? I don't think so. Bokill?"

"Bollocks, more like! Try sticking an extra bit at the beginning or the end of it, if you must," Theo said.

"Such as *Bokilly*, I suppose?" She paused, as if considering, then spoke animatedly. "Actually, Theo, I quite like the sound of that, but it needs something more. Bokilly Clay or Bokilly Holdings maybe. Tell me what you think."

He didn't say anything for a couple of minutes, and she knew he was mulling over the name in his mind.

He finally growled at her in his usual fashion. "It's the best so far. I'll go along with that. And what I think is that you've just conned the conman. Now get out of here and leave me to my bed and the bloody whisky bottle."

She went home feeling elated. This had been a good day. The suggestion about the booklet could be put aside for now, but it would eventually give her many hours of pleasure after the undoubted trauma of signing half her life away was done. Melodramatic maybe, but she knew she would never have the same affinity for Bokilly Holdings as for Killigrew Clay. But times were changing, and she had to change with them.

She had brought back the box of photographs with her, along with her article outline, and she put them away until the time was more convenient for her to think about them. The stability of the business was the most important thing now, and when it came to the new name, Theo's gout had probably proved more of a help to her than a hindrance, she thought with a smile.

Though, regaling Nick that evening with the nonsensical result of her cousin's temper, it made her realise just how unpredictable he could be.

"I should probably have got his agreement to the proposed name in writing," she said, remembering it too late. "But he more or less believes he had the final say on it, so let's keep our fingers crossed."

"Then the sooner we get the next meeting over and everything agreed between all parties, the better. The rally has been fixed for the tenth of September."

"We should let David Kingsley know it then, since he'll want to cover it for the *Informer*. And I had better warn you that Olly wants me to give him an exclusive interview—"

"That child?" Nick said sceptically. "I suggest you'd better write it yourself unless you want it to sound like a schoolboy essay."

She reacted at once. "Give him some credit, Nick. He needs to do this and I'm not going to alter one word of it – once I've checked that he doesn't distort anything I say. Not that I think he will for one minute," she added hastily. "And he's not a child any longer, either."

"If you say so."

But by the following week when the new partners were due to meet again in Bodmin, Theo was confined to bed with a serious flare-up in his foot and leg that the doctor pronounced as phlebitis. Betsy informed Skye on the telephone with an unsympathetic note of I-told-you-so in her voice.

"He's not allowed to put his foot to the ground, and if he don't rest it he's in danger of losing his foot to the surgeon's knife. So that's put the wind up him, I can tell you, but he's driving me demented with his constant whining and demands for attention. I'm to tell you that Seb will be bringing you a signed note confirming your chosen name for the new company. He says 'tis secret until 'tis all agreed."

"So it is," Skye said, sure that by now Theo was quite convinced he'd thought of it himself. "Please tell him I'm sorry he's ill, but I'll let you know what's decided the minute I get back from Bodmin."

She couldn't help a sneaking feeling of relief. Everything always proceeded more smoothly when Theo wasn't around. She was sorry for him, though. Phlebitis could be very painful, as she knew from tending the soldiers in the field hospitals who had suffered from it in the Great War. Even worse, she had witnessed the physical and mental effects of gangrene and amputations . . . she shuddered, wishing such memories hadn't entered her mind.

She tried not to think of them as she and Nick drove to

Bodmin, as this was to be a momentous day. She wondered what name the Bourne and Yelland partners would produce and how many arguments there would be on the choice of a new company name.

In the end it was all a damp squib.

"My clients have thought of several names, but none that meet with any enthusiasm," Mr Pascall said tetchily. "So we await your suggestions in the matter."

"Then perhaps you will consider Bokilly Holdings," Nick said. "It is an amalgamation of the original names and has a substantial authority about it."

The look of relief on the other three faces told Skye that there had probably been considerable harassment between them all during this past week, and that they were simply thankful that someone else had taken the initiative. It was quickly apparent that the end result suited them all.

"Thank heavens for that," Skye said later, when they were on their way back to Truro to get Theo's signature on the documents. "Though it all feels a bit like an anti-climax, Nick. I was expecting fireworks and we didn't get any."

"That's because your cousin wasn't there. Even if it was his idea – or he thinks it was – he'd still have made some kind of fuss."

It was sad too, she thought. Such a huge decision to make, and it all been settled in a matter of minutes. And yes, crazy though it was, damn it, she had missed Theo's fireworks!

Incapacity certainly hadn't softened his temper. He was as irascible as Betsy had said, sitting up in bed with a huge wooden cradle over his leg beneath the bedclothes to keep any pressure off his painful limb.

"So how did it go?" he growled. "Did the buggers put up much of a fight?"

Skye saw him wince for a moment as he eased himself up higher in the bed, and thought how old he looked. Pain did that, of course, and he was no longer a young man. He was sixty-one years old, and looked every day of it right now.

"They agreed to Bokilly Holdings without any arguments, Theo," she told him. "In fact, they hadn't even been able to think up a title of their own."

215

"Typical," he sneered. "I always knew we were dealing with dullards when it came to using a bit of brain power."

Skye mentally counted to ten. He really was insufferable, and rarely gave anyone else any credit but himself. Zacharius Bourne was an intelligent and astute businessman, regardless of any underhand dealings. She didn't know Gideon Yelland that well, but he had certainly not struck her as a slouch. She was about to defend them, but Nick forestalled her with a sharp glance. She read it correctly. Once they got into any kind of arguments here, Theo was just as likely to refuse to sign the title document until he'd given it more thought.

The news had come through only that week that both the Vogl and Kauffmann firms had slimmed down their orders for raw china clay, so they couldn't afford to let anything go wrong now. If they must look for more home orders than exports, they needed this merger more than ever before. As yet the German orders were only slightly less than the previous ones, but with the uncertain European situation it could be the start of a more general slide.

"The other partners have signed the title document, Theo," Nick said crisply. "It only needs your signature."

He held out the document and the pen, and Skye saw her cousin give a sly smile.

"Gives me the final say, don't it, cuz?" he said. "If I choose to change my mind on this."

"I hardly think you'd be so foolish," she said. "After all, you've wanted this merger all along, and you made the final choice on the name, so I can't think why you would go back on your own triumph."

She was giving in, but she just wanted to get out of here, with its cloying sick-room smells and the overwhelming sense of betrayal that could still unexpectedlly stab her.

He signed quickly, and thrust the document back at Nick.

"Now leave me be to get some rest," he snarled. "I need to be fit for the rally, and I ain't planning to be wheeled there in a bloody bath chair."

They left him and declined Betsy's offer of tea. It was done, and it gave Skye no sense of satisfaction at all.

"I feel terrible," she said, once they reached the car. "Right until this moment, it never seemed quite real, but now it is and there's no turning back. You know damn well the clayworkers won't oppose anything with the bonuses Theo and Bourne are dangling in front of them. The rally will be no more than a farce and I don't want to be there."

"You have to be there, Skye. You have to show them that this was the only way Killigrew Clay could progress. It's part of something bigger and better now."

"Is it?" she said bitterly. "Oh, I know you're right from a business point of view. But I can't separate my head from my heart, and my heart still tells me it's wrong, and that something very precious has gone for good."

"That's why you're going to write about it," he said calmly. "So that what it was will never be forgotten."

He started up the car while she stared unseeingly ahead. He was so right, and she had the means and the skill to do something that no one else could do. So that something precious would never be forgotten.

"I'm so glad I've got you," she said thickly.

"Well, thank you, ma'am," he said, in a pseudo-Amercan voice to echo her own. "I'm glad I've got you too."

Her prophecy about the rally was proved correct. Where in times past, hundreds of clayworkers had gathered in belligerent fighting mood, or marched to the meeting-house in St Austell to argue their rights, this time it was a reasonably orderly mob who stood shuffling their feet in the hot sunshine of a September morning.

Each of the partners was to give the clayworkers their spiel, assuring them that they had their best interests at heart, and that this merger would benefit everyone. Zacharius Bourne was eloquent enough, but his partner declined at the last minute owing to a throat infection that rendered his voice hoarse and useless.

"More like a convenient way o' not riling the workers," Theo jeered. "None of 'em has much faith in the likes of that shirt-lifter."

Skye felt her face flame. Whatever Theo thought about Gideon Yelland, and she had begun to have similar suspicions, it was best kept to himself.

"It's a good thing you and I are seen to be so normal then, isn't it?" she hissed at him under cover of a rousing cheer as the bonuses were outlined. "If normal is the right word for a pig of a man," she added beneath her breath.

But she had to admit that he gave his speech his roaring best, interspersed with blasphemies that were undoubtedly his style, and one that the men knew and accepted. Then it was her turn, and she had barely begun when it was clear there was going to be some organised heckling.

Nick shouted back at them to give her a chance, but she stopped him with a glare and stood firm on the small platform that had been erected for the speakers.

"I thought you were all intelligent men with the gumption to know that what's being done is in your best interests, but if you aren't prepared to listen to me, then I suggest you all go back to work while you've still got a job to go to," she snapped.

"Who d'you think you are, missus, all done up in your fancy clobber and telling we what to do?" a few voices jeered.

"She ain't Morwen Tremayne, that's for certain sure," yelled another. From the look of his grizzled face he must have been near eighty years old, Skye thought, and still devoted to the clay and the old ways. It gave her a lead.

"No, I'm not Morwen Tremayne, nor ever could be," she said in a clear voice. "Some of you knew her, and those who didn't, knew what she stood for. I'm her granddaughter, and from the moment I met her, what I wanted most in the world was to be like her. I've done everything in my power to uphold her views and ideals and to preserve Killigrew Clay in the way my family controlled it."

"You should have thought o' that before selling out." A lone voice continued to yell amid more subdued mutterings.

"*Sir*," Skye said passionately, "I assure you it's the saddest thing in the world for my cousin and myself to accept that we can no long continue alone, and that Killigrew Clay has to be merged with another company. But many of you here know the integrity of Bourne and Yelland and that none of this has been considered lightly. Together we can grow stronger."

"So what's this new company to be called?" the grizzled one shouted. "You'm taking our clayworks, and the rumours say you'm taking our name too, and I ain't working for no Bourne and Yelland fancies."

"Leave it, Theo," she said, as he began to add his roars to the sudden outburst. "We all agreed that this was my time."

She was shaking inside. The new title, that had sounded so grand and perfect, was already stamped and registered, but these people had to be pleased. They had been a law unto themselves many times in the past, and could be now, if they chose to go on strike. And with the autumn despatches imminent, however much the orders were depleted, it was a risk she couldn't afford to take.

She held up her hand for silence, and spoke with as much dignity as she could.

"In any merger, just as in any marriage, both sides have their opinions, and the new title has been thought out carefully and agreed by all of us. We will no longer be Killigrew Clay –" she had to pause for opposing shouts and cheers – "but neither will we be Bourne and Yelland Holdings. Instead we have merged the names of the companies together and come up with a sensible solution. The new company will be known as Bokilly Holdings."

There was silence for a moment and then some slow handclapping from the back of the crowd was taken up by the rest. Like bloody sheep, Theo muttered. But knowing that David Kingsley and Olly were here, writing their reports for the *Informer*, Skye wasted no time on Theo's sneering asides.

It had been left to her to do this, and she had given up wondering if it had been a good idea. She just wanted to get the rally over and get back home. When the noise finally died down, she continued.

"As for working conditions, nothing will change. You all know your duties under your pit captains, and the central distribution of the china clay will be an administrative matter. When we have your ayes on it, you will separate into your old company groups and, as an act of goodwill, the bonuses will be paid out personally and immediately to each of you by Mr Bourne and Mr Yelland and by Mr Tremayne and myself."

"That's the blackmail, be it, missus?" a final heckler bawled out. "Once we've got our bonuses to sweeten the pill, there's no going back on it."

She gave him a wide smile, recognising him at once.

"That's about right, Ned Forest. I've learned a few of Morwen

Tremayne's tricks in my time, and I still don't know which of us is getting the better of the other. Do you?"

There was a ripple of laughter at this and the heckler was silenced. But once they had given their ayes on it, the lines were organised and they began to separate into two factions and shuffled forward to receive their bonuses, overseen by the two lawyers.

"By God, with all this money jingling in their pockets there'll be some business for the local kiddleywinks tonight," Theo muttered, handing out the packets into the grasping hands, and still begrudging the fact that he was willingly parting with his money.

"My Lord, I haven't heard that word in years," Skye said to him, as one and another clayworker touched his forehead to her by way of acknowledging their pay packets.

"They'm all called inns and hostelries now," Theo scowled. "But they still serve the same gut-rotting ale and clog the lungs wi' foul-smelling smoke."

But the thought of it filled his senses with an unexpected sense of nostalgia, and he knew he bloody well intended being in one of them tonight, whatever poncey name they gave the places now. He'd done his duty to Betsy for a good few years now, and he was feeling more like his randy old self since his medication had done its stuff.

Oh, yes, a few roisterous jars at a kiddleywink and a trip down memory lane – if that was all he could manage – at Miss Kitty's bawdy house, was definitely on the agenda for tonight. Even if it killed him.

# Fifteen

The Pengelly girls read their mother's latest letters with varying emotions. Far away in New Jersey, sitting in the shade of an apple tree in the fruit farm where she was now firmly ensconced, Celia gazed into the distance and let the pages fall from her hands on to the grass.

"Bad news?" a voice beside her said, and as Jarvis's shadow passed between her and the sun, Celia smiled quickly.

"No, at least I don't think so. Not for me, anyway, and my mother seems quite positive about it."

"So are you going to tell me about it, or do I have to guess?" he asked encouragingly.

She laughed, gathering up the pages and stuffing them back into the envelope.

"It's just a merger between two china-clay companies in Cornwall that you wouldn't even have heard about, if I hadn't told you about my family connections. It's like the end of an era, of course, and I know I should feel sad, but somehow I don't. Life has to move on, doesn't it?"

"And there, fellow students, class of '38, speaks the voice of the nation," he said solemnly.

"Oh, very noble! Are you aiming to be the head of your college debating society or what?" she teased.

"Not really. I'd rather have a certain person agree to wear my college pin," he said, so coolly Celia thought she had misheard him for a minute.

And then she knew she hadn't.

"Jarvis, for pity's sake, you'll have your mom and poppa on my back for cradle-snatching," she said, scrambling to her feet. She gathered up her letter and the newspaper reports of the rally and the newly formed Bokilly Holdings. She was amazed at how astute her little brother had been in his exclusive interview with

221

their mother. But as the American boy's face flushed darkly, she realised she had humiliated him, and put her hand on his arm.

"I'm sorry. You know I didn't mean that. It's just that – well, you know how fond of you I am, of *all* of you," she emphasised. "But you're only just starting your college education—"

"And I'm lame," he said bluntly.

She stared at him, genuinely startled. "Do you think that would ever be an issue for someone who loved you, Jarvis?"

"Probably," he said. He turned away from her, his shoulders stiff, his frustration and anger making his limp more pronounced as he walked away.

She ached for him. He was more vulnerable than anyone might suppose, despite his brash manner. It was obvious that he had taken a real shine to her. Maybe it was time she moved on, too . . . except that she didn't want to. She loved it here. Anyway, Jarvis would be starting the new semester at college soon, so he wouldn't be a problem.

There were hints of a long-term position here for Celia. As well as helping with the various fruit harvests, she would be a child-minder-cum-book-keeper, and try to straighten out the chaotic accounts Poppa Stone returned to the IRS.

They had such a warm and relaxed way of life. Working with the younger ones, and as good as being a general dogsbody to the admittedly slapdash Momma Stone, would hardly be stretching her mind as the prestigious post in Berlin had done. But since all that was no longer part of her life, she was definitely tempted.

Besides, she thought, breathing in the sweet-scented grass of the orchard, what did she have to go back to Cornwall for? She would miss her mother, she still did, but she was too old for any of that homesick nonsense now. Her stepfather would definitely disapprove of any long-term arrangement here, of course, and would point out the wasted years at a Swiss finishing school.

Too bad, Celia thought defiantly. It was her life – and you had to be tough to survive these days. And anyway, what about Wenna's wasted academy years, which had led her to singing in a London nightclub!

Wenna burst into tears the minute she read her mother's letter. Fanny looked at her in dismay.

"Gawd Almighty, what's wrong, duck? Your Ma's not been taken ill, has she?"

"No," Wenna said, as soon as she could speak. "I'm being silly, that's all. I mean, I knew it was coming, but now it's settled, and it just seems so sad and final, that's all."

Fanny smiled faintly. She'd heard enough about the proposed merger of the clay companies to guess immediately what Wenna was getting at. Privately she thought it just made good business sense. She put her arms around the girl.

"You're just too soft-hearted fer yer own good, my duck. It's this clay-company stuff, I s'pose?"

Wenna nodded, her face full of misery. "Mom sounds so brave, and there's a bit in the letter where she tries to make me laugh about Uncle Theo smashing up his television set."

"Oh, my good Gawd!" Fanny said, staring. "You folk never do things by halves, do yer?"

"But I know she's really sad about it all," Wenna went on passionately. "Killigrew Clay was – well, I wouldn't go so far as to say it was in her soul like it was in my great-grandmother's – but it was so much a part of her life."

"Now you just listen to me," Fanny said briskly. "So these two companies have become one, and I'll refrain from makin' any funny-cum-naughty remarks about that, 'cos I can see yer ain't in the mood. But bleedin' 'ell, darlin', nobody's *died*, have they?"

As she paused for breath, Wenna felt her face flame with embarrassment.

"Oh, Fanny, I wasn't thinking. Poor Georgie—"

"I wasn't thinking about that neither, so stop yer frettin'. All I meant was, when it comes down to it, the most important thing in this world is having yer 'ealth and strength, and yer mother's got that in plenty. I bet by now she's thinkin' of other things, and she won't let any of this get her down for long. So don't you, neither. The last thing she'll want is a sob letter from you or a tearful phone call, so you just keep your pecker up, d'yer hear?"

She got a watery smile in return. "I know you're right, Fanny. But I've got to say something, just so she doesn't think that I don't care."

Fanny hugged her, her eyes suddenly moist. If she'd ever wanted a kid, she thought, she'd have wanted one exactly like this one.

223

"She knows you care, lovey."

Wenna wriggled free and continued perusing the letter with only the occasional sniff now. "She also says she might be doing some writing again. Proper writing this time – a sort of historical booklet."

"Fancy that now," Fanny said, never having had any inclination to do anything that sounded so dull, but readily admitting that Skye had quite a brainbox on her shoulders. Writing about anything, and especially about boring historical stuff, was well outside Fanny's limitations, but somebody had to do it, she supposed cheerfully.

"Anyway, Mom says the new company will do well, so I'm sure she means it. She's a great survivor," Wenna added proudly. "All our family were, wouldn't you say so, Fanny?"

"Course they were," Fanny said, not knowing the half of it, but thankful that Wenna was recovering fast.

For a minute she'd been afraid she would want to rush back to Cornwall and vegetate, when already there were big plans afoot to launch her in a Saturday spot in the new year, when Gloria del Mar would be starting rehearsals for a coveted role in a Broadway musical. Now might just be the right time to push ahead with the plans for Wenna, to cheer her up. It would cheer Georgie up too, she thought hopefully, knowing how his dark depressions over his parents came and went.

Lately they had got more frequent, and decidedly darker, she thought anxiously. He kept predicting that things could only get worse, that they had only seen the tip of the iceberg yet. She always hated it when he talked like that, as if he carried the weight of the world on his thin shoulders.

In November, Georgie Rosenbloom had another letter from an old friend that he couldn't bear to show even to his wife. The agony of what was happening in Germany was starting to affect him deeply, but the most recent news of what was virtually a massacre burned into his very soul.

According to Jackie Cohen, there had been an organised reign of terror carried out throughout the country; Jewish-owned shops had been looted, and innocent Jewish citizens beaten senseless. Thousands of people had died in one night. The reality

224

of it was only just dawning on many of his countryfolk who were fleeing Germany in panic.

"I won't leave," the letter went on. "This is my home. Here I was born and here I will die, old friend, just as your mother and father did. All I will say is, pray for me, and for our brothers and sisters. I will write again when I can."

Georgie brooded over the letter continually, until the day Fanny discovered him silently weeping and she demanded to know what was wrong. Everything else faded out of existence as she held him in her arms. Whatever she had been in the past she was completely devoted to her Georgie, whose dry wit had sadly deserted him in recent times. It broke her heart to see him suffer like this.

Once she had got the gist of it, she was outraged.

"We must bring Jackie here to safety, and any others who want to come with him," she said at once.

He shook his head. "He won't do it. You've read the letter. He's a proud man and an old one. Why should he leave? The old ones are stubborn, but it's the children I'm sorry for. They're the innocent ones caught up in this evil. There's nothing we can do for them."

He was steeped in pessimism, and there was nothing she could say to comfort him. He spent long hours at the synagogue and she let him go, knowing it gave him strength, but privately thinking it did no good at all. Fanny admitted that her religious faith began and ended with what people could do for one another, not in some mumbo-jumbo candle-lighting rigmarole, or whatever it was they did.

The newspapers were soon full of the latest outrage, and the government was starting to take action, she reported to him. Many parts of the empire were offering to take in refugees, including Britain, the way it always had.

"I daresay," Georgie said, with a rare bitterness. "But your pompous Mr Chamberlain also says there's a limit to how many refugees Britain can accept."

"I s'pose there is. But he ain't my Mr Chamberlain," Fanny said vigorously. "I never voted for 'im."

"You never voted for anyone," Georgie reminded her.

She looked at him anxiously. If ever he needed a boost, it was now, and she knew just the way to give him one. She smothered the smile she felt coming on, knowing how she would have put a double meaning on her words on another day – another age, it seemed now.

"Wenna's going home to Cornwall for Christmas. I think we should go too. You know the invitation is always open to us, and it will take us out of ourselves."

"It won't change anything."

"It won't change anything by staying here, neither. Bleedin' 'ell, Georgie, think of something else for a while, can't yer? Think of *me*."

He looked at her in surprise, as if only just realising she was there at all, but the tortured look left his eyes for a second to be replaced by something else.

"There's nothing wrong, is there? If I thought I was losing you too—"

"No, there's nothing wrong," she scowled, almost wishing that there was for a minute, so he'd have something else to worry about. That was a wicked thing to think, because at least they both had their health and that counted for a hell of a lot in this world. "So shall I sort it out with Skye that we all go down there for Christmas?" she persisted. "She'll be glad of the extra company now Celia's gone to America."

"I doubt that she'll care if we're there or not, but do what you like," he said listlessly. "It's all the same to me where we are, since I won't be celebrating anything."

"Well, yer not going to put a bleedin' damper on things, neither," she snapped. "So yer can get that into yer head right away, my son."

"Yes, Mamma," he said, with the first ghost of a smile she'd seen on his face in weeks. But the smile was more haunted than Fanny realised.

Skye read the front-page features in the London newspapers as well as the *Informer* with growing horror. The headlines were huge and black, underlining the seriousness of the whole situation. With practised ease, she skimmed every article, picking out the essential facts. The tension grew with every day that passed and following Hitler's march into Czechoslovakia, it seemed obvious that his fanatical goal was to conquer Europe, if not the world. To do what he was doing to an entire race of people, was to fill every decent person with shame and outrage.

The small matter of their own European markets shrinking for both china clay and White Rivers pottery, seemed petty in the extreme now, compared with the suffering that was being endured elsewhere. It looked as though nothing was going to stop it.

"I've heard from Wenna," she told Nick one evening, "and she says Fanny and Georgie want to come here with her for Christmas. They'll be closing the Flamingo Club for a couple of weeks apparently, and Wenna says she'll have some exciting news to tell us about that. You don't have any objection to them all coming here, do you?"

Her eyes dared him to do so, and he shrugged, saying he could always keep himself occupied if Fanny's coarseness and Georgie's laboured humour all got too much for him. But then he relented, seeing the indignation on her face.

"Of course I don't mind. The poor devil's had enough to put up with lately, anyway. This house is big enough for an army, and it may be the last Christmas of its kind that we'll see for a while, so let's enjoy it while we can."

Skye wouldn't comment, knowing exactly what he meant, and refusing to put it into words.

"I'll call Fanny this evening, and tell her we'd love to see them," she said.

But before she could do so, Fanny called her. It wasn't a long call, she just stated the facts in a strange, calm voice that didn't sound like Fanny's voice at all, then she said that she had to go away and see to things.

Wenna came on the line, and the mood was totally different.

"Oh Mom, it was terrible," Wenna wept hysterically. "One minute everything was fine, and then – and then – oh, I don't know how to say it—"

"Just slow down, honey. Take a deep breath and tell me exactly what happened," Skye said.

Wenna gave a huge gulp. "We were having dinner, and Georgie wasn't eating a thing. He just sat staring at his plate, and Fanny was scolding him, you know the way she does. Then suddenly Georgie got up from the table and said there was something he had to do, and we were to get on with our dinner and not to wait for him."

"And?" Skye prompted.

"So we did. Got on with our dinner, I mean, which just seems so awful now, but we didn't know, did we? How *could* we have known?"

"Then what happened?" Skye asked sharply.

"Well, we didn't have to open the club as it was Sunday, and when he didn't come back Fanny got the hump as she calls it, and said we should go to bed. So we did, and in the middle of the night there was a loud hammering on the door that woke us both up. I heard Fanny go downstairs to answer it, yelling to Georgie that for two pins she'd make him stand outside all night if he'd forgotten his key. A few minutes later I heard her screaming."

Wenna found herself reciting the story parrot-fashion, as if to hold the horror of it all at bay.

"I ran down to see what was happening, and two policemen were holding her up. One of them told me to fetch her some brandy. Then they told me that Georgie had walked calmly along Westminster Bridge, climbed onto the parapet and jumped. If a passer-by hadn't seen it and reported it, they might not have found him for days. His wallet was still in his pocket, which was how they identified him."

"Dear God," Skye said, horrified, visualising it all too well. "That poor sweet man! His state of mind must have been in turmoil for him to do such a thing."

"I know. And now Fanny's blaming herself for not seeing it coming. But how could she? Georgie kept everything so much to himself these last months. And I – I just don't know what to say to her any more."

Skye heard the bewilderment and grief in her young voice, and knew at once what she had to do.

"I'll be with you in a day or two, darling, just as soon as I can arrange it, and I won't leave until you're both ready to come back to Cornwall with me."

Cornwall. Where she had once believed in her naivety that everything could be solved, and all ills could be healed.

As she thought it, Skye realised how foolish and infantile that had been. Nothing could heal the pain that Fanny was going through now, except time. And pathetic though the platitude sounded to her, Skye knew it was true.

\*     \*     \*

"You're going to London?" Nick asked.

"I have to. Fanny needs me, and so does Wenna. Once the funeral's over I'll bring them both back here as soon as possible. They were coming for Christmas, anyway."

"A bright Christmas it's going to be, isn't it?"

"What would you have me do then – leave them to spend a miserable time alone in that flat above the empty club? I thought you had more compassion than that," she said angrily. "Fanny must be in a terrible state, and this has obviously hit Wenna hard. She was so very fond of Georgie."

"I'm sorry, darling," he said, contrite at once. "You're right, and they must come down here as soon as possible."

"What I also have to do is write to Celia," she said uneasily, her thoughts leaping ahead. "We all know what demons drove Georgie to this, and I wonder if it will affect any remaining feelings she has for Stefan von Gruber."

"Why on earth should it? You can't stamp all Germans in the same mould as that madman, Hitler. You of all people know that. Herr Vogl would never have been a party to such evil doings, and nor would any other sane person going about his daily business."

"I know. But I can't help being thankful that nothing more came of the romance between Celia and Stefan. What would have become of them if they had married and their countries were heading for war – as you keep reminding me they are?"

She shivered as the enormity of it filled her mind, blocking out for a moment the horror of what had happened to Georgie Rosenbloom. But their fates were all linked together, and in those moments she found it hard to separate the one from the other.

"I'm sure Celia's glad she's well out of it," Nick reassured her. "Now, I'll find out when there's a suitable train for you, and I suggest you get some sleep, darling."

But she insisted on going into her study and writing to Celia first. She couldn't put it off. How could she ever sleep, when once her head touched the pillow she knew it would be filled with images she didn't want, but couldn't avoid. Images of Georgie jumping off Westminster Bridge and sinking into the sinister dark water of the Thames and giving no resistance while he was sucked under and drowned.

Her forehead was beaded with sweat as other, unwanted,

images crowded into her mind. Were her family and everyone they touched cursed with this same awful self-destructive urge? She remembered how Granny Morwen's friend Celia had drowned herself in a milky clay pool all those years ago. How Theo's father Walter had walked into the sea when everything became too much for him. Now Georgie Rosenbloom. Was there a terrible pattern to all this that none of them could avoid . . .

"Drink this, Skye," ordered Nick. A glass of spirit was thrust into her hand. "You can't take on everyone else's burdens, my love."

"It seems to me that's just what Georgie did," she said, as she swallowed the bitter spirit with a grimace. "And I know it can't be done."

"Then write your letter and come to bed. And maybe later you can write a personal obituary for the *Informer*. People here won't have known Georgie, but they'll know of our connection with him, and it may help them to understand things happening in Germany more personally. It will help you, too."

She didn't speak for a long moment and then she shook her head. "I love you for your understanding, Nick, but I don't think that's a sensible idea. I'm afraid it might just remind people of the time we brought the German youths here to work, and stir things up all over again. We're all involved in this now, whether we like it or not. In our own small backwater way, we're already at war, aren't we?"

The thought of it loomed ahead of her like a spectre. Already, times were changing at a breakneck speed and there was no way it could be stopped, not by ineffectual governments or by personal tragedies. Only a fool could deny it.

Two days later she reached London at the end of a long and wearisome journey, and took a taxi to the Flamingo Club. Wenna fell into her arms and began to cry helplessly.

"I'm so glad to see you, Mom. Fanny's being so odd and working feverishly, and the place is full of strangers."

"What kind of strangers?"

"Policemen and doctors and reporters and accountants and clients from the club, of course, and the new manager."

"What new manager?" Skye said, starting to feel like an echo as her daughter faltered.

230

Wenna sniffed back the tears and linked her arm in her mother's as they went up to the flat with her suitcase.

"The one Fanny called among all the other people she's been calling. It seems tasteless to me, but she keeps saying it's what Georgie would have wanted, that he hadn't built up this club from nothing to see it all fall apart, so she sent for Martin Russell, an agent-manager, who comes here often, and asked him to take over the running of the club in the new year. We shan't re-open until then."

"And you don't think it's right for Fanny to have contacted this Martin Russell so soon?" Skye said, ignoring the rest of it.

"I think it's awful. Why couldn't she have waited? Georgie's not even buried yet and I've even heard her laughing with this other man."

Skye sensed her outrage. Youth had such fixed ideas. She had known Fanny a very long while and knew that laughter could also hide tears and heartbreak.

"Honey, everyone faces grief in their own way, and no single way is the right one. Remember how Adam turned inwards and became almost a recluse after Vera died, and how Lily furiously cleaned her mother's house until no speck of dust would have dared to enter it? If this is Fanny's way, then it's the only way for her, and we have no right to question it. Now then, dry your tears and stop letting your resentment show, while I go and find her."

She left Wenna sitting on the bed and sought out the sitting room where the noise was coming from. Fanny was surrounded by a small group of people, but the moment she saw Skye she turned to her and held out her hands.

"I knew you'd come," she said simply. "Come and have a drink, fer Gawd's sake. You look fair perished."

Only someone who knew her well would have seen the anguish in her eyes and recognised the tremor in her voice. Fanny was suffering all right, thought Skye, but she'd never show it. She was a real trouper and if the show didn't have to go on until the new year, it would bleedin' well go on then, she thought in Fanny's style.

"This is Martin Russell who's takin' over the management of the club," she said next. "I ain't a businesswoman, Skye, so I need somebody I can trust, and me and Martin go back a long way. He'll be handling Wenna's future, too – I should say Penny Wood's, o' course. Me mind plays tricks these days."

Skye wasn't surprised. As the moments passed and the chatter resumed with no mention of Georgie at all, she began to feel as if she was in a kind of charade. Fanny was acting out the part of hostess so well, talking too loudly, making sure everyone had a drink, and putting people at ease. It was more like a social occasion than a pre-wake, and it alarmed Skye. Despite what she had said to Wenna, it wasn't natural. It wasn't right.

It was only when they had all gone and it was just the two of them sitting together on the sofa, that Fanny's shoulders drooped and she looked old for the first time since Skye had known her. Gone was the brashness and the brittle tarty look, and in its place was a broken woman who had just lost her husband and didn't know how to handle it except by surrounding herself with people.

"I know Wenna thinks I'm wicked and that I don't care," she said, pouring herself another drink with shaking hands. "But she don't understand, Skye. It's because I care too much about Georgie that I can't just sit back and weep. I daren't even let myself think too much. I just have to go on. *You* understand, don't yer?"

"You know I do. We went through too much together during the war not to know how grief affects different people."

"And I can't cry in front of 'er, can I? She's too young to know how it feels. And I can't cry in front of anybody else, neither. I ain't cried at all yet, Skye. It's like I was waitin' fer somebody's shoulder. It used to be Georgie's, but now there's nobody."

"Yes there is, Fanny," Skye said softly. "There's me."

She held out her arms, and as she did so, Fanny gave an agonising cry like that of an animal in pain.

It went straight to Skye's heart as Fanny leant heavily against her and cried her heart out. It went on and on, while she poured out all the details of her personal and passionate life with Georgie that Skye didn't need to hear but couldn't avoid.

At one point during the hours of sorrowing, she saw Wenna's frightened face over Fanny's heaving shoulders, as she stood hesitatingly at the door, and she shook her head as she motioned her daughter out of the room. This was Fanny's time, and one that she desperately needed.

\* \* \*

The following day Fanny was nearly as brash as ever. Only her shadowed eyes showed evidence of a night's releasing weeping. Wenna made no more criticisms of her behaviour, and simply put her arms around her.

"I'm sorry. I didn't understand," she whispered. "I'm glad Mom's here."

"So am I, duck," said Fanny crisply. "So when are yer goin' to show her the poster?"

"Oh. I thought after – you know—"

"After we've seen Georgie on 'is way to the sweet bye-and-bye? Nah. He wouldn't want yer to miss out on yer bit of excitement. Go on now."

"What's all this?" Skye asked, when Wenna had gone hurrying to her room.

Fanny smiled faintly. "There's no point in making the poor little bugger suffer on account o' Georgie's passing, is there? She's been dying to let yer know what's happening in the new year, and we was goin' to spill the beans at Christmas, but now seems as good a time as any."

"You're still coming to Cornwall, aren't you, Fanny?" Skye said urgently. "I'm not going back until you agree."

"O' course I am. Me and Georgie are looking forward to it." She stopped abruptly. "Bugger it. I'll have to get out of the habit of speakin' fer two, won't I?"

Wenna came back into the room, relieving Skye of finding a reply that didn't sound trite. She turned to her daughter quickly as she unrolled the poster and held it up.

"My Lord!" Skye exclaimed.

Wenna grinned. "I thought you'd be surprised. There's going to be a bigger one outside the club, and these smaller ones are going to be distributed around the area. This one's a souvenir for you. Are you impressed?"

Skye scanned the words surrounding the photograph of her daughter – a sensuous, yet still tasteful photograph, showing the glowing sapphire eyes to best advantage, the mouth half-smiling, and the dark hair curling provocatively around her heart-shaped face.

"Celebrate the New Year of 1939," she read, "with the opening Saturday evening debut of the beautiful Cornish songbird, MISS PENNY WOOD."

"My Lord," Skye said again, as if they were the only words she knew.

Fanny chuckled. "Are yer praying, or just thanking the Almighty fer giving yer such a luscious daughter?"

"Both," Skye said at once.

"Oh Mom," Wenna said, embarrassed. "It was all down to the photographer's skill, though Georgie was as flattering as usual and said it didn't even do me justice."

She clapped her hand over her mouth at once, her eyes full of dismay, and Fanny wagged a finger at her.

"Now look here, my gel. If yer goin' ter stop using Georgie's name, it'll be as if he never existed at all, and I won't have that. My Georgie was a good judge of yooman nature and he loved yer like 'is own."

"I know," Wenna said, her voice catching.

Already Skye could see that they had moved on from the depths of shock and sorrow that should have drawn them together, but had instead driven them temporarily apart.

She asked about the plans for the new-year opening, and learned that Martin Russell would play a big part in promoting, as well as managing, the club in future, which clearly went some way to mollifying Wenna to his existence.

"So when is Mother coming home?" Oliver said resentfully to his father, on hearing the news that Skye had gone rushing up to London.

"Soon. As soon as the funeral's over, and Fanny feels ready to travel."

Nick looked at his son through narrowed eyes. He was only fifteen, but there was already a hardness about him that reeked of David Kingsley's influence. David was constantly reiterating that a newsman had to be hard-headed and unemotional, no matter how harrowing the story, and God knew it was the same for a lawyer, but sometimes Nick thought his son was taking the advice too far.

"They'll still be suffering from shock after Georgie Rosenbloom's death," he went on. "We must make this Christmas as comfortable for Fanny as possible in the circumstances."

"I still think I could ask her to give me some comments on how she sees the German situation," Olly said.

"That's exactly what you are not going to do," Nick snapped. "Do you have no sensitivity at all? If you can't be tactful then I suggest you stay away."

"That's just what I'll do then," he shouted. "Lily said I can have Christmas dinner with them if I wanted to, and I jolly well will. It's not going to be much fun here, is it? Adam's going there for the day too, so you can all stew in your own juice for all I care."

"Oliver, come back here," Nick raged, incensed, but his son banged out of the house and went pedalling furiously away on his bicycle in the direction of Truro.

So much for a family holiday, Nick fumed. Not that it would have been any easier with Olly around. They constantly rubbed one another up the wrong way lately. It was probably better like this, though he wasn't at all sure that was how Skye would see it. She was a great one for family get-togethers and it looked as if this one was going to consist of just themselves, Wenna and Fanny Rosenbloom.

Theo's family were also spending the holiday in their own home, with Justin coming down from London. There had been a time, thought Nick, when this old house had been bursting with people at the least opportunity, but all that was changing. He regretted the fact his elder daughter seemed to have no inclination to come home at all.

# Sixteen

Fanny Rosenbloom, née Webb, was nothing if not resilient. However much crying she did in private she did none of it in public. She had been born illegitimate, living hand to mouth with her feckless mother in London's East End, and learning how to survive. Once she was alone in the world she had clawed herself up from nothing, through good times as well as bad, and meeting Georgie had been the best thing of all. They had made a good and respectable life for themselves, and she wasn't letting go of it now. She owed it to him to follow his dream, and to make the Flamingo Club a success.

But if Georgie had been a dreamer, Fanny was also a realist. Throughout the funeral service, eyeing the men, in their bespoke tailored black suits, who had come to honour and remember him, she noted that they were of a class who wouldn't have given her their nose-droppings in her early years. It was all due to Georgie's modestly warm and generous personality, of course, and together with Martin Russell's management and her new star in the making, she vowed that it would continue. There was work to be done.

By the time she and the protective Pengelly women were on the train bound for Cornwall, Fanny's eyes had lost much of their haunted look, and she was already thinking positively about the future. Yesterday was gone, but a brighter tomorrow was just around the corner, she thought cheerfully. You had to bleedin' well believe it or go under.

"I want ter say something, Skye," she announced, after they had all dozed for a while as the train clattered westwards. "I don't want gloomy faces on my account, and Georgie wouldn't have wanted it neither. If yer planning parties and suchlike, yer must go ahead wiv 'em."

"We weren't, actually," Skye began.

"Why ever not? It's Christmas, ain't it? Bleedin' 'ell, ain't yer planning a knees-up or nothin', gel? I might as well have stayed at home and looked at me four walls!"

Wenna started to laugh. "Oh, Fanny, you're priceless!"

"Oh yeah? And what's that s'posed ter mean?"

"Just that I love you," Wenna said quickly, in case she thought she was being patronising.

"We all do," Skye said. "And if it's a party you want, then a party you shall have. Just as long as you're sure."

"I'm sure."

Skye raised her eyebrows slightly as she glanced at her daughter. How anybody could think of a party at such a time was beyond her, but if Fanny wanted it and needed it, they would have it. It wasn't right to spoil everyone else's Christmas, anyway, even though she had been prepared to do it. But there were others to think about, she thought guiltily. There was her husband and her children.

"Olly said *what?*" she asked Nick, some time after they had arrived at New World late that night, and Wenna and Fanny had gone to bed.

"Don't worry. I put him off the idea damn quickly."

"I should think so, indeed. How could he think of interviewing Fanny at this time? How dare he think about dissecting her feelings? And I suppose you both argued about it as usual," Skye said, touchy after the endless train journey and not needing to hear any of this.

"When did we not?" Nick retorted. "But I made him see sense. Anyway, he's now planning to spend Christmas Day with Lily and David—"

"He certainly is not! He'll be here where he belongs, and they'll all be invited too, and so will Adam. People need to be together at Christmas. It's bad enough that Celia will be so far away without the family splitting up unnecessarily."

She felt angry and ridiculously tearful at that moment and dashed the feeling away. But with the recently revealed instructions about what everyone should do in case of war, and now news of the government spending an exorbitant amount of money on air-raid shelters, it made the prospect seem desperately real. She felt an urgency to gather her family around her like a mother hen with her chicks.

Nick's arms held her close and she leaned against him. They had been apart for more than two weeks, and she desperately needed him in a way that Fanny could never physically have Georgie again.

The thought sent a wave of erotic sensation through her and, while it shocked her, it was an unchangeable fact that she and Nick were warm and alive, with normal feelings and emotions. Whatever happened to the world around them, they mustn't lose that feeling.

"Can we sleep on it, honey?" she said huskily. "Let's talk about it tomorrow."

"Of course we can," he said at once. "I was forgetting how exhausted you must be, darling."

"I'm not," she whispered against him. "I just want to go to bed and to feel you holding me."

She raised her face to his, with all the love she felt for him mirrored in her eyes. His answering kiss was very sweet on her lips.

Lily was uncertain, and openly shocked.

"Are you sure this is what Fanny wants?" she asked Skye, while making a duty visit and guiltily relieved to find that Fanny and Wenna had gone out. "As far as I'm concerned, I'll be delighted to let your people do all the Christmas cooking, but is it right?"

"If you mean, does she want to forget Georgie, then of course she doesn't, and she won't. But this is her way, Lily. She wants what she calls a good old knees-up. I don't know that we'll go that far, but she needs people around her, and I want to humour her before she and Wenna go back to London."

"Well, if you say so. I hope David will agree once I explain, and anyway, our boys love it here."

"They'll make all the difference," Skye assured her. "Children make Christmas, and although Fanny never had any, she always says she enjoys other people's, because she can always hand them back."

"I know the feeling," Lily said with a grin.

"Oh, and one more thing, please prime David and Olly – well, I think you know what I'm trying to say."

"Don't worry. I've already warned them to walk on eggshells when they come in contact with her."

"Well, you didn't need to go that far. She's marvellous as always, and full of the big splash that Miss Penny Wood is going to make in the new year," Skye said, and remembered to show her Wenna's advertising poster.

"This is wonderful," Lily said. "You must let David see it. Wenna really is going places, as they say. And how about your plans?"

Skye looked at her blankly. What plans did she have, apart from wondering if Bokilly Holdings was really going to be the success they hoped, or if the shock of the drastically reduced china-clay orders from Kauffmann's was going to make Bourne and Yelland wish they had never suggested the merger at all.

"Your writing, Skye!" Lily reminded her. "The booklet you were planning."

"Good Lord, I haven't given that a second thought. There's plenty of time for all that, and right now I don't have the heart for it." She felt something akin to anger at even being reminded of it.

"Well, don't let other people's worries eat into you the way you always do. They have to sort out their own lives."

"There's no danger of that," Skye said dryly, hearing the raucous laughter that heralded Fanny's homecoming. Tinged with hysteria it may be, but it was laughter all the same.

Celia telephoned on Christmas Day, and Skye told her to wait a minute until she closed the door to the drawing room, as she couldn't hear a thing for the noise.

"What's happening there, Mom?" Celia yelled. "It sounds like a herd of elephants rampaging through the house."

"No. It's just Fanny organising them all in a game of charades," Skye replied.

"Good God. It didn't take her long to get back on form, did it? Anyway, I can't talk for long, or it will cost Poppa Stone a fortune – and he won't let me pay for the call. I just wanted to wish you all a happy Christmas, and to thank you for the gifts you sent – and I wish I was there too."

"I wish it too, honey. So when are you coming home?"

"Well, not just yet. I'm going to be doing some extra work for Poppa Stone. It is all right, isn't it, Mom?"

"Just don't stay away for ever. We miss you."

240

"I miss you too. Listen, I'll have to go now, but say hello to everyone for me, won't you?" she said, before she choked up altogether.

She hung up the receiver on the wall hook, blinking the tears from her eyes. What an idiot she was to get so emotional when she had just made up her mind to stay here for a few more months at least. But it wouldn't be for ever, she vowed. This place was heaven, but it wasn't home.

She could visualise them all there now, with Fanny holding court and being the life and soul of the party. And for one scintillating and completely unexpected moment, Celia identified with Fanny totally. She understood that need to throw yourself into a brash and noisy party atmosphere, as if it could blot out the pain inside. But it wouldn't make Fanny forget, even for a moment, her love for that funny little Georgie Rosenbloom.

Just as if it could make *her* forget, even for a moment, the love that she had felt, and would always feel, for Stefan von Gruber.

"Are you coming back to the party?" Jarvis Stone's voice interrupted her thoughts. "Did you manage to call your folks?"

"I did, and yes, I'm coming back," she said brightly, and then squealed as Jarvis caught her under a sprig of mistletoe and just missed her mouth with his enthusiastic kiss as she managed to twist her head away.

"Nearly caught you that time!" He laughed.

"Go find your sweetheart, Jarvis," she said, laughing back, and more than thankful that he had at last found a sweet little farm girl to court. Then she was being chased by the younger Stone siblings who all screeched and hollered as they fought to kiss their adored Celia under the mistletoe, and for a few blissful minutes, it was almost like being home.

Skye was thankful that the holiday passed smoothly after all. Once it was over she was relieved to have no more of Fanny's enforced exuberance, though she was sad to see Wenna leave for London. But the feeling was reversed when Lily arrived a few days later to show her a belated Christmas card and letter from Ireland. Skye's eyes widened as she read it.

"I'm sure Wenna doesn't have any serious feelings about Ethan now," Skye said. "But the news that he and Karina have a child might have revived them again."

"And so soon after the marriage," Lily said meaningly. "No wonder it was all so hastily arranged. But they seem to be doing well enough with their pigs and sheep."

Skye pulled a face. "It's not something I ever imagined them doing. I can still remember the awful farmyard smells whenever I visited Aunt Em in Padstow. Poor Em," she added wistfully. "I never thought the 'flu would see her and Will off so quickly. They always seemed so strong."

"That doesn't mean a thing, apparently. I'm sure Karina will be writing to you as well, but I thought you'd like to know that there's now a Ryan Pengelly in the family."

"I'll telephone and congratulate them," Skye said, trying not to mind that Lily had got the news first. But since Karina had been part of her household for quite a while, she supposed it was understandable.

Ethan might have been embarrassed to speak to Nick, she conceded, since it was obvious that the child had been conceived before their marriage. She readily forgave them for any lapse of protocol.

"So how are you, now that you've got the house to yourself again?" Lily went on.

"How am I?" She considered the question. "Lonely. Quiet. Missing Wenna. Missing Celia. Missing Fanny too."

"Well, that sums it all up neatly. And what about Olly? Don't you miss him?"

"Well, yes. Does that mean you're tired of him?"

"Of course not. I love having him around. It's just that you didn't include him in your list of missing persons," Lily said shrewdly.

Skye gave a sigh. "I'm afraid he and Nick clash more often than they agree these days. I know it's an awful admission to make about my own son. I love him dearly, but the house is much calmer when he's not around."

"Calm? Lonely? Skye, I'm worried about you!"

"Why on earth should you be? I'm perfectly fine."

Lily shook her head. "I don't think you are, darling. You look peaky, and I think you're losing weight. It doesn't suit you, and perhaps you should see the doctor."

Skye began to laugh. "I promise you there's nothing wrong with me, Lily, and I'm not going to turn into a hypochondriac like cousin Theo. Betsy tells me he calls the doctor out on any pretext now, the old buffoon!"

"You're not going to divert my attention by telling me any tales about Theo," Lily said sternly. "Promise me you'll think about yourself for a change instead of thinking about everybody else, and about business worries. It will all survive without you, Skye."

"Oh, well, that really fills me with confidence! Are you suggesting I'm about to hang up my boots at any minute?" she said. The accompanying small shiver reminded her that she shouldn't tempt fate.

"Of course not. You're indestructable, darling, and in any case, what would we all do without you?"

Lily blew her a kiss as she took her leave. Skye was still smiling in the doorway as she drove her car away at her usual gear-crunching speed. But once she had gone, all was silent again, and Skye turned slowly back indoors, and felt the smile slipping away from her mouth.

There was nothing wrong with her, she thought, at least nothing that a new interest wouldn't put right. The pottery was in good hands now, with Adam and Seb doing such good work, and the showroom was under the control of an efficient manager and an assistant.

She certainly wasn't needed at the clayworks, nor was she obliged to be present at any meeting other than the quarterly meetings of the four new partners of Bokilly Holdings. Orders, shipping, accounts and audits were all taken care of by others, and the lawyers kept their eagle eyes over it all.

Once, the clay bosses had been deep into every facet of the industry, knowing where every penny was spent, and dealing with every problem, large or small. Now, providing her signature was obtained on each document that needed it, she was no more than a figurehead.

Perhaps that was the reason Theo Tremayne had turned in on himself, she thought suddenly. He was no longer the chief of the Indians, either, and studying and querying his own health was one way to keep attention on him. It was the way old folk behaved, and it wasn't going to happen to her, Skye thought in panic.

She knew she should make a start on the booklet she was

promising to do, but somehow she couldn't even gather up the stamina or the interest in it, and that was alarming too. The combination of remembering Theo's antics, which didn't seem so funny any more, and Lily's anxiety about her, was beginning to remind her sharply that she too was middle-aged. And she didn't like what she saw.

"Tell me something, honestly. Do you think I'm getting old?" she asked Nick that evening.

"Not by my reckoning," he said with a laugh, and then he saw that she was serious. "Of course you're not getting old, no more than the rest of us. What's brought this on, anyway?"

"Oh, just something Lily said. I'm being silly to take any notice of it. I've probably got too much time on my hands lately. Which reminds me of the reason she came here. Ethan and Karina have had a son."

"And they haven't let us know themselves?" Nick said, anger flaring in his eyes. "Well, that's rich, I must say, considering that Ethan's my brother and that we took the girl in. It happened mighty quickly, didn't it?"

"Don't let's judge them for that, honey. I'm sure Ethan felt too embarrassed to tell you himself. Anyway, I telephoned them this afternoon, and Karina's not too well." She hesitated. "Actually I wondered if I might go over there for a few weeks to help out. What do you think?"

"Why should you? She's not your responsibility."

"But she doesn't have anyone else, and Ethan's busy with the farm. You could always come too. He is your brother, and I'd love to see the baby."

Nick was clearly more put out than she was that Ethan hadn't let them know about the child, but finally he nodded.

"I couldn't spare the time to stay away for long, but I'll take you and stay a few days, and then fetch you back when you're ready. Just don't stay away too long, Skye."

"Don't be crazy. It won't be for ever," she said.

She was guiltily relieved that he would only stay for a few days. London had been harrowing after Georgie died, and although Fanny had been in fine form over Christmas, Skye had still felt obliged to keep an eye on her, and on Wenna too, who had loved Georgie like a substitute father. There had been all the trauma over the recent business merger, and even a satisfactory conclusion could take its toll on the nerves. She hadn't even realised, until this new opportunity arose, that she needed time to herself; time to get away from everything. She would find peace and tranquillity in Ireland, and the sweet remembered joy of caring for a new baby.

She smiled ruefully as these thoughts assaulted her. Oh yes, she may not be getting old in Nick's eyes, and thank heaven for that, but she definitely felt the need to slow down and take stock of her life.

"My mother's going to Ireland for a few weeks," Wenna said to Fanny, after their weekly telephone call.

"What the 'ell would she want to go there for? They have pigs and sheep and chickens running in and out of their houses, don't they?"

"Oh, Fanny, I'm sure they don't!" Wenna said, laughing. "Although my relatives do have a small farm."

"There you are then," Fanny said. "What relatives are these, anyway?"

"Karina's a sort of Irish cousin, and her husband happens to be Nick's younger brother," she said, almost surprised to note that there were no painful palpitations in her heart as she said the words.

"Blimey, gel, you do like ter keep it in the fam'ly, don't yer?" Fanny said, not for the first time. "Yer ma's parents were cousins as well, weren't they?"

Wenna nodded. "It makes you believe in fate though, doesn't it? I mean, my grandfather was born and brought up in America, and my grandmother was as Cornish as the clay. But they found one another out of all the people in the world. Don't you think that's beautiful?"

Fanny suddenly gave her one of her bear hugs. "I think you're a sentimental sweetheart, that's what I think. No wonder yer can put so much feelin' into yer songs."

"Well, you have to live the words, don't you?"

And she certainly did that, Fanny thought happily. She put her heart and soul into every song she sang, and the Flamingo audiences were well aware of it. On this very Saturday night little Wenna Pengelly, alias Miss Penny Wood, was going to be their shining light.

Her delight faltered just for a moment, thinking how much Georgie would have loved all this. Georgie had loved *her*, his little Cornish cup-cake, loved her like a daughter.

"Fanny, are you all right?" Wenna asked her now.

"Course I am, duck. And this afternoon you and me are goin' round the sales to buy yer a new frock for tonight."

"But I've got my blue, and I don't need anything else."

Fanny shook her head. "White and virginal is what yer need to set off them lovely blue eyes and dark hair, my duck. Trust me and never mind the coffers."

In the audience at the Flamingo Club that night there was a theatre critic sent along, under protest, by his editor. More used to covering plays and revues for the weekly theatre guide, it wasn't Austin Marsh's idea of an interesting night out to visit a small club well away from the West End. But his editor had been sent details of a new female singer called Penny Wood by an agent friend, and had decided that their paper may as well cover it. Austin had been given the assignment, and taken along a bored woman colleague in the interests of remaining incognito.

"It's better than some, I suppose," she commented. "Nice enough decor, anyway, and the clients look well-heeled."

Austin glanced around at the black-suited gentlemen and their ladies. He really hadn't known what to expect of the Flamingo Club, some low dive, perhaps, but this certainly wasn't it. It had class, he thought in surprise. At least he could report on that, even if the singer wasn't up to much. He'd seen enough amateur nights to last a lifetime, and he didn't hold out much hope for some little country girl from the wilds of Cornwall.

An hour later he had completely reversed his opinion.

"Put your eyes back in their sockets, Austin," his companion said in her usual cynical drawl, drawing heavily on her cigarette before exhaling blue smoke and blurring his vision for a moment.

He ignored her. He was too intent on watching and listening to the lovely girl on the stage, who had already enchanted the audience with her singing and piano playing. Her performance was magical, but it was more than that. He had never believed how a beautifully straight posture that curved so deliciously into a slender waist could be so erotic. Now, after an interval, someone else was playing the piano, and the vision in the sensuously silky white gown was weaving her way slowly around the audience as she sang a plaintive love song in that soft, husky voice that surely touched the heartstrings of everyone who heard it.

For a hard-bitten theatre critic who had seen and heard it all, Austin Marsh was completely bowled over by this angel whose eyes were more lustrously blue than any eyes he had ever seen before. He reminded himself severely that he was here to make a report for his column and not to fall in love.

Wenna had almost reached their table. He could breathe in her subtle perfume. He could see the delicate sheen on her faintly flushed skin and the perfect contours of her face. Her seductive shape was caressed by the white silk dress and he felt an urge to replace that white silk with his hands and touch that lovely warm young body.

"Come back, Austin. She's not for you," he heard his colleague say, and he glanced into her so sophisticated eyes that were a world away from those of the girl nearing them.

What would Maggie Stubbs know who was and wasn't for him, he thought resentfully. Her mission in life was to get her claws into him, as well as every other man on the paper, but he had never fallen for it. She was too brash, in a worldly, unfeminine way that wasn't to his taste. Until now, he had never met a woman who was.

Until now . . .

The golden-voiced girl had reached their table. Several people had reached out to shake her hand as she slowly circled the room, and she had made each of them feel important, as if she sang especially for them.

Austin stretched out his hand to clasp those slim, ringless fingers in his for a moment, and smiled into her eyes. He was positive he saw them widen imperceptibly, and the flush in her cheeks deepened, but it may just have been a trick of the lighting – and then she had moved on.

He applauded with the rest of the clientele as the performance came to an end, and finished his drink quickly.

"I'm going to ask for an interview," he said briefly.

Maggie gave him a knowing look. "My God, I do believe you're smitten. She's no different from a hundred other girls singing for a crust."

"Yes, she is. She's very different."

The woman pulled her fake fur stole around her shoulders and gave a disinterested shrug.

"Well, you can hang around here if you like. Personally I'm bored by the whole thing. I'll leave you to it and see you at the office tomorrow."

"I'll call a cab for you."

"Don't bother. Just be sure and tell me tomorrow if you made a conquest."

She went out laughing, and Austin immediately forgot her as he wove his way between the tables to where the blowsy woman who owned the club was watching his progress.

If this handsome bloke thought he was going to make a play for her Wenna, Fanny thought keenly, he was out of luck.

"Mrs Rosenbloom?" he asked her, and thrust his business card under her nose. "Is it possible for me to have a few words with Miss Penny Wood? I was very impressed by her, and I intend to give her a good review, but I'd like some personal background information for my readers."

And for yourself, I'll bet, thought Fanny. But now that she had seen the credentials on his card, she knew better than to refuse him. This could lead to something big for Wenna.

"Wait here, and I'll see if she's prepared to talk to you," she said, as cool as you like.

She left him and went to the little dressing room where Wenna was sitting motionless on a stool, gazing at her reflection in the mirror. She turned at once, her face more flushed than ever.

"Was I all right, Fanny? Do you think they liked me? I couldn't really tell, though there seemed to be plenty of applause. I was a bag of nerves from start to finish."

"Sweetheart, you was the tops and you know it. And we ain't the only ones. There's a theatre critic bloke who wants to talk to yer. Martin says he's all right, so do yer want me to send him in? He don't look the type to start any funny business, but in any case I'll be right outside the door."

Wenna laughed, her nerves starting to unwind at last at Fanny's threatening words.

"Oh, let's get it over with, then I can change out of this dress and have something to eat. I'm starving."

"That's just reaction," Fanny told her. "Here's the bloke's card then, and remember, I'll be right outside."

Wenna glanced into the mirror again as she heard the tap on the door and called to the stranger to come in. It was only an instant before she turned round to face him, but it felt like an eternity. It was one of those weird moments in life that you wanted to hold on to for ever, knowing it could never come again.

She shook off the feeling and rose quickly to shake the man's hand. She felt the same tingle in her fingers that she had felt before. Somewhere in the back of her consciousness she remembered Celia telling her about a similar sensation the first time she had touched Stefan von Gruber's hand. With a small sense of something like fright, she almost snatched her hand away from Austin Marsh's as she asked him to sit down.

"I thought you were marvellous," he said simply.

"Oh – well, thank you."

He had taken her by surprise. She had expected the kind of interview that David Kingsley was so good at, and that her brother Olly was emulating, firing crisp questions at her that were as unnerving as they were efficient. But this man – this Austin Marsh with the almost autocratic features and crisp dark hair – seemed content to simply look at her for long moments, which was just as unnerving in a different way.

"What did you want to ask me?" she said huskily. "My brother works on a newspaper in Truro, so I know the form."

She felt her cheeks burn. It sounded so pathetic, as if she was trying to prove that she was a sophisticated Londoner like himself, which she certainly wasn't. In fact she felt all fingers and thumbs. He gave a small smile.

"I hope your brother has such delightful assignments as mine has been tonight," Austin went on. "Is Truro your home?"

"Nearby. Do you know the area?"

He shook his head. "I've never been to Cornwall, but I've heard that the scenery is stunning and that Cornishwomen are beautiful. Now I know that much is true."

Wenna blushed at the blatant compliment. She wasn't used to such outspokenness from strangers, and asked him again what he wanted to know.

He took out a small notebook. "I can write a review of what

249

I've seen and heard here tonight, and I assure you it will be a good one," he said, more briskly. "But our readers like to know a few personal details too. For instance, do you mind telling me your age, Miss Wood?"

She smiled at the name, still not used to it. Even though she had been working on and off at the club for some time it seemed suddenly unreal that Wenna Pengelly was being interviewed for a London theatre guide.

"I'll tell you mine if you tell me yours," she said mischievously, without stopping to think.

Austin paused in surprise, and then laughed.

"I'm twenty-five, a bachelor of this parish, and I live in an apartment overlooking the Thames."

"My goodness, that sounds very grand," Wenna said.

"Not really. My parents bought it for me as a university-leaving gift. So now that you know more about me than I know about you, are you going to come clean, or are you about to show me a picture of a female Dorian Gray in the attic?"

For a moment she looked blank, and then remembered the story by Oscar Wilde, and she laughed.

"I'm nearly nineteen," she told him.

"What a wonderful age to have the world at your feet," he said, scribbling in his notebook.

"I don't know that I want the world at my feet," she heard herself say. "I just want what every other woman wants."

"Oh yes?" he said, interested at once. "And what's that? Marriage? Children?"

He merely asked the question to get a useful quote to add to his review. She didn't answer immediately, and when she did, her voice was husky again.

"Of course marriage and children, when the right man comes along."

"But how will you know? I'm sorry, this is becoming far too personal, but as a mere man such comments intrigue me. Women always seem to have an instinct about these things."

"Especially Cornishwomen," she said softly.

Right at that moment, right on cue, as if to disperse the suddenly charged atmosphere between them, her stomach rumbled. She gasped and pressed her hand to the offending object.

"I apologise for that, Mr Marsh. I never eat before I perform, and this is the result."

"Then would you let me take you out to supper? I promise that nothing you say will be taken down and used in my review, cross my heart. But only if you'll call me Austin and allow me to call you Penny."

"I'd much rather you called me Wenna, since it's my real name. But you must promise not to reveal it in your paper."

"Your secret is safe with me, ma'am," he said solemnly.

"Then perhaps you'd wait in the club while I change," she said pointedly, when he made no attempt to move.

"I'm sorry. It's difficult for me to take my eyes off you, and I find myself wanting to look at you for ever."

But he left her then, and she had changed out of the white gown with shaking hands by the time Fanny came into the little room.

"Is everything all right, duck? He was a mighty long time in here, and Martin's talking to 'im now just to make sure he's who he says he is. He's on the up and up all right."

"He was absolutely delightful," Wenna said dreamily. "And he's taking me out to supper."

Fanny's face changed. "Is he now? I ain't sure I approve of that. I'm sure yer ma wouldn't approve of yer going out wiv a man yer've only just met, neither. Maybe I should come wiv yer as a chaperon."

"Well, you said yourself that he's on the up and up, so I'm sure you can stop worrying. And I don't want him to think I'm a baby, do I? I'm sure he's perfectly respectable, and I can take care of myself, truly."

She knew she was talking too fast to justify the fact that wild horses wouldn't have permitted her to let Fanny come along. She turned away to continue with her toiletry, afraid that her eyes would reveal what her heart was already telling her, with every bit of Cornish intuition bursting forth in her veins.

That he was the one. He was the one.

251

# Seventeen

S kye felt her stomach heave as the boat lurched, dipped and then threatened to fall into eternity on the choppy Irish Sea. It was icy cold at the end of January, which had been the earliest time that Nick could get away. He had flatly refused to let her make the journey by herself. She was more than thankful for his company now, as the apparantly endless voyage continued. Yet it was such a short distance compared with the great adventure she had made all those years ago, travelling from New York to Cornwall, and finding love on the way.

She could think of Philip with fond affection now. She remembered both their passionate love and the difficult last years when he had suffered so badly from the effects of the Great War, as if it had happened to someone else. She was oddly detached from it all, and if she stopped to think about that too deeply, the feeling alarmed her.

These days she seemed detached from everything. Her children had all gone; Nick was kept ever more busy with his legal work; the clayworks and pottery got along very well without her; she wasn't needed by anyone. She was useless. Not even Nick guessed how desperately she clung to the hope that Karina really needed her to help with the baby. It had begun to feel like a lifeline to her.

"What's wrong, darling?" Nick asked quietly, when she had said nothing for a long while, but gazed unseeingly out at the pewter-grey water.

"Nothing, really."

"Please credit me with more sense than that, Skye. There's clearly something wrong," he said, eyeing her pinched face as she sat huddled up in a thick coat and scarf, her hat pulled well down over her ears to keep out the wind, her hands clenched tightly together in her leather gloves.

She forced a smile to her cold lips, trying to reassure him without revealing the awful hollow feeling in her stomach. "I guess I've lost the knack of being a good sailor after all these years, honey. The Atlantic was never as rough as this."

He looked relieved. "And that's all? You're just feeling seasick and nothing more?"

"Well, if you call that *all*, then yes," she said with a touch more spirit. "I'll be fine once we get onto dry land."

"I hope so. Ethan's meeting us, so let's hope it's not too far to the farmhouse and that it's good and warm."

She was glad she'd planned to stay for a month. Years ago, making the pilgrimage from her home in New Jersey to meet her Cornish family, she had so longed to be in Cornwall, and now she couldn't wait to get away from it. She couldn't even begin to understand why. She didn't even want Nick around any longer than the several days he planned to be here. She didn't want anything any more.

She was intelligent enough to know it was her mid-life crisis, and dumb enough to have thought it would never affect her the way it did other women. She had imagined she would sail through it all, keeping busy, keeping her interests alive, living vicariously through her children's careers.

Her thoughts went off at a tangent, and she allowed them to do so to take her mind off the heaving sea. Olly was becoming hard, which wasn't such a bad thing in a newspaper reporter, but he was still barely sixteen and she mourned the passing of his childhood. Celia had always been self-sufficient, needing no one, and would overcome all the knocks life threw at her. And Wenna . . . Skye's face softened, remembering her daughter's phone call a few nights ago.

"His name's Austin, Mom, and I'm sending you a copy of my review from the paper where he works. Isn't it funny that he's in journalism too? His father's a member of parliament and his mother's so nice. I met them both at the weekend."

"So soon? I thought you hardly knew this man, Wenna."

She had laughed happily. "Oh, well, you know how it is with some people. You feel as if you've always known them, don't you? That's how it is with Austin and me."

Skye had felt a lump in her throat, hearing in her daughter's voice all the things she wasn't yet prepared to say: all the tremulous, first-love words that were too private to reveal to anyone but the beloved – if it had gone that far.

"Wenna, be careful. I think you know what I mean."

"I do, and you really needn't worry, Mom. Austin is an honourable man, and I know you'll love him."

"I'm going to meet him then? And incidentally, what does Fanny say to all this?"

"Fanny thinks he's lovely now that she's invited him round for tea and given him a proper once-over, as she grandly calls it."

Skye had felt utterly cheated at that moment. Fanny was doing all the things she should be doing. Fanny had met the man that Wenna had obviously fallen head over heels for, and Skye had been left out in the cold. Ridiculous as it seemed, she hadn't been able to shake off that feeling. She prayed uneasily that she wasn't thinking of this baby of Karina's as a substitute for her own lost chicks.

"Not long now," she heard Nick say, and felt a surge of relief as the land became more evident. All she wanted was to get off this boat and on to dry land before the bile in her throat came up and humiliated her.

A short while later, as the flat grey coastline merged into recognisable shapes and contours, they saw Ethan on the quay. At last they left the boat behind, and were being clasped in his arms.

"It's so good to see you both," he said, "but come to the car quickly, for you must be frozen. Karina's got a hot meal waiting for you at the farm."

Skye realised he was nervous, rightly so, she supposed. His news had been a shock to everyone, but the child was here, and had been born in wedlock, and she was sure she would love him as much as they did. Ethan had grown in stature, she realised. He was a husband and father now, and he looked every inch of it.

"How is Karina?" she asked, once they were in the welcome warmth of the car and driving away from the quay.

"She still doesn't have much energy, and the doctor says she's anaemic. She's desperately looking forward to having you here, Skye. She regards you as a second mother, you know."

"Does she? I thought that was reserved for Lily."

"Not at all. It was always you she wanted to please."

The sincerity of his words helped to settle some of the akwardness of the reunion, and the queasiness she still felt in her stomach – though she hoped that the hot meal was going to be a plain one.

She concentrated on watching the changing countryside as the two men talked, and fell in love with the greenness of it, with the smoky blue hills in the distance, in just the way her Uncles Freddie and Bradley must have done all those years ago when they first came here. There was a family tradition here too, she thought, and the charm of it warmed her heart.

Once they reached the valley and glimpsed the white-painted farmhouse with the curl of smoke drifting straight up into the sky, she knew exactly what had drawn them here.

She was shocked to see how thin Karina had grown. When she hugged her, Skye could almost feel her bones through her woollen dress. She needed pampering, and she was going to get it. When Ethan brought the baby down from his crib upstairs and put him in Skye's arms, she looked into his blue eyes and fell in love all over again.

"He's beautiful," she said, "and I hope you'll let me care for him while you get your strength back, Karina. That's what I'm here for, remember."

She breathed in his baby smell and felt her heart lift.

"Just as long as you don't overdo it," Karina said. "You don't look so well yourself."

"I'll be fine once I settle down after that boat trip."

But she wasn't. It took a few days before she felt anything like her old self, and caring for Ryan took more energy than she had expected. It was too cold to take him out in his baby carriage for more than short walks, but she was more than content to hold him by the fire and croon to him, the way she had always done for her own children.

By the time she had been there a couple of weeks, and Nick had long since returned to Cornwall, she had become used to the easy pace of life, even though she knew it couldn't last for ever. It was an idyll, no more, a month out of time, out of her life, to pause and take stock of herself. She still hadn't come to any conclusions as the days sauntered on towards the end of February.

"It suits you," Karina said with a smile, when she came

downstairs one afternoon from her regular afternoon nap, to find Skye dozing by the fire with Ryan sleeping in her arms. Karina was so much better now, and the doctor's pills were restoring her colour and her health.

"What suits me?" Skye asked lazily, still half asleep.

"You with a baby in your arms. Did you never think of having any more children, Skye?"

"Don't you think three was quite enough?" she said with a laugh. "Anyway, it's a little late now!"

But even as she said it, she knew immediately what had been wrong with her all these weeks.

The queasiness, the irritability, the disorientation, the tearfulness at the least provocation, she had put it all down to the mid-life changes in her body. Now she was just as certain that the absence of her monthly periods meant something quite different.

"Skye, are you all right? You look quite pale. I haven't said something to upset you, have I?" Karina said.

"No. Just a goose walking over my grave, that's all," she replied quickly, because no one was going to hear about the spectacular thing that was happening to her until Nick heard it first. Until she was reassured by his love and his care that he was delighted by this late-stage child.

At the thought she gave a shiver. Because it was a late-stage child, of course, and anything could go wrong. She was no longer a young woman. She was forty-seven years old, and Nick was fifty-two. They had three adult children. How would they view the prospect of a brother or sister? She didn't know how they would react to this news.

"If you're ready to take over this little honey-bee," she said to Karina, in as normal a voice as possible, "would you mind if I go and lie down in my room for a while? I have quite a headache."

"Of course. Can I get you anything?"

"No. I'll be fine after a little while."

As she reached the door, she heard Karina speak softly.

"You miss them all, don't you, Skye? A month is a long time to be away, and you'll be glad to see Nick again."

"I expect that's what it is," she murmured.

She realised she was nervous of seeing him again. What if he hated the thought of another child? What if he rejected the very idea? But why should he? It would be her fourth, but Nick's first-

257

born. Her thoughts raced on. What if her own children despised her for putting them in an embarrassing position? She lay down on her bed as the imaginary headache became a real one and she pressed her hand to her belly as if to protect the child against all comers.

If it actually was a child. Her imagination began to make nightmare images, wondering if it there was a hideous cancerous growth inside her instead. She turned her head into the pillow with a sob, wondering if she was going mad.

She had forced herself to think more soberly before she went downstairs again. Nick was due to arrive in a few days' time, and she decided to judge the effect of the infant Ryan Pengelly on him, and to see her own doctor to confirm just what was wrong with her before she said anything at all.

He had dire news. Wenna's latest letter was full of indignation and jitters because thousands of air-raid shelters were going up in London in the event of bombing.

"They look just like horrid steel tunnels," Wenna had written, "and Fanny's saying she wouldn't be seen dead in one of them if her life depended on it."

"Which makes sense to Fanny, if not to the rest of us," Skye commented as she read the words aloud to their hosts.

"So what else do you have to tell me?" she asked Nick, knowing there was more to come.

"Both our main German outlets have cut their orders by half," he said brutally, "and Herr Vogl has sent a personal letter of apology in his usual pompous manner, saying it's doubtful they will be able to continue to do business with us if all the portents are to be believed."

"In other words, if war comes."

"No, my love. *When* war comes," he said. "Why else would all this frantic government activity be going on, if it wasn't inevitable? We have to face it, and make plans."

"What plans?" she said, the ever-threatening tears beginning to surface. "What do you expect us to do? Go and hide away in some South Sea island out of harm's way until the conflict is all over?"

"You could stay here. Move to Ireland and be near us. That would be perfect," Karina said eagerly.

Skye gave her a half-smile. She was so young. She didn't know what it was to go through a war. But Skye did and Nick did. They had both lost people in the last one, and the prospect of a new horror was too awful to contemplate. But one thing was certain. They didn't run away from it.

"Honey, I wasn't being serious," she told her. "We belong in Cornwall, and that's where we'll stay, whatever happens."

"At least Celia's safely away from it all," Karina went on unthinkingly. "You'll be glad of that."

Skye didn't answer. Glad of it? With so much uncertainty on a world scale, and so much uncertainty in her own heart?

What she wanted more than anything was to have all her family around her, to know that every one of them was safe. Like a mother hen, she thought again, she needed her brood.

"Oh, by the way, Herr Vogl included a letter for Celia," Nick said. "I sent it on to her before I came here."

Skye looked at him listlessly. If Herr Vogl was thinking of offering Celia her old job back, he was a bigger fool than she took him for! But it wouldn't be that, of course. In the circumstances, she thought with a shudder, the sooner all foreign workers got out of Germany, the better.

Celia recognised her stepfather's handwriting on the bulky envelope, and put the letter aside to read later, as the younger Stone siblings clamoured for her attention. It wasn't until after supper that she remembered it. There was just a short note from Nick, enclosing another letter that had arrived for her recently. The second envelope bore a German stamp, and her heart leapt as she recognised Stefan's handwriting. She tore the envelope open.

'My darling Celia,' she read, noting at once the carefully correct words that were always so stilted, no matter how deep the sentiments.

It's been so very long since we were together, and I must apologise contritely for my tardiness in not contacting you before. I tried to do so after I left Berlin, and I assumed that you did not care to continue our association. Since then I have learned that you went home to Cornwall, but I cannot leave things as they were without knowing if your feelings are the same as mine.

My life has been turned upside down since those halcyon days, and God knows when we will be together again. You will be as aware as I am of the precarious situation between our two countries, and how dangerous everything seems these days. Some of our Jewish workers have simply disappeared and no one can trace them. I fear the worst, and although it would be my dearest wish to come to you, or to beg you to come to me, who knows what disaster that would produce in the future?

On a different level, I have to tell you that my circumstances have undergone a radical change since both my parents have died. I have many people dependent on me for their livelihood now and I cannot abandon the estate unless I sell it. I suspect that this will be my course eventually, as I've no heart for the family business. But until this present situation is resolved, I feel the best thing to do is to sit tight, as you English say, and await developments.

Or come here, Celia found herself imploring him silently. Come to America where we are both safe.

The most important thing I wanted to tell you, my Celia, is that I loved you then and I love you now, and nothing will change that. Whatever happens in the future, I ask you to believe in us, and to believe that one day we will be together for always. Please write to me if you can, for who knows how long such a correspondence will be available to us?

These last words struck a black chord in her heart. It seemed more ominous that anything else she had heard lately. Being so far away from home had removed the sense of urgency that she realised everyone in Europe must be feeling now. Reading Stefan's words made it seem even more real. Both sides were going to suffer. It wouldn't only be governments that were at war, ordinary people would be affected too. Just as employing some German youths soon after the last war had resulted in violence and murder in the clay industry, there would be no place for lovers whose countries were on opposing sides.

She swallowed a huge sob as the enormity of it sank into her brain. Her earlier thought about being safe here seemed hollow now, as she remembered that America had been drawn into the last conflict. If that happened again, there would be no safe place for lovers like Celia Pengelly and Stefan von Gruber.

The portly Poppa Stone found her in the family room, staring into the distance, her face as white as chalk. He put his head on one side, as if trying to read her mind.

"Is this some kind of Cornish trance, honey?" he said with a chuckle. "If so, I don't want to disturb it, but Momma Stone and me were wondering if you'd care for a game of cards now the young 'uns have gone to bed?"

"Do you mind if I don't?" she said in a choked voice. "I have a lot of thinking to do tonight."

"My Lord, you don't want to do too much of that, girl. It rots your brain," he said. His voice grew anxious as he realised how serious she looked. "What's wrong, honey?"

She took a deep breath. "I think it's time I went home," she said slowly, her eyes wide and dark.

She had expected him to argue with her, but, as perceptive as any Cornishman, he nodded and hugged her.

"If you think it's time, it's time," he said.

But first of all she wrote to Stefan, to tell him she understood everything he was careful not to put into words, that her feelings for him had never changed, and never would. She told him what she had been doing all this time, and that now she was going home to Cornwall. She told him she loved him with all her heart.

What she didn't tell him was that part of her reason for going home was because she would feel a little closer to him without an ocean separating them. They would then only be divided by the evil intent of a madman who wanted to conquer the world.

"Celia's coming home," Skye said joyfully to Nick, when they had been back at New World for two weeks.

She had still said nothing about her suspected condition. Every time she was about to do so, something held her back, and now she attributed her reticence to this new development. Celia was coming home, and that was a good omen. Once her daughter was here, that would be the time.

She still felt unwell for hours on end. When Nick told her angrily that she should see a doctor, she simply told him it was perfectly normal for a woman of her age going through these changes, and that he wasn't to fuss.

"Are you sure it's no more than that?" Lily had already asked her. "You're not – good God, Skye, you're surely not—"

"Don't be ridiculous," she had snapped. "A woman of my age? People would be staring at me as if I had two heads or something. Imagine my having to tell Olly!"

But Lily's incredulity and her own embarrassment seemed to sum up what she felt. It also filled her with guilt, as if she was rejecting the child she was sure she was expecting. Once Celia came home, she was just as sure she would have her support and that everything would be all right. She clung to that fact like a talisman.

It was the middle of March before they finally welcomed their daughter home. Sebby had insisted on going to Falmouth to meet her from the ship and bring her home to New World. Once they had all fallen on one another's shoulders with hugs and kisses and tears, and he had discreetly left them to it, Celia addressed her mother in a shocked voice.

"What the heck have you been doing to yourself while I've been away, Mom? You look terrible!"

"Well, that's a nice way to greet your mother, I must say," Nick commented.

"Well, can't you see it? Have you seen a doctor, Mom?"

"Not yet," Skye said weakly. "I intend to, though."

She really meant it. It had to be done soon, if only to see if she needed iron for her blood, the way Karina had done. She felt so weak these days. In fact, right now, she felt as though the room was starting to spin, and she fought to hold her senses together. It would be a terrible homecoming for Celia if she passed out here and now.

She was vaguely aware of drifting in and out of consciousness for what seemed an age, but when she came around properly, there was a terrible dragging ache in her belly.

She realised she was in her own bed. The doctor was looking down at her accusingly, and Nick and Celia looked strained and anxious.

"Why haven't you come to see me before, Mrs Pengelly? We could have prevented this. Your age is no barrier to producing a healthy child, providing sensible precautions were taken, but that would include not subjecting yourself to excursions on the Irish Sea and taking on another woman's burden."

"It is a child then?" she asked huskily.

It seemed an age before he slowly shook his head. She saw Celia and Nick clutch one another's hands as she heard the doctor speak more gently, in the tone he always used whenever he had to give bad news.

"My dear, I'm afraid you've suffered a miscarriage."

"Skye," Nick pushed past him to take her cold hand in his. "Why didn't you tell me? I had a right to know."

She turned her face away. It wasn't easy to speak of personal, womanly things, even to the one you loved the most. It was the stupid indoctrination of the age they lived in, but now she realised too late that by her stupidity, she had denied him something precious. She should have allowed him to share in these early weeks of anticipation. He could hate her for not doing so, just as she hated herself now, and wept inside for the child that was never to be.

But he didn't hate her, and although it took her months rather than weeks to get over the trauma, he was always there when she needed him, and if he wasn't, then Celia was. Her beloved Celia, who had come home when she needed her most.

"My grandmother's best friend was called Celia," Skye told her one morning when they were sitting outside on a warm June day. "And you needn't think I've gone crazy to mention it without reason," she added. "We named you after that other Celia. Did I ever tell you that?"

"Only about a hundred times," Celia said uneasily. "What made you think of that now, anyway?"

"I was thinking how Granny Morwen picked herself up so many times when things went wrong, and here am I, wallowing in my own troubles, when all around me the world is facing disaster. What right do I have to feel so sorry for myself?"

"Every right. You're a person, aren't you?"

She looked at her daughter. "And so are you, my love. And I never asked you properly why you happened to come home exactly when I needed you. Was that Cornish, or what?"

Celia hesitated, and then spoke truthfully. "I'm afraid it was what, Mom. I had a letter from Stefan at last, and I thought coming home to Cornwall would bring me that much nearer to him. That's crazy if you like, isn't it?"

"No darling, it's not crazy," Skye said. "It's exactly what I would have done for someone I loved. Why don't we go for a walk on the moors and you can tell me all about it?"

"Are you sure? You haven't wanted to go anywhere lately, let alone take a strenuous walk."

"It's high time I did. Good Lord, people must be sick of coming to visit me when I'm not even ill. How selfish can you get, for pity's sake? I need to get back in the world again!"

"That's my Mom," Celia said thankfully.

"My mother's better," Wenna told Fanny, putting down the telephone. "Celia says she's going out of the house at last and seeing people. Thank God. I still feel horribly guilty that I haven't been home to see her."

"Now you know yer Dad said you wasn't to make her feel bad about taking yer away from yer work. And she takes such pleasure in seeing all them good reviews yer keep getting now, my duck."

"I know, and not just from Austin, either," Wenna said, cheering up at once. "He's the best though, isn't he, Fanny?"

"If yer say so," Fanny said dryly.

"I do. And you'll never guess what else Celia said."

"Well, that's for sure, unless yer tells me."

"They're going to offer to take in some London children at New World for families who want to evacuate them to the country. That's just like Mom, and of course, Celia's been looking after children in New Jersey until recently, so I daresay she'll have a hand in it too. It makes the threat of war seem even more certain, though."

"Well, I'll tell yer one thing, gel. I ain't going to be evacuated on account of old Hitler, no matter how many bombs he drops on London," Fanny said determinedly.

"Neither am I," Wenna declared. "And neither is Austin. Whatever happens, we'll stick together like the three musketeers, won't we?"

"If yer say so. Though in your case, I reckon it'll be more like the two bleedin' musketeers stickin' together, if yer get my meaning. Yer won't want a third party around when you do yer canoodlin'.

"Oh, Fanny, you'll make me blush," Wenna said, laughing.

"Good. That means yer still taking care of yerself then."

"Of course I am. And Austin's taking good care of me too, so stop fishing for details, because you're not getting any!"

All the same, she was more than thankful that Austin didn't pressure her to go further than she wanted to go. He was more worldly than she was, and he had a passionate nature. So did she, Wenna had discovered, but there was an unspoken rule between them that dictated how far they would go with their lovemaking.

Kissing and touching – fondling even, Wenna thought with a thrill at the erotic-sounding word – was permitted on both sides. But doing the actual thing was going to wait. She was young yet, but one day they would be married. They were so deeply in love that nothing else would do.

This summer was turning out to be so wonderful for her career. People were coming to the club time and time again on Saturday nights when she had the star spot, and Fanny was delighted with the good business her little Cornish songbird was bringing in. It was almost as good as being discovered for the movies, Wenna told Austin, although she had never wanted to be an actress.

"Singing's a kind of acting, sweetheart," he pointed out.

"Yes, but I don't have to say anything. I know I'm giving a performance, but I can forget my shyness once I throw myself into the words and the melodies, and just live the emotions."

He laughed, pressing her to him as they strolled arm in arm along the riverbank on that warm, still evening. It was high summer now, and London had never looked so beautiful, the elegant bridges bathed in the reddening sunlight, the ethereal colours of the sky reflected in the water.

"Sometimes I think your shyness is something of a myth, Wenna," he teased. "At least as far as I'm concerned."

"Only as far as you're concerned," she retorted, her cheeks warm, knowing how hard it was for him to resist their mutual desires at times, but loving him all the more for his patience and understanding.

"I know it," he said, more soberly. "And I consider myself the luckiest man on earth to have found you. Do you realise that if my paper hadn't persuaded me to go along to the Flamingo Club that evening, we might never have met?"

"Oh, but we would," Wenna said with supreme confidence.

"You're sure of that, are you?" he said with a grin.

"Of course! I'm Cornish, and we know these things. You and I were destined to meet, and no power on earth was going to stop that!"

"Not even—"

"Don't say it," Wenna broke in quickly. "I don't want anything to spoil this lovely evening, Austin."

Especially not thoughts of a German dictator and his machinations. The colour of the sky deepened still more as the sun began to slide below the horizon, and the river, so serene and beautiful just moments ago, turned an ominous blood-red.

# Eighteen

"The bastards have done it then," Theo Tremayne bawled, bursting into New World while Skye and Celia were enjoying an afternoon cup of tea in the garden.

His presence was hardly a surprise, since they had heard the screech of his car as it roared to a halt, and had been relishing the few moments' peace before he found them.

"Would you like some tea, Theo?" Skye asked mildly.

"I don't want your tea, cuz. I want to know what we're going to do now that the bloody Germans have pulled out of every contract they had with us."

Celia got to her feet. "I think I'll leave you two to sort out your business problems, Mom," she said. "In any case I have a meeting in Truro this afternoon with the ladies' evacuee committee."

"What's that?" Theo said, diverted for a moment as he watched her trim figure go back into the house. "You're not going through with this daft idea of bringing London brats down here, are you? Outsiders don't belong here."

She had long been thought of as an outsider, too.

"I don't remember you objecting when we brought the German boys over here years ago," Skye pointed out. "In fact, it may even have been mostly your idea, Theo."

"It was a bloody bad one, whoever thought of it." He scowled, not admitting anything. "And now look what's happened. You are acquainted with the situation, I suppose, in between your flower-arranging and poxy female occupations."

Skye held on to her temper with an effort at his patronising sneer, and snapped back a reply. "Naturally I know what's happening. And if you mean do we have to think of where else to sell the clay, then no, we don't. Our partners have got it all under control, and we should be thankful they have their other outlets."

267

His eyes narrowed in his florid face. "You're in a mighty forgiving mood, considering you never wanted us to merge with 'em in the first place."

"Times change," she said evenly. "In fact, I've been giving the whole business serious thought lately."

"Oh ah," he said, alert at once. "And what wonderful conclusions have you come up with?"

His tone implied that it could be nothing of major importance, especially coming from a woman. He was in one of his most belligerent and macho moods, but she had never been afraid of standing up to him, and she wasn't afraid now.

"Perhaps it's time we sold out completely after all," she said coolly. "And before you throw a fit, hear me out, Theo."

But she could see that he was too dumbstruck by her words to say anything at all for a moment. She certainly hadn't meant to blurt it out. It had been no more than a seed of an idea at first, but one that had steadily grown in her mind, as insidiously as the mist descending over the moors.

He sat down on the chair vacated by Celia and folded his arms as best he could over his bulging belly.

"Go on," he snapped. "I'd never taken you for a turncoat, so your reasoning had better be good."

"I'm tired," she said flatly. "Very tired. The miscarriage took more out of me than I realised, and although Celia and Nick think I'm perfectly well again, I know I'm not. I'm telling you this in confidence, Theo, and I'm appealing to your better nature, if that's not an impossibility."

"Go on." He grunted again, for once not making any snide comment at her frankness, but not missing her pallor.

She spoke slowly, needing to explain her thoughts to herself as well as him.

"I've come to realise that I don't have the same interest in the clay that I once did, Theo. My heart is no longer in it, and I don't think yours is, either. Our day is past, and it's time we realised it before it's too late."

"Too late for what?"

"Too late for all of us to make any profit out of a business that's dwindling rapidly. Bourne and Yelland are in a much better position than we are. They have the goodwill of the paper mills and medical supplies trade, but without the regular German firms buying our clay, we're doing no more than giving lip service to the partnership. That embarrasses me, and I've no wish to feel like a poor relation."

"And how do you think our grandmother would see this backing down of all she stood for?" he couldn't resist sneering. "So much for your fine principles, cuz."

Skye bit her dry lips. "I have a feeling that Granny Morwen would applaud my common sense. There's a time for holding on and a time for letting go. I think we've reached that time."

"And do you think our offspring will think the same about losing their inheritance?" he demanded.

"It's not for them to say whether or not we decide to sell. Naturally, they'd all be compensated. But I suggest we put the matter to them all to see what they think."

He leapt to his feet, his ungainly bulk blotting out the sunlight from her gaze, his eyes spitting fire, his brief sense of compassion gone.

"I'll tell 'ee exactly what they'll think without askin' their bloody opinion. Yes, they'll get compensated all right, but your girls couldn't give a tinker's cuss about the clay, and your son's got so toffee-nosed with the newspaper trade he won't care, neither. Justin's already turned his back on it all to become a doctor, so that leaves only one, don't it?"

"It's Sebby I'm most concerned about," Skye said carefully. "I do understand, Theo—"

"No, you bloody don't! You came here from America and stepped right into your grandmother's affections. For all the rest of us knew, you wormed your way right into her will an' all. You knew nothing about what my father had worked for all his life, and his father and brothers before him. You knew *nothing* except for some romantic idea of where your parents came from – and it's mighty kind of you to be so concerned about Sebastian," he added, seething with sarcasm now. "But if you're that bothered, why don't we go and ask him what he thinks about selling out, and by-pass all the rest?"

"*Now*?" she said, appalled at his vindictiveness, and his smouldering resentment of her that she thought had been dead and buried long ago.

"Yes, *now*," he snapped. "While we're both in the mood."

\*     \*     \*

269

Seb Tremayne looked up from his work to see the small deputation making their way through to the workroom from the White Rivers showroom. When he saw the expressions on their faces he grinned wryly at his working partner.

"Stand by for fireworks, Adam. When these two get together with that look, something's definitely up."

Seb stopped working his wheel and slid the pot expertly on to the base board before wiping his hands on a rag as Skye and his father came into the room.

"To what do we owe this pleasure?" he asked. "Checking up on us, are you, Father?"

Theo scowled. The boy had far too sharp a tongue on him, he mused, and just as quickly conceded that it was far too much like his own for comfort.

"We've come to talk to 'ee on an important and personal matter, boy," he stated.

"Then I'll leave you folks to it," Adam said.

"No, you stay, Adam. Whatever business there is to discuss, we'll do it in the open air," Seb said at once, taking command.

This was his domain, his and Adam's – and Skye's, of course, he thought, though she didn't look too well. He wondered at once if they should discuss whatever it was indoors after all. But it was too late now, and she was already following his father outside again.

"Shall we walk over the moors, or would you prefer to sit in the car to talk, Skye?" he said. "You do look weary."

"I'm well enough," she said. "Let's walk."

She had had enough of sitting beside Theo in the confines of his car. He had never smelled too sweet and it seemed now that he never bothered to keep himself particularly clean. How Betsy must hate it, although maybe she preferred his natural bodily stink to his reeking of the floosies he used to visit. Skye gave a shudder, thankful that her husband was a decent man.

They strode across the moors in the heady summer freshness, until they reached the outcrop of smooth rocks where they could sit down and take a breather. In the distance was the Larnie Stone, the tall, holed standing stone, from where you could see the distant sea, and where Morwen Tremayne had once glimpsed her lover, Ben Killigrew, after taking a witchwoman's potion.

Skye pushed the thoughts out of her head, even though they

were never more vivid than here, where it had all begun. The sweet liaison had become a powerful dynastic concern, which she and Theo were about to dissolve. A sob caught in her throat and she wondered after all, if she was doing the right thing.

"Are you sure you're feeling quite well, Skye?" Sebby asked her again.

"She's all right, boy," Theo said crudely. "Just listen to me, and give us your thoughts without interrupting."

He listened silently as his father explained what he and Skye were contemplating.

"Is this really what you want to do?" he said, turning to Skye. "I can hardly believe you want to turn your back on the clay-works."

He ignored his father. It was Skye he was most concerned with, the lovely woman who was looking more careworn than he had ever seen her before. She was still beautiful in middle age, but so fragile and so vulnerable. It was not the way he liked to see Skye Pengelly. Impulsively, he caught at her cold hands.

"Skye? Have you really had a hand in this, or have you been pushed into it by my father?"

He heard Theo give a raucous laugh.

"Well, if that ain't a proper show of confidence in your father, I don't think!" he said angrily. "The woman can speak for herself, and always has done."

"Then why don't you let me?" Skye said, her quiet voice echoed across the rustling bracken. She looked at Seb. When they were children her daughters had always called him a prize pig, and so he had been in those days, but not any more. Now, she had the greatest fondness for him.

"Sebby, it was my idea," she said gently. "I feel it's time I stood aside, and naturally, you'll have your opinion on it, but it's not only the clayworks I'm thinking of selling."

Both men gasped as she said the words that seemed to fall from her lips of their own accord. But once said, she knew it was the way forward.

"I also know how important the pottery is to you and to Adam. You may hate the idea of working for someone else—"

"Neither us would agree to it," he said sharply. "I'm sure I speak for Adam as well as myself. If you're going to sell out, then you must give us first refusal."

271

His reply took her aback. It was what she had tentatively intended to offer, but Seb's response was immediate and decisive. She had expected remonstrations, perhaps anger, but not quite such swiftness of thought that turned a negative situation into a positive one. She should have expected it. Sebby was a man after old Morwen Tremayne's heart, her eyes stung as the sweet thought slid into her mind with consummate ease.

"Now wait a minute, boy. Never mind the bloody pottery. 'Tis the clayworks that's the main concern here. Shares should come to you and the rest of 'em by right, and there are things to discuss –" Theo began hotly.

"There's nothing to discuss as far as I'm concerned, Father. The pottery is Skye's property, and once I've discussed it with Adam, I'm sure we'll be able to make an offer for it with my share of the money from the sale of the clayworks. I don't imagine you'll get any opposition from my brother and cousins, providing you see us all right on that, since we'll be losing our true inheritance. Is that your plan, Father?"

Skye could hardly contain her smile at his so-innocent words. He could sum up a situation in a moment, and oh, Theo, she thought, you may have scored over a thousand people in your lifetime, but you'll never put one over on your own son!

"Of course," Theo said coldly. "You're agreeable then?"

He held out his hand and Seb grasped it firmly. Then it was Skye's turn and, as she felt Seb's fingers close around hers, she could have sworn she heard a faintly cackling laugh creep over the moors, as if in triumph that the Killigrews and Tremaynes were to be finally severed from all that had been theirs for nearly a century.

But when she looked around quickly, there was nothing there, except a small breeze blowing through her heart.

Nothing could be done swiftly. There had to be further meetings between all the partners and their lawyers to ensure the best deal on all sides. Skye knew that Nick was openly relieved that she had finally decided to relinquish her interests in business matters. Though he was surprised she had decided to sell the pottery as well.

"I surprised myself, but it just seemed the right time," she said "and I won't be losing all my interest. The pottery will still be a family concern with Seb and Adam taking charge, and Lily minding the shop in Truro. I won't be letting go entirely."

"You'd have had to, if Seb hadn't offered to buy," he pointed out. Then he saw the look on her face.

"My God, you had no doubt of it, did you, woman? Did you prime him on it beforehand?"

She shook her head. "Truly I didn't, Nick. But I knew in my heart what would happen. He's the right one to carry on. Him and Adam. I rather like the idea of their partnership, don't you? It cements our two families."

"I thought the two of us had already done that pretty effectively," he said meaningly.

Skye laughed, but the laugh was shaky as she turned away from him. The memory of of what might have been still lingered in her mind with a great sadness. As the weeks and months passed, the time for their baby to be born would soon be here. It was as though she had to go through the normal gestation period as a time of mourning until she was completely whole again. It wasn't even something she felt able to discuss with Nick, whom she loved more than life. It was her pain and her sorrowing, and hers alone.

She felt an undoubted sense of relief now that the idea of selling out had been approved by all concerned. It had only needed the resolve to carry out what her heart had been telling her for months. To free herself of business responsibilities she had never sought, and be herself. A wife and mother and, above all, a woman.

True to what she and Theo had surmised, neither Oliver nor Justin had raised any objection to the plans. And her girls had openly applauded the decision.

"It's time you took things easy, Mom," Wenna had phoned from London. "You've worked far too hard all these years, and you're not young any more."

"Oh, really! And what was that all about?" Skye had asked, hearing the explosive noise in the background.

After a few minutes Wenna's voice came back on the line, full of suppressed laughter.

"It was Fanny telling me off for implying that you're past it. She's a scream, isn't she, Mom?"

"Is that what you think, then? That I'm past it?"

"Good Lord no! But you won't be worrying your head about how much money the businesses are making or losing from now on, will you? You can be a proper lady of leisure at last."

"That's not quite what I had in mind," Skye said mildly.

"Well, I'm glad you won't be rushing around so much, because Austin and I plan to come down for a visit at the end of August."

Skye was diverted at once. "That's marvellous news, darling! So I'm going to meet this wonder man at last, am I?"

"And we'll have some special news to tell you then. But I'm not going to spoil the surprise by telling you now. I'll give you a tiny hint, though. Austin will want to have a word with you and Daddy."

She would say no more. Skye was fizzing with excitement when she hung up the phone, guessing at once what the tiny word was going to be. Austin Marsh wanted to marry her daughter. And when he did, Skye would become a mother-in-law, and in time, a grandmother. The thought of it was at once thrilling and alarming.

Time moved on, and with it, so did she. Not for the first time when she had something on her mind, whether good or bad, she felt an oppressive need to get out of the house. Like all the Tremayne women before her, she needed the clean invigorating air of the moors to be able to think clearly.

It was funny, but she had naturally expected Celia to be the one to bring this news home. Celia was more forceful, more sure of herself, and had fallen in love first. For all her early flirtatious ways, Celia had become a one-man-woman, Skye thought with deep affection, and until Stefan was free to come to her, there would be no one else. While Wenna, shy, quiet Wenna, had fallen just as hard.

It occurred to Skye as she drove to the moors and parked her car before striding out aross the short stubbly turf, with the whole of St Austell bay shimmering far befow in the sunlight, that she had never met either of the men her daughters were so determined to marry. But that didn't matter, as long as they were happy and fulfilled. Happiness was all that counted in this world.

Nick's peevishness, for example over who had been told first about Ethan and Karina's baby had faded away the moment they saw how blissful they all were in their idyllic Irish farm.

She and Nick might have been just as blissful with their own baby being born any day now . . . the mortality that was everyone's destiny would have been continued in a new son or daughter.

In a weird way, the loss of that child had been one of the things that had prompted her desire to sell her partnership in the clayworks and the pottery. She needed time to do what had been no more than a vague idea suggested to her some time ago by David Kingsley. She wanted to perpetuate what had always belonged to the Killigrews and the Tremaynes, and now the Pengellys. She *would* write that booklet, so that all the children that followed, would know – and that those who remained, wouldn't forget . . .

"What noble thoughts be goin' round and round in that pretty head o' yourn, my fine lady?" she heard a wheezing voice cackle close by.

She didn't need to turn around to know who was hobbling up behind her. Perhaps she had come this way especially for the sake of coming face to face with old Helza, for whatever reason fate decreed, thought Skye. How old was she now, she wondered, as the old witchwoman literally rocked on her spindly legs as if they would barely hold her up.

"I'm looking for answers," she said simply, the words escaping her lips without any forethought. She felt as light-headed as she always did when faced with this self-styled all-seeing, all-knowing old creature. She began to wish she had stayed safely at home.

"Before 'ee can find answers, there must be questions, my pretty," the wizened old woman croaked, her head cocked to one side like an enquiring bird.

"But how can I find the answers when I don't know the questions?" Skye said, knowing she was being ridiculously enigmatic.

Helza's eyes screwed up to slits in the brightness of the sun, accentuating the corrugated lines of her ancient face to gargoyle proportions.

"Mebbe the answer is inside yourself, lady. You're strong enough to find it wi'out anybody's help."

With that she turned and hobbled away. She seemed to disappear into nothingness, but common sense told Skye it was simply a dip in the hillside that hid her from view.

She stood motionless for a while, letting the warm, caressing breezes of the moors wrap softly around her. She had already found the answer. Life didn't end, even if her own baby's had ended before it had begun. In the great overall plan of things, life went on, and she had already decided what she was going to do with hers.

August, that had once seemed an eternity away, was into its middling days now. The sun was hot, reviving the spirit, and the countryside she loved was serenely beautiful. Her sky tips, no longer strictly hers, but which would always be so in her heart, were sparkling like diamonds as she turned towards them to reach her car. In essence, they would never change, and nor would she.

Thoughts of wars, of conflicts that were none of her making, nor of anyone who belonged to her, were as far removed from her mind as that distant life-giving sun. The solidity from deep inside the earth in the form of the pure white china clay that was her heritage, always gave her a feeling of peace, as it had done for all the women in her family.

She was much calmer by the time she reached New World once more, where she found Celia in a state verging on hysteria. There had been a telephone call from Stefan.

"He's in Gstaad for a week or so, and he asks if I can meet him there." Her voice shook with excitement, and Skye felt her heart stop at the yearning in her daughter's face.

"I wouldn't even try to stop you, honey, if you're sure it's what you want to do."

"I have to go to him. It's unwise for him to come here, for if the worst comes to the worst, there's a great danger that he'd be interned, and he forbids me to go to Germany. But in Gstaad we shall be on neutral ground. You understand, don't you, Mom? I couldn't bear to miss this chance of being with him again for a short while."

Skye hugged her, feeling the tension in her taut young body. "Of course I understand. In your place I would do exactly the same. Daddy will make all the arrangements—"

276

Celia shook her head. "Too late. I've called David and he's organised everything through his connections. I fly out tomorrow afternoon on a private aeroplane."

She gave a gulp. Her eyes were huge and vibrantly blue as she looked at her mother. "I'm so excited – and so scared. What if we take one look at each other, and everything's changed?"

"Do you believe that's how it will be?" Skye murmured.

"No. But I just can't believe it's really true that we're going to be together again," Celia said tremulously.

"Not for too long," Skye said, hating to take the sparkle from her eyes, but obliged to remind her that this was no more than a temporary reunion. "Stefan will have to go back to Germany, honey, and you'll be needed here once the evacuee children descend on us. I'll be depending on you."

"I know. But I'd rather spend a week with Stefan than a lifetime with anybody else. And if a week is all we have . . ."

They hugged one another, and into Skye's mind came the fleeting thought that it wasn't only a clayworks and a pottery that had been the family legacy. All the women had felt this passionately about their lovers, and that passion had given them strength, in the way that women everywhere had found the strength to send their men away when necessary. It was a sweet and sobering thought.

But such introspection had to take second place to Celia's frantic haste to prepare for her journey. Every moment she and Stefan were apart was obviously a moment wasted, for who knew whether or not this lovers' meeting would be the first of many, or one that must last for ever?

Celia was realistic enough to know how lucky she and Stefan were to have this second chance. If she hadn't come home when she had, she might still have been halfway across the world in New Jersey. Stefan wouldn't have been able to contact her from Gstaad in time for her to get there before he returned to Germany. She shivered, thinking how fragile and dependent on coincidence life could be.

These thoughts were far behind her when at last she took the taxi cab to the hotel in Gstaad where they had first met. The town was pristine and fragrant now, the meadows and foothills of the mountains clothed in wild summer flowers, turning the

277

whole area into a fairyland of colour. The man who rose from the window table to greet her was dear and familiar, and the love of her life. She whispered his name and was enfolded in his arms.

"God, how I've missed you," Stefan breathed against her mouth. "How I've wanted you and ached for this moment."

"And so have I. Oh, so have I, Stefan."

They could hardly bear to break apart, and had it not been for the amused stares of other hotel guests they might have stood there all day, locked in one another's arms. But they both had other needs, and although for the sake of her reputation as well as the hotel's, he had booked them into separate rooms, Celia knew they would not be apart that night, nor for any of the nights to come.

Later, when they had had dinner and drunk a bottle of the hotel's best wine, they retired to their adjoining rooms, and she undressed nervously. It had been a long time since they had been together and when she heard his tap on her door, she opened it with shaking hands. Her drew her into his arms and looked down searchingly into her darkening eyes.

"Are you afraid, *liebling*?" he said softly.

She shook her head. "Only of not pleasing you. Of not being everything you expect of me."

"You are all that and more, and always will be, my Celia. And if I don't possess you this minute, I think I shall go mad. Does it not shock you that I'm so impatient to feel your body next to mine?"

She felt her heart soar to meet him. "No, it doesn't shock me! It only makes me love you more, if that's possible, because I feel the same way."

She could say no more as he swept her up in his arms and took her to the bed, kissing her mouth every step of the way.

Then he removed the silky nightgown from her shoulders and let it fall to the ground, pausing a moment to gaze down at her as if to imprint her luscious shape on his mind for eternity, before disrobing and sliding into the bed beside her.

They had all night . . . but they had been too long apart and their need was too great. Hands and mouths sought and found their goals, and the sensations were at once new and erotically familiar, and then she felt him enter her and she cried out with the sheer remembered pleasure of it.

A long while later, when their passion was spent, they still lay in one another's arms, dreaming impossible dreams of a future together, and finally coming back to reality.

"*Liebling*, if this was all we had, I would die happy tomorrow," he whispered against her mouth, and her eyes stung, because it echoed her own thoughts so much.

"This won't be all we have, Stefan," she whispered back. "However long it takes, we'll be together again, I know it."

"Is this your famous Cornish intuition speaking?"

"No. I know because I love you," she said. She was glad to her soul that it was her Cornish passion that allowed her to say these words in such an uninhibited way.

"Then I must tell you the special reason I wanted us to meet here, *liebling*. In time I intend to move here to Gstaad, possibly to go into the luxury hotel business. I will not desert the people who depend on me, and I ask you again to accept that decision. But when the time is right I will ask you to marry me and to start our life together here. I do not ask it now, while the future is so uncertain—"

"But I will give you my answer now," Celia broke in, knowing that his words became more formal the more nervous he became, and loving him for not taking her for granted. "Whenever you ask me to marry you, I will marry you, Stefan, whether it's today, tomorrow, or a hundred years from now."

"I trust it will not be so long to wait," he said. "But if you're sure—"

"I was never more sure of anything in my whole life."

"Then I will ask you formally. Will you do me the honour of marrying me, Celia?"

Her answer was on her lips before the question was properly ended. By the time she returned home to Cornwall, on the third finger of her left hand was a pearl and garnet ring that had belonged to Stefan's mother. They knew that contact between them might well become sparse or non-existent in the days to come, but to Celia, the ring was a talisman and a sweet reminder that love never died.

It was ironic that Wenna's arrival back in Cornwall coincided with the day that Skye's baby would have been born.

She woke with a heavy feeling in her heart and spent a few self-pitying moments weeping into her pillow. Nick found her there, and held her close while she finally spilled out all her emotions.

"Did you think I didn't know – or didn't care?" he said gently. "We both knew this day must come, and tomorrow it will be over. Isn't that the way you've always coped with things, my darling? Even the worst, most heartbreaking things?"

Her snappy reply died on her lips as she looked into his tortured eyes, and knew that her pain was also his. All this time Nick had had to face this day too, and she had never considered his feelings.

"We have to go on, don't we?" she whispered.

"It's the only way," he said evenly. "But we go on together, and we're luckier than most. We'll have all our family around us soon. Wenna and Austin will be here by tonight, and Celia will be back from Gstaad tomorrow. Olly's keen to meet this beau of Wenna's, and is insisting that we have a family party at the weekend, just our own crowd for once, and not all the rest of the horde. But you only have to say no if you don't feel up to it."

She drew a deep breath. "Of course I'm up to it. When did you ever hear a Tremayne woman refuse a party?"

"Or even a Pengelly one," he said.

So on the last day of August, Wenna and Austin Marsh boarded the train for Cornwall, having decided it was far too long a drive for his old boneshaker of a car. By the time they arrived at New World it was late in the evening, and once the ecstatic reunion was over and Austin had been welcomed and silently approved, Wenna spoke soberly.

"It was a ghastly journey, Mom. We hadn't realised how many children were being sent out of London to the country today, so the trains were full of the poor little things, all with labels round their necks and carrying their bags and gas masks. A lot of them were crying. It was horrible, I can tell you."

She looked around the familiar surroundings with huge affection, wanting Austin to see it all exactly as she saw it. A refuge, a haven – or more properly, a heaven on earth.

"I can understand why you and Celia want to bring some of them here," she went on. "I really envy them their first sight of the moors and the sea."

"But you're just as determined to go back to London, I presume," Skye pointed out.

Her daughter smiled at the young man sitting beside her. "I belong there now just as much as Austin does. I never thought I'd say it, but it's true. We have a good life there."

She was so grown up, Skye thought, with a catch in her throat. She had not only changed, she had blossomed. Skye doubted that it was just her career that had done that for her. She was so clearly in love with the handsome young man who patently adored her.

"I'm so glad you came home today," she said, without thinking.

"What's special about today?" Wenna asked in surprise.

Skye caught Nick's glance and smiled into his eyes.

"Nothing at all, except that your father and I are old-stick-in-the-muds and like having our children around us."

"Well, you've got one more now," Wenna teased. "That is, if you'll have Austin as a sort of extra son."

"Wenna, not yet—" Austin said, getting a word in at last in this exuberant family gathering, but she brushed him aside with a squeeze of her hand.

"Oh, they all know why we're here, don't you?"

"You're here to make this day a special one," Nick said, in the small pause that followed, and the glance between him and his wife was one of perfect understanding.

They were all glad Wenna and Austin had got here in advance of Celia, so that their own news wasn't overshadowed by Celia's. Celia wore her betrothal ring on her finger, even though her future was so uncertain. Olly was full of dire and excited predictions about what would happen in the next few days.

"Olly's an out-and-out newspaperman," Wenna confided to Austin as they strolled on the sands below New World and looked out towards the horizon and the stately progress of the ships way out on the Atlantic Ocean. "A real one, I mean, and is always bragging he has advanced news of world affairs."

"He probably has," Austin said. "But anyone would have to be wearing blinkers not to know that we're on the brink of war, my love."

She hugged his arm, suddenly afraid. Down here, far from the capital, she had expected the urgency of the crisis to be left behind, but she hadn't been able to forget the sight of those evacuee children. It seemed as if everything was closing in on her.

"What will it mean to us, Austin? How will life change for us, personally, I mean?"

"Oh, I'll probably enlist and be a war correspondent, and you'll sing to the troops at camp concerts and have every soldier swooning over you," he said jokingly.

"You don't mean it – about enlisting?" she said.

"Every red-blooded man will want to do the same," he retorted, and then he saw the panic in her eyes. "Hey, sweetheart, I'm not planning to get shot, I promise you!"

"Nobody ever does," she muttered. "But it happens."

"Well, don't let's spoil our few days here worrying about what might happen. We've got a party tonight, and I've heard rumours that the Pengelly parties are famous around here."

Wenna pulled a face. "So they are. Mom intended this one to be just for us, but word got around, and now you'll meet the rest of the clan. The house will be bursting at the seams as usual. You may as well know what you're in for in one fell swoop," she said with a grin.

"It'll be bursting with evacuee children pretty soon, won't it? Your sister was telling me she's involved with the billeting committee in Truro and they'll be allocated with however many your parents are prepared to take in."

"I know. And although I think Mom's crazy, she's looking forward to it. She thinks we don't know how she grieved over losing that baby, and she misses having children around, but she couldn't keep us children for ever."

"Thank God," Austin said, cementing the words with a very satisfactory kiss.

In the end the party was a noisy and frenetic affair, with Theo and Betsy and Seb arriving with Justin, down from his university term, an unexpected visit that tempered Theo's normally sarcastic manner.

Lily and David Kingsley came with the twins, and Lily reminded Celia that it was a foretaste of how the house would be disrupted when the evacuees arrived, and to everyone's surprise Adam brought along a lady friend. The festivities went on until the early hours of the morning, and Skye gloried in the fact that they were all united in friendship and love. There were no enemies here.

At that moment, she caught sight of Celia's face as she took a breather outside on the terrace. Skye's heart turned over, thinking how very alone she looked in the midst of this family gathering, and the reason for it was crystal clear. Soon, very soon now, Celia's beloved Stefan would be classed as one of the enemy. It was an impossible position for lovers to be in. She went outside in the cool of the evening air, and tucked her arm through her daughter's.

In the comparative quiet of the lovely starlit night, with the laughter and noise muffled inside the house, Celia spoke softly without needing to turn her head to acknowledge her mother's presence. "Do you see that star, Mom? That very bright star that's brighter than all the rest? That's our star, Stefan's and mine. As long as that star still shines, we know that some day we'll be together, no matter what happens. We pledged to look at that star every night that we're apart. Don't you think that was a beautiful thing to do?"

To Skye, it seemed as if she was compelled to repeat the words like a mantra. It was only when she had finished that she turned to look at her mother with brimming eyes. They hugged one another close. Skye looked back through the years, knowing exactly what war could do and how it could tear people apart; while Celia looked ahead, full of uncertainty and dread, and ultimately hope.

"Let's go inside, darling," Skye said huskily. "There's a party going on, and we'll be missed."

They still held on tightly to one another, and as they went back into the house, it seemed to Skye as if the rest of their close-knit family was drawn towards them by an invisible thread. She could hear Olly's eager chatter with Austin Marsh, as to the part he too would play as a war correspondent, if he got the chance; Wenna's eyes were full of guilty dreams as she imagined herself on a makeshift stage surrounded by adoring homesick soldiers.

Celia turned to Skye with a smile that reminded her so startlingly of her own mother that she drew in her breath.

"As long as we always have one another, we'll be all right, won't we, Mom?" she said softly.

"Amen to that," Nick said, coming closer and circling them both in his arms.

Skye looked up at him, her beloved Nick, older and wiser, and knowing better than any of them that no day was ever going to be the same again, and that they had to hold on to the lovely memories of this one for as long as possible.

This precious day, whose stars were already beginning to fade with the coming dawn of a perfect September morning.